If you feel a little strange w[...]
If you sense some greater p[...]
With the skies arching above you
If you're touched by the presence of something unseen
When walking in the woods
Then come with me
And enter the world of Stonewylde ...

Kit Berry is an amazing natural storyteller, as much a magician in her effect as any of her characters. There is nobody who has taken the spirit of modern British Paganism, and infused it into a thrilling tale, as convincingly and alluringly as she. Her people, her places and her plots are all so vivid that they would in themselves establish her as a major novelist of what can be termed 'fantastic realism'."

Professor Ronald Hutton of Bristol University

The Stonewylde books are absolutely at the top of the league of unputdownable novels. The author's descriptive powers indicate a deep love of landscape and an acute observation of nature, while the brutality of some of the action brings a disturbing tension to the story. These books are such a terrific read that I have absolutely no reservations about recommending them to anyone.

Jerry Bird of Merry Meet

Also available from Moongazy Publishing by Kit Berry:

Magus of Stonewylde
Moondance of Stonewylde

THE STONEWYLDE SERIES

SOLSTICE
at STONEWYLDE

by

KIT BERRY

MOONGAZY
PUBLISHING

Published by Moongazy Publishing Ltd
22 Cross Hayes
Malmesbury
Wilts SN16 9BG
United Kingdom

October 31st 2007

ISBN 978-0-9551439-3-9

Cover design Big Blu Design Bristol

Printed in Palatino by Cox and Wyman Ltd
Reading, Berks

www.stonewylde.com
www.moongazypublishing.com

The Stonewylde Series
is dedicated to the memory of
Jean Guy,
my best owl aunt.

STONEWYLDE

ACKNOWLEDGEMENTS

Thanks once again to Clare Pearson of Eddison Pearson Ltd, for her professional and personal involvement in the Stonewylde Series.

Love and thanks to my three gorgeous boys George, Oliver and William. They endured all sorts of horrors whilst I was pouring every drop of my energy and effort into writing. I neglected them terribly and now they've grown up and flown the nest. Luckily they too love Stonewylde!

Thanks to all my lovely friends and family who've given me unfailing support. Getting this far wouldn't have been possible without so much encouragement and help from them.

Thanks once again to the wonderful Rob Walster at Big Blu Design for his superb creation of yet another stunning cover, and for being so responsive to all my quibbling demands.

Real heartfelt thanks to all the people, most of whom I've never met, who've read the books and loved them. Their excitement and support for Stonewylde has ensured publication of this third book. I've been so inspired by their e-mails, reviews, enthusiasm and praise . Thank you everyone

Finally – Mr B! Without him, this book would still be in manuscript form, and lurking in a dark corner somewhere. As would I! He's my own personal magus and with his magic touch has transformed all my dreams and fantasies into reality. I'm the luckiest woman alive to have such a special partner.

SOLSTICE
at STONEWYLDE

**BOOK THREE
IN THE
STONEWYLDE SERIES**

MOONGAZY
PUBLISHING

Ghostly wreaths of mist clung to the great stones, partially obscuring the sinister images painted all around. Black crows with outstretched wings, leering white skulls, grinning Jack o' Lanterns; the emblems of Samhain loomed ominously. Two old women, grimy shawls clutched tightly around them, entered the Stone Circle. Black feathers and white bones hung from the branches of elder that arched over the entrance to the sacred space, brushing their whiskery faces as they shuffled beneath the archway. It was silent and eerie inside the Circle and the sisters surveyed the menacing scene with grim approval. A labyrinth delineated by smooth black stones was laid out on the soft earth. The ancient cursal pattern filled the area, and the path it marked led to the centre where a great pyre had been built. The women hobbled across to the Altar Stone, decorated with boughs of yew. A great crow painted on the stone above looked down at the black cauldron sitting on the altar, squat and baleful.

The crones lit cracked clay pipes, puffing contentedly at the stinking smoke. They both took a good swig of cloudy liquid from an old glass bottle and smacked their lips with satisfaction.

"'Twill be strange, sister, both our boys here with us tomorrow."

"Aye, you speak right. Blessed be that Magus fetched Jackdaw home, his banishment over. My own dear son back again."

"Things'll change now. Magus brung him back to deal with the brat. Dark Angel didn't want the boy up on Mooncliffe at Hunter's Moon. But tomorrow, sister, at Samhain! Magus must have a clear path. Stop the boy interfering with the moongazy maiden. Magus needs her magic, like his father afore him with that Raven. Hah!"

They cackled hoarsely at the memory of Raven.

"Moongazy as they come but didn't save her, did it? Nought but a pile o' ash under the Yew! Old Heggy got it wrong there."

They spat in unison, then knocked their pipes against the stone.

"Work to be done now, sister. Best get on with it. We need to be ready for tomorrow night, when the Angel comes a-walking in the Stone Labyrinth. When the Dark Angel comes looking for his own."

CHAPTER ONE

Magus strode purposefully along the Tudor gallery leading to the rooms at the end. He had much to do, with the festival so close, and no time to waste today.

"You're not still in bed!" he said irritably. He stood with Miranda in the girl's bedroom gazing down at Sylvie as she lay against the pillows, white and exhausted. She pointedly looked away, refusing to meet his eyes or answer him.

"You should be up and about by now, young lady," he continued. "A week in bed is more than enough. Don't you agree, Miranda?"

"I'm not sure if she's quite ready yet," said her mother. "She's still very weak. Look at the shadows under her eyes."

"Rubbish!" said Magus firmly. "Remember that I know best in these matters. I've warned you that Sylvie is prone to malingering and attention seeking. It's Samhain tomorrow and she should be preparing for the festival along with everyone else. This is all put on - she's absolutely fine. Leave us now, Miranda. I want to speak with her alone."

Reluctantly Miranda left the room and Sylvie struggled to sit up. She stared hard at him, her eyes pools of icy water in her white face.

"I'm not putting it on," she said in a small voice.

"You're being pathetic, Sylvie," he said tersely. "All you did was stand on a rock for a few hours. I can't understand why you're making such a fuss over nothing."

"I'm not making a fuss over nothing! You know what I went through that night! You had no right to do that to me. How could you be so cruel? I'm not doing it next month. I won't let you take my moon magic ever again."

Magus's lips tightened into a hard, white line and he sat

1

down on the bed next to her. He leant forward and pushed his face close to hers, black eyes glittering.

"You'll do exactly as I tell you," he said in a voice of steel. "Everyone else does and you're no exception. You know full well why you were brought to Stonewylde and what I need from you. You will go to Mooncliffe every month for as long as I want."

Sylvie closed her eyes, trying to summon the strength to stand up to him.

"I won't," she whispered. "I'll leave Stonewylde rather than go on that rock for you again."

He chuckled at this and reaching out, gently stroked the hair back from her face. She flinched at his touch but was unable to move away.

"No, you won't leave Stonewylde, Sylvie. Your mother's expecting my baby and she'll never leave. You wouldn't abandon them here, surely, wondering how they'd cope with my anger and displeasure. To say nothing of what I'd do to your sweetheart Yul. You will stay here for their sakes. And you'll do exactly what I want."

Sylvie stared at him helplessly through a mist of tears. She had no energy to fight. He continued to brush the hair off her forehead. The feel of his sure fingers made her skin crawl.

"Is Yul alright?" she whispered, vaguely recalling his dramatic arrival at the moonrise but unaware of what had happened to him after that.

"No, not really," he laughed. He stood up and looked down at her with a pitiless smile. "And by the time I've finished with him, he'll never be alright again."

"I hate you," she whispered, even more softly. "I really hate you."

Magus laughed again and then called her mother back in. He put his arm around Miranda, his other hand resting proprietarily on her swollen belly.

"Sylvie is to get up now. She's not ill. She's just wallowing in self-pity. She's far too keen on playing the martyr, expecting us all to run around after her. Get her out of bed now and make her eat. Do you understand me, Miranda?"

"Yes, Magus, whatever you say. You know best."

He smiled and patted her stomach.

"Yes, I do. Make sure she's ready for Samhain. That's an order, Miranda. I want her down in the Village tomorrow and taking part in the festival. This attention seeking behaviour is going to stop as from now."

The Village Green was alive with activity as Magus trotted along the cobbles. He reined Nightwing in, holding the black stallion in check as he surveyed the scene before him. The Green Labyrinth was almost complete. Scorched lines marked the pattern on the grass, which was picked out further with white pebbles interspersed with tiny candles in coloured glass jars. In the centre of the seven coiled labyrinth the Villagers had build a large wicker dome, and many people were busy now adding the finishing touches. Tomorrow the labyrinth would be the spiritual focus for the day's events.

Magus swung the horse around and urged him towards the open doors of the Great Barn. Peering in, he nodded with satisfaction at the preparations taking place. The ancient building was decorated in the same manner as the Stone Circle, with black birds, skulls and Jack o' Lanterns. Twigs of the elder tree and slips of yew hung all around the walls and rafters, tokens of the trees sacred to Samhain. The elder was the tree of the crone, the waning and dark face of the Triple Moon Goddess. The yew was the tree of death and regeneration. The elder was thought to guard the gates to the Otherworld and the dark mysteries of the dead. All around were emblems of death, and Magus smiled grimly. Death was exactly what he had in mind for the ashen-faced boy lying up in the byre. Yul had led a charmed life, thanks to that meddling old crone. But maybe this Samhain her binding spell could be side-stepped. Maybe at last the Dark Angel himself would intervene to break her spell of protection for the brat.

He wheeled Nightwing around and trotted down one of the lanes radiating like spokes of a web away from the Village Green. He'd already visited three of the families involved, and had one more call to make this morning. Maizie saw the tall figure of Magus through a window and hurriedly opened her door. She'd been worried ever since receiving a message from Magus the day after the Hunter Moon. He'd informed her that he was keeping her son up at the Hall for a few days following an incident with Sylvie at Mooncliffe. The implication was that Yul had committed a serious misdemeanour. Maizie's heart had sunk at this news, and she now greeted Magus with some trepidation. He dwarfed the cottage parlour. His head brushed the beams as he gazed down at the anxious woman before him.

Despite seven children and a brute of a husband, he recognised the spark in her that had so attracted him all those years ago. The dark curls and slanted grey eyes, the rosy cheeks that burned now with aroused emotion, just as they had once done for entirely different reasons. Her dimples were the same, and her proud chin. He shook his head to dispel the memories and sat down in an armchair, indicating that she too should sit. A little girl came running in from the kitchen, freezing when she saw the grand figure of the master of Stonewylde seated unexpectedly in her home.

"Blessings!" he smiled, and held out a welcoming hand. Shyly she approached and he lifted her onto his lap. He looked down at her pointed little face and ruffled her dark curls gently.

"She's so like you, Maizie," he said. "Not in Nursery yet? Or do you like to keep her at home with you?"

"She won't be three till Imbolc, sir," replied Maizie. "Time enough then for Nursery."

"Nearly three years? Doesn't time fly?"

"Like a crow, straight and true. Have you come to tell me, sir, what's happened to Yul?"

"No, Maizie. I wished to speak to you about your husband. I think that ..."

"But what about my boy, sir? When will he be coming home?"

"I'll be keeping him at the Hall for a little longer."

"I don't wish to be disrespectful, sir, but last time you had Yul up at the Hall back in Midsummer you nearly killed him. Whatever he's done, surely he don't deserve that?"

4

Magus looked deep into her eyes and remembered how he'd once felt about this woman, only a girl then. There'd been women aplenty, but this one was different. She'd been with him all through that long spring and summer. He'd worked himself to the bone, struggling to rescue Stonewylde from the slough of neglect that was the legacy of his father, uncle and grandfather. Three bad masters in a row, and the very fabric of Stonewylde almost torn apart by their laziness and greed. It was a daunting task for the young, idealistic man who'd abandoned his burgeoning career in the Outside World to return home and put things to rights. Maizie had been his saviour that year. Her vivacious prettiness and uncomplicated sense of fun had been the only light in those dark days of endless labour. His ray of warmth right up until the Winter Solstice, when everything had fallen apart so cataclysmically.

He sighed and smiled sadly at her.

"Now, Maizie, you must trust me on this. We both know that Yul is wilful, disobedient and a complete troublemaker. That's why poor Alwyn had such a difficult time with him over the years. It can't have been easy bringing up a son as rebellious as Yul."

Maizie regarded him steadily, also remembering the past. She'd once loved this man so desperately. Part of her would always love him. She took a deep breath.

"We both know, sir, that Yul is no son of Alwyn's. Now that the man's ill and not likely to recover, we can speak openly. After all this time, surely you can acknowledge the boy as your own."

There was silence in the small parlour. Magus's black eyes glittered dangerously. He tapped his whip against his boot, mouth tight with displeasure.

"I thought we'd agreed never to discuss this subject? The matter was dealt with years ago. You were already pregnant at the time of that Moon Fullness up at Mooncliffe. If I'd known that, I'd never have taken you up there that night. Nor carried on with you all summer and autumn. I don't make love to women already pregnant by another man. You deceived me, Maizie. You even admitted it just before your Handfasting

5

with Alwyn. Yul is not my son."

She gave him a hard stare, then looked away, her cheeks burning fiercely.

"I was not pregnant then and you know it. Anything I admitted was because 'twas forced out of me. I'd never lain with anyone other than you, not till after Yul was born. You and I both know that night of the eclipse was my first time. And we both know right enough why you've denied Yul all these years. But Mother Heggy's just a mad old biddy and you should never have taken heed of her foolish words."

"It was nothing to do with that, Maizie."

"You know 'twas! And because of it, you condemned me to a life of misery with Alwyn. And condemned your own son to suffering beyond belief!"

"You're wrong, Maizie. I ..."

"No I'm not! All these long years I've kept quiet! All these years I've held my tongue and stood by silently. Had to, because of Alwyn. But he's not around any more and at last I can speak plain. Any fool can see Yul's yours."

"Yul's nothing like me! He has dark hair and grey eyes."

"Yes, he gets those from me. But he has your build and height, your way of moving and riding, your hands, your eyebrows and cheekbones – I could go on for ever. He's clever like you, determined, quick witted and so strong willed. He won't be told what to do unless he wants to do it. And he has your temper."

"Maizie, you're all of those things too. You're strong minded and bright. And he was born eight months after the eclipse up at Mooncliffe. That was our first time together. So you obviously conceived before then."

"No! He came a month early! 'Tis not that unusual! Would I have been up at the Stone Circle for the Midwinter Solstice if he'd been due then? I thought I had another month to go! I was as shocked as anyone when he was born up there during the ceremony, with me squatting on the earth while everyone looked on, and Mother Heggy capering about and laying him on the Altar Stone all bloody and screaming. Not the best way of birthing your first child. And not expected neither."

She stared angrily at Magus, her nostrils flaring and grey eyes flashing. He was reminded forcibly of the boy who now lay like death up in the byre, for this was just how Yul looked when he was angry. He knew that Yul would have been a worthy son, someone to groom as his heir, as the future magus. The boy had courage, pride and leadership qualities. He was tough and intelligent and passionate about Stonewylde. But since Yul's birth he'd been haunted by Mother Heggy's prophecies. By acknowledging the boy as his own, he would surely be opening up the possibility of their truth? *Conceived under a red moon, born under a blue one, the fruit of his passion. This child would one day rise up with the folk behind him to overthrow him at the place of bones and death.* He'd woken in the middle of many a night in cold, sweating panic. The thought of a child of his growing up at Stonewylde, whose destiny it was to destroy him, was like something from a Greek tragedy.

He shook his head and once more denied his paternity, hoping as always to thus negate the prophecy. He looked across at the pretty woman before him, his face implacable.

"I'm sorry, Maizie, but you're wrong. I shall be very displeased if you continue to make these false allegations. Yul remains at the Hall whilst I investigate his latest insubordination. I'll deal with him exactly as I see fit. I am the magus and it isn't for you to question the punishment I choose to administer. So keep your remarks to yourself. I'll hear no more about it. You'd do well to remember your place."

"I'm sorry, sir," she said, lowering her eyes, although her anger was palpable. She was still so attractive; he always had preferred women with spirit. He glanced down at the child sitting silently in his lap. She gazed up at him with enormous green eyes that seemed to search his soul.

"Bad man," she said clearly. "Bad, bad man."

"Leveret, come here!" said Maizie sharply. Magus handed the tiny girl over to her mother.

"The matter I actually came here to speak about is Alwyn. You know there's been no improvement following the stroke? He's still alive but he can do nothing for himself and doesn't seem to be aware of anything. He's shrunk to skin and bones and has to be forcibly fed. I wanted to ask if you were in agreement to Alwyn entering the Stone Labyrinth this Samhain for the Dance of Death. I personally think he should go, but as his nearest relative you have the final say. You know the custom. Permission can only be granted by the closest member of the family."

She took another deep breath to calm herself. If there was one thing Maizie had learnt from living with Alwyn all those years, it was self control. She nodded.

"Yes, I agree he should go. Let the Dark Angel decide. 'Tis the best way."

"Good," he said, smiling briskly. "I'll arrange for it to be done. Well, I must be off."

They both rose and he gazed down at her as she stood before him, Leveret on her hip. His dark eyes softened and he took one of her hands.

"Maizie, let's not spoil things between us now. Not after all this time and all that's happened. You've always been special to me. You were such a lovely girl and you're a fine woman."

She frowned at him and removed her hand from his.

"Thank you for calling on me, sir. Samhain Blessings to you."

By mid-morning the next day the heavy mist had once again lifted, although the day was overcast and grey. Children ran around the Village excitedly, desperate to get on with the festivities. Every fire in the Village had been extinguished and everyone must fast until the feast in the evening. The trees encircling the Green had already shed their leaves, victims of a gusty storm that had raged the day after the full moon. They'd now taken on their skeletal winter appearance. The remains of the messy rooks' nests had blown away too in the south-westerly gales. Only the great yew remained clothed in glossy dark-green, its slips like the barbs of a bird's feather. It was the last day of the pagan year. It was the day of ending the old. It was the day of death.

In the morning the Samhain drama prepared by the young people was acted out in the Great Barn. It was a spectacular event, full of dance and music with everyone masked and costumed. Sylvie hadn't taken part, feeling far too weak; she'd missed all the rehearsals anyway. Magus noticed her absence and at mid-day left the festivities to summon her from the Hall. She sat now in the jolting cart beside her mother, huddled miserably in her black cloak. This was her first time outside since the night of the Moon Fullness over a week ago. She hadn't wanted to come, but Magus had stormed into their rooms. He'd insisted that she go immediately to the Village to take part in the afternoon and evening ceremonies. He'd become very angry when she'd refused. Miranda hadn't batted an eyelid when he'd slapped Sylvie hard, shouting at her and throwing clothes at her to put on. Her mother had merely looked on as he dragged her, crying and struggling, out of the rooms and downstairs. He'd bundled her towards the waiting horse and cart, his one concession to her weakness.

"Behave yourself, girl!" he'd hissed menacingly into her face, dumping her on the seat in the back of the cart. "I told you yesterday you were to take part in the festival. There's nothing wrong with you. Snap out of it and stop being so pathetic!"

Shivering in her cloak, she tried now to stop the sobs that escaped every so often. She felt ill and weak, but a dull anger burned inside her.

Then Sylvie realised it was Tom sitting in front holding the reins and she managed to pull herself together. Once Magus had ridden on ahead, she leant forward and whispered to the ostler.

"Tom, do you have any news of Yul? Is he alright?"

The old man turned and gazed down at her in consternation. He was unsure of how honest to be, for this poor girl looked little better than the boy. But she deserved the truth.

"I'm not to speak of it, but reckon you won't spread the word and get me into trouble. So no, miss, Yul's not alright at all. He's alive, and that's a miracle in itself, but he's in a bad

9

way. He can't stand nor barely sit and he can't take no food. I done what I can, and Mother Heggy's sent potions. But … well, 'tis not looking good."

"What did they do to him?" she whispered, closing her eyes in anguish at the thought of Yul suffering. "Was he whipped again?"

"Why no, miss, they done nothing to him. He was brung up to the Hall the day after the Moon Fullness. That Jackdaw carried him into the byre like a brace o' rabbits slung over his shoulders. I reckon Yul's been poisoned. His eyes aren't right. He don't know who he is or nothing."

Miranda pulled her back onto the seat.

"What are you whispering about, Sylvie? Don't talk with the servants like that. You know Magus wouldn't like it."

Sylvie glared at her. Even with the hypnosis, she couldn't understand how her mother could behave like this.

"All you ever think about is Magus. How could you have let him hit me just now, Mum? *You've* never hit me. You always said it was wrong. Don't you care about me any more?"

Miranda looked away uncomfortably.

"Of course I do. But Magus is right. You can't just take to your bed for half the month. If you insist on dancing on that cliff, you'll have to put up with feeling tired afterwards. And he didn't hit you. It was just a little slap."

"That's not true! Why do you always take his side?"

"Because he knows best. He says I've been too soft with you all these years and I think maybe he's right. We have to obey him, you know that. Please don't be difficult, darling. It makes life so unpleasant and I don't want to make him angry. I have the baby to think about, after all."

Sylvie turned her back on her mother, seething with outrage. When they reached the Village, Tom helped them out of the cart and Sylvie managed to whisper to him again.

"If you get the chance, tell Yul I love him. Please, Tom?"

"Aye, miss, I will that."

Sylvie stood shivering at the entrance to the Green

Labyrinth marked out on the Village Green, waiting her turn to go in. Her face was so white and thin that she hardly needed a skull mask. She pulled the thick black cloak tightly around her. The atmosphere on the Green today frightened her. It was so different from the joyous maypole dancing at Beltane or the holiday fun of the Summer Solstice. Everyone she saw today wore a hooded black robe or cloak and many wore skull masks. A thin line of smoke trickled from the wicker dome in the centre of the labyrinth, but the cottages seemed strangely lifeless without their habitual plumes of smoke. It was quiet too, despite the many people thronging around the cobbles. She wanted very much to cling on to Miranda, who stood nearby. But that was out of the question given Miranda's earlier remarks. Her mother had made it very clear where her priorities now lay. Sylvie felt vulnerable and alone.

A man wearing a crow mask stood at the arch of elder branches, identical to the one up at the Stone Circle. He let young people into the sacred space nine at a time, one by one. As Sylvie's group waited, he reminded them of the significance of what they were about to do. This was a pilgrimage and time of deep meditation. The walk through the labyrinth was symbolic, representing the journey towards death. When they entered the dome in the centre they entered the Otherworld, the Realm of the Dead. They shed their past life and lay in the Otherworld, reflecting on what they'd discarded and left behind. Then they were reborn from the dark womb and began a new life, a new journey starting afresh as they retraced their steps and followed the path out of the maze. Sylvie watched the children already in there. They walked very slowly, guided by the white pebbles as they followed the symmetrical, tortuously curved path. They kept their heads bowed as they walked, making sure they kept the distance between them until they reached the entrance to the dome.

Sylvie didn't want to enter the labyrinth. The whole thing was macabre. She swayed on her feet at the entrance. She'd barely eaten all week and couldn't shake off the overwhelming exhaustion that smothered her. She knew Hazel had put her on a drip for the first few days; her arm was still bruised. Her legs were shaky and her stomach hollow. She wanted to cry as she surveyed the great coiled labyrinth ahead. There was nothing on the path to hold on to if she felt faint. She wanted to cry at Magus' harshness towards her. It was all his fault. He'd put her through the terrible ordeal up at Mooncliffe. She couldn't help being slow to recover after feeding him her moon magic. She'd never be able to take this every month. She looked across to the wicker dome in the centre and hoped she'd make it that far without collapsing.

"This is a very solemn journey," continued the crow man. "'Tis not one to be undertaken lightly. As you walk towards your death, take stock of the past year and all that you've done. Have you achieved all you hoped for? Have you made mistakes or failed in your intent? When you are inside the Otherworld, confront your weaknesses, your failures. Then clear your minds and savour the darkness. In the dome you'll be given a drink, symbolic of the blood of death and the blood of birth. When you emerge newly born, remove your death mask and with a bright face look to the New Year ahead. As you walk back along the path, think hard on what you hope to achieve this coming year, on what you can do for Stonewylde, for our community. Think of our Magus and all that he does for us. Try to be like him, giving of your time and energy willingly for the sake of Stonewylde and the folk who live here. You'll be given a slip of yew as you finish the journey to remind you of your rebirth. May the Dance of the Green Labyrinth at Samhain be sacred to you all."

As the gate opened and the group began to move forward, Sylvie glanced across and saw the tall black-robed figure of Magus staring intently at her. His face was impassive but his dark eyes burned into her. She shuddered and stepped under the arch of elder, the black feathers brushing her white face.

"Pull your mask down!" hissed the crow man, bundling her in and blocking the exit behind her.

CHAPTER TWO

Yul's eyes stared straight up at the cobwebbed ceiling of the stone byre. Enormous and glassy, his pupils were so dilated that the grey irises had all but disappeared. His face and lips were ashen and his heartbeat very slow. He was very cold. His hands were as white as his face as he lay unmoving amongst the scattering of mouldy straw that littered the stone floor.

Earlier in the day Magus and Jackdaw had looked in on him. Magus was pleased to see the boy was now at least conscious, if not in good health. Unbeknown to him, Mother Heggy's medicine and Tom's care had pulled Yul away from the brink of death where he'd been hovering. The hallucinogenic substances in the cakes he'd been fed were grown and harvested on the estate, and fairly harmless if only taken occasionally in small doses. But Yul had been forced to swallow a great deal on the night of the Hunter's Moon, and they'd proved almost fatal. A week later he still lay in the straw covered only by an old horse blanket. He was alarmingly thin and white, his cheekbones and chin sharp and pointed, the hollows of his cheeks and under his eyes deep and shadowed. His black hair was lank and matted, his eyes strange. The bruises where Magus had hit him so hard around the face up on the clifftop were stark on his pale skin.

When they came in and shut the door, Yul tried clumsily to cover his face. The harsh light was blinding. Jackdaw stood cracking his knuckles as he looked down at the still figure. Magus sat on a straw bale and also surveyed the boy.

"Can I work him over a bit, sir?"

Magus hesitated.

"It's tempting, but I think not. He still looks very fragile and I want him with us for the ceremony tonight at Samhain. Sorry to disappoint you, Jackdaw. Just see if he can stand, would you?"

Jackdaw bent and hauled the boy to his feet as if he were a marionette. Yul crumpled immediately, falling first against Jackdaw and then onto the floor in a boneless heap.

"Nah, he can't."

"Oh well. Go and get him some food from the kitchen, something light. We'll see if that does the trick."

With Jackdaw gone, Magus dragged Yul over to another bale and propped him upright. The boy was cleaner than Magus had thought he'd be, and he wondered if Tom had been showing any misguided kindness. But nevertheless, he was in a terrible state; limp and passive, staring blankly with enormous eyes from his skeletal face.

"Cat got your tongue?"

Yul looked at the silver Magus cat and nodded slowly. The cat had played with him for so long. It had chased him all over the floor of the byre, in and out of the straw, tormenting and teasing him. He knew now it was easier to play dead than try to escape.

"Do you realize it's Samhain today?"

Yul showed no reaction at all and Magus sighed in disgust. This was no fun. He enjoyed breaking someone's spirit only when the person was aware of it being broken.

"Well, just in case anything is reaching your addled brain, you'll be joining me up in the Stone Circle tonight. For the Dance of Death. You know what that means."

Yul gazed at him vacantly and Magus sighed again.

"Oh dear, oh dear. Looks like we've got a new Village idiot."

Jackdaw returned with a tray of food.

"Bloody hell! That sour-faced old cow in the kitchen hasn't changed much since I left Stonewylde. Marigold gave me a right tongue-lashing. You'll have to speak to her, sir. I ain't putting up with that, not from a woman. Very tempted to ram her tea-towel down her bloody throat."

He put the tray down on a bale.

14

"Here's the grub, then."

"Good."

They looked at each other.

"Well feed him then!"

"What - me, sir?"

"Yes, you!"

With a grunt of annoyance, Jackdaw sat heavily on the bale and started to shovel food into Yul's mouth. Yul vomited repeatedly, unable to stomach the food crammed so relentlessly into his mouth. Magus stood up in revulsion and waved his henchman away.

"Goddess, that's disgusting! Enough, Jackdaw. We'll try again later."

The men stomped out of the byre, snapping off the electric light and locking the door behind them.

Yul lay now in the gloom, cold on the stone and straw. In the weak afternoon light that filtered through gaps under the door he could make out the tray of food. His vomit was spread in a splattered pool on the flagstones. A ray of light stirred in his brain. He blinked. Then he carefully sat up, the room spinning around him. He realised where he was. But this time there was no Alwyn, no excruciating pain in his back. He had vague recollections from the past days of Jackdaw leaning over him, slapping his face and shouting at him. But he wasn't sure if that was a dream.

He saw the jug by the door. On his hands and knees he crawled over very slowly, hoping it contained water. He drank deeply and splashed his face. Then he crawled back to the meagre remains of congealed food on the tray. Avoiding the mess on the floor, he ate what little was left. He felt queasy but managed to keep it down. Trembling with weakness and the aftermath of the poisons still in his body, he lay back against a bale and tried to think. His mind was a kaleidoscope of images and he didn't know which were real and which imagined. In the murky light, Yul closed his eyes and tried to make sense of the chaos in his head.

Behind the mask and under the hooded cloak, Sylvie felt

private and sheltered. Despite her misgivings about this bizarre experience, she did as instructed and reflected on the past year. So much had happened. Her life had been turned upside down. She thought of her joy when she'd first come to Stonewylde and believed she'd found paradise. And she thought of the reality now. Magus' words rang in her ears – *You know full well why you were brought to Stonewylde and what I need from you.* As she shuffled along the convoluted path of the Green Labyrinth, careful to keep within the white stones that marked the way, she felt a surge of rebellion rising up. She understood exactly how Yul felt and why he defied Magus, even though he knew he'd be punished. She would not obey that man, nor would she serve him. It wasn't why she'd been brought to Stonewylde at all.

Sylvie didn't understand the forces at work in this special place; the moon magic spirals up at Hare Stone, the Earth Magic in the Stone Circle, the green magic in the Village Green. Nor did she understand the evil that stalked Quarrycleave and the coiled malignance at Mooncliffe. But she knew she hadn't been brought here to serve Magus' needs. She must dance at Hare Stone at the rising of the full moon, just as Yul must stand on the Altar Stone at sunrise and sunset. Together they seemed necessary to both ground and release the energies that worked so powerfully here. They were both crucial to the very fabric of Stonewylde.

And she must be with Yul. She loved him. They belonged together; their souls and destinies were linked. But if Magus had his way, they'd be kept apart forever. If Magus had his way, Yul would be treated so badly that eventually he must die. And she would become Magus' vessel. She'd be used every month to feed his hunger for moon magic, then confined to her bed, too weak to move, when he'd taken his fill. She couldn't live like that. She could never obey him or accept his cruelty towards Yul. She'd rather not exist at all than exist on those terms.

Tom was back at the stables again with the cart. He knew that Magus was down in the Village and took the opportunity of visiting Yul briefly. He was delighted to find the boy sitting up and aware of who and where he was. The stench of vomit was strong, but he couldn't risk cleaning it up.

"'Tis good to see you back in the land of the living, Yul," he said, going over and tousling the boy's matted hair.

"I'm glad to be here," said Yul, the words sounding strange to him. He hadn't spoken for a week. "Could I have some more water please, Tom? I'm so thirsty."

Tom quickly refilled the jug from the tap outside and helped him to drink, cradling the frail boy as he struggled to sit upright and hold the heavy pottery vessel.

"I daren't stay long," Tom said hurriedly. "I'm not meant to be in here at all, and that brute Jackdaw's about somewhere. Look, I've some more of Mother Heggy's remedy here. Can you drink it now?"

Yul put the little bottle to his lips and swallowed the draught, fighting the nausea that rose instantly.

"I just saw your girl," Tom said, trying to hide the pity he felt for the boy. Yul looked up desperately, his eyes huge in his bruised face.

"Is she alright? Was she ill? I don't even know what day it is. Is it long since the Moon Fullness?"

"Aye, 'twas a week ago. You been on this floor all that time. 'Tis why you're so weak. But the young lady is fine. She's been ill too, but she's down at the Village right now in the Green Labyrinth. She had a message for you. She said she loves you."

Yul closed his eyes, relief sweeping through him. Knowing Sylvie was alright was the best medicine of all.

When Sylvie reached the centre of the labyrinth she was admitted into the dome. It was very dark inside with only a little light filtering through the densely woven wicker. The smoke from the small fire, the only one that burned at Stonewylde today, hurt her eyes and throat at first, but she found she got used to it quite quickly. A robed adult in a skull mask pointed for her to sit cross-legged on a mat with the others, in a circle round the fire. Real bones and many black feathers hung from the low ceiling of the dome. Once all nine of the group were seated, the figure began to chant in time to the drums played softly by another crow-masked person.

"Enter the darkness of the tomb, the darkness of the womb."

A tray of small, white bowls was passed around, looking like babies' skulls full of blood.

"Drink of the blood of death, and the blood of rebirth."

They took off their masks and gingerly sipped the deep crimson liquid. It was sweet, aromatic elderberry wine made from the fruits of the tree of death, and laced with something that made their heads spin. One by one they lay back on the mats and let their minds drift away. Above them the black feathers and white bones moved gently in the swirling smoke. Sylvie's head jostled with strange images – a black raven, white rocks, a chevroned serpent, a circle of hares. But too soon the robed figure commanded them to stand. They obeyed, unsteady on their feet.

"'Tis time to leave the Otherworld. As you leave this womb you will be reborn. 'Tis the beginning of a new life, a new start. As you walk, think on how you want life to be in the year ahead. Farewell."

One by one they left the dome, blinking in the afternoon light and inhaling the fresh air in gulps. This journey was uplifting, a real new beginning. Sylvie focussed on what she wanted for the coming year. She must join Yul in the fight against Magus and mustn't give in, whatever the outcome. She'd be as brave and strong in her defiance as Yul was. She thought of Mother Heggy's wisdom. The old woman knew something of what lay ahead and Sylvie must take heed of her advice.

She walked slowly, her eyes fixed to the ground, guided in the grey fading light by the white pebbles. She had to stay at Stonewylde. Despite her threat to Magus yesterday, leaving here wasn't an option. She had to be with Yul, and he would never leave Stonewylde. He was a part of the place, his very bones the rocks and his skin the earth. His soul was rooted here and he could never go far. Therefore neither could she.

She'd stay at Stonewylde for ever until her bones too became the rocks, and her skin the earth. Her body would become part of the substance of Stonewylde for eternity. She knew this with sudden, piercing certainty. Shuffling along the path of the labyrinth, her body cloaked in black and her face masked with death, Sylvie realised the full impact of where her thoughts had led. She'd fight Magus to the very end. And she would rather die than live under his dominion.

The exit of the labyrinth was ahead. Sylvie was handed a slip of yew and then she was out. She wandered not over to the Barn with the others, but into the cavernous gloom under the great yew tree itself. She cast her mind back to her birthday, the Summer Solstice, when she and Yul had had their first kiss in this magical place. She'd thought at the time that nothing else in the world mattered, compared to that moment of perfect joy. She realised now she'd been mistaken. Many other things mattered a great deal. She sat for a while on the bare earth littered with dead, brown barbs of yew. She thought hard of Yul, trying to reach him. She felt the cold, smelled a foul stench, sensed pain and a body so weak and frail that it barely functioned. Sylvie hung her head in sorrow, sending her love to him wherever he was.

Just after Tom left the byre, Clip arrived. He was on his way to the dolmen where he liked to spend Samhain night. He'd felt a twinge of conscience as he remembered Yul and his plight. He'd called in briefly during the week and had realised there was nothing he could do for the boy who just lay there like a corpse. Clip knew from experience how it was when the soul was away on a journey to other realms. The body left behind was an empty shell. Other than keeping it warm, there was nothing to be done until the soul returned. Unlocking the door, he wrinkled his nose and peered in. He'd hoped that Magus had released the boy by now. But then he saw him sitting up, propped against a bale in the near darkness.

"Ah, there you are," said Clip. "You've come back from the journey then. How are you?"

"You were there that night," said Yul slowly. "You know

what he did to me. You know how powerful those cakes were."

Clip frowned.

"I can barely see you in this gloom. What is that disgusting smell?"

"I was sick. There's a light somewhere. I think the switch is outside."

In the glaring electric light, Clip's face dropped at the sight before him. He realised it was now over a week since Jackdaw had been sent to collect the boy from the cliff top. The time had flown by. He looked at Yul and was deeply shocked. The boy was a living corpse; face white and skeletal, eyes sunk in his head. His pupils were still dilated and stared darkly from deep sockets.

Clip felt a sharp twist of guilt. He should never have been a part of this. He should never have been involved in causing this boy's or Sylvie's suffering. Why did he always allow Magus to over-ride him? Why did he never find the courage to stick to what he knew was right? He stood there indecisively. He wanted to get Yul out, but he was frightened of Magus' reaction. He was also terrified of Jackdaw. The man was so intimidating, and there was something about the way he looked at Clip with such contempt that made him feel uncomfortable and inadequate.

"Is there anything I can get you?"

"I'd like some food please. I'm very hungry."

While Clip was gone, having locked the door behind him, Yul reflected on his predicament. His mind was suddenly clear, completely clear. Maybe vomiting up everything earlier had flushed his system. He didn't know what had been happening during the past week, but knew he must escape from this prison before Jackdaw and Magus set to work on him. He shuddered to think what they had in store for him. Perhaps Tom would help him to get out – or even Clip. He'd recognised the look of guilt on the man's face. Maybe he could be persuaded to help.

Clip returned from the kitchens with a plate of sandwiches. He watched in revolted fascination as the boy devoured them, only to be racked by excruciating pain the moment he'd finished. He doubled over, clutching his stomach in agony. Clip stood back in case he was sick again. After a while the danger seemed to have passed. Yul realised he should have eaten only a little and very slowly.

"Can I go home now?" asked Yul casually.

Clip stared at him in consternation, his indecision plain.

"Well … you're hardly in any fit state to leave."

"But my mother will be so worried about me. You are the master here really. You could help me get home."

"No, I don't think I ought to," said Clip. "I think Magus wants you here a bit longer. If …"

"Too bloody right he does!" said a deep voice.

They both jumped in fright. Jackdaw's powerful bulk filled the doorway. He was unshaven and the stubble glistened greasily on his jaw and head. His massive arms and chest were exposed by the leather waistcoat he wore, even in this cool weather. His bulbous muscles, covered in writhing tattoos, bunched menacingly. He came inside and sauntered over to where Yul sat.

"Nice try, kid. But we all know Magus has got something else in mind for you. The last thing you'll be doing is going home."

"Er, I think I'd better be off," said Clip, edging towards the door.

"Sounds good to me," said Jackdaw, his lack of respect for Clip blatant. "Here, did you bring him food?"

"Yes, yes I did. He was very hungry."

"Oh, what a shame! You should've waited for me. I'd have enjoyed feeding him again."

Jackdaw lowered his bulk onto a bale, watching Yul closely. His bright blue eyes gleamed. The boy seemed much better now. Clip sidled away and out of the byre, closing the door behind him. Jackdaw smiled, revealing a gold tooth. Yul eyed him warily, remembering all the incidents of humiliation at Quarrycleave.

"Just you and me now, mate," said Jackdaw. "Are you thinking of old times? Because I am."

Yul nodded and stared down at the stone floor, too frightened to speak. Jackdaw chuckled. He cracked his knuckles and spat into the corner.

"It's good to be back. Pity I ain't got longer with you. You and me, we got so much catching up to do. No! Don't look like that, my son. You know you missed me too. It was fun back in the summer, weren't it? Happy days at ol' Quarrycleave. And now they're here again."

Jackdaw fished in the breast pocket of his waistcoat and pulled out a pack of cigarettes and lighter. He lit a cigarette and inhaled deeply. He examined the glowing tip and glanced down at the quaking boy at his feet.

"Maybe I could show you some of my tricks with a lighted fag. You still look a bit dopey to me. After that long sleep you need waking up good and proper. Yeah? Let's get that shirt off you, then."

When the all young people had been through the Green Labyrinth, the candles along the path were lit and the adults began. The afternoon wore on, the light slowly fading from the sky. Sylvie sat alone on a bench outside the Barn wrapped in her black cloak, watching the spectacle on the Green. It was an amazing sight. The entire labyrinth was ringed with glowing lanterns forming a great circle of light in the dusk. Hundreds of tiny candles in coloured glass jars twinkled amongst the white pebbles. The paths of the labyrinth were scattered with silent figures in black hooded robes, their faces turned to skulls, shuffling slowly towards or away from the wicker tomb in the centre. Sylvie looked up and gasped. The leafless trees surrounding the Green were clotted with birds. She knew there was a rookery in some of the chestnut trees, but this wasn't only rooks. There were crows, jackdaws and hundreds of starlings too, all perched up in the bare branches watching the Dance of the Green Labyrinth taking place below. It reminded her of the funeral.

"Incredible, isn't it?" said a mellow voice next to her, making her start. Magus sat down close beside her on the bench. She began to tremble.

"Sylvie," he said quietly, "I'm sorry. I've treated you badly. I want to apologise and make amends."

He paused and looked at her. She stared straight ahead, watching the silent black figures and the birds, still alighting on the branches to swell the numbers even further.

"I don't blame you for being angry. But I'm going to show you over the next month that I'm not such a terrible person. I've let my love of Stonewylde blind me to how hard I've been on you. The only thing that matters to me - the only thing in the world - is Stonewylde. This place is my whole life. Can you imagine what it's like to be the magus here? The responsibility of it? Apart from the spiritual guardianship of the place, there are so many people dependent on me."

He sighed heavily and sat back in the bench, stretching out his legs. Sylvie remained huddled in the corner. His voice was silky and gentle.

"And lately … for some reason I'm no longer getting the same energy from the Stone Circle. I used to come away from the ceremonies up there buzzing with it. It helped me in the weeks ahead when I struggled to get through all the work. When that power started to ebb, I became so exhausted. And then that night up at Mooncliffe, I found that you were able to channel moon energy into the great rock. I know now that it's been done before. I've been told that my mother too had the ability to do it."

Sylvie retreated deeper inside herself. He put a gentle arm around her hunched shoulders and pulled her close to him. He turned her face with a finger under her chin to make her look into his eyes. They glowed dark and bright and she knew he'd been soaking himself in the moon magic. He oozed it from every pore. He exuded power and energy and it was like a magnet, even to her who hated him. He smiled at her and she thought again how very attractive he was, despite being so cruel. There was something beautifully vicious about him. He squeezed her tightly and kissed her forehead.

"I'm so pleased you and your mother came to live here. I was delighted to heal you when you were so sick. And now, in return, I'm grateful for your gift to me of moon magic. It's the

New Year tomorrow. Could we start again as friends? And that which I've forced you to give, can you think about giving freely? I need your moon magic, Sylvie. I need it so desperately. If I'm going to run Stonewylde as it should be run, I need the energy only you can give me. I can get Clip to use his hypnosis to help alleviate the discomfort for you. Sylvie, if you do this for Stonewylde, I'll be in your debt forever. Nobody else shares your gift. Nobody else can do what you can. You'd be like a queen here. You could have anything you wanted."

She sat stiffly despite his arm holding her so close.

"There's only one thing I want," she replied shakily, scared at the way he made it sound so simple. Scared that she wouldn't be strong enough to resist the full assault of his charm and persuasion. "I want Yul to be free from you. I want you to leave him alone. And I want to be allowed to see him and be friends with him."

His face tightened and his voice changed.

"Sylvie, we've been through this many times. We had a deal, didn't we? I'd leave Yul alone if you stopped seeing him. And who broke that deal? You've brought this on him by not keeping your side of the bargain. This is your fault and it's too late now for any more deals. The boy has pushed it too far this time."

"What do you mean? What have you done to him?"

"I've done nothing to him yet."

"But yesterday you said …"

"I was just winding you up, Sylvie. It's not difficult. You made me angry, threatening to leave Stonewylde. I wanted to get back at you."

"So where is he?"

"He's been around. It's you who've been out of action, not him. He's actually taking part in a ceremony tonight up at the Stone Circle. Alwyn will be there too. It's the custom for the son to go with the father. Yul's quite happy to take part."

"So he's alright then?" she asked eagerly, her eyes wide with hope. "I'd heard he was really ill."

"I don't know who told you that, but I can assure you he's

alive and kicking. He's in the hospital wing with his father. Alwyn's a very sick man and hasn't got much longer now. Again, it's a custom. But you must forget Yul. I don't want to talk about that now. In the morning, in the New Year, we'll discuss this. Things will be different then. And now I must go. It looks like most of the folk have performed their Dance of the Green Labyrinth. We need to move across to the Playing Fields to light the Samhain Bonfire and start cooking the food. Come with me, Sylvie. Lean on my arm and you can help me. I want your role in the community to be acknowledged. You can start by assisting me this evening. Everyone will know how special you are, and what a fine thing you're doing every month for me. And for Stonewylde."

He spoke as if she'd already agreed but she felt too tired to argue now. It was easier to let it go; let him think what he liked. She remembered her resolution made in the labyrinth. She would never give in to him.

It was some time since Jackdaw had left the byre and Yul huddled up alone in the darkness. His mind was now completely clear, although in many ways he wished he was still lying in a stupor. At least then he wouldn't be able to feel the awful pain that Jackdaw had inflicted so casually, just to while away the time. He didn't dare try to imagine what further torture Magus had in mind for him. He hugged his knees and closed his eyes, shivering in the cold byre and desperate for some more food. He wished now with all his heart that he'd listened to Mother Heggy's advice. He should never have gone up to Mooncliffe for the Hunter's Moon. He hadn't helped Sylvie at all and because he'd acted so rashly he was once again at the mercy of Magus. There was nobody to help him escape, despite what Tom had once promised. It was too much to expect the man to risk his own safety. Yul was alone and he was scared.

He knew that in the Village, people would be gathered in the Playing Fields with Magus to light the Samhain Bonfire. They'd dance in great circles around the bonfire, several people deep, symbolising the wheel of the year turning and never ending. There'd be singing and fireworks, which he'd always enjoyed. The food would be cooking on the fires around the field and people would eat to their heart's content, hungry after a day of fasting. His mouth watered at the thought. After games and fun, the dancing and drinking would continue into the small hours of the New Year. Yul also knew of the other rites that would take place up at the Stone Circle. He'd never witnessed them, for only a few chosen acolytes took part in the ceremony with Magus. But everyone in the community was aware of what happened in the Stone Circle at Samhain. It was after all the festival of the dead.

Yul heard footsteps approaching and shook with fear. Jackdaw filled him with terror in a way that Alwyn had never done. His father had been a bully who relied on brute force; Jackdaw was more subtle and shared Magus' enjoyment of a slower paced cruelty. The light snapped on and the door opened. Jackdaw beckoned, huge in the doorway. Slowly Yul tried to stand, his legs giving way beneath him at first. But he stood upright and then attempted to walk across the byre. Everything tilted and spun around crazily. He put out a hand to steady himself but the wall wasn't where it should have been and he fell heavily to the floor. Jackdaw stood watching and laughed at his clumsiness.

"Hurry up, boy! I ain't got all bloody day."

Yul tried again but couldn't manage to walk across the room. He'd thought his head was clear now but the poison must still be in his body. And he was very weak from lack of food.

"You're pissing me off now, Yul. If you can't walk, then crawl. But get a move on."

Yul started to crawl shakily on all fours across the stone floor to the doorway. Jackdaw swore at his slowness and hauled the boy to his feet. Yul felt himself sway and hoped that Jackdaw wouldn't let him drop to the ground again. He felt so fragile. The man picked him up and tossed him over his shoulder as if he weighed nothing. They left the stable area and headed round the back of the Hall to the Hospital Wing.

Jackdaw strode inside, nodding to the nurse on duty. He

made his way to a room near the end where he dumped Yul to his feet. Inside here it was very quiet. There were four patients: three old people and Alwyn. Standing confused and unsteady, Yul was shocked at the sight of his father. He'd always been a large man, and in his later days, obese. Now he was shrivelled and withered, the skin hanging off him in folds. His piggy eyes were lifeless and droopy. Most of his hair had fallen out and he sat in a wheelchair like a dummy. Two of the other people lay on beds, ashen faced and clearly very ill. The third was in a wheelchair but shaking severely and breathing with difficulty. All of them wore white tunics tied with white cords, their arms, legs and feet bare.

Yul stared at them. It slowly dawned on him that these were the Death Dancers who'd be going to the Stone Labyrinth tonight for the special ritual. But why was he here? Then it hit him like a stone between the eyes. Surely Magus wasn't going to make him take part? As if in answer, Jackdaw pointed to a white tunic and told Yul to put it on and then sit on the remaining wheelchair. Jackdaw left him amongst the dying people. The four were unaware of him – indeed, unaware of anything. Yul's heart thumped with dread. Magus couldn't mean for him to die with them tonight up in the Stone Labyrinth. It must be a horrible joke, just another of Magus' cruelties. Carefully, he shuffled to the door but it was locked. He stumbled back to his wheelchair, head reeling. He sat there for what seemed like hours, but without a window he had no idea of time. The ragged breathing of the four was awful. Yul wanted to scream with horror. He found he was shaking uncontrollably even though it was warm in the room. Too warm in fact. He began to sweat, a clammy wave of dizziness washing over him.

When the door finally opened he almost choked with relief. Jackdaw wore a long black cloak and his face was grim. Yul tried to stand up but Jackdaw cuffed him round the head, making the room spin once more.

"Stay there and don't bloody move," he growled.

He wheeled out the others, one by one. Eventually he came back and pushed Yul's chair down the corridor and out into the night. A large cart was parked outside with two black plumed horses in the shafts. Jackdaw scooped Yul out of the wheelchair and laid him along the width of the cart next to the dying people. All five of them now lay like sardines. Jackdaw threw a blanket over the lot of them, pulled up the tailgate and went round to sit beside the driver. Slowly the cart rolled forward, jolting on the track.

The old person's shrivelled skin rubbed against his and Yul felt a wave of revulsion. He was young and healthy. He didn't belong with the old and the dying. He tried to move, tried to sit up, but he was so weak. His body wouldn't respond, and he'd never manage to escape even if he could somehow get out of the cart. So he lay jostling against the dying person next to him as they trundled onwards. The track forked off just before the Village. As they approached it, Yul smelt the wood-smoke and roasting meat. He heard wild shouts and laughter as the community celebrated the festival.

He started to cry, sobs choking his throat, tears running hot down the sides of his head and soaking into his hair. He'd never again take part in the ceremonies, the dancing, the feasting. Never again be with his family and the folk he'd known all his life. Never see his cottage, the Village, the woods, the hills – none of the places he loved. Everything was coming to an end this night. He loved life, loved Stonewylde. He didn't want to die.

The sounds and smells of the Village receded and the cart rumbled up the track of the Long Walk. In the lantern light Yul saw the skeletal branches of the trees above, interlacing into a tunnel. He remembered all the times in his life he'd walked along here, to and from ceremonies at the Stone Circle. The feelings of excitement and magic he'd experienced there, of being part of something beautiful and powerful and in tune with the Earth Goddess and her forces. He'd never imagined this horror – the Dance of Death before he'd even reached adulthood.

The cart stopped and Jackdaw hauled him out roughly. He was dumped onto a wooden sled with his arms crossed on his chest. The air was cold on his bare skin for the white tunic was skimpy and thin. He lay silently as the other four were put onto similar sleds. They were just outside the great stones of the Circle. Yul turned his head and saw flickering light inside. The cart rolled away and the sleds were lined up side by side. Yul heard voices approaching, people getting closer. Then Jackdaw loomed into view again, black cloak flung back to reveal an enormous glistening torso covered with dark swirling tattoos. He crouched down, knees crushing Yul's chest as he leaned forward to leer into the boy's face. His breathing was heavy, his eyes gleamed with excitement. He produced a tiny bottle and forced Yul's mouth open with a grimy finger.

"Swallow!" he growled, pouring the liquid down Yul's throat. Yul gagged on the bitterness but swallowed. Jackdaw smiled, his gold tooth glinting. His face started to swim and melt away and Yul's fears were confirmed; he'd been drugged once more. Jackdaw laughed as he saw the change in Yul's eyes.

"That's a good boy, Yul. Taking your medicine nicely now, ain't you? We don't want you getting up half way through and trying to leg it. This'll stop you moving but it won't knock you out. Magus wants you conscious."

Jackdaw stood up as people approached, and positioned himself by the sleds. Yul could see and hear although everything was strangely distorted and elongated. He found he couldn't move a muscle. The group wore hooded black robes and skull masks. Reality spiralled out of reach.

"How many folk wish to enter the Stone Labyrinth tonight?" asked Magus, his voice formal and ceremonial.

"Five," answered Jackdaw, now wearing a bird mask. He looked like a real jackdaw.

"The five who enter the Stone Labyrinth must perform the Dance of Death. Are they prepared for this?"

"They are."

"Have their closest relatives agreed that they should perform the Dance of Death?"

"They have."

"And are these Death Dancers prepared for the Dark

29

Angel, who may tonight come in their midst and take their souls to the Otherworld?"

"They are."

Magus paused. He looked in turn at each of the bodies on the sleds. He was quite terrifying in the skull mask.

"Bearers, step forward."

Five of the robed people stood before him and he addressed them solemnly.

"Tonight you bearers may look Death itself in the face and you must turn away, for you belong in the Realms of the Living. Before you enter the Stone Labyrinth, you must be fortified. This wine is the fruit of the elder, the sacred tree of the dead. It represents the blood of the earth, the blood of death, and the blood of birth. Drink deeply of the wine. It will prepare you for the part you must play in the Dance of Death."

A squat female figure with a small cauldron and ladle came forward. One by one the bearers knelt before Magus, who held a ladle of the dark liquid to their mouths for them to drink. He then moved to the white figures on the sleds and poured a tiny amount of wine over their unresponsive lips. But when Magus came to Yul, the bearer stood aside. Jackdaw crouched and lifted the boy's head, tipping it back and opening his mouth. He winked as Yul's terrified eyes met his, only centimetres away. Magus slowly poured a whole ladle full of the wine down his throat, giving him time to swallow. Yul felt the thick, warm wine slide down into his empty stomach. Jackdaw looked up and nodded, and Magus gave him another ladleful.

Yul, already drugged from the little bottle of liquid, felt his body melt into paralysis. It was as if his bones were dissolving. Before him he saw Magus flex his claws and purr with pleasure. The Jackdaw strutted forward and bowed to the Cat. Then the bearers took up the ropes and began to drag the sleds of the Death Dancers towards the entrance of the Stone Labyrinth.

CHAPTER THREE

Within the Stone Circle the transformation was complete. The circus of joy and celebration was now a carousel of death. Painted emblems of the dead danced and flickered on each great stone, lit from beneath by flaming torches. The lines of the labyrinth were defined with black stones and candles in red glass jars, glimmering like tiny pools of blood to mark the sacred path. In the centre of the Stone Labyrinth rose a flat topped pyre, a raft of death large enough for the consuming of several corpses.

The first bearer dragged his sled under the arch of elder, brushing beneath the hanging feathers and bones. The black robed figure and his white-tuniced burden stepped onto the path of the labyrinth and the Dance of Death began. Yul knew that the pattern itself marked the dance, and led the dancer to the Realms of the Otherworld. Tonight, because the veil between worlds was so thin at Samhain, the dead would be visible. The drums were like heartbeats thudding their final rhythm and a lone voice chanted eerily in a song for the dead. The birds of the Otherworld were now here. Crows, jackdaws, rooks, blackbirds and starlings roosted on every stone, forming a ring of black feathers and bright eyes.

Finally it was Yul's turn to enter the labyrinth; he was the last. His bearer tugged and the sled moved forward, sliding on the soft earth. It was a strange sensation, lurching but gliding, and very slow. Reality had vanished for Yul. His world had imploded into this circle, this pattern; the red flickering lights below his vision, the torches and capering skulls and crows above. The drumming and chanting were deep and unearthly. The circle was slightly misty. The temperature was dropping and his skin was cold. His feet and hands were numb already.

31

He tried to close his eyes, wanting only to block out this vision of horror, but he couldn't. The Dance of Death was inexorable.

The Great Barn rang with merriment and laughter. The community had feasted well and all were now drinking cider and elderberry wine freely. Young children were in bed, and the older children and adults were having a riotous time. The Barn looked fantastical. The candles inside the pumpkins and skulls were lit. Flocks of black papier-mâché birds moved in the hot air or perched realistically on the rafters. The dancing was wild, the musicians tireless. Miranda sat on one of the benches at the edge fanning herself. She was hot and uncomfortable, too pregnant to join in the galloping dances. Sylvie sat listlessly next to her. Her earlier resolve to fight Magus had seeped away. All she wanted was get back to her bed. It had been a long day and she was exhausted. Magus wasn't here so she couldn't ask to leave. Would he be angry if she went back to the Hall now, having made such a fuss this morning about her joining in the celebrations?

She thought wearily about what he'd said to her earlier. He made it sound so simple – just give her moon magic willingly for the good of Stonewylde. Give in to him and do what he wanted, like everyone else did. She wondered if it would help if Clip hypnotised her again. Her tired head was a jumble of confusion. If Magus was going to talk to her again in the morning, she needed to sleep. She'd need all her strength to stand up to him. Maybe she could use her gift of moon magic as a bargaining tool to help Yul? She closed her eyes, trying to block out the noise and heat of the celebration. The only thing that would make it bearable here tonight was if Yul were around. She wanted so much to see him, to make sure that he really was alright as Magus had said. She wondered what he was doing up at the Stone Circle tonight. What sort of ceremony was taking place up there? She concentrated hard, imagining his face, his hair, his long limbs, his smile.

Suddenly an image flashed into her mind. Hundreds of black birds perching on stones looking down. Drumming and chanting, slow and sinister. Red lights flickering, black hooded figures with skulls for faces dragging heavy burdens after them. She felt terror, a suffocating sensation of being trapped and unable to move. A certain knowledge that something terrible was going to happen. She opened her eyes with a jolt, her heart thudding.

She noticed Rosie getting a drink and stood up.

"I'm just going to speak to someone, Mum."

Miranda nodded.

"Alright, and then shall we go home? I've had enough. I'm sure Magus won't mind us leaving."

Rosie was pleased to see Sylvie but concerned that she looked so ill.

"It's okay, I'm off to bed in a minute. But I wanted to ask you what Yul's doing up at the Stone Circle tonight. Is he alright?"

Rosie frowned.

"The Stone Circle? I don't know, miss. I haven't seen him since the last Moon Fullness. He's been at the Hall ever since. We've all been very worried. So you ain't seen him neither?"

Sylvie shook her head, dread growing inside her.

"Magus told me this afternoon that Yul was fine. Although Tom from the stables told me earlier that Yul was in a bad way. And Magus definitely said that Yul was going to the Stone Circle tonight."

"Well, our father's up there. He's a Death Dancer and he'll meet the Dark Angel tonight. 'Tis time for him to let go of life, to pass on into the Otherworld. But not Yul ... I'm really scared, miss. Something's not right here."

The two girls stared at each other, their eyes wide with fear, united in their concern for Yul.

"I think he's in danger," said Sylvie. "I felt it a moment ago. He's trapped somehow and can't escape."

Rosie nodded.

"I think you're right. I'm going to find Mother now and tell her. Are you alright, miss? Hold on to me a minute. You look so faint. Take deep breaths. You go on to the Hall, and I'll let you know what happens. I'll get a message to you. I promise we'll find Yul."

The first sled had finally reached the centre of the labyrinth. The elderberry wine and potion had effectively paralysed Yul. He showed no more signs of life than the other four bodies, except for his eyes. As his sled lurched along its tortuous path, his beautiful grey eyes were once again wild and dilated, darting around to watch terrors real and imagined. At last his sled entered the centre and he was pulled around to face the pyre.

Seated on the top was a gruesome figure; a crone dressed in shreds of grey rag that hung from her sagging body. Her wiry hair sprang madly from her skull in long grey strands. She wore no mask, but white unguent of some sort had been rubbed into her skin. It gave her a cadaverous look and accentuated the wrinkles and seams that furrowed her face. Her toothless mouth was a cavernous hole, her eye-sockets pools of shadow. She held a lantern on her lap which shone up into her hideous face creating macabre shadows. She cackled as Yul was turned to face her, and even in his hallucinatory state he recognised the evil laughter of Old Violet.

Magus, Jackdaw and a crow-masked figure stepped forward. Jackdaw climbed the wooden steps to the flat summit of the pyre. He stood behind the crone, enormous and dark, his arms raised. He now wore a death mask. Magus began slowly to circle the centre around the sleds and pyre, chanting to the drum beat. It was very dark, for there was no extra light and the torches on the stones only lit their immediate area. The cold was intensifying as the night grew later. Mist curled in wisps just above the ground, glowing red above the tiny lights.

"You have completed the Dance of Death," intoned Magus. "You have reached the gateway to the Realms of the Otherworld. The dead are waiting. They peer through the veil to watch who approaches. They are beckoning, inviting you to join them. Death is merely a rebirth into another world. Now is the time to let go your hold on this life and move onwards to the next."

He paused, looking up at the sinister figures of Jackdaw

and the old woman on the pyre.

"It is almost the hour of midnight. The old year is dying, the new one beginning. The Dark Angel draws near. He alone will decide who accompanies him to the Otherworld. The Dark Angel will choose. Now is the time for the living to leave this circle and return to their realm. Bearers, depart!"

The bearers left the centre in single file and wended their way back around the path of the labyrinth. Finally they arrived at the edge of the Stone Circle, joining up with the others there – the drummers, singers and a few relatives of the dying people. One robed person started to organise a procession back down along the Long Walk. It was the custom to leave Magus and a couple of acolytes up in the Circle, alone with the dying. Nobody wanted to be in the Stone Labyrinth at midnight for the summoning. There were whispered tales of things that had happened over the years. Nobody wished to encounter the Dark Angel and look him in the eye.

Magus and the attendants who'd remained in the centre now stood on the platform of the pyre. Yul could see them clearly from where he lay helplessly, hallucinating and in a state of terror. They seemed huge and grotesque so high up above him.

"By the power of the sacred Stone Circle and the wisdom of the dark birds, I summon the Dark Angel to the portals of this world," called the crow-masked man, and Yul recognised Martin's voice.

"As the Crone of Samhain, I call on the Dark Angel as the veil stretches thin!" cried the hag. "We summon you now to the Stone Labyrinth. We ask you to take these souls with you tonight to the Otherworld."

"These five are ready and they await your presence this Samhain," said Martin, his robe flapping like wings. His beak nodded upwards repeatedly in exactly the movement of a crow.

"We summon you to the Circle tonight to take these five souls!" cried Violet, her withered arms outstretched and face hideous with excitement. "Take them tonight, Dark Angel!"

She and her son Martin bowed to Magus and made their

way down the steps to the ground. They joined the others at the arch of elder leading out into the Long Walk. Only Magus and Jackdaw now remained with the five bodies. Yul glanced around as far as his eyes could move, for his head wouldn't turn at all. He knew that soon Magus and Jackdaw would leave too. And then the Dark Angel would come. Then he would die.

Just as the procession was about to leave, there was a commotion under the trees of the Long Walk. Magus looked up sharply and in the flickering torchlight made out a woman. She was pulling at the bearers and drummers, pushing at the crone and her sister who blocked the entrance. The woman was held fast by the crow man, but was trying to get into the labyrinth. She shouted and cried, and even in his drugged state, Yul recognised his mother's voice. He struggled to move, to show her where he was. Despite his very best efforts he couldn't move a muscle. He could hear her calling him, her voice frantic.

"Bloody woman!" hissed Magus. "What the hell's she doing here?"

"Shall I go and deal with her?" asked Jackdaw quietly.

Magus hesitated.

"No, Martin seems to have hold of her. And I don't think she'd dare come in here. It's a sacred space. She knows that."

Yul's slow heartbeat quickened slightly. Maybe there was a chance after all? Could she rescue him? But he thought of Jackdaw's brutality and knew the man would have no qualms about hurting a woman. The images swirled around in his brain but the effects of the elderberry wine seemed to be wearing off, for he was thinking a little more clearly.

"Magus, have you got my boy in there?" Maizie called desperately. She was surrounded by the bearers who barred her way, and Martin still restrained her. The two old women capered about, plucking at her shawl and poking her. Magus stood up high facing her across the Circle, the paths of the labyrinth flickering with the tiny red lights. The centre was dark and Maizie couldn't see clearly what was there. Who exactly lay on the sleds.

"It is not the custom to come here and question the magus at this crucial time of Samhain," he called sternly. "You are displeasing me and you will answer to me tomorrow."

"Have you got my son in there?" she called again, ignoring the threat as if he hadn't spoken.

"I have your husband Alwyn here," said Magus. "You are disturbing his journey to the Otherworld. Woman, do you have any idea how serious this is? You ..."

"I don't care about that! Have you got my son in there? That's all I want to know. I won't go away until you've told me the truth!"

Her voice was shrill with fear and anger. Magus swore softly.

"Just lie to her," said Jackdaw quietly.

"She knows I've got him," replied Magus. "Somebody's told her."

"Let me go and deal with her," repeated Jackdaw. "It'll only take a minute to shut her up and she won't bother you again."

"No," said Magus. "That wouldn't go down too well in the Village. It's alright, I can put her off."

Yul lay as if made of stone, praying that his mother wouldn't be put off.

"Maizie, listen to me," called Magus, in his most reasonable and conciliatory voice. "I have got Yul here. He's eaten something bad, a poisonous mushroom or something, and he's very ill. He can't move. He's dying, I'm afraid."

There was a loud shriek of anguish and Yul heard her sobbing.

"Why didn't you tell me?" she cried. "Why didn't you come and get me? Has the doctor seen him? How could you bring him to the Stone Labyrinth without letting me know?"

"I'm sorry, Maizie. It all happened so quickly. The doctor's said he can't possibly survive. So I thought it best for him go tonight at Samhain, with proper ceremony, to meet the Dark Angel."

Yul could hear his mother sobbing and crying, screeching her grief and desolation. His heart felt as if it would break at the sound of her suffering. Then suddenly her sobs quietened.

"No!" she cried. "No – that isn't right. You told Sylvie this afternoon that he was fine. Yet you knew then that he'd be up here tonight. You told her so. You're making this up! I don't believe you! You're lying!"

She started to struggle again. Martin and the bearers did their best to hold her as she flailed her arms and tried to wrench away from their grip. Magus swore viciously.

"Maizie," he called sadly, "I promise you I'm not lying. You ask Martin and Old Violet there. They've only just left the labyrinth and they've seen for themselves. The boy is completely paralysed. He's only barely alive now and his breathing is very slow. He's dying. It won't be long now."

"NO!!" she shrieked. "I never gave my permission for him to enter the Stone Labyrinth! 'Tis not allowed to take anyone in there without their closest relative's say so. I never agreed! I want him out now! *Now*, Magus! If Yul's dying I want him to die in my arms, not in there with those old bodies. You bring him out!"

"I can't, Maizie. It's too late."

"NO IT'S NOT!! You need my permission and I don't give it! I don't give it, Magus! I'm going back to the Village now and I'll bring all the folk up here and let them see what you've done! You took my son in there without my agreement! Everyone will know!"

She was almost screaming with hysteria, a heady mixture of panic and fury. Magus swore strongly again and Jackdaw fidgeted, begging to be permitted to silence her once and for all. Magus stayed him with one hand and took a deep breath. He looked down at Yul. The boy lay like a corpse but his dilated eyes were wide open and watching everything. Magus smiled down at Yul. In the flickering light his face grinned with wicked glee, like the Jack o' Lanterns painted on the stones.

"Maizie, listen to me. Stop shrieking and listen. I didn't ask your agreement because I didn't need it. I myself decided to bring Yul in here tonight. I gave the permission myself."

"You can't do that!" she screamed. "You can't do that,

Magus!"

"Oh yes I can!" he shouted triumphantly. "I can because I'm his closest relative too. I'm his father!"

Yul thought his heart had stopped in his chest. *Magus his father?* Could he be? He heard Maizie howl in anguish, a cry of pure pain as if someone had stabbed her.

"NO!! You can't do this, Magus! How can you do this? How can you be so cruel?"

She sobbed uncontrollably, unable to speak any further. With his eyes swivelled as far as they could go, Yul saw her sink to her knees, head in her hands. He knew then that it was true. Magus, this sadistic tyrant, was his father. Magus laughed, the sound ringing out around the great stones.

"Go back to the Village, Maizie! You're not allowed to stay up here now, as the time approaches. Come back in the hour before dawn with the other relatives. Then we shall know whether or not the Dark Angel has chosen to take our son to the Otherworld."

Yul saw the group leave, surrounding his distraught mother and bundling her away. She was crying pitifully, overwhelmed with despair. His hopes plummeted. He was very cold and had no way of getting his circulation going. He realised then that the thin tunics must be the means of ensuring death for the old and dying.

"Do you want me to stay on here, sir?" asked Jackdaw, climbing down from the pyre.

"No," said Magus. "Go up to my office and I'll meet you there. I want a word first with this boy, just the two of us. I'll join you in a while and we'll have a drink and warm ourselves up. There's brandy in my office. Martin will show you. We don't need to return until early in the morning. I'd rather not spend any more time than I need to in the Circle at Samhain. Just so long as we're back here before all the relatives turn up. Bring the cauldron over before you go, would you?"

Jackdaw passed him the cauldron and ladle and left.

Magus walked around the sleds feeling for the pulses in the neck of each person. When he came to Yul, he crouched down. His fingers lingered, stroking the boy's throat almost tenderly.

"Well, son, here we are then. Just you and me," he said softly. His long fingers caressed the skin around Yul's windpipe. "I hold your life in my hands. A tiny squeeze and it's snuffed out forever."

His fingers paused, pressing slightly and then a little harder. Yul thought that this was it. But Magus released the pressure and continued to stroke Yul's neck.

"You began life in this Stone Circle and soon you'll be ending it here too. The circle of life. I remember the night you were born, the Winter Solstice and the rising of the blue moon. Both together – a very rare occurrence. What a night that was! And you've been the angel of my nightmares ever since, haunting me at every turn. Never out of my thoughts or dreams. I've watched you grow up over the years, Yul. I've looked on as Alwyn did his best to knock the spirit out of you, to break you. This year I've watched you make the transition from boy to man, and start to challenge me in a way nobody else at Stonewylde would ever dare. Just as it was foretold. Old Heggy was right all along. It's strange, you know. None of my other children even begin to measure up to you. I almost feel proud of you. You're so very like me. Flesh of my flesh."

He sighed deeply, running his fingers over Yul's hollowed face, pushing the tangled curls back from his forehead. He reached across and took a ladle of the rich elderberry wine. He sipped it, savouring the heady taste. Then he knelt and lifted Yul's head, cradling it almost lovingly. Yul's eyes were locked in to his. Locked in fear at this new facet of Magus. This apparently tender side scared him almost more than the cruel side.

"It should be easy to end your life now, Yul. I gave you life one magical night under a blood red eclipsed moon, when I took your mother's virginity. And I should be able take your life away so easily. Just a little pressure would do it. You're very cold now, aren't you? Your body's shutting down and I can feel your pulse is slow and weak. But I can't do it. Not because I care and not because I don't want to. Your death is something I've dreamed about. But all these years you've been protected by that old hag Heggy. Bound by her spell, cast here in the Circle on the night of your birth. I can't take your life, much as I long to. If I were to do that, the Dark Angel would take me also. That was the binding spell that Heggy cast. But tonight – this is different. It's not my doing if you should die. The Angel himself will decide on your fate."

Yul stared up at him, unable to move or look away. He felt the man's power as he cradled him, the force within him that was nothing to do with Sylvie's moon magic. Magus eyes, so dark and bright, gazed down into his and Yul sensed the iron will in his father's soul. The hard cruelty that drove him. His absolute faith in his own strength and superiority.

"In a minute I shall leave you here on your own. You've defied me, challenged me, tried to put yourself above me. And now I want you to suffer, Yul. Tonight you will know real fear as the Dark Angel walks the labyrinth. You'll probably die during the night, for you're cold and weak. But if you should survive, your death will be even more terrifying. Remember the custom of Samhain and the journey to the Otherworld? In the hour before dawn, if you cannot move or show a sign that you choose life, then you will be burnt on the pyre. A kindness for those poor souls who wish for euthanasia to end their suffering. I know you won't be able to move. Old Violet's little bottle of potion you willingly drank earlier, from Jackdaw's hand of course, will prevent any movement for many hours yet. When I ask who chooses life, you won't move or show any sign. Your choice, Yul, not mine. Not my hand in any of this. I shall be safe from the binding spell. Jackdaw will put a torch to the pyre and you'll burn with the corpses."

He chuckled, and drank more of the wine.

"This is very strong stuff. I must go easy. I don't want too many visions myself. I want to savour every single moment of this night. The night when I finally rid myself of you. I've looked forward to being free of you for so long. But you – why, you can have the wine. Visions and dreams whilst you're lying here will get you through the night, as you contemplate your death."

Still cradling Yul's head, he ladled wine down the boy's

throat slowly and carefully. Yul had to swallow or choke. Magus took his time, ensuring Yul drank plenty. He tenderly wiped the boy's lips with the sleeve of his robe.

"There, that's more than enough. That should ensure some powerful visions. I can feel something myself and I've only had a small amount. Now I must leave you on your own with these four bodies. Did I tell you they're already dead? No pulses. Just you, the corpses and the Dark Angel. You're surrounded by death. You're very brave but tonight even you will know terror. Look out for the Angel, Yul. He's here, that's for sure. Goodnight, my son."

Magus bent and kissed Yul's forehead. He rose and stretched, looking down at the boy. His dark eyes glowed in the dim light and his mouth tightened momentarily. With a farewell salute, he turned and walked out of the Circle, leaving Yul alone with his visions and dreams.

The small silvery creature sat up high on one of the great standing stones, a crow on her shoulder. She waved at him and smiled, then floated down to the misty ground. She skipped along the labyrinth path, her ragged dress flimsy in the wisps of mist and hazy red lights. Her feet were bare, as were her thin white arms and legs. She was small and delicate and her face was beautiful. Her hair was a wild silver bird's nest of tangles and burrs.

"Blessings, Yul," she said softly in a tiny angel voice. "We meet again, my grandson."

She threw her head back and laughed, revealing tiny sharp teeth. Her laughter tinkled in the air and wove a web of silver around the four dead bodies.

"You hold fast, my little Yul. 'Tis the place of your birth, but not the place of your death. I'm here to help you through this long and lonely night. Old Mother Heggy summoned me to protect you."

He tried to smile at her, feeling better for knowing he wasn't all alone as the Angel drew near. He glanced upwards and saw the birds still perched above, watching him with bright beady eyes.

"Don't be scared of them. They're your friends, come to watch over you. Especially my crow. You'll see."

The night wore on, growing colder and colder. Yul couldn't feel any part of his body now. Everything was numb. Only a little kernel of his mind still functioned, and that in a bizarre way, for the visions followed thick and fast. Many people joined Raven with him in the labyrinth. A host of people, all long gone, from centuries and centuries past. They poured through the veil and crowded in to gaze at him, appearing and then fading. But Raven let nobody come close to Yul. She sat by his side and held his hand in hers, guarding him.

Several times Yul saw in the corner of his vision a tall, black robed figure processing around the Circle. At first he thought it was Magus come back. Then Yul realised with a burst of recognition that it was the Dark Angel himself. He stalked the labyrinth, the blackness around him deeper than it should be. Yul knew he must not look into the Angel's face. He must not get a glimpse of those eyes, or he would be lost.

"Yul, Yul," called the silvery voice later on, when the darkness grew thicker all around him. "Don't go! Don't leave! You must stay and fight, Yul."

She blew softly on his face, stirring his curls. He forced his eyes open. They were very heavy. He was so tired. All he wanted was to float into soft, grey sleep and never wake up. It was so tempting, so alluring. Just sink into goose-down slumber and peace.

"YUL!! Do you want Sol to win? Do you realise what will happen if you die tonight? You must fight, Yul! You're the only one at Stonewylde who can defeat him. Think of your moongazy maiden! He'll never have his fill of her. He'll drink her life away, sip by sip. She'll die from his greed, as I died from his father's greed. You saw what happened to me, didn't you Yul? You saw that night on the cliff top how he devoured me, ripped me apart. You're the only one who can stop it happening all over again, but this time to your beloved girl."

Yul's eyes shot open. He'd forgotten about Sylvie! He had to protect her from Magus. He couldn't give in now. He saw the Dark Angel leave the labyrinth and melt into the edges of the night. And then he heard voices.

"I reckon he'll have snuffed it."

"I don't," said Magus. "That boy's strong. He'll have survived. But he won't be able to move, so he'll burn at dawn with the others. You must do that, Jackdaw, for I can't."

"Aye, and I'll say the words, right enough," came a cackly voice. "I know 'em well. I'll speak the words for you, so 'tis not your doing and the binding spell's not crossed."

"Yes, Violet, you do that. Leave me out of the whole thing this year."

The four cloaked figures walked briskly around the labyrinth path and arrived in the centre. Raven shielded Yul from them, whispering comfort in his ear.

"You won't die here tonight, Yul. 'Tis not your destiny. I'll help you. You'll choose life."

"Well I'll be damned!" exclaimed Jackdaw, seeing Yul's eyes still open and watching. "You were right, sir. Tough little bugger, ain't he?"

Magus laughed dryly and glanced down at his son. It was still night and the torches were burning low. Many of the red lights on the path had gone out. It was very cold and their breath clouded out in the still air. The four arrivals were snug in their thick cloaks. Magus' cheeks glowed and Yul could tell he'd charged himself up with moon energy during the night. He was full of life and vitality and his eyes burned brightly. The four of them looked down at Yul lying on the wooden sled in his thin white tunic with his arms and legs bare. He was pale and unmoving, and but for his dilated eyes, looked like a corpse. Every one of the four wished him dead.

"Soon 'twill be time, Yul," cried the silvery voice. "You must try to stir your cold blood. Move your toes and fingers, boy. Move them!!"

He tried but nothing happened. He kept on trying, willing his body to move even a fraction, but nothing whatsoever happened. He was completely numb and paralysed. Magus crouched down and felt his pulse again. He gazed deep into Yul's frightened eyes and his black fire blazed in exultation.

He smiled slowly and nodded, straightening up.

"He's still alive but only just," said Magus, "He's not going anywhere. We have about an hour until dawn. The relatives will be here soon. Have you got everything you need, Martin? The oil so they burn well? The wreaths for their heads? The lighter? Good. As soon as Violet's said the words, you two men get the bodies up on the pyre as fast as possible. I want this over with quickly and I can't give you any assistance. Nothing must go wrong."

Then Yul heard them coming, and so did Magus and the others. There were far too many voices. It was customary for the closest relatives to attend the burning. But now, in the coldness of the hour before dawn on New Year's Day, a great throng of people came up the Long Walk. Yul could just see if he swivelled his eyes. He made out a huge crowd of Villagers led by his mother, all carrying burning torches. His heart leaped. There was still a chance!

Maizie stopped by the arched entrance and peered into the centre of the Stone Labyrinth. It was very dark inside the Circle and all she could make out were the four figures in their dark, hooded robes, and five still, white shapes on the wooden sleds.

"I don't believe it!" snarled Magus. "She's brought bloody reinforcements!"

But he began the ritual as if the size of the great crowd was entirely normal. The Death Dancers were invited by the crone to choose between life and death. They were commanded to show some sign if they wanted to stay in this world, or remain still and silent if they wished to be sped to the Otherworld and have their mortal remains burnt. The four corpses remained still and silent. Yul tried to move, tried to call out or move his hand. He tried with every fibre of his being. But his numb, drugged body wouldn't respond. He could hear his mother's voice calling to him from the entrance, begging him to make a sign. He could hear her choking on her sobs, pleading with him to choose life. She'd been convinced he'd be dead already. But now, although she couldn't see him clearly at all, she felt somehow that he still held on to a thread of life. She kept on and on calling to him, but try as he might, he could make no movement at all. Then he heard the other voice, the voice of his grandmother.

"Come, Yul! 'Tis time and you *have* to move. If you don't show a sign now you'll be burned alive. Call on the Earth Magic, Yul! This Circle is your special place. You are the chosen one. Summon it to you, Yul! Call the green magic now to give you strength!"

He was some way from the Altar Stone where the force was most powerful. But he knew she was right. The energy was here in the Circle if only it would seek him out. He was so weak, so cold. But he remembered that night in August at the Corn Moon when he'd run round and round, calling up the storm. In his mind he started now to run, his limbs free and strong. Round the Circle, round the stones, calling on the power of the Earth Magic, raising the energy up, up into his soul … Raven rubbed hard on his frozen hands crossed on his chest. She chafed them with her small, rough hands, exhorting him to move. Her mass of tangled silver hair fell across his face and tickled him. He called and called, summoning the hidden power of the ancient Stone Circle, the power tapped by his ancestors, the green magic of old … He called on the Earth Goddess who'd chosen him to lead Stonewylde.

"Sir!" whispered Martin urgently. "I saw his nose move. It twitched."

"What?" hissed Magus. "Don't talk rubbish! He's paralysed. He can't move a muscle."

"No, look! His fingers moved as well. Look, sir!"

Magus then saw too.

"Give him some more of the potion quickly! Where is it? Quick!"

"'Tis over yonder by the Altar Stone," said Violet. "There's more in the chest. But something's amiss here. I feel another close by. A shade … something, someone from the Otherworld who has no place here. We must …"

"Never mind that now! Go, Jackdaw! Get the bottle quickly!"

But as Jackdaw tried to fetch the paralysing draught, a great crow launched itself from a standing stone and flew straight into Jackdaw's face. It flapped and pecked in a wild flurry of black feathers, beak and claws. Jackdaw swore violently and tried to swipe it away. But the more his arms thrashed, the harder it attacked, coming from all angles, pecking and beating its wings, cawing crazily. He couldn't get out of the centre; couldn't move from the spot.

"What the hell is going on? Violet, say the last words! You two – get the bodies up onto the pyre! Quick!"

"I ask for the final time! If you choose to live, give us a sign. For now 'tis the hour of the burning. Do none o' you choose life?"

"Move, Yul, move! I can feel the life force rising in you. Raise your hand!"

There was a cry from the crowd.

"He moved! I saw him move!"

"YUL!" screamed Maizie. "Are you alive, my boy?"

"Here, my sweet grandson, take my hands! Let me help you."

He gazed into her silvery moonstone eyes and felt such love and kindness flowing from her. She took his cold hands in hers and tugged with all her strength, raising his hands above his chest. He felt the green energy snaking across, seeking him out, finding its path to him under the labyrinth. With a sudden explosion of power, the Earth Magic poured from the ground beneath him up into his body. Yul sat up in one fluid motion, bolt upright on the sled. It was like someone rising from the dead.

The crowd of Villagers roared its delight, everyone cheering and laughing.

"He chooses life, Magus!" screamed Maizie, beside herself with joy. "He's moved and now he can live. You're not burning my son! I'm coming to fetch him!"

Nobody knew the protocol for when a Death Dancer decided to live. It had never happened before in their memory. Only the very sick or the very old took part, and the cold night had always finished them off by this stage. But Maizie began to trot along the path of the labyrinth, hurrying around the twists and turns until she entered the centre. Magus glowered

47

at her in silent fury, his face white. Jackdaw cracked his knuckles ominously and Violet muttered. They all stepped back from Maizie as she threw herself down beside Yul. She kissed his cold face, taking his icy hands in hers and rubbing them. She carefully laid him back down on the sled, for although he'd somehow sat up he couldn't move at all now. She pulled off the warm shawl wrapped around her shoulders and tenderly covered her son, stroking his cheek as her tears fell on his chilled skin. His deep grey eyes gazed up at her, pouring out his love.

She glared up at Magus.

"You knew he was alive!" she whispered. "Yet you were prepared to burn him, your own son. I won't forget this, Magus. Nobody will forget this. The folk know what you've done here tonight. They all know now of your wickedness."

"Maizie, you must …"

But she stood abruptly, ignoring him. She found the rope tied to the sled and began to pull. Slowly it moved away from the centre and down the path. Several of the men in the crowd came forward to help and soon they were out of the Stone Labyrinth.

Tom had brought the cart and Yul was lifted up and laid carefully in the back, covered with people's shawls and cloaks. The crowd surrounded the cart as it moved away, the procession lit triumphantly by their blazing torches. The few grieving relatives who remained watched in silence as Magus and his assistants continued with the Samhain rite of burning the bodies.

Magus' face was as dark as the crows and rooks that perched on the stones. The pyre whooshed into crackling life and the birds rose as one. As the ashes floated high above the Stone Circle, the air was filled too with the beating wings of hundreds of birds, speeding the four souls to the Realms of the Otherworld.

CHAPTER FOUR

Magus stood looking out over the grey gardens. Dew and cobwebs laced the shrubs around the French windows like a shroud. The trees reached up to the overcast skies with bony black fingers. There was a desolate feel to the early morning that belied the excitement of the festival the previous day. Sylvie paused silently in the doorway of the office, loathe to disturb the reverie of the man before her. He seemed dejected. There was something bleak in the set of his shoulders and his absolute stillness. He wore a dark business suit which gave him an Outside World air.

Sylvie had been summoned by a dour-faced Martin, who'd informed her coldly of Magus' request. He'd barely spoken a word as they made their way along the gallery and into the main body of the Hall. His wintry grey eyes and air of disapproval had quashed her attempts at conversation. Sylvie still knew nothing of Yul, for she'd seen nobody else yet this morning. Her mind raced with speculation as to why Magus should send for her so early, before everyone else was up and about for the New Year's Day breakfast.

Her tentative feelings of sympathy for him, standing so alone and pensive, were quickly dispelled when he turned suddenly and fixed her with an icy glare.

"Come in and close the door behind you," he said tersely.

They sat on the sofas and his gaze scoured her face.

"I told you yesterday we'd speak today. But this isn't the conversation I'd envisaged. Due to ... unforeseen events, I'm now going away for a week or so. There're a couple of things I need to say before I leave in a minute. I've obviously reached you before you heard the gossip that will doubtless rage at the breakfast table today, once it's filtered up from the Village."

Her heart jumped at this, dreading his next words.

"I wanted to tell you this myself, in case you get ideas about anything changing."

He paused and saw the fear in her eyes. His face was impassive as he continued.

"Last night during the Samhain rituals up in the Stone Circle, I made an announcement. I let it be known to all that Yul is my son."

He waited as the news impacted on her consciousness. She stared at him in mute incredulity and he watched the succession of emotions flit over her face, before finally reaching acceptance and understanding.

"You ..."

He waved her to silence.

"I'm not discussing it now. Other than to remind you that you are forbidden to have any contact with that boy. This changes nothing."

"But surely ..."

"No! He remains an ignorant, uncouth woodsman and nothing more, despite being sired by me. You're out of his league and you're to keep away from him. That's my final word on the matter."

Sylvie's eyes met his and she tried to mask her intentions, knowing only too well how perceptive he was.

"Is he alright? There was something wrong yesterday. I could feel it."

"Yes, he is alright. And I heard of the part you played in this. Thanks to your meddling and scaremongering, my plans for the future are now in jeopardy. You've a lot to answer for, and when I return I shall make sure you do. In the meantime, you're to attend all your classes every day and ensure that you work extremely hard. I've left a note for your tutor. When I get back I expect a full report from him on the progress you've made since coming here in March, and a record of your attendance. You're slothful and lacking in motivation. Your attitude is a mockery of all that we strive for at Stonewylde. This is your final year of secondary education and at this rate you'll fail your exams miserably. It's not acceptable. So whilst

I'm away I expect you to make a concerted effort to cover the work you've missed. Now go back to your rooms and tell your mother that I wish to see her immediately. That's all, Sylvie. You may go now."

"But it's not …"

"I said *that's all*. I shall take this up with you when I return."

His face was like stone. Sylvie stood up, smarting with injustice. She knew exactly what she intended to do at the first opportunity.

Miranda returned a little later with an equally grim expression.

"Come on – breakfast time. Get a move on, Sylvie."

As they made their way down the long gallery she turned on her daughter.

"Things are going to change, Sylvie, starting from today. I've been far too soft with you. You're to sit with me at meal times so I can make sure you're eating properly. When you've finished breakfast this morning you're to see your tutor and find out what you need to do to catch up with your work. Then go and see Hazel in the hospital wing. Magus had told her to do a complete health check. And your weight's going to be monitored closely."

"What? But Mum, why is …"

"I don't want to hear it, Sylvie. Your attitude is just not good enough. You're going to spend every evening working in our rooms where I can keep an eye on you. You have so much ground to cover."

"But it's not fair! I only missed so much school because he made me ill! If you …"

"Don't be so ridiculous! It's not Magus' fault. That's typical of your inability to accept responsibility for your own shortcomings. You've been selfish and lazy, expecting us all to run around whilst you take to your bed and deliberately make yourself ill. I used to worry that you were anorexic. But I can see now how you refuse food in an attempt to weaken yourself deliberately and then get us all fussing over you. Well it's going to stop. I have the baby to think of now. I don't have the time or inclination to pander to you any more. Magus is very annoyed and it's up to me to sort you out."

Sylvie's tutor, a rather grumpy middle-aged member of the Hallfolk who was staying at Stonewylde for a couple of years whilst he completed his thesis, was also curt. He'd compiled a list of coursework and areas of study where she must catch up. Her heart sank. She'd never really taken to him but had found him to be generally amenable if not disturbed too much. Now he glowered at her, furious to have his New Year's Day holiday taken up like this.

"I've had to speak to all your subject teachers at extremely short notice. We thought we had the day off. Now that I've looked into it more closely, I'm appalled at your attendance since the summer. You made a reasonable start in the spring, but it very quickly deteriorated. You're behind in every subject and you have a considerable amount of work to catch up with. I want to see you every morning with the fruits of the previous day's efforts. The last thing I need is Magus breathing down my neck. You've let us all down with this hypochondria. You now have some serious work to do, young lady, if you're going to even scrape through your exams."

Even Hazel, usually supportive and friendly, was cool. She gave Sylvie a comprehensive medical and drew up a chart to record her weight. Sylvie by this time was feeling thoroughly depressed by the turn of events. She recognised Magus' attempts to punish her for alerting Maizie to Yul's presence in the Stone Circle the night before. She was still desperate for news of him, although judging by Magus' displeasure, Yul must be alright. Hazel frowned at her as she sealed the blood and urine samples in a box to be sent off for analysis.

"I'm disappointed in you, Sylvie," she said. "I feel responsible for you being here, and I was so pleased that you'd apparently made a full recovery from your illness in London. But this – this is something different. Magus says you're deliberately malingering to get attention, and that there's nothing physically wrong with you. I must say that apart from your obvious exhaustion after the full moon, and the fact that you lose so much weight through refusing food, I'm inclined to agree with him."

"But it's his fault, Hazel! He makes me stand on the rock up at Mooncliffe and it drains my energy. He knows exactly what's wrong with me!"

"Oh come on!" said Hazel sceptically. "Don't start fantasising as well as faking illness. I know all about that rock. That's a load of nonsense."

Sylvie stared at her helplessly.

"But Hazel ..."

"No, Sylvie. Magus warned me you'd try to put the blame for your apparent malaise on someone else. You've got to face the facts. You enjoy all the attention that illness brings and that's all there is to it. It's a common enough syndrome but not something I'd have expected from you."

"But I don't pretend to be ill! It's real!"

Hazel shook her head and stood up, firmly ushering Sylvie from her office.

"I'm sorry, Sylvie. I just don't believe you. Of course if these tests throw up anything, I'll reconsider. That's why Magus ordered them. To be absolutely sure we're not misjudging you. But you need to do some hard thinking about your life at Stonewylde. You didn't come here to mope about being pathetic, did you? Don't try and get my sympathy. Because if you put me in a position where I have to choose sides between you and Magus, I'm afraid you'd be the loser. That man has been so kind to you. It's about time you woke up to that and started acting a little more appropriately to your situation. I'll see you tomorrow morning for your weigh-in."

The only brightness in the dull days of endless school work and disapproval from all the adults responsible for her, happened a couple of evenings later. Harold caught Sylvie alone as she walked through the Tudor gallery. He emerged from the shadows of one of the doorways leading to guest rooms, and had clearly been waiting for her to pass by.

"Sorry, miss, to startle you. I got a message from Rosie for you."

"From Rosie? Brilliant! Thank you, Harold."

Sylvie was so relieved. She'd heard gossip and had gathered that Yul was now safely at home, but other than that there'd been no news yet. She'd been wondering what to do; how to find out more. She desperately wanted to see him but didn't know where to meet. She smiled encouragingly now at Harold, who shyly scuffed his shoe along the deep wooden wainscot of the gallery. He was the same age as Yul, but much less sure of himself.

"Rosie said Yul's on the mend now. But he's still very weak and their mother's keeping him indoors. She said Yul wants you to go to their cottage and see him. Any time you like, he said. And he misses you. And … he loves you."

They both looked embarrassed at this but Sylvie grinned with bubbling happiness.

"Please tell him, or Rosie if that's easier, I'll be down to the Village just as soon as I get the chance. Everyone's on my back at the moment but I promise I'll visit. Tell him I love him too. Sorry, Harold. This is awkward I know. I wish he could read, then I'd write him a note."

Harold looked up and nodded eagerly, his eyes alight.

"I told Yul I'd teach him."

"You can read? How come?"

"I'm learning. Teaching myself. I'm not very good yet but I'm getting better."

"Good for you! Le me know if I can help you. And do try to persuade Yul to learn too. Magus would hate it! Did you know Magus is his father?"

"Reckon the whole of Stonewylde knows that now, miss. What a thing! Who'd have thought it, the way Magus has treated him. Mind you, I always thought Yul was a bit special."

"So did I," said Sylvie with a smile.

It took several days for the effects of the paralysing draught to wear off and for Yul's body temperature to normalise after the hypothermia. But he was young and fit and began to recover from the near fatal experience that Magus had subjected him to. Maizie kept him indoors and made him up a bed in the parlour. It seemed that most of the Village turned up to wish him a speedy recovery and bring him little gifts. She couldn't have them all trooping up and down the rickety wooden stairs to the attic where he normally slept.

In the Village there was a backlash of anger against Magus. The main cause, apart from his brutal and inexcusable treatment of Yul, was the re-appearance of Jackdaw from his banishment. Most people had been kept unaware of his presence at Quarrycleave earlier in the year, and he hadn't shown his face in the Village then. But now the man had been brought back to Stonewylde without any explanation or apparent retribution, and many felt he hadn't been punished at all. People muttered and held whispered conversations. But such was Magus' power that nobody would dare to criticise him openly. So solidarity was displayed in a show of support for Yul. He became the focal point for the Villagers and Maizie found her house crowded every evening with well-wishers.

Sylvie managed to get away one morning during a rare free hour. She'd been working as hard as she could in the evenings and was beginning to make a little headway in catching up with the work she'd missed. She was still struggling to cope with everyone's censure, but persuaded Hazel that a daily walk was beneficial to her recovering good health. She slipped out of the Hall and went straight down to the Village to find Yul's cottage, having checked with Harold exactly where it was. She was nervous about going into the Village like this. She'd been at Stonewylde long enough now to know what was acceptable and what wasn't. And Hallfolk didn't visit Villagers in their homes.

She received puzzled looks from the Villagers out and about on their business. There was no festival and it wasn't the Dark Moon. Why would Hallfolk be coming down here? The Village was bustling with women wrapped in warm shawls, wicker baskets on their arms, gossiping to each other as they went about their errands. A group standing outside the baker's collecting their daily bread turned and stared, but she wished them a cheerful good morning and they smiled and greeted her in return. It was the same by the butcher's, the Village pump, and the laundry. Her presence in their territory was startling to them, and every time she passed a group she felt all eyes upon her and heard their barely concealed squawks of surprise. But Sylvie found that her friendliness was returned each time, so she continued her walk around the Green and along the track leading to Yul's cottage.

She began to feel anxious as she approached, never having seen Yul like this before. Their friendship and developing relationship had been conducted entirely out of doors in the fields, woods and hills of Stonewylde. She was also a little scared of meeting his mother face to face. But she found the cottage and walked up the path to the front door, her heart beating faster and her mouth dry.

Maizie recognised at once the beautiful ethereal girl, shimmering on her doorstep like a star. She smiled warmly, dried her hands on her apron, and opened the door wide. Yul, lying on his made up bed in the corner, looked up as the door opened and his wan face flooded with joy at the sight of her. Sylvie's shyness with his mother was forgotten as she flew across the room and knelt by his bedside, flinging her arms around him. She sensed Maizie's discreet withdrawal into the kitchen and held him in a fierce embrace, tears welling up and scalding her cheeks. She clung to him, her face buried in his dark hair, feeling his arms holding her as tightly as she held him. She knew then just how much she loved him. She'd never let him go. He was more precious to her than anything or anyone. She knew in that moment with absolute certainty that they truly belonged together.

Sylvie cried as she held him tight, understanding how close she'd come to losing him forever. He was so thin under the shirt; she could feel his ribs and shoulder blades. They finally pulled apart and she looked into his deep, smoky eyes. She saw that he still wasn't right. His pupils were a little dilated and his eyes seemed enormous in his white, hollow face. His suffering was very apparent, worse even than the time when he'd been beaten and starved and then worked like a slave up at the stone quarry. And something else was different. It was as if he'd been to a place where nobody should go; had seen things that nobody should see. Yul had looked death in the face and had turned away only at the very last minute.

"I've been so scared for you, Yul," she sobbed, the tears streaming down her face. "I don't ever want to be without you again. I love you so much."

He tenderly wiped away her tears with his sleeve and kissed her mouth, gently but leaving her in no doubt that he felt exactly the same. Then he held her tight again, pulled her into his chest, kissing her hair and cradling her in his arms.

"We're almost there now, Sylvie. We've just got to get through the next few weeks until the Winter Solstice and then we'll be free of him."

There was a cough from the kitchen and Maizie appeared with rosehip tea and cakes. She smiled again at Sylvie and sat down with them, Leveret following her in from the kitchen. The little girl stared in fascination at their beautiful silver-haired visitor. She stood in her home-spun pinafore dress with woollen socks slipping down her tiny legs, and shook the mop of dark curls out of her eyes exactly as her oldest brother did. Then she too smiled and Sylvie was enchanted by her dancing green eyes and white pointed teeth. Maizie gathered the child up onto her lap and surveyed Sylvie with equal intensity.

"Well, I can see why my son's been so moon-struck these past few months," she said, in the embarrassing way mothers have. "And I must say 'tis good to be called on by Hallfolk for a friendly visit."

"Oh please, don't think of me as Hallfolk. I really hate all that stuff. I'd much rather live in the Village and be one of you. I'm not very popular up at the Hall. I don't belong there at all."

Maizie nodded at this.

"Yul says that you're one of Magus' victims too. He's told me about your moongaziness. I'm sorry you've suffered so much, my dear."

"Yes, but nowhere near what poor Yul's been through at his hands. At least Magus wants me alive. That man's got a lot to answer for."

"Aye, he has!" agreed Maizie, her face grim. "And he will answer for it too. I'm sure o' that."

Sylvie managed to spend quite a bit of time with Yul over the next few days, snatching precious minutes alone with him in the cottage as his mother went about her daily routine. Sylvie went down to the Village every day, ostensibly on a healthy walk when lessons were finished, and found she was warmly greeted now by everyone she met. Word had spread that she was Yul's sweetheart even though she was Hallfolk. People had plenty to gossip about already with the news that Yul was Magus' son. Sylvie still found this fact hard to accept, although now that she knew, it was obvious. Their difference in colouring had masked the likeness between them but she wondered why nobody had realised before. She discussed it with Yul on one of her visits, not sure how he felt knowing that their enemy was in fact his father.

"In some ways it's a relief," he said. "It explains why Alwyn treated me the way he did. I've spent my whole life wondering why he hated me so much."

"So he knew all along?" asked Sylvie.

"Mother says it was impossible for my father to be anyone other than Magus. She and Alwyn didn't get together until after I was born. Apparently Alwyn had been keen on her for ages, although she never encouraged him. He was very jealous of Magus. But he was a Villager and couldn't compete with the master. Village men keep away from a woman if they know that Magus is interested."

"How mediaeval – the droit du seigneur. Why did Alwyn pretend you were his when he knew you couldn't be?"

"Magus insisted. It was all part of the deal. After I was born he ordered Maizie and Alwyn to be handfasted straight away. Alwyn had to accept it because you don't question Magus. He was delighted at taking Mother for his wife because he'd wanted her for a long time. But he hated having to acknowledge me as his own son. He took it out on me because he couldn't take it out on Magus. I suppose it's understandable."

"No it's not!" said Sylvie fiercely, remembering the bruising and scarring she'd seen on Yul and realising that was just the tip of the iceberg. "It's child abuse and that's never understandable! It wasn't your fault anyway."

"True, but Mother says that every time Alwyn looked at me he was reminded of Magus because I'm so like him. I can't see it myself. Alwyn started mistreating me when I was still very young, and Mother was terrified he was going to go too far one day and kill me. She went to see Magus and begged him to take me in as a Hallchild. But he refused and wasn't concerned at all about my injuries. He never said anything to Alwyn. Never told him to lay off me or control his violence. So Alwyn realised then that he could do whatever he liked to me and Magus wouldn't interfere. It was as if Magus wanted me dead. And of course now we know that's exactly what he hoped would happen."

"And it's because of this prophecy?"

"Yes. And you must go and see Mother Heggy, Sylvie. I'm not allowed out of the house yet, and my mother's been through so much recently I don't want to upset her by disobeying her. You know Alwyn died at Samhain? It was no great loss and I won't pretend I'm sad, because I hated him. But it's not easy for Mother. They were hand fasted for years and he was the father of all the other children."

"Are they alright?"

"Yes!" he chuckled. "He might have been their father but they hated him too. They had to watch him beating me remember, and they were terrified of him. Please go and see Mother Heggy, Sylvie. Today if you can. The crow keeps visiting me and pecking at the window. It's driving Mother mad. I'm sure it's a message."

"Yes, I've seen it too. I'll go now. I'll make up some excuse about being late back."

"Take her some of this stuff people have brought me. We've got so much jam and wine and cake. She'd appreciate some treats, poor old thing."

The crow was hopping around outside as Sylvie left with a

laden basket for Mother Heggy. It flapped up onto her shoulder, cawing loudly in her ear.

"Yes, I understand," she said with a smile as it scrabbled to hold on. "I'm on my way now."

It stayed with her for some time as she walked through the Village, gripping clumsily onto her jacket. Several Villagers noticed and pointed it out to each other, remembering the crow on Yul's shoulder at the Summer Solstice ceremony. They knew it was Mother Heggy's creature. Many made the sign of the pentangle in the air and touched their chests. Everyone now understood that Yul and Sylvie were under her protection.

"My little bright one!" crowed Mother Heggy at the sight of Sylvie on her doorstep. "At last you've come. And only just in time, for 'tis the Dark Moon tomorrow."

She pulled Sylvie inside the smelly cottage, shooed a cat off the chair and sat her down. The crow hopped about on the table after a scrap of meat. Sylvie handed over the basket to the old woman.

"Very tasty too," cackled Mother Heggy, smacking her shrivelled lips as she rummaged about inside it. "And how is my boy? Is he healing well? I've been sending some reviving potions for him."

"Yes, but ... he's changed. There's something different about him. I don't think that will heal."

"No, 'twon't. He saw the Dark Angel at Samhain. He'll never be the same. There's a shadow on his soul now. But 'twill make him stronger and he'll need that strength. We're on the final path now, Sylvie. You know Magus must die, and 'twill not come about easy. Yul will need all his power and energy. Tell him to get up to that Circle just as soon as he can."

"You're not saying that Yul is actually going to kill Magus?" asked Sylvie, shaken at the thought. "Surely that isn't right? I mean ... well, I don't know if Yul would do that, or even could do it."

Mother Heggy shrugged, peering myopically at a jar of bramble jelly she'd unpacked from the basket.

"I don't know how 'twill happen," she said finally. "I only see so much. The old prophecy that came to me like a thunderbolt when the boy was born was clear enough. Magus would be destroyed by the fruit of his passion, conceived under the red moon and born under the blue moon. In the brightness at the darkness – that's the full moon at the Winter Solstice, the darkest day. So I know 'twill happen this Solstice, when Yul becomes a man. 'Tis the Moon Fullness on the eve of the Solstice this year. He will rise up with the folk behind him. And are they not all gathering behind him now? At the place of bones and death. We know where that is, right enough. 'Tis six weeks to the Solstice. But Sylvie," she gripped the girl's arm with her claws, peering almost sightlessly into her eyes, "there may be a prophecy from long ago but that don't mean all will go right. I seen something else of late, but 'tis not clear. There may be more than one death this Solstice. I see the number five, always the number five. But 'tis too many! Not five deaths, surely? I cannot see who must die, but I know one thing for sure. You and Yul are in great danger from Magus. Do you understand, girl? The man is evil. Yul would've died at Samhain but for Raven. I summoned her back through the veil. 'Twas down to her that the boy survived. Has he told you my girl was there in the Circle with him that night?"

"No," replied Sylvie. "He's hardly spoken about it. He said he has terrible nightmares every night."

"Aye, the Death Dance will haunt him for some time to come, poor boy. Maybe for the rest of his days. Well, you must listen to old Mother Heggy, my silver one, and do as I say. The prophecy may yet go unfulfilled and that's what Magus will hope for. He'll do everything in his power to stop it coming about. If he can get past the Winter Solstice, he'll be safe. The prophecy will lose its magic once the Solstice is passed, and then Goddess help us all. We must fight him, we who stand against him. Are you with us?"

Sylvie nodded, her eyes wide with apprehension.

"I love Yul. I'd do anything to stop Magus from hurting him."

Mother Heggy pursed her lips at this and patted Sylvie's

smooth hand with her withered one.

"Much will be asked of you, my bright one. Almost too much. You must be brave and strong. 'Twill be a cage of sorrow for you. A cage that binds the silver nightingale with bars of gold. You'll see, you'll understand my words when you're captive. And the first task is this. You must bring me something of Magus - hair or nail. I need something of his body for my spell."

Sylvie looked sceptical but Mother Heggy was unperturbed.

"You don't believe but that is of no matter. Just bring me something. You must, without fail, bring it tomorrow. 'Tis the Dark Moon and the spell must be cast tomorrow night, when the banishing is at its most powerful."

"I won't be part in murdering anyone," said Sylvie a little shakily.

"You are as much a part of this as Yul or me or Magus or anyone at Stonewylde," replied Mother Heggy tetchily. "You were part of it from the moment you were conceived in the woodland under the red Harvest Moon. You ask your mother. She knows right enough 'twas no ordinary conception. Now, we have two more weeks till the next Moon Fullness. We cannot let Magus feed on your moon magic again."

Sylvie closed her eyes wearily, sick of the whole thing. Stonewylde had seemed like heaven on earth when they'd arrived here. Now it was just a battleground.

"Aye, 'tis that," said Mother Heggy, pulling her filthy shawl closer around her bony shoulders. "And who do you want to win – Magus or Yul? For if you fail to get me what I need for my spell tomorrow, then the boy may well die at the hand of his father this Solstice. And the very spirit of Stonewylde will be broken. I can promise you that."

Sylvie stumbled back up the track to the Hall as the early November darkness closed in around her. The fallen leaves formed a soggy carpet on the ground and several times she skidded and slipped, for she was always clumsy at this time of the month. Rooks were cawing noisily around her, their voices raucous and abrasive. It was cold and damp and she was scared. How was she going to find hair or nails belonging to Magus? He was still away, but it might've been easier if he were around. She'd have to look in his rooms. Although she knew where they were, she'd never been anywhere near them before. She was terrified at the thought of what she must do.

Miranda looked up from her knitting as her daughter entered their small sitting room. She sighed, rubbing her swollen belly. The baby was very active today. He'd had the hiccups this afternoon, which had felt uncomfortable. Sylvie had never done that. This pregnancy was very different, which was why she was so sure the baby was a boy. She pictured him as a tiny Magus, complete with silvery blond hair and brown eyes like dark chocolate. She was missing Magus since he'd been gone, and longed for his return. He'd be pleased with the way she was handling Sylvie. Her daughter had really knuckled down. She was eating properly now and making progress with her schoolwork in the evenings.

"Why are you back so late? It's dark outside. You've been gone ages."

"I lost track of the time."

"Well don't do it again, Sylvie. You won't be allowed to go out walking if you come back this late."

Sylvie shrugged and went into her bedroom, closing the door on her mother. She'd never thought they'd be like this, having always been so close. She'd lost her mother, who'd been so loving and devoted to her. She felt as if everyone was against her. Not only her mother, but the teachers, her tutor, the doctor and of course the other girls. Everyone was on her back. And now she had this other thing to worry about. Would Yul really die if she didn't help with Mother Heggy's spell? She couldn't believe it, but didn't dare risk not doing her bidding just in case the old woman was right.

Sylvie sat with Miranda in the dining room picking at her meal. She was too nervous tonight to enjoy the food, and with her mother now watching every mouthful she swallowed, mealtimes had lost any pleasure. They were surrounded by many other Hallfolk, all talking and laughing together at the long tables. The servants scurried about, refilling plates and glasses and ensuring the Hallfolk had everything they needed. During the meal Sylvie could feel Holly and her gang staring and whispering. Holly had gathered quite a crowd over the past few months; the older ones including July, Wren, Fennel and some of the other boys, and Rainbow and the younger ones she'd gone around with during the summer holiday when her original gang were abroad. They were a large and noisy group and Sylvie felt uncomfortable, knowing that she was being talked about and given the eye. Holly was very open about it. Her dark eyes held contempt and undisguised scorn as she glared insolently at Sylvie. Her pretty face twisted into an expression of malice whenever she caught Sylvie's eye, and she flicked back her thick, shoulder-length hair in a gesture of challenge. Sylvie could sense that Holly was building up to a major confrontation, and dreaded it. She knew how Holly had decided at the Autumn Equinox to make a play for Yul, who had of course brushed her off. Sylvie wondered now if Holly had somehow found out about her and Yul's relationship. That would explain this increase in hostility.

Sylvie kept her eyes down and tried to avoid any kind of non-verbal contact with anyone on Holly's table. She had far more important things to worry about than girl-warfare. As the pudding was served, Sylvie sensed a good opportunity to go up to Magus' rooms. All the Hallfolk were in the Dining Hall and would be for some time, as coffee was also served in here. The servants were busy with the meal and the clearing away.

"Excuse me, Mum. I don't want any pudding and I need to do some research for my coursework. I'll see you later."

"Have some pudding first, Sylvie."

"Really, Mum, I'm full. You know I've put on weight and Hazel's happy."

"Alright. Where are you going? The library or computer room?"

"Probably both. I don't know yet."

She didn't want to be searched for.

"Okay, Sylvie. See you later. Make sure you work hard."

Sylvie left the great Dining Hall, having to walk down alongside the table where Holly sat. She steeled herself to go past the large group, feeling her cheeks burn as they all stopped talking and turned to stare. It was as intimidating as if they'd insulted her. She nearly bumped into Martin on the way out. He stood deferentially to one side to let her pass, watching as she hurried down the corridor. She sped across the hall and up the main staircase, wide enough for several people standing abreast. Paintings, banners and shields hung everywhere. At the top she turned towards the front face of the vast building where Magus had his rooms. Her heart pounded and her hands were trembling. She also had the dull nagging ache that told of her imminent period, and her head throbbed.

She entered the front wing and looked down the corridor stretching darkly away. There were other rooms further on, which she knew nothing about. But she knew the huge oak door under the stone arch before her led into Magus' rooms. She took a deep breath and thought of Yul, telling herself this was to help save his precious life. She opened the door and stepped in quickly, shutting it behind her. Hopefully now she wouldn't be disturbed. Nobody would come in here with Magus away.

Inside the room, it smelt strange; old and woody, and aromatic with some kind of incense and the exotic scent Magus always used. Sylvie breathed deeply again to steady herself, and felt as if the essence of Magus himself had entered her lungs. She shook with nervousness. She could picture his reaction if he were to suddenly appear and discover her purpose here. It was totally black inside the room as it was almost Dark Moon and a cloudy night anyway. There were no street lights of any sort at Stonewylde and the rooms downstairs were shuttered to the night. She groped across the expanse, her feet silent on the thick carpet. She bumped into a small table and felt an electric lamp on it. The room sprang into vision and she gasped, looking around in wonder. It was enormous – a bigger floor-space than many people's houses.

Set in the oak panelled inner wall was a vast stone fireplace, and a great mantle-piece ran along the top of this. Above the mantle-piece hung a mirror of huge proportions, making the room seem even larger. An enormous leather sofa stood before the fire, and over against another wall was an antique desk, with a leather chair and computer. There were more sofas and chairs positioned around the room, a large television screen, a dining table and chairs in a recessed alcove, and paintings and sculptures everywhere. Everything in the room looked priceless. Along the outer wall in front of the diamond-paned mullioned windows was a long window seat, set behind a huge stone arch. The massive wooden shutters hadn't been closed against the darkness, but Sylvie imagined that when Magus was in residence, with the great fire lit and the shutters drawn, it would be very comfortable and even intimate in this luxurious room.

She knew she had to find hair or nails, and if they were to be anywhere it would be in his bedroom or bathroom. She crept across the room and into the connecting one, for like her rooms, this was a Tudor wing and each room opened onto the next. The corridor outside must have been a later addition. The next room was a dressing room, the walls lined with panelled wardrobes, tallboys and chests of drawers. She couldn't begin to imagine how much all his clothes must be worth, for he was a man of expensive and exclusive tastes. She decided she'd look in here if she had no luck elsewhere, as there was just a chance there may be a hair on one of his jackets.

The opposite door led into his bathroom, almost Roman in its masculine opulence. She pulled the light cord, and soft, concealed lighting filled the room. It was of black marble, with onyx and jade accessories, gold fittings and a thick white carpet. There were piles of luxurious white towels on every surface. The spa-bath was large and circular, the shower roomy enough for several people, and there were gold framed mirrors twinkling reflected light everywhere. Sylvie had a flash of a naked, tanned Magus emerging from his bath like a god from the pool of immortality, and quickly banished the thought.

She went over to the two adjacent wash basins and looked for his personal things: a razor, hairbrush, or anything that he may have left behind when he went away. There was a carved jade set – hairbrush, comb and clothes brush – on the black marble top, but all were immaculately clean. She couldn't imagine Magus tolerating any untidiness whatsoever, and pitied the servants who were responsible for looking after his rooms and clothes. She opened the cabinets one by one above the basins, looking for nail clippers or a stray comb, but everything was spotless and arranged with precision. There were rows and rows of expensive toiletries; every possible product available for a well-groomed man who cared about his appearance and personal hygiene. But no hair or nails.

Feeling a rising sense of desperation, Sylvie closed the doors and moved into the next room – the bedroom. She found a switch on the wall and the room glowed with intimate lighting. She gasped again; how much luxury could one person command? This room too was massive, a lair of crimson silk-lined walls and deep carpet smooth as velvet. The bed was antique, a great carved four poster large enough to sleep several people. The trimmings and covers were of exquisite Chinese silk, embroidered gold and scarlet on black, and the mound of pillows sumptuous. Sylvie had a Goldilocks-like urge to lie down on the great Father Bear bed just to see what it felt like. She looked carefully at the pillows, but of course the fine Stonewylde linen would have been changed since he left. Knowing Magus and his taste for luxury, he probably had the linen changed daily. She went over to the dressing table and examined that minutely, but there was nothing. She sat down on the embroidered stool in misery. This was impossible. She'd never find hair or nails. Mother Heggy would be very cross; the spell wouldn't work and Yul may die.

Sylvie sensed the movement rather than saw it. Reflected in the ornate mirror, the door behind her, which had swung silently closed as she'd entered, slowly moved open. She was already in a state of nervous arousal; she now broke into a sweat, her heart drumming frantically in her ribcage. She looked desperately around for a place to hide. She considered dashing over to the bed and throwing herself underneath, but there was no time. She was in direct view of the door, which was opening slowly by the second …

The face that peered at her in the reflection, as pale and anxious as her own, wasn't that of Magus, but Cherry!

"Sacred Mother, you scared me to death, Miss Sylvie!" she whispered, coming into the room. "What in Goddess' name are you doing in here?"

Sylvie swivelled around, waves of relief pouring over her, and suddenly felt very dizzy. She grabbed hold of the dressing table to steady herself.

"I … I …"

"Hold on, miss," cried Cherry, hurrying across the room. She put one arm around the girl to support her. "Are you faint? You've gone as white as a linen sheet. Put your head down between your knees. There, that's better."

She stood holding on to Sylvie, clucking and fussing. After a minute or so Sylvie sat upright. She felt a little better but had no idea what to say.

"Don't look so rabbit-scared, miss! You won't be the first maid to come in here unbidden," said Cherry, shaking her plump jowls. "I seen it afore. Even known the more brazen ones creep in there," she nodded towards the massive bed, "and wait for him."

"Oh no!" cried Sylvie in disgust. "Oh no, Cherry! I'd never, ever do that!"

As soon as she spoke she realised what a good excuse it would have been to explain her presence here, but too late. Cherry smiled at her genuine horror.

"Aye, well … I was wondering, seeing as how I heard that you and our Yul were sweethearts," she said. "I know you go up to Mooncliffe with Magus at the Moon Fullness, but I'd heard that he forces you to go. 'Tisn't the usual thing he wants from you up there. Saves that for afterwards with someone else. He uses you up there for moon magic, I heard. Is that right?"

Sylvie nodded, her eyes still round and nervous. Cherry

patted her shoulder kindly.

"So you didn't come here to get into his bed, or rub your cheek against his clothes, or splash about in his bath, or any of the other daft things I've seen girls do when he's got 'em in his thrall. So I wonder why you did come? You must hate the man if he's made you suffer up at Mooncliffe. And for what he's done to Yul."

Sylvie nodded again. She was so bad at lying, and racked her brains for a plausible reason why she'd sneaked in here. Cherry regarded her steadily, lips pursed as Sylvie sat on the embroidered stool in an obvious dilemma.

"Have you heard of Lily? What happened to her?" asked Cherry eventually.

"No, I haven't."

"She's the poor maid who was hand fasted to that brute Jackdaw. You've come across him?"

"Oh yes, and Yul's told me about him. He murdered his wife, didn't he?"

"He did that, and was banished for it right and proper. But now Jackdaw's back! And why? Magus is mocking us, that's what! Treating us like fools, like we have no feelings. Thinking he can do exactly what he likes to us. Lily was my sister Marigold's girl, and my niece. Apple of my sister's eye, Lily was. 'Twas bad enough at the time, but now that Jackdaw's back, 'tis like Lily's murder never mattered at all. So don't you worry about me knowing you hate Magus. Never thought I'd say this, but I find that I hate the man too. As does my sister."

Sylvie looked up at her in relief.

"But you still haven't told me - why are you in Magus' bedroom, Sylvie?"

She noticed the 'miss' had been dropped.

"I came looking for something."

"Aye?"

"Something that somebody sent me to find."

"'Twouldn't be a certain old woman who lives outside the Village, would it?"

"Yes."

"And would you be looking for something of Magus for a banishing spell, by any chance?"

"Yes."

Cherry roared with laughter and clapped her on the back. After this revelation they searched together, looking everywhere in the four rooms. It wasn't long before both realised the futility of their hunt.

"I'm in charge of these rooms," explained Cherry. "'Tis more than my life's worth to allow any mess or dirt here. We'll never find anything. We'd better get out now before someone realises we're in here. That Martin is always wandering and creeping about like a ghost. Come on, my girl."

They turned off the light and left the rooms. Instead of going back down the main stairs they carried on along the corridor, past several more closed doors. They reached the end of the wing and went quietly down the wooden back stairs leading straight into the servants' quarters.

"We'll talk to my sister Marigold. She may have an idea."

Marigold, so like Cherry in looks, size and temperament, hugged Sylvie to her generous bosom once she was filled in on the details. All notions of Hallfolk and Villager seemed forgotten in their united purpose of helping Mother Heggy with her banishing spell. They sat in the cook's parlour, a small room next to the kitchens, and were quite private here.

"Many of us feel the same," said Marigold, "but we have to be careful. 'Twouldn't do if some little weasel went and told Magus that people were gathering against him, would it?"

The three of them talked for some time, trying to think how they could get hair or nails before the next night. Magus was due back any day, but nobody knew exactly when. Sylvie was thinking along the lines of DNA, and wondered if Hazel would have any samples in her office, maybe some of his blood. But even if there was any it would probably be under lock and key. Then Marigold shrieked and slapped her great thigh so hard it quivered.

"I know, I know! Cherry, remember the album? The album old Rosemary used to keep of the boys?"

"Of course! Are you thinking of the locks of hair?"

"That I am, dear sister. That I am. I'm sure there's hair in there."

"What?" squeaked Sylvie in excitement. "What album? Where?"

"Well, my dear, when the two little boys, Sol and Clip, were growing up they had their own nurse called Rosemary. Poor old thing, she was. Doted on them boys and they treated her terrible, especially young Sol. See, their mother had nothing to do with them."

"Raven?"

"That's right. Raven."

They exchanged glances.

"You're thinking I look just like her, aren't you?"

"Well yes, my dear. You do. Peas in the pod."

"Why did they have a nursemaid? Why didn't Raven care for her sons?" asked Sylvie.

"Oh no, she couldn't do that. They were kept away from her out of harm's reach," said Marigold. "Raven lived with Mother Heggy, and sometimes she lived wild in the woods, especially in the summer. I reckon she would've killed them boys if she could. Hated 'em as much as she hated their fathers. She was ill-used, the poor girl, first by old Basil, and then Elm. No reason to love the children she was forced to bear, especially Sol. He was a thug as a boy, a real bully. Used to fight the Village boys and beat 'em badly. Elm sent them away to school in the Outside World when they was older."

They poured some more tea, but much as she wanted to hear all this, Sylvie was very conscious of the time. Her mother could be looking for her and she had to get the hair to Mother Heggy tomorrow.

"So you think there may be some of Magus' hair in this album?" she asked.

"Aye. Old Rosemary, she used to keep an album all about the two little boys. Photographs, drawings they'd done and suchlike. And I'm sure she kept locks of their hair in that album as they grew up. Now where would it be, Cherry? Can you remember, sister?"

"'Tis in that room where old Siskin works sometimes. You

know, where all them papers and framed photographs are kept. We'll have to rummage."

Sylvie started to get up. They both looked at her in surprise.

"Not now, maid!" said Marigold. "'Tis too late now. The Hallfolk are about. They'd see us if we started rifling about now."

"We'll have a look tomorrow, dear," said Cherry. "Don't you worry. I can go in that room nice and early to get the cleaning done and nobody'd think twice. We have to be careful of Martin, for he'd snitch as soon as look at us. But in the morning, he wouldn't question me going into any of the rooms. If that album's still about, and I don't see why it shouldn't be, I'll find it and get the lock of hair to you."

"It's Dark Moon tomorrow, and Mother Heggy must have it by the evening she said."

"We know. We'll get it to you in time. And be happy to do it."

"Anything that will help rid Stonewylde of Magus. Dark Angel take his wicked soul!"

CHAPTER FIVE

The two women didn't let her down. After breakfast Sylvie returned to her room to find a twist of paper on her pillow. She opened it and stared at the small silver-blond lock of hair. She felt a sharp twinge of emotion looking at the tiny piece of Magus' childhood, so small and silky in her hand. It must have been difficult for him growing up without a mother, in the care of a harsh father who was interested in nothing other than his own base pleasures. She pictured the little boy tearing around Stonewylde getting into mischief, fighting with other boys and earning a bad reputation. Unloved by anyone except an old nursemaid. Lashing out at the world, trying to control others with his strong will and angry fists. Nobody to nurture him and bring out his gentle side. Then sent away to a tough boarding school where he'd learnt to hide his darkness and present an amiable face to the world.

She stroked the silver lock, curled like a tiny crescent moon. She wondered if she held in her palm the means to Magus' downfall. Maybe to his death. But she pushed the guilt and pity away and thought instead of Yul, still recovering from the terrible ordeal Magus had put him through. Whatever the reasons behind Magus' cruel nature, the fact remained that Yul was in danger from him. Sylvie hurried to Mother Heggy's cottage before her misgivings got the better of her.

"I don't know if it's any good," she said, breathless from climbing up the hill in the chilly November wind. "It's from when he was a child. It's all I could get. I'm sorry, Mother Heggy."

"'Twill do," wheezed the old crone, fingering the lock of hair with gnarled fingers. "Shouldn't matter how old it is so long as 'tis his own. Now I can get to work."

"Will ... will the spell actually kill him?"

"No, not on its own. 'Tis not that powerful magic. I'm old and on the wane myself. Not like I used to be. But 'twill weaken him just as I weakened Alwyn. 'Tis like a symbol of intent. I do what I can to help the boy. He's the grandson of my Raven and the one with the Earth Magic. The Goddess chose him, as I knew she would."

"But Mother Heggy, I don't understand why you hated Magus so much when he was a child, and yet you don't hate Yul. Magus was Raven's own son, after all."

"'Tis true, but he was conceived from her suffering. She should never have borne children. If you could only have seen it ... My poor little Raven! Just a tiny, delicate little thing she was. And he a great brute of a man. 'Twas terrible how he forced her every single month, like his brother afore him, while she was moongazy and weak and couldn't defend herself. And he brimming full o' the power and energy he'd leeched from her through the stone. Capering about like a wild tom cat and greedy with the moon-lust. No child of such a cruel union could ever be loved. Not by me and not by her. But 'tis different with Yul. True he has his father's blood, but not his father's evil. The power and the strength without the cruelty. And Maizie was willing. She loved Sol, and in his own way he loved her. That conception was not cursed."

She gave Sylvie some potions for Yul and said that he must visit her as soon as he could. Then Sylvie left for the Great Barn. She must join all the other women there for the Dark Moon gathering, and didn't relish the prospect. She'd felt so awkward and lonely last month, and the situation with Holly was worse than ever.

When she walked into the Barn, she noticed Holly and her gang over on one side of the enormous space. Once again they'd commandeered the pile of squashy cushions and were lying about on their backs, laughing and talking loudly. Another group of older Hallfolk women sat at a distance from them, examining a great pile of rushes. She decided to join them. Hazel looked up at her arrival and the smile faltered on

Sylvie's lips. The doctor was still cool with her, despite the daily visits when Sylvie tried to get back to their previous friendliness. Magus had done a thorough job of turning Hazel against her.

"Can I join you?" she asked diffidently.

Hazel nodded, pulling several of the dried rushes from the pile. The women were making mats for the Villagers' cottages. The rushes had been harvested in the autumn from the marshes where the river flowed into the sea. The new circular mats they were making now would replace the worn out ones on the stone kitchen floors. Sylvie sat down and watched how they selected the rushes and smoothed them out, before binding the ends with thin reed and beginning to plait. It was more difficult than it looked.

"I had the results back from your tests just after you left my office this morning," said Hazel, plaiting efficiently. "Magus is due home very soon and he'll be pleased to see them."

"Are they alright? Is there anything wrong with me?"

"No, there isn't. So Magus was right all along."

Sylvie's heart sank. Although she hadn't wanted anything to be seriously wrong, this would only strengthen Magus' case that she was faking the lethargy and exhaustion she suffered after moondancing for him.

"He'll be pleased too that I've put on weight, won't he?"

"I expect so, although you haven't gained that much. And the blood tests show that some of your levels are far too low, indicating malnourishment. He won't like that."

"I am eating properly now, Hazel. I couldn't help not eating when I felt so ill. I was asleep for most of the week after the last full moon."

"Excessive sleeping is just another way of not facing up to life. Maybe it's time you woke up, Sylvie."

A couple of the women in the group were Sylvie's teachers, and they looked across at her.

"I hope you've finished that history coursework," said one of them sternly. "Magus has requested a full report on his return, and I've got your history ready for him. There are still gaps in what you've submitted so far."

"It's almost done," said Sylvie. "I'll finish it off tonight I hope."

"Too late for the report though."

"How's the revision going?" asked another. "You know your mock exams start soon. Have you caught up yet?"

"Nearly," said Sylvie quietly. "I've been working hard."

"Pity you didn't try that earlier. The mocks will prove just how little effort you've put in over recent months. I always say they're a wake-up call."

"Just what she needs," said Hazel grimly. "What a good job Magus realised in time how far you've slipped, Sylvie. You're lucky he's taken such an interest in you."

She swallowed the bitter retort, fighting down the tears of frustration and injustice that made her throat ache.

"And I hear your maths is quite dreadful," continued the history teacher. "I think you've left that too late to turn around. William isn't happy. The maths results are usually very high. He's annoyed you're letting him down. Magus is always particularly proud of the maths results achieved by Hallfolk. He'll be furious."

"I'm doing my best," said Sylvie, bent over the plaiting to hide her burning face.

"About time too. Oh for Goddess' sake, girl! What are you doing with those rushes? What a dreadful mess! Unplait all that and start again. Or go and do something a little simpler that you can manage."

Sylvie stumbled miserably over to the group working again on patchwork quilts. She wanted to avoid the Hallfolk girls who were eyeing her malignantly across the barn. The group of Village women welcomed her warmly and moved around to make space for her. Maizie and Rosie were in the group and were especially pleased that she'd joined them. Rosie swapped places to sit next to her. Remembering Sylvie's clumsy attempts the month before, she offered to teach her how to sew properly. Sylvie tried hard to copy the girl's tiny neat stitches as she hemmed her hexagons, but wondered glumly if she'd ever find anything she was good at. The conversation was mundane but comforting, revolving around simple things such as whose house pig was next due for slaughter, and when to shut the bees up for winter. Sylvie started to relax a little, managing to block out the strident laughter coming from the group on the cushions.

Then the women in her group turned to the favourite topic of the moment – the return of Jackdaw. He and Magus had been away for over a week now, but it was known that Magus was due home. The servants always fed any Hallfolk news back to their relatives in the Village. There was speculation now as to whether or not Jackdaw would return with the master.

"I reckon he will. His things are still in the rooms over the stables where he was sleeping," said Tom's daughter.

"He better not show his face in the Village," said Edward's wife grimly. "There'll be such trouble if he does."

"Marigold said he comes into the kitchens for food like he owns the place. Swaggering about and giving out orders. She's tempted to add a little Death Cap or Destroying Angel to one of his pies, she said."

"She wouldn't do that!"

"Well, the poor woman has good cause to."

"Aye, but then she'd be no better than those two old hags, Violet and Vetchling, with their nasty brews."

"I'd poison him myself if I could," muttered Rosie.

"Rosie! Don't say such things!" said Maizie sharply. "He'll get his justice for what he's done to Yul without your hand in it."

Sylvie glanced up at them and saw the naked hatred on Rosie's face.

"What did he do to Yul? Do you mean at the quarry last summer?"

"No!" said Rosie, almost choking as she tried to explain. "What he did at Samhain."

"When he took Yul into the Stone Circle?"

"No, before that, when he had Yul at his mercy in the byre. He burnt him."

The group of women and girls stopped their sewing and

looked across at Rosie's flushed face. Maizie nodded, her eyes hard and bitter.

"Yul's covered in tiny round burns," she said. "Jackdaw did it. Yul told us everything, after we noticed the marks all over him. Jackdaw did it just for fun, Yul said. My poor, poor boy ..."

Tom's daughter put an arm around her.

"Don't you fret, Maizie. That Jackdaw will be taken by the Angel, you'll see. There's justice in this world, and not only at Magus' bidding."

"Aye, and I'd like to see him dead too."

The women fell silent, bending their heads over their sewing once more as the ripples of this shocking comment reverberated amongst them. Now it had been said openly, and by a woman who'd always loved him. The dark clouds were gathering and Sylvie shuddered, thinking of the pitiful lock of silver hair in the Wise Woman's withered hands.

Yul meanwhile, knowing that many of the women and in particular his mother would be in the Barn for most of the day, slipped out of the cottage to visit Mother Heggy himself. He wasn't as strong as he'd thought, and by the time he arrived, was pale and exhausted. She fussed over him, sitting him down and making a reviving brew in the old stone mug.

"You have but two weeks to get your strength back, boy," she told him. "He must not take her to Mooncliffe this next Moon Fullness in November. He must be as weak as possible when the Solstice comes in December. So no moon magic this month."

"I know," said Yul, worriedly. "I need to organise it properly this time. Will I be well enough by then?"

"Aye, you should be. Get up to the Circle, my lad. That'll help. Sunrise and sunset. This time of year, 'tis easy enough. Days are shorter. Keep yourself warm, for you'll feel the cold in your bones for a while yet."

Yul sat back, closing his eyes. He was so weary. Even when resting and sleeping he worried about Sylvie and the next full moon. He couldn't let her down again.

"I can't take her to Hare Stone, can I? That's the first place he'd look."

"No, you must get her far away, somewhere he won't find her. But nowhere near Quarrycleave. That's a place of death, and the big stone there at the head of the quarry, 'tis the same as the stone at Mooncliffe. 'Twill hold her moon magic just like the other one does. 'Tis where he got the rock to make those stone eggs he uses."

Yul found himself getting angry just thinking about the eggs. He'd love to smash open the chest and steal them away. That would give Magus a nasty shock when he came for a fresh one to boost his dwindling energy.

Mother Heggy chuckled, and patted his arm.

"Now you're thinking a-right, my boy. It must be your plan, not mine. You must use your wits. You may have the Earth Magic in you, but Magus is still bigger and stronger than you. Use your mind to outwit him. Get things ready aforehand. Think it clear. Use his own greed against him."

"What about Jackdaw? He's very strong and as cruel as Magus. I can't take on both of them at once."

"Those who stand against you will fall, one by one."

"You mean Jackdaw?"

She chuckled, and shooed him out of the cottage.

"Go home and sleep. Eat and get strong. Make your plans. Let me get on with my banishing spell."

After lunch in the Barn, Sylvie and Rosie along with many of the women went outside for a walk around the Green before resuming the afternoon's work.

"I'm pleased to speak alone," said Rosie. "Yul gave me a message this morning. He said to meet him under the tree before you go back to the Hall tonight."

Sylvie smiled and nodded, wishing again that he could read and write.

"I've got some medicine in my bag for Yul," she said. "I'll give it to you to take back for him in case I forget when I see him. He has that effect on me."

Rosie grinned at this, but then looked serious.

"Be careful with Mother Heggy, Sylvie. And don't let on to Mother about going to see her. Mother has a real wasp in her shawl about Old Heggy. She says all of this is her fault. If Heggy hadn't made that prophecy, Magus would've taken Yul as a Hallchild and wouldn't have turned against Mother. She'd never have been handfasted to Father and Yul would've grown up happy and loved. Mother blames Old Heggy for everything that's happened, and she's told Yul he mustn't visit her again."

Just then they heard a shriek of laughter and Sylvie groaned. Holly and her friends had come onto the Green and were heading their way.

"Hey, Sylvie! Wait for us! We'd so like the pleasure of your company!"

"You'd better go back to the Barn, Rosie. Don't get involved in this."

"Are you sure? I don't want to butt into Hallfolk talk but I think ..."

"It's not that. They're going to have a go at me and I'd rather you weren't around to get mixed up in it. I'll see you back inside."

Rosie turned and walked off, ignoring the rude comments as she passed the approaching group of girls. Sylvie quickened her pace, continuing the circuit of the Green. Holly came running up and overtook her, capering about in front of her and laughing. Holly was fit and athletic, and Sylvie had a sudden memory of the time when Holly had leapt from the apple tree and landed on Yul, wrapping her muscular legs around his hips. She swallowed and kept her head down.

Behind Holly came the rest of them – July, Wren, Dawn and the group of younger girls.

"Why are you ignoring me, Sylvie?" asked Holly. "Do you only mix with scummy Villagers now? You've been sitting with them all day, haven't you?"

"No," said Sylvie. "I sat with Hallfolk earlier on."

"Not for long. You've been with Yul's mother and sister most of the time, I noticed. You're very friendly with them, aren't you?"

"Not especially," said Sylvie.

"But you are, Sylvie. And I heard some interesting gossip this morning. I heard that you and Yul are sweethearts!"

Sylvie's heart sank. Holly fell into step beside Sylvie as the rest of the girls caught them up. Sylvie felt Holly's dark eyes watching her, sizing her up.

"So you're not denying it then?" she asked, spoiling for a fight.

"I'm not saying anything to you!" retorted Sylvie.

"So is Yul your boyfriend? I want to know, Sylvie, and I'll find out if I have to go and ask him myself."

"It's none of your business!"

"Ooh! I take it that's a yes."

"Take it however you want, Holly."

Sylvie strode as fast as she could, not looking at any of them, her long silver hair wafting around her as she marched doggedly on around the Green. She was now taller than Holly by quite a way. Despite Holly's slim fitness, Sylvie's legs were much longer and Holly had to trot to keep up with her.

"We're sick of this, Sylvie," said July. "You know that Holly's keen on Yul. Why are you stealing away another of her boyfriends?"

"Yeah, you're just a prize bitch really," said Wren. "First you take Buzz away from her, and now you're taking Yul too."

Despite intending to ignore them, Sylvie found herself drawn into the argument.

"Have I missed something?" she asked. "Is Yul your boyfriend then, Holly? How can I take him away from you if he's not?"

"Shut up, you cow!" snarled Holly.

"Why? Because what I'm saying is true? I heard that Yul won't go anywhere near you, doesn't want to know. That's got nothing to do with me."

"Yes it has! He was keen enough till you came here! It's just like what happened with Buzz, the same thing all over again!"

"We think you're a real slag," said Rainbow. "First Buzz, then Magus and now Yul!"

"Greedy! Can't get enough of it! She is a slag!"

"Stop it!" said Dawn, frowning at them all. "There's no need for that."

But they started to chant and dance around her, taunting and jeering. Sylvie was reminded sharply of her school life in London.

"I wish you'd never come here!" cried Holly, skipping to keep up. "Nobody likes you! Why don't you go back to where you came from?"

"Why should I? I live here now and I'm not going anywhere. So get used to it, Holly!"

"We don't want you here! Do you realise just how unpopular you are?"

"It's your fault Buzz was banished! And now you've got your hooks into Yul, just because Holly wants him. You better leave off him, Sylvie!" warned July.

"Yeah, and Magus too!" said Wren, still besotted after her stint as the Corn Mother at Lammas.

"You can't have them both!" cried Holly. "It's not fair! Goddess knows what they see in you anyway, you skinny bitch! Does Magus know about you and Yul? I bet he doesn't! I might just tell him. That would make him really mad and it would serve you right!"

Sylvie stopped. She was almost back at the Barn now. She had to deal with this situation, although she wasn't sure of the best way.

"Look, Holly, if you're interested in Yul you won't say anything about this to Magus. It's not me he'd be mad with. He'll take it out on Yul. You must've heard what happened at Samhain. If you really like Yul you won't say anything. Do you want him to suffer?"

"Don't be stupid, of course I don't!"

"Then leave me alone and stop stirring it up!"

"You haven't heard the last of this!" hissed Holly as the crowd of girls swept in through the great doors of the Barn.

As the afternoon drew in and the light began to fade, the women in the Barn packed away their projects ready for the morning. The Barn was used every night by different groups and all must be left tidy. The rushes and patchwork quilts were put to one side, along with the flax for spinning and the wool for felt-making. The women bid each other a good evening, and the Villagers hurried home to get the supper cooking. The Hallfolk were not so rushed for the servants would be busy on their behalf up at the Hall.

Outside the Barn, the sky was pink and pearly to the south-west where the sun was setting. The birds still sang up in the great circle of trees that surrounded the Village Green, and Sylvie thought of the professor and all that he'd told her about the history of this part of Stonewylde. She remembered the great carved wooden face set into the wall of the pub, and the photo of Yul that the professor had given her back in the late summer. The photo was her most treasured possession. Sylvie knew that Yul was the embodiment of the Green Man and all that he represented at Stonewylde.

She smiled to herself, remembering the funny little professor. They'd kept in touch since he'd left in August, e-mailing each other occasionally. She must write again. He knew nothing about what had happened at Samhain and she felt he should know. He'd made it clear that he was on her and Yul's side. It was obvious that Stonewylde meant everything to him and she thought again how cruel Magus was, only allowing him back for a few weeks a year. The old man would have loved to spend his last years back in the place where he'd grown up and where he belonged. There were plenty of empty rooms at the Hall. Sylvie vowed that when Magus had gone, she'd make sure Professor Siskin was invited to return to Stonewylde for good.

The sky above was now soft violet and grey; the sunset a vivid flamingo pink. The air was quite mild for November, and Sylvie stood outside the Barn and breathed deeply. A stable hand had arrived with the large painted cart and two horses that were used to transport Hallfolk to and fro between Hall and Village. Several Hallfolk women climbed in and settled themselves on the padded seats. Sylvie watched the cart roll away across the cobbles, soon overtaking the large group of women who'd chosen to walk the couple of miles up the track to the Hall. She heard the gang of girls up ahead still making too much noise, and breathed a sigh of relief.

All was now quiet and peaceful. She lingered in the shadows waiting a little longer, her heart thumping with anticipation at the prospect of seeing Yul. She didn't notice Holly, who also lingered around the side of the Barn. When Sylvie thought the coast was clear she hurried across the Green to the yew tree. Holly saw her disappear into the half-light but was careful not to follow too closely. She saw Sylvie melt into the shadows of the circle of trees, and waited before moving forward herself.

As Sylvie entered the yew's sphere, she felt the atmosphere alter. The air was somehow different. Time was a little changed and her skin felt strange. She thought of the scientific explanations possible. Perhaps the oxygenation process caused by the transpiration of such a huge tree ionised the air all around it. But her heart told her it was the magic of the tree spirit causing the changes. She smiled. In her old life she'd have laughed at such a theory, but now she knew it to be the truth.

Yul leant against the massive trunk of the tree, dark curls falling across his face, his grey eyes shadowed. She felt a starburst of excitement at the sight of him, tall and pale and waiting for her. She ran the last few steps and was enfolded in his arms, his lips bruising hers as he kissed her long and hard.

"I can't stay long," she gasped, pulling away eventually. "Mum will wonder why I didn't return with the others. They're all on my back at the moment and I must be careful. How are you feeling?"

"Much better thanks. Tomorrow I'm going up to the Circle. And Old Greenbough's said I'm not to go back to work for a while. He's on our side, Sylvie. He said if we need help, he'll do anything he can."

"That's good news. We've got Marigold and Cherry up at the Hall too, and they said there are many others who feel the same way."

"I think most of them do. The time is coming closer. Sylvie, we need to make plans. The next Moon Fullness ..."

He felt her shudder as he spoke and held her close against his body, stroking her hair.

"Sylvie, I let you down last time and I swear it'll never happen again. I'd die rather than allow him to feed off your moon magic on that rock again."

"No, Yul."

She pulled back a little and looked up at him in the fading light. She could see the shadows in the hollows of his lean face.

"Dying wouldn't help. Awful though it is, I can survive the moongazing on the rock. Don't sacrifice yourself for nothing."

"No!" he said vehemently, shaking his hair. "He won't do it to you again. I've sworn an oath to myself. Next Moon Fullness I need to get you away before the moonrise. Not so early that he has time to look for you, but not so late that there isn't time for us to get far away. You understand we won't be able to go to Hare Stone?"

She nodded. "I'll do whatever you say. I can't think or act rationally at moonrise, so you just do what you need to."

"I'm going to find a place where we can hide. Once the moon's risen and it's high, the danger's mostly passed. But we need to make him think everything's fine at the moment. He mustn't lock you up or get Clip to put another spell on you. I know it's awful, but you must go along with whatever he says over the next couple of weeks. Can you do that? Make him think you're coming round to his way of thinking. If he found out we're meeting like this …"

"I'll try. I'll make him think everything's fine. He's due back very soon, and I know he's going to give me a hard time. But I won't stand up to him …"

She stopped as he bent and started kissing her again, his tongue skilful, his hands now more assured and practised than the first time they'd kissed under the very same tree at the Summer Solstice. She'd wanted him then, but the feelings were now infinitely stronger. She'd grown up a great deal since June. Everything was more intense and she felt herself dissolving into a wave of pure desire. Sylvie wondered if Yul felt the same, little appreciating just how tightly he controlled his longing for her.

"Stop, Yul," she said shakily, pulling away from him. "It'll show. Mum will know what I've been up to. I must go."

She stumbled a few steps towards the grass.

"Will you be in the Great Barn tomorrow?" he called softly.

"Yes. I'll see you here again?"

"You will. But a little later, after sunset. Wait here for me if you can. I love you, Sylvie."

She smiled and blew him a kiss as she turned away. Leaving the thrall of the ancient yew tree, she hurried home with wings at her heels.

Yul waited a while under the boughs of the yew. He knew there was some special magic here; not the Earth Magic but something else. Something primeval which called to him and fed a hunger in his soul. He belonged in this place and always had done. He leant back against the flaking bark of the great bole and shut his eyes, his mouth still tingling from kissing Sylvie so hard. He took a deep, shaky breath. His body was highly aroused. His hands trembled from the torture of wanting her so badly but knowing he must rein himself in whenever he was close to her.

Darkness was almost complete as Yul pulled himself away from the massive trunk and ducked out from under the boughs onto the Village Green. He looked up at the moonless sky, glittering with bright stars. He felt the magic of the Dark Moon deep inside. He began to make his way across the grass, heading for home and the food he knew would be waiting for him. His heart still soared wildly from the encounter with Sylvie and the prospect of seeing her again tomorrow.

Nothing in the world compared to the feel of Sylvie in his arms; so willowy and pliant, so willing and passionate. Every moment they spent together was snatched and stolen. One day Yul knew he would wake to see her face next to his, feel the whisper of her breath on his cheek as they lay close together. He quivered with another rush of longing and then miraculously felt her hand slip into his as he walked across the Green. She'd come back! He turned, smiling, but his face froze into a mask of disappointment. It was Holly.

Immediately he shook the hand out of his with a gesture of dismissal.

"What do you want?" he muttered angrily.

"That's not very nice, Yul!" she replied in a hurt voice. "We've known each other all our lives. There's no need to be nasty to me."

He continued to walk briskly, trying to throw her off as she trotted to match his strides.

"I need to talk to you," she said. "Please - just for a few minutes."

"I've got to get home," he said. "My supper will be waiting."

"It's important. Just a couple of minutes."

"Alright then. But be quick."

She slid her hand around his arm and guided him under the nearest tree, for they'd now crossed the Green and reached the other side. It was a very different atmosphere under the chestnut tree. Most of its leaves had been shed and now the bare branches and twigs made an intricate pattern against the starry night sky. Holly stopped and Yul turned to face her, anxious to get this over with. He remembered how jealous Sylvie had been in the orchard during the apple harvest. He didn't wish to do anything that might upset her again.

"What do you want then?" he asked brusquely, barely able to see Holly in the darkness.

"I want some of what Sylvie's been getting," she replied and threw her body against his. She flung her arms round his neck in a limpet grip, trying to pull his head down to hers. Her lips brushed his as he jerked his head away and tried to shake her off. She clung on tightly, deliberately pressing herself hard against him. Despite himself Yul felt a jolt of desire, aroused as he was from his earlier passion with Sylvie.

"*Get off me!*" he snarled, grabbing hold of her arms and flinging her away from him. She stumbled backwards, shocked by his vehemence.

"Don't be like that!" she wailed. "Why do you hate me? What have I done to you?"

"Nothing! Everything! I don't know!"

He was angry with himself for the momentary lapse, for wanting her even if only for a split second.

"Please, Yul. Sit down and talk to me," she said, her voice small and unhappy. She sat on the wooden seat built around the trunk of the tree, and patted the spot next to her. Yul shook his head and remained standing.

"Okay, stay up there, but I'll have to speak louder and anybody could hear. It's about you and Sylvie. I know what's been going on."

Reluctantly he sat down.

"I don't know what you're talking about."

"Oh yes you do! I know what you've been up to, under the tree with her. How long's it been going on? She gets about, doesn't she?"

"What do you mean by that?" he demanded.

"First Buzz, then Magus, now you. She can't get enough of it."

Yul stood up abruptly, not trusting himself so close to her. He had an urge to slap her nasty little face.

"I'm not listening to this! You've got it all wrong. She's never been interested in Buzz or Magus."

"But she's interested in you?"

"No, I ..."

He stopped, realising he'd made a blunder. She jumped in.

"I saw her going under the tree with you, Yul. I saw everything. We both know it's not allowed between a Villager and Hallfolk, not like that. I'm going straight to Magus."

"*No!*"

He sat down next to her again and grabbed her wrist, peering at her in the darkness. He could only make out her shoulder-length blond hair but knew her face well enough to imagine how she'd look right now. Her pretty feline features would be smug with malicious self-satisfaction.

She didn't struggle in his grip but almost melted into him,

reaching into his jacket to caress him.

"Yul, stop fighting me. What's she got that I haven't? You and I could have such fun."

"Stop it! Get off me! Look Holly, you mustn't go to Magus. Please don't."

"Who'd suffer the most if I told him – you or her?"

"I don't know," he said, not sure how best to play this. She was clever and manipulative and at the moment, at least one step ahead of him.

"Because I don't want you to be punished again, Yul. Although it would be nice if she got into trouble. I could tell Magus that ..."

"NO! Don't, Holly, please. You mustn't say a word to him."

"What's it worth?"

He shrugged, at a loss to understand what she wanted from him.

"You're very slow, Yul, aren't you? I want you to kiss me like you kissed Sylvie."

"No! I couldn't kiss anybody else like that!"

"Then try, Yul. I'll be patient with you. Come on, it's not much to ask in return for keeping your secret. Magus would be so angry with both of you. My silence for a little kiss, just for old times' sake. You were keen enough once and I haven't changed. Come on, Yul."

Reluctantly, knowing this was madness but unsure what else to do, he allowed her to link her hands behind his head and pull him down. Her lips fastened onto his and she kissed him. He remained passive, not responding in any way. She pulled away from him.

"What's the matter? Come on, it's not so bad. It's only a kiss, Yul, and Sylvie will never know. Kiss me properly or I'll go straight to Magus and tell him everything."

So he did, hating himself for it and hating Holly even more. It was mechanical and soulless. It felt wrong, she felt horrible, and she tasted different. Finally, unable to endure it any longer, he wrenched himself from her clinging grasp. He stood up again, wiping his mouth hard with the back of his hand in the ultimate gesture of disgust.

"Alright, I've done it! Now let me go home. And leave Sylvie alone, Holly. If I hear you've been upsetting her …"

"Yes? You'll do what, exactly? Don't threaten me, Yul! Or I might tell Sylvie what we've just been doing. She wouldn't like that, would she?"

The light from the pub just illuminated her face as she looked up at him. Her eyes glinted and he could see her smile of triumph.

"That was very nice for starters, Yul," she purred. "Although a little more passion next time, I think. It's not long till our Rite of Adulthood, remember."

He turned on his heel and strode off, ignoring her laughter. He'd betrayed Sylvie and hated himself for it. He'd made a stupid mistake giving in to Holly but it was too late now to go back. He must just make sure it never happened again. As he crashed in through the door, Maizie and Rosie exchanged glances. It was a while since they'd seen Yul in one of his black moods.

CHAPTER SIX

The next morning whilst it was still dark, Yul left his cottage wrapped against the chill November air. He started up the track that led to the Long Walk and the Stone Circle, and was surprised to find Edward waiting in the tunnel of bare trees. Edward was one of the key men on the estate. He was young to be a farm manager, but intelligent and hardworking and well respected in the community.

"Blessings, sir!" said Yul, taken aback.

"Blessings to you, Yul."

They fell into step together. Yul was pleased to see that he was now almost as tall as Edward, although he had a long way to go to match the man's huge physique.

"Why are you up here this morning, sir?" asked Yul. He kept an eye on the sky through the trees, not wanting to miss the sunrise.

"To look after you," replied Edward with a smile, thinking the lad would resent this.

"But I ..."

"Mother Heggy's orders. She says you need the Earth Magic. That you must come here every day, sunrise and sunset. If Magus realises what you're up to, he'll send Jackdaw to stop you. 'Tis why I'm here. There's nought I'd like more than a fight with Jackdaw. So no arguing, young man. I'm coming whether you like it or not. We need you strong. There's a lot of folk counting on you, Yul."

Yul was silenced by this. He knew Edward to be one of Magus' staunchest supporters, and wondered what had brought about this change.

"Thanks, sir. I hope you don't mind. You must be busy at this time of day."

"I'm happy to do my bit. We need to hurry now. 'Tis almost sunrise. And Yul – you can drop the 'sir'."

They entered the Stone Circle and despite himself, Yul began to shake uncontrollably. This was his first visit since the night of Samhain. The crows and skulls were still painted on the stones and would stay there until the preparations for the Winter Solstice. In the centre the ashes from the pyre marked a darker spot on the earth, although all remains of the fire had been cleared. The black stones and tiny red candles had gone and every trace of the labyrinth had vanished. But Yul felt sick with dread, remembering the stalking Dark Angel, the white corpses on the sleds, and his own paralysis from the poison. He knew that but for Raven's help he would certainly have died in this place. He shuddered and Edward put a strong arm around his shoulders.

"You were very brave that night, Yul. Braver than any of us would've been. Come on, up on the Altar Stone and forget about death. Think instead o' life - the life force o' the Earth Goddess."

Yul nodded gratefully, unable to speak as the emotions choked him. He clambered up onto the stone, not yet strong enough to leap as he usually did.

Immediately he could feel the throbbing, pulsing energy of the earth pushing up through the atoms of the stone, channelled into his body. He felt it building as the sun came closer to the horizon. It was cloudy and grey, but the sun was approaching whether or not the human eye could see it. The magnetic energy of the sun slid into alignment with this spot where the magnetic energy of the earth was strong and focussed.

The sky remained a dull pewter grey, but Yul knew the moment when the sun appeared over the horizon for he felt an almost orgasmic jolt to his body. He stood with outstretched arms and the energy flooded through him, into every carbon atom of his being, electrifying in its intensity and power. He felt filled, charged, fired up with the Earth Magic. He took a deep breath and relaxed, letting it saturate him. Gone were his fears and terrors. He could now slay any foe who dared to challenge him.

About ten minutes later when the sky was much brighter, he opened his eyes. He smiled across at Edward who stood some way off, leaning against one of the great stones. Edward was silent as they walked back towards the Village, and after a while Yul broached the subject on his mind.

"You were angry with me in September, Edward, at the Apple Harvest, for speaking against Magus. Yet now you say that everyone's counting on me. Why the change of heart?"

Edward looked across at Yul, tall and filling out with hard muscle, but all said and done still a boy and not quite yet a man. The long dark curls and slanted grey eyes had put them all off the track, but now it was plain to see. He was so clearly his father's son, powerful and strong and a natural leader. The air around Yul crackled, although he didn't seem to be aware of it himself. Nor of the tiny sparks arcing from his fingertips. There was no doubt whatsoever that the Earth Goddess now blessed Yul with her green magic. Edward felt over-awed at what he'd just witnessed.

"I used to admire and respect Magus with all my heart," Edward began. "And in many ways I still do. He saved Stonewylde and made it a great place again, after the years when his father, uncle and grandfather had allowed it to rot. But somehow he's missed the true path and gone wandering up the one that leads to the precipice. I've heard of his future plans for Stonewylde and I don't like 'em. I have young children and I don't want them growing up in a place that's gone bad. Seems to me Magus is abandoning all we hold sacred. He wants to build more homes for Hallfolk. He wants to increase the yields of the land and farm more aggressively. I don't hold with that. The Earth gives us what she can. She mustn't be forced."

Yul nodded at this. It was one of the most fundamental principles of honouring the Goddess in the landscape. Take and enjoy her bounty, but never be greedy.

"And there's also the matter o' Jackdaw," Edward continued. "You know Lily was a relation? We all trusted Magus to punish Jackdaw fairly for killing her, and banishment was the just retribution. But Magus has gone back on that, and not even had the decency to explain why. I don't feel I can trust the man any longer. Especially a man who tried to burn his own son alive."

He glanced across at the boy, still bearing a haunted look of suffering, but also surrounded by an aura of energy that danced about him like a cloud of gnats.

"And lastly, Yul, there's you yourself. You're the one who receives the Earth Magic now. Greenbough and Tom both told me so afore, and I believed 'em, for they are good men and always speak true. Now I seen it for myself I shall tell others too. 'Tis not us but Stonewylde herself that chooses the magus. You are the one, Yul. I'm behind you every step o' your path."

They reached the Village and with a farewell salute, Edward mounted his great grey mare and rode back to the farm.

Before joining the fertile women of Stonewylde for the second day of menstruation, Sylvie went first to Hare Stone for the sunrise and then a walk along the ridgeway. She found increasingly that she was able to sense the serpent lines of energy in the earth, just as Yul could feel the silver moon energy as well as the green magic of the land.

Walking along Dragon's Back up high in the hills was exhilarating and set her spirit soaring. She could literally see the bigger picture when surrounded with great sweeps and swathes of green hills and valleys, the recumbent form of the Goddess in the land. She walked along the green spine of the earth feeling the late autumn wind blow away the cobwebs, breathing deeply of the magical essence of Stonewylde. Arriving late at the Great Barn, all eyes turned to her as she made her entrance. She was windswept and rosy-cheeked, her eyes sparkling and hair whipped into silver tails. She resolved to spend a peaceful day in the Barn and try hard to avoid any trouble.

At the end of the day Sylvie watched the girls get into the cart to go back to the Hall. She savoured the peace once they'd left, standing amongst the trees and looking up at the bare branches feathery against the pale mauve sky. A blackbird sang sweetly, the liquid song pouring into the clear evening. Sylvie closed her eyes for a moment, feeling a thrill of pleasure at the thought of seeing Yul. She walked across the grass and waited under the yew tree for him to return from the Circle. She was alive with excitement, longing for him to join her in their special place.

He arrived silently, appearing under the boughs in the shadowy enclosure of the yew. They gazed at each other, suddenly shy. Yul held back, crawling with guilt at the kiss with Holly. Sylvie was overwhelmed by his presence. She felt the difference in him straight away now that he'd visited the Stone Circle at sunrise and sunset today. He buzzed with energy, his eyes sparkling and long fingers plucking at the bark of the tree.

"It's because I haven't been up there for so long," he explained, taking her hands in his. "It's always stronger then. After a few days, it'll settle down."

Sylvie was a little scared of him when he was like this, restless and vibrant with life and almost ready to explode with the magic. His eyes seemed to pierce her. He overflowed with power and energy; she felt it tingling in his fingertips. When he tried to take her in his arms she pulled away, apprehensive of the strength of the Earth Magic that hummed within him.

"I'm sorry," she whispered, stroking his cheek. "You're too much for me tonight, Yul. It's as if anything you touch will burst into flames. You set me on fire as it is. Tonight you'd consume me completely."

He smiled at this and contented himself with running his hands through her silky hair as they stood close, all the time watching her for signs that she'd been told about his kiss with Holly. It seemed the girl had kept it to herself and he prayed that she continued to do so. He considered confessing to Sylvie, but thinking how angry and hurt she'd be, he decided not to.

He was edgy and nervous, fiddling with her hair and shredding slips of yew, scuffing his boot in the ground. They talked of Magus' and Jackdaw's imminent return to

Stonewylde and how careful they must be not to attract attention. Sylvie started to explain about the banishing spell that Mother Heggy had made on the night of the Dark Moon, and then without warning Yul lost his temper. He was furious when he heard about Sylvie searching Magus' rooms. He swore vehemently and kicked hard at the soft earth beneath the tree with barely suppressed aggression.

"Mother Heggy had no right to put you in danger like that!" he said angrily. "Don't you ever put yourself at risk again!"

"There wasn't any risk. Magus wasn't home so he couldn't have found me there."

"He could've come back unexpectedly. And he still may find out what you've done. Sylvie, please don't do anything that could make him angry with you. He's so cruel, so sadistic. I can't bear to think of him hurting you. Goddess, I'm really annoyed that Mother Heggy made you take a risk like that! How dare she?"

"Yul, she didn't make me do anything," said Sylvie in a placatory voice, anxious to calm him down. "She asked me to help and I agreed. I want to do my bit to defeat him. It's not just your battle; we're all in it."

"Yes but you're more at risk from him than anyone else."

"We're all at risk from him, Yul. Everyone at Stonewylde who crosses him is at risk."

"So don't cross him!"

"I will if that's what it takes to destroy him."

"Sylvie, I'm the one who's going to destroy him, not you! It's not your fight, it's mine. You keep well out of it and leave it to me!"

She turned away angrily. It was almost dark and she needed to get home. She started to walk off.

"Don't turn your back on me!" he snapped, eyes flashing in the gloom. "Come back here! I'm still talking to you!"

"Don't speak to me like that!" she retorted. "You sound like your bloody father!"

She marched away and he tried to grab her.

"Sylvie, don't go! I'm sorry, I …"

She shook him off, running out from under the shelter of the yew tree onto the Green where she knew he wouldn't risk anyone spotting them together.

"Think about it, Yul! If you end up just like your father, what's the point in having a new magus?" she said, over her shoulder. "I'll see you around, when you've learnt to control your arrogance."

Yul was so angry after she'd gone that he decided to see Mother Heggy right away and speak his mind. He reached her cottage quickly and stormed in after a cursory knock.

"Blessings, Yul," she wheezed from her rocking chair by the fire. "Close the door. 'Tis cold out there."

"Mother Heggy, I ..."

"Come and sit awhile, boy. I hope Edward found you out today at the Circle?"

"Yes thanks, but it's the other matter I've come to see you about. You had no right to send Sylvie snooping in Magus' rooms for stuff for your spells. NO RIGHT!!" He banged his fist on the table. "She is *not* to be put in any danger. I am the one who will destroy Magus, not you or her or anyone else. In the end it's between me and him, and I won't let you interfere or put Sylvie at risk. Do you understand?"

He quivered with anger, grey eyes flashing. He glared at the old crone, a bag of wrinkles and whiskers. She peered up at him blindly and smacked her gums together.

"Spoken like a true magus."

He glared even more fiercely.

"Do you understand, Mother Heggy?"

"I take orders from nobody," she muttered. "We are in this together and we must all do what is needed. You love Sylvie and want to protect her, I know. But she too has a part to play in his downfall and you can't deny her that."

"But I don't want her taking risks! And I don't want your spells! I want to kill him myself!"

"And you shall. But 'twill help weaken him, and it gathers the people behind you. Everyone knows I've cast a spell. Cherry and Marigold have seen to that. Never could hold their tongues, them two sisters. The folk will all look at him with new eyes, watching for weakness or strangeness. 'Tis part of casting off the old magus and adopting the new one. Keep your temper under control, Yul. Save it for them that deserve it, not we who are on your side."

He hung his head, curls falling over his face, trying to calm his rage. He was so full of passion at the moment. She continued rocking as he fought to contain himself. After a few minutes he looked up.

"I'm sorry," he said, his eyes no longer sparking fury. "I have no right to order you or anyone else about. But please, please, don't put her in danger. She's the most precious, most special, most …"

He stopped, choking on the words.

"Aye, but she's also brave," said Mother Heggy, "which is why she's a worthy partner for you. She's not made o' petals. And she certainly won't take no bullying from you."

He grinned ruefully at this.

"I know. She's already put me in my place about it."

"Then listen to her and stop acting in passion. In many ways she is far beyond you. She's clever and been in the Outside World most o' her life. She knows far more than you, who's nought but a simple, ignorant Village boy. Don't make her see you as a fool. You too have to be worthy of her."

"But how? I know I'm ignorant, but …"

"When this is over, all will change. You have much to learn, Yul and you're very young. But at the Solstice, when you take the mantle of magus and also become a man, you will have a difficult lesson to learn. Being leader o' Stonewylde means sacrifice as well as power. Your sacrifice may be that you face your ignorance and swallow your pride. You will have to get proper learning to match hers. Maybe in the Outside World. The struggle don't end for you at the Solstice, my dark boy. 'Tis when it begins."

While Yul was running up the path to Mother Heggy for his confrontation, Sylvie walked angrily up the track towards the Hall. She was furious with Yul for speaking to her in such a high-handed way, and also for his attitude about the struggle with Magus. She felt hurt that he was shutting her out, and not acknowledging either her important status in the conflict or her wish to help. She seethed with resentment at his arrogance. All around her the night was closing in. She heard an owl calling in the distance, and then the sharp scream of a vixen from the woods nearby.

"Hello, Sylvie!"

Holly appeared before her on the track, just visible in the falling darkness. Sylvie groaned. The last thing she needed tonight was Holly's cattiness.

"I thought you'd gone home on the cart."

"I did, but then I got off. I wanted to speak to you in private. I've been waiting for you, Sylvie. You weren't long tonight. Not as long as last night."

"I'm not in the mood for it, Holly. Just leave me alone."

Holly laughed her false, irritating laugh.

"I can guess what you're in the mood for! Just left lover-boy under the tree, have you?"

"What?"

Holly laughed again, skipping alongside Sylvie in a state of glee.

"I know where you meet Yul and what you get up to! Don't try to deny it!"

"Go away, Holly! You know nothing about anything."

"That's where you're so wrong! I know everything about it. Has Yul told you what happened last night, after you'd left him?"

"What are you on about?"

"No, I thought he wouldn't tell you! Ha! Would you like to know what he got up to with me?"

Sylvie turned and grabbed Holly's sleeve, shaking her with uncharacteristic fury.

"Just shut up, you little cow! I don't want to hear anything from you!"

Holly shoved Sylvie away, her face splitting into a grin of pure malice.

"Are you sure about that, Sylvie? You don't want to know

what Yul and I did under the chestnut tree on the Village Green, just after you'd gone last night? You really shouldn't leave a boy all worked up like that, Sylvie. All worked up and needing more. It's just asking for trouble. Poor Yul! Lucky for him I came along. Still, if you're absolutely positive you don't want to know what we did ..."

With a laugh she took off, running up the track leading to the drive, her laughter becoming fainter in the distance. Sylvie didn't try to catch her. She wondered just what had happened the night before. Surely Yul wouldn't have done anything with Holly? Or maybe he had, which was why he'd been so nasty to her tonight? And he'd liked Holly in the past. Enough to fight with Buzz over her. She gulped back her tears, misery squeezing at her heart. She could cope with anything if she had Yul by her side. But if he betrayed her, she'd never have the strength to stand up to Magus.

Candlelight gleamed all down the long white tables as the Hallfolk ate dinner. Conversation bubbled, glasses and silver cutlery chinked and the servants hurried to clear away soup dishes and bring on the next course. Sylvie sat miserably next to Miranda, huddled in her seat trying to force down the meal. Miranda chattered non-stop, excited at the prospect of Magus' imminent return. There was a general buzz of anticipation in the air. Sylvie seemed alone in dreading his return. Holly turned several times to gloat at her, sniggering with her group of friends. Sylvie wished that she were anywhere but here tonight. She noticed Hazel sitting up on the high table, near the head where Magus would dine if he should arrive in time. Several of her teachers had given her meaningful looks already and she knew what they were thinking.

Just as pudding was served, the double doors were opened wide and Magus made his entrance into the Dining Hall. All went quiet and then he was greeted by cheers and a crescendo of noise as he strode down the long room to his seat. Sylvie felt her heart thudding faster but knew it to be fear rather than excitement. Miranda had flushed at the sight of him and was now giggling and talking too loudly, along with many of the females. He sat in his great carved chair, smiling at those around him and accepting a plate of food from Martin, who fussed over him deferentially. Sylvie noticed how the servants in the room had jumped to attention and become more nervous and jerky. She caught Harold's eye but he quickly looked away, denying their new friendship.

Sylvie gazed up the table at Magus, the returning hero. He glowed with health and vitality which she knew was thanks to her suffering on the rock. He wore a dark business suit with a snowy shirt and silk tie. His blond hair gleamed like burnished bronze. His dark eyes flashed with cleverness and energy. The candlelight gleamed on his skin, as smooth and rich as marble, hollowing his cheekbones, etching the strong nose and chin, emphasising the curve of his lips.

Sylvie was struck forcibly by his likeness to Yul. How had she never spotted it before? Looking at Magus, she could picture how Yul would be at this age and knew she'd want him then just as much as she did now. Magus was so very attractive and every woman in the room watched him. Some were obvious, like her mother, Hazel, and Holly's group, and others more discreet. All were caught up in his magnetism and beauty. Would it be the same with Yul, Sylvie wondered. Would she have to share him with every woman at Stonewylde?

At that moment, Magus looked up and across the room straight into her eyes. She felt her cheeks flushing and her eyes widen, but couldn't look away. His dark eyes bored into her and he inclined his head, his lips tightening into a half smile. This was not lost on Holly, whose head shot round to glare at Sylvie. She whispered to Rainbow next to her, and both continued to stare at Sylvie throughout the rest of the meal. Sylvie felt awkward and embarrassed and couldn't eat any more after that, her stomach churning. She wondered what he'd do if he found out about the missing lock of hair from the old album. She also wondered when Mother Heggy's spell would start to work, because he certainly looked as strong and powerful as ever right now. She shivered with fear, dreading the weeks ahead.

Sylvie sat in one of the school rooms in a maths lesson. William had just humiliated her in front of all the others by revealing her complete ignorance of quadratic equations. Maths had always been a weakness and she'd missed the block of teaching on equations back in July. Sylvie stared at the text book before her, cheeks burning with chagrin as Holly swaggered up to the whiteboard and solved the complicated calculation easily. William smiled and nodded.

"Good – well done, Holly. You see, Sylvie? It's not that difficult if you put your mind to it. I suggest you apply yourself to the relevant chapters which you've clearly never even bothered to look at. Work through the examples and complete all the exercises this evening and I'll take a look at them tomorrow."

"But this evening I have to finish my ..."

Magus poked his head round the door.

"When the lesson's finished, I'd like a word with Sylvie in my office."

Ignoring the whispers and daggered looks from the others, she tried to concentrate on the rest of the lesson. At last it was over and she made her way to the office at the back of the Hall.

Magus sat at a desk working on a computer, but stood as she entered. He beckoned her over to the sofas and sat down opposite her. He regarded her steadily, his expression neutral. She quaked inside.

"Well, Sylvie, I see you've made a complete recovery."

"Yes."

"And I hear from Hazel that there is absolutely nothing wrong with you other than deficiencies brought on by under-eating."

"Yes."

"She tells me you've put on some weight, and Miranda says you're eating sensibly now and applying yourself at last to your studies."

"Yes, I am."

"Good. I also have a detailed school report here from each

of your teachers. The news there is not so good, as I'm sure you're aware. Everyone is disappointed with your progress and lack of diligence over the past months."

"I'm trying really hard now."

"I'm sure you are. And will continue to do so. Miranda also tells me you've been asking about new clothes for winter because you've grown so much taller."

"Yes please."

"Mmn. I'll have to consider that request. You may of course visit the Village stores and pick up some material to make clothes for yourself. Everyone's entitled to that."

"I'm ... I don't know how to make clothes."

"There's also the dressmakers. You can ask them to run you up something to wear."

"Yes, thank you."

He fell silent and watched her. Then he smiled, his eyes amused.

"I expect you'd rather hoped to order some fashionable things on the Internet, like all the other Hallfolk teenagers do."

She looked at her hands, unable to keep eye contact with him.

"I'll go to the Village dressmakers," she said quietly. "I know I can't buy anything."

"We'll see. It rather depends on you. You're in an awkward position, aren't you, Sylvie? All the others have wealthy and successful parents to provide for them. You don't. Miranda may ostensibly work as a teacher here, but over the months she's missed a lot of work through caring for you during your "illnesses". She's barely earned your keep."

"I'm sorry."

"I'm pleased to hear it. Maybe now you'll appreciate the consequences of your actions."

"I hadn't thought of it like that."

"No, I don't expect you had. Let me remind you that nobody at Stonewylde gets a free ride. Everyone here works for their living in whatever capacity they can. Be it ploughing the fields to grow our food, rearing children to provide future labour for Stonewylde or teaching the next generation of doctors and lawyers, nobody takes and gives nothing back. All your contemporaries are at the Hall School because their parents pay me expensive fees, just like any other boarding school. You're the only one here who doesn't. And yet you expect me to provide you not only with education, accommodation, food and the necessities of life, but also a fashionable wardrobe."

"No, I'm sorry … I didn't think. It's alright, I can manage."

"Good. Because I'm a generous man where it's deserved, but I won't be taken for a fool. When I became magus I jettisoned all the spongers and leeches. I don't intend to start allowing them back in."

Sylvie felt embarrassed. She'd expected a lecture about school work, but not this. She wished her mother had never said anything about her needing new clothes.

"However, there's one thing you can do for me that's worth more than every hour of labour given on the entire estate. I think you know what I'm talking about."

She swallowed hard and nodded.

"Look at me, Sylvie, when I'm talking to you. You know what I need from you. You know what you alone can give me. Have you thought about it since our last talk, when I was so angry with you for interfering at Samhain?"

She nodded again.

"So will you freely give me the moon magic I need from you? Or will you persist in fighting me, threatening to leave, and starving yourself so you become weak and too ill to moondance properly and give me what I want?"

"I'll give it freely," she whispered. "I'm sorry I refused. I didn't realise how selfish I was being."

He smiled and it was like the sun irradiating the land after a thunderstorm had passed.

Life at the Hall became unbearable for Sylvie. The teachers continued to exert pressure on her in every lesson and she was loaded with extra work in all subjects. None of them had a good word for her, despite the effort she was putting in. She began to feel worthless and stupid. The daily visits to Hazel continued and her weight rose slowly, aided now by Magus himself. He demanded that she sit by his side at every meal, and monitored her eating carefully. He controlled everything she ate, always insisting she take more than she wanted or could comfortably manage. She felt like a turkey being fattened up for Christmas. All the fuss he made of her didn't go unnoticed. The girls were beside themselves with jealousy and took delight in making nasty remarks. Holly in particular tormented her and had plenty of ammunition. Sylvie's unpopularity with the teachers was seized on, and Holly teased her constantly about her failure to keep up with the class. She commented on Sylvie's eating and weight gain, and especially on her lack of winter clothes. Sylvie felt frumpy and plain in the summer things she still wore, topped with jumpers to keep warm. Holly swanked around in smart outfits and took pleasure in humiliating her rival at every turn.

One morning Sylvie sat alone in the Dining Hall surrounded by the debris of breakfast. She'd been forced to eat a hearty cooked meal, and coming after a huge dinner the night before she now felt uncomfortably over-full. Magus had just left. He'd spent nearly an hour plying her with food, watching her swallow every mouthful. He'd stayed with her as everyone gradually left the room just to make sure that she ate it all. Holly had given her a particularly venomous stare as she left for the first lesson of the day. Sylvie was now almost in tears, trying to decide whether to make a dash for the bathroom or wait a few more minutes. She wasn't sure whether or not she'd make it there before she was sick.

"So you are in here," said Holly, poking her head round the door. "Not still eating, are you? Greedy pig - you're going to get so fat! Brambling said to hurry up, he's waiting to start the French lesson."

"I don't feel very well," said Sylvie weakly. "Tell him to start without me and I'll come as soon as I can."

"You can't just skip lessons because you stuffed yourself at breakfast," said Holly, coming into the great Dining Hall and standing in front of Sylvie. "You're thick enough as it is. You can't afford to miss any more lessons. Brambling's not impressed. He's furious you're not there after all the fuss that's been made about your attendance. You should hear what he's saying about you. Everyone's killing themselves laughing at his impersonation of you trying to buy a rail ticket in French."

A young servant came in quietly and started clearing away some of the serving dishes from the long sideboard. Holly threw the girl a look, but otherwise ignored her.

"Tell Brambling I'll be along soon."

Sylvie wished she'd go; the nausea hit her in waves and her waistband dug in tightly. Holly glared at her disdainfully.

"Seen lover boy lately?"

Sylvie shook her head, unable to open her mouth to speak.

"Well I have. I saw him yesterday when I was out riding. Looking as gorgeous as ever, he was, up at that stone on the top of the hill near the ridgeway. I told him about our chat, and he wasn't pleased that you knew about me and him. He told me he'd wanted us to keep it a secret from you. That way he could have us both. A bit like you with him and Magus. I suppose now that Magus is back, you'll have to keep away from Yul. Which means I'll have him all to myself, just like in the good old days before you came here. Yul and I always did have an understanding. Did you know we're going to be partners at our Rite of Adulthood?"

"Go away, Holly!" whispered Sylvie.

The Village girl came back in to get more dishes, and glanced over at the two Hallfolk girls.

"Get out!" yelled Holly. "We're having a private conversation!"

The girl scuttled off and shut the door behind her.

"Bloody half-wit! Yeah, now that Magus is back, you'll have to stop seeing your bit of rough, won't you? And haven't you just got Magus wrapped around your little finger? Goddess, it makes me want to puke watching him with you. Fussing over you, spoiling you. He was practically feeding you breakfast just now. Does he like you being his little girl? That's sick!"

At that point, Sylvie threw up over the littered table, unable to hold it any longer. With a shriek of disgust, Holly leapt back.

"You revolting bitch! You did that on purpose!"

Sylvie sat ashen faced and perfectly still, holding a linen napkin to her lips. Holly made for the door, then stopped, hand on the brass doorknob. She turned and looked speculatively at Sylvie, sitting motionless at the table waiting for the tide of nausea to recede.

"Or maybe you didn't? Maybe it's morning sickness! Now there's a thought. Mother and daughter both up the spout! We know Magus is the father of your mother's baby, but I wonder if he's the father of yours?"

One night not long after this, Sylvie sat in bed trying to finish her geography revision. Outside she heard the wind rising, and from her bed could see dark clouds scudding across the large silver moon. The wind rattled the diamond window panes and Sylvie shivered slightly, feeling warm and safe in her bed, but not free of the fear that haunted her. Every night she saw the moon growing and she still didn't know what was going to happen on the night of the Moon Fullness.

She hadn't seen Yul since their argument under the yew tree when he'd been so arrogant. It was probably just as well, for now she'd had time to calm down and reflect on what had happened. She realised they'd both been overwrought and was quite prepared to forget the whole thing. The business with Holly was not so easy to forget, however. She was desperate to know what had really happened between the two of them. But Magus had been watching her so closely that there'd been no chance at all to escape the Hall and find Yul.

Magus was being strict and still a little disapproving with her. Every meal time he beckoned her to sit with him, he looked in on every lesson, found her in the library in all her free periods, made her walk with him in the formal garden if she said she needed fresh air. He even visited every night to check she'd gone to bed and was not staying up late. He'd started coming into her bedroom to say goodnight and turn her light out, like a stern father. She hated it. She felt suffocated by his patriarchal attention. But she endured it because she didn't want to arouse his suspicions. Yul had said she must go along with what Magus wanted and she was doing her very best.

She put the dull text book aside and opened the drawer next to her bed, pulling out her battered copy of Wuthering Heights. It fell open immediately to reveal its secret – the hidden photo of Yul that Professor Siskin had given her just before he'd returned to Oxford. He'd printed it on heavy photographic paper, and despite Sylvie's constant handling, the photo was still clear and smooth.

She gazed at Yul's beautiful face, golden in the sunlight, smeared with green lichen and brown earth, his glossy curls long and full of twigs and leaves. His slanted, long-lashed grey eyes gazed sleepily out at her, and a half-smile played on his lips. All around him was bright green foliage forming a halo of leaves. Whenever she felt unhappy - unable to cope with Magus' attention, the nastiness of Holly and the girls, her mother's indifference, the criticism of her teachers or the loneliness of not seeing Yul for so long – she'd look at the photo and feel comforted by the sight of her own Green Man, so beautiful and magical.

Suddenly there was a pattering at her window. Sylvie rose from her warm bed and looked out into the darkness, just making out a figure with pale upturned face standing on the grass below. It waved and disappeared, and a minute later there was a knock at the wooden door in the corner of her room, leading to the staircase.

"Yul!"

She was overjoyed to see him. He stood in the arched doorway, his head almost brushing the top of it. The wind had whipped his face into a rosy glow and his hair into wild ringlets. His eyes sparkled brightly and he stood there slightly out of breath, obviously having run all the way. Sylvie had learnt that Yul never walked anywhere if he could run. He wore an old leather jacket against the November cold, and dark trousers and boots. He was tall, lean and devastatingly good looking. She had a vision of him in the Outside World, maybe at college or university, surrounded by adoring girls all unable to keep their hands off him. She closed her eyes, blocking the image, and opened them to find him standing directly in front of her.

"Are you alright, Sylvie?" he asked, holding her at arm's length and looking into her eyes.

"I'm fine, just fatter. I've wanted to come and find you but I haven't been able to get away. Magus is watching me like a hawk. How are you feeling now? You look good."

"I'm really well, almost back to normal. Sylvie, I need to talk with you. I'm really sorry about how I spoke to you that night at the Dark Moon."

"It's okay. It was nothing really. I just don't like being bossed about. And you sounded so like Magus. It's bad enough with him dominating me."

"I know, and I shouldn't have spoken to you like that. It won't happen again."

She laughed.

"Don't make promises you can't keep, Yul! I'm sure you'll do it again loads of times. Just understand that I won't take it and you'll never get away with it."

He grinned at her and relaxed a little.

"I've brought you a present to say sorry," he said, fishing inside the leather jacket. He produced a small woodcarving of a leaping hare, exquisitely made of polished golden wood. Sylvie gasped and took it gently in her hand.

"It's a moondancing hare. I made it from a piece of our tree, the yew on the Village Green."

She flung her arms around him and hugged him, kissing his cold cheeks and smelling the November night in his hair.

"It's the most beautiful thing I've ever seen!" she exclaimed. "Apart from you of course."

He laughed but then his face clouded over.

"There's something else we must talk about."

"Come and sit down," she said, but looking around realised the only place was the bed. Her chair was covered with a pile of school books. She was wearing her long nightdress made of fine white Stonewylde linen. Although it covered everything except her hands, feet and face, she suddenly felt shy. But he seemed not to notice and sat on the bed, frowning. She sat down next to him.

"I don't know how to start, really. I don't know quite how it happened, and I ..."

"If it's about Holly, I already know."

"I was worried you might," he groaned, his face downcast. "I saw her again the other day when I was up at Hare Stone looking for you. She started bragging that she'd told you what had happened. I was so tempted to slap her. I don't know how I controlled myself. I despise that girl! Sylvie, I ..."

"Look, Yul, I don't know the details and I don't think I want to. I know how manipulative she is. I expect she tricked you, did she?"

"Yes, in a way. But I was a fool and I knew it straight away. She'd followed you and seen us together. She threatened to tell Magus if I didn't kiss her like I'd kissed you."

"And did you?" whispered Sylvie, her throat tight and aching.

He nodded in shame, looking beseechingly into her clear grey eyes, now full of pain that he knew he'd inflicted.

"I'm so sorry, Sylvie! If it's any consolation, I hated it."

"Oh Yul! How could you? I'd hoped it was just talk. I didn't realise you'd actually *kissed* her."

His face twisted with guilt. He shook his head and half turned from her, unable to face her distress. She sat silently, fighting the jealousy that raged inside her.

"Do you want me to leave?" he mumbled.

She glanced down at the little golden hare still in her hand. It was perfect, completely capturing the essence of hare in its long ears and lithe body. He must have spent such time and care on it. She shook her head. He wrapped his arms around her and pulled her down with him onto the bed so she half lay on top of him. He held her face just off his, her silver hair hanging down like a veil around them, and gazed deep into her eyes. She saw then his love for her. She felt herself dragged down into his soul where she knew there was a place

110

for her alone and nobody else. Holly withered into insignificance.

"Kiss me, Sylvie," he whispered softly. "Show me you forgive me. You know it's you I love."

She began to kiss him, slowly and gently at first. She teased him with her softness and lightness, enjoying the control she had over him, the way he strained towards her so desperately. But soon her teasing gave way to the urgent need she felt blossoming inside, and her kisses became deep and hard. She felt his hands on her body through the soft linen of her nightdress, his leather jacket stiff between them as he clasped her hard against him, his mouth ravenous for hers. All around the walls of her bedroom disappeared as she entered the dark labyrinth of desire and took her first tentative steps along the path. Nothing else mattered but this journey.

Yul sat up in a sudden and fluid motion, taking them both upright. But still she clung to him by the mouth, her arms locked around his head, unwillingly to release him.

"Enough!" he mouthed around her lips, and gently but firmly held her away from him. His eyes were almost black with passion and he laughed unsteadily, shaking the hair from his eyes. "Sylvie ..."

She closed her eyes for a couple of heartbeats, then opened them to stare at him, her face pale and hollowed with longing.

"I don't ... Yul, I've never felt like this before."

He grimaced, brushing her messed-up hair away from her face with a trembling hand.

"You're lucky then. I feel like this all the time. Every time I see you or even think of you ..."

He took a deep breath, his steely control slipping back into place, and gazed into her eyes once more.

"You don't know just how much you fill my days and my nights," he said softly. "Thinking about you, wanting you, dreaming of how it will be one day, when we can make love and be together all the time. You're my whole universe, Sylvie. Holly is just an irritating speck of dust. I can't begin to tell you just how much I love you and how much I need you. Don't ever doubt it, whatever happens."

He stood up and pulled her up too, his eyes searching her face.

"I must go," he said quietly. "It's dangerous being here. But it's the Owl Moon very soon and I have to tell you the plan. I'll come and get you in the middle of the afternoon. It gets dark early, now that the Solstice is near. Have lunch as normal, and after a while, say you're feeling sleepy and want a rest before the evening. He'll approve of that. Tell your mother that you don't want to be disturbed. Then come up here and put on your warmest clothes. Lots of layers, because it'll be cold. Make up your bed so that from the door it looks like you're in it, and pull the curtains shut so it's dark. Then wait. I'll come and we'll get away as fast as we can."

"Okay. Sounds a good plan to me. But what if the outside door's locked?"

He grinned at her.

"I now have a key! Harold borrowed it and Tom got it copied by the blacksmith. So even if the door leading outside is locked, I can use my key to get you out."

"Brilliant! I feel so relieved knowing you'll take me away where he can't get me. I've been really frightened about it. You'd better go now, Yul. It's quite late and Magus has started coming in here to say goodnight to me. He could come at any time. He's insisting on early nights, along with the force feeding. He wants me strong and healthy so I can give him all my moon magic. He goes on about it all the time."

He kissed her quickly but longingly.

"Well he'll be disappointed, won't he? See you at Owl Moon then. Any problems, send a message with Harold or Cherry and I'll come straight away. I won't let you down this time, Sylvie, whatever happens."

It was as well he left then, because five minutes later Magus knocked on the door and came in almost immediately. Sylvie was back in bed reading, the photo and golden hare safely hidden away in her drawer, her love locked inside her heart.

"Time for lights out, young lady," he said, smiling at her. He sniffed the air and glanced around the room, but then came across to her bed and took the book from her hands. "What are you reading? Oh, Wuthering Heights. Are you enjoying it?"

"Very much," she replied, lying down in bed and pulling the covers up high. "It's one of my very favourite books."

He stood looking down at her as she lay there, her hair spread on the pillow. He stared and stared and she began to feel uncomfortable. Then he sat down on the side of the bed, and the covers were pulled tight over her, trapping her. He began to stroke the hair back from her forehead. She shivered with fear, remembering him doing this before when she was weak and he was angry with her. His eyes were deep and unfathomable, dark as a moonless night. He gazed at her as she lay trembling at his touch.

"Are you cold?" he asked softly.

"No."

"Then what's the matter?"

"Nothing."

She was terrified, her mouth too dry to speak. His fingers, so like Yul's, began to trace her eyebrows and then down to her cheekbones. She remembered Yul doing the same, but she'd welcomed his touch.

"You are growing up, Sylvie," he said, voice like velvet. "Almost a woman now."

His fingertips continued their slow journey down the line of her jaw. His thumb gently ran along the contours of her lips, still slightly swollen from the passionate kissing of only ten minutes ago. She didn't know how to stop him without offending him. His eyes were compelling, and so close. She saw a muscle in his cheek twitch and his nostrils flare very slightly. She could hardly breathe, she was so scared. But she needn't have worried. He bent and brushed her cheek with his lips, his exquisite scent entering her lungs.

"Sweet dreams, my moongazy girl. I'll see you in the morning."

He got up, turned off her light and left the room, shutting the door firmly behind him. Only then did she breathe freely again, although his presence seemed to linger in the darkness long after he'd left.

The next day after another large breakfast, Magus took Sylvie into his office again. She could feel every pair of eyes in the Dining Hall following her as he led her out of the room, his hand under her elbow to guide her. She knew the rumours that Holly had been spreading after she'd seen Sylvie being sick the other morning. She walked glumly by Magus's side, trying to hold her head up, feeling ill from the heavy food he'd forced her to swallow. She knew she might be sick again and hoped that whatever he wanted to say to her would be over and done with quickly.

He ushered her into the office and she saw Clip sitting on one of the sofas. He had a cake tin by him and brushed some crumbs off his jacket. He looked pale and faraway, his face strained and eyes dull. Sylvie was reminded of some wolves she'd once seen in a zoo, their beauty and spirit marred by enforced captivity.

"Good morning, Sylvie," he said. "You're looking well."

"She's very well now. She's taking care of herself properly at last," said Magus smoothly, guiding Sylvie to the sofa opposite Clip and sitting down next to her. He took one of her hands in his and rubbed it encouragingly.

"She's seen sense at last, haven't you Sylvie? I'm so pleased with her, Clip. She's willing now to make that little sacrifice every month for me. For Stonewylde. She knows what I need and what she must do for me."

Sylvie stared at her knees, wondering how she could pull her hand away without making him cross. She didn't like him touching her. He gripped her quite tightly, and she looked up suddenly. Clip was gazing at her intently, his pale grey eyes with the dilated pupils huge in his face.

"She's seen sense then. No more fighting," he said softly, in his voice that was like Magus', but not as deep or resonant. Sylvie stared at him, remembering something, something she mustn't forget …

"No!" she cried. "No, Magus, you promised! You said the other day I didn't have to be hypnotised again if I co-operated. Please, no!"

She started to struggle, trying to pull away. Magus gripped her arm harder so she couldn't stand up.

"Just keep still, Sylvie, and it'll all be over with very quickly. This is for your own good to make it easier for you. Come on, stop struggling. You know I'm far stronger than you."

"Please, Magus, I beg you! I'll go to Mooncliffe, I'll do whatever you say, I promise! I won't fight you and I'll charge up all your moon eggs. Just don't hypnotise me, please!"

But he only chuckled, his grip as tight as ever as he held her down on the soft sofa. Clip moved over and knelt in front of her, taking her head between his hands so she couldn't look away. She closed her eyes, desperately trying to shake her head out of his grasp, whimpering for him to stop.

"Stop fighting, Sylvie. Stop! Just give in. It's so much easier, believe me. Now look at me, look at me. Look very well, Sylvie, right deep into my eyes. That's right, good girl. When I count to three, you'll wake up and you won't remember this. Just like before. Now, remember what I told you last time about Mooncliffe? It's where you like to be at Moon Fullness. The only place you want to be. You love to stand on the great stone up there. You want to please Magus. You're desperate to give him all your moon magic. If anyone tries to stop you, you will fight them and resist. You must go to Mooncliffe, Sylvie!"

He let go of her head and turned to Magus, his eyes resigned.

"Alright? Anything else, or is that it?"

Magus smiled, releasing his hold on Sylvie's arm. She remained sitting exactly how she'd been before, still staring ahead. He chuckled again.

"It's so easy, isn't it? No, I think that will do for now. There may be another thing, but that can wait for a bit."

"I've told you, Sol, this is the last time ever. I refuse to abuse my gift like this again. And I'm not coming up to bloody Mooncliffe with you either, so don't even ask."

"I don't need you, dear brother. Jackdaw's coming with me. I think he'll be far more effective than you were.

Especially if our friend Yul turns up on another rescue mission."

"Sol, don't overdo it this month, will you? I know what Jackdaw's like – and you. Be careful, please. Sylvie's only a girl. Remember what happened to our mother."

"That was an eclipse," said Magus tersely. "Ordinary moongazing won't kill her."

"Don't force her to carry on for hours on end, will you? And make sure she's warm enough."

"You sound like a bloody nursemaid. What's with the sudden concern for her welfare? What's she to you anyway?"

Clip shrugged, and reached wearily for another cake.

"She's very vulnerable. And you're a cruel bastard. You take such pleasure in making others suffer for your own gratification. I don't like to see you hurting people."

Magus laughed.

"Very touching. Bad memories, eh?"

"You could say that."

"That was just an adolescent thing, Clip. I'm not like that any more."

"Yes you are, Sol. You're just as bad. In fact, I think you might be worse. The only thing that's changed is now you're so much better at hiding it."

CHAPTER SEVEN

The night before the Owl Moon, Yul called on Sylvie again. As soon as she returned from dinner, he raced silently up the back stairs and tapped on the arched door leading into her bedroom. He knew he had a little time before Magus would arrive. She opened it immediately, her face lighting up at the sight of him. She put her arms around him but then groaned, pulling away.

"What's wrong?"

"I'm so full. I feel sick."

"Are you ill?" he asked anxiously, taking her hands.

She sat down on the bed weakly.

"I'm not ill, but I've always had trouble eating large meals. I used to have allergies and things. I hate being made to eat. Magus forces me to eat so much and I just can't take it. I'm often sick after meals."

"Does he know?"

"No. Every day he looks at my weight chart and he's angry because I'm not putting any on. In fact now I'm being sick all the time I've started losing it again. So the next day he makes me eat even more."

He sat next to her, holding her hand sympathetically.

"I just came to check that you're alright for tomorrow. You remember the plan?"

"Yes, I know what to do. It'll be easy because he said I must stay in my room and rest all day tomorrow anyway. I'm looking forward to spending the afternoon with you."

"Good. Wrap up warm because it's cold now in the evenings. I'd better go then."

"But Yul, I have to get back before the evening."

"What do you mean?"

"I must get back here before the moonrise. I'm going up to Mooncliffe with Magus."

He laughed and stood up.

"No, Yul, it's not funny. I have to dance on the stone at Mooncliffe tomorrow. I want to give Magus my moon magic. You do understand, don't you?"

She looked up at him earnestly, her eyes great pools of moonstone grey. His face fell in horror.

"Oh Sylvie, they've got to you again! The bastards!"

"What do you mean, got to me? I don't understand."

"Never mind," he said shakily.

He couldn't believe it. There was no chance now to get her to Mother Heggy before the moonrise tomorrow night, not when she was watched so closely. He felt like crying with frustration.

"You just make sure you're ready tomorrow afternoon, alright?"

"They've put a spell on her again!" shouted Yul, pacing the tiny room. The crow squawked indignantly, flapping its wings.

"'Twas to be expected, however much she seemed to agree to do what he wants," mused Mother Heggy. "He's taking no chances. It just shows how desperate he is for the moon magic. Did you get to steal some of the eggs, boy?"

"Yes, the key worked, after a bit of twisting. Edward helped. There were a few eggs left in the chest. The ones lying on the grass outside the chest were the used up ones. There were so many of them! He's been gorging on her moon magic. So we took most of the good ones from the chest and replaced them with used ones. I've hidden the charged eggs in the woods. They're so powerful, those eggs. I hated having to touch them, knowing what they took out of her."

"He'll be spitting angry when he finds they're missing," cackled Mother Heggy. "Especially when there's no new ones this month. Heh heh!"

"But he will get new ones this month! That's why I'm so worried! She's under the spell again and she wants to go to

118

Mooncliffe tomorrow night!"

"For Goddess' sake, Yul! You're a man now; she's nought but a slip of a girl. Who's the strongest?"

"Yes, but I can't force her to stay with me."

"Course you can, silly boy. You must bind her tight till the moon is good and high and 'tis safe to release her."

He looked at her in horror.

"I couldn't treat Sylvie like that!"

The crone pursed her lips and tutted, shaking her head at his misplaced sensibilities.

"Well, there is another way, Yul, now I think on it. Up by Ash Wood, right up beyond the Dragon's Back, there's a grove of old sycamore trees. A whole group of 'em have split trunks. They were coppiced long ago and then forgotten. They've grown strangely and we called them the tree-cages. When I were a girl, the woodsmen put naughty lads in there to punish 'em. They'd bind around the trunks with rope and make cages so the boys couldn't get out. You could put Sylvie in one o' them. She'd be imprisoned, right enough, and you must gag her if she makes a noise, but 'tis not as bad as trussing her up. Sounds cruel I know, but 'tis only to help her. 'Tis for her own good."

Jackdaw tapped at the French windows of Magus' office and was beckoned inside. Magus wrinkled his nose at the stench of stale tobacco that clung to him. Jackdaw was particularly unsavoury today; greasy and unshaven, his protruding blue eyes bloodshot and bleary. He smelt unwashed too, and Magus decided not to bring him inside the Hall again. They'd have to meet elsewhere in future. He opened the French windows wider on the misty morning.

"You understand what's involved tonight?" he began. "You'll help with the eggs, and ensure that damn boy comes nowhere near the cliff-top."

"Aye, sir. Looking forward to a bit of action at last. But I don't see why I can't deal with the little bugger now. I could take him away, up to Quarrycleave maybe. Have some fun with him first and then snuff him."

Magus shook his head.

"It sounds easy, but it's been proven to us twice now that his time isn't yet up – last Moon Fullness at Mooncliffe and again in the Stone Labyrinth at Samhain. He should by rights have died on both those occasions, but clearly the Dark Angel didn't want him."

He saw Jackdaw's scepticism.

"You've been away too long, Jack. You've forgotten the reality of Stonewylde, tainted as you are by the Outside World. The Dark Angel might sound like some fairytale fantasy to you, but I know only too well just how real that spectre is. I believe now that Yul will continue to live a charmed life until the Winter Solstice. And it's only me who'll be able to finally destroy him. It's his destiny and mine. They're linked. But you can keep him at bay if he tries to rescue Sylvie. I can't stress how vital it is that I take her moon energy tonight. I need to be extra powerful for the Solstice. There are only a few charged eggs left and I want her to do the full load tonight, and maybe more if she can take it. I've had some extras made up. She's much stronger this month. I've seen to that."

He stood up, anxious to remove Jackdaw from his office and clear the air.

"Keep well away from the Village today," he continued, ushering Jackdaw towards the French windows. "Martin tells me there's a lot of ill feeling about your return. The Villagers are muttering and complaining."

"Bloody load o' peasants," growled Jackdaw, forgetting his own origins. "There's a few of 'em I'd like to put in their place. Especially that old sow Marigold."

"Once this Moon Fullness tonight is done, we'll smooth things over. Now, I want you up there by mid-afternoon stacking all the empty eggs around the rock ready for me. I'll bring the girl up myself just before sunset. You've got the walkie-talkie and charged it up?"

"Aye sir. And I'll make sure the boy don't trouble you," said Jackdaw, rubbing his bristly jowls. He grinned, the gold incisor glinting amongst dark teeth. "I know Yul's yours to finish, but there's a whole month till the Solstice, ain't there?

Time enough for a bit of fun with him, if you don't mind. I'd enjoy that. He's a tough little nut to crack, and they're always the sweetest."

"We'll see," said Magus, eyeing the brute of a man with distaste. "Depends on what you have in mind. But it could be useful to have him out of the way in the lead up to the Solstice, especially if you can weaken him for me. I'll think about it. We'll get through tonight first and discuss it tomorrow. Remember, Jackdaw - tonight you must keep your eyes open and your wits about you."

By mid-day the tree-cage was ready. Yul had found the sycamore grove, a good five miles from the Hall up in Ash Woods. He'd chosen an enormous tree to be Sylvie's prison. Its huge trunk grew to almost a metre and then split into seven separate trunks, each one nearly as thick as a telegraph pole and just as straight. The gap between each trunk was thin, not big enough for even a slim person like Sylvie to squeeze through, except for one gap which he himself could just manage to slip between.

Inside the cage of trunks it was surprisingly roomy. The bole of the tree had collected leaves over the years and was now carpeted with a thick floor of soft moss, covered by this year's fallen leaves. There was space enough for a person to sit or lie curled up, and easily to stand. Yul had ropes ready to tie across the larger gap once she was inside, and water and a lantern to hand.

Edward had lent him the beautiful grey mare, which had saved a great deal of time in preparing the tree cage. He would have liked to ride up here with Sylvie, but if she started to fight or thrash about it would scare the horse and make her bolt. He decided eventually to compromise and tether the horse half way.

Finally, checking that all was ready and that the finer rope and a piece of cloth were in his bag in case she proved difficult, he mounted the mare and trotted off along the path towards the Hall. The mare was quiet and gentle, very different from the exhilaration of Nightwing, but Yul enjoyed riding her all the same. He had an affinity with horses and had always wanted one of his own. He thought often of Nightwing. He'd vowed that one day the dark stallion would be his.

He urged Edward's horse into a canter and they flew down the woodland path. The dark haired boy and the milk-white steed were like a beautiful picture from a book of fairy tales. They rode through the bare-branched trees to the palace ahead to rescue the imprisoned princess. Yul managed to stay in woodland until he was just outside the Hall, not wanting to be seen by any Hallfolk out in the open country riding Edward's horse. He tied the mare to a branch and continued the last part of the journey on foot. It was now about an hour after lunch time at the Hall and she should be ready and waiting. His heart pounded as he turned the handle of the outside door leading to the staircase to her bedroom. It was locked.

Yul peered through the keyhole and realised that the key was missing. Magus must have removed it to keep Sylvie captive. He felt in his pocket and found the key that Tom had had made for him. It worked, after a bit of jiggling, and the door opened. He crept up the stairs, as quiet and terrified as a field mouse. His fear was not that Magus would catch him and hurt him, but that it would all go wrong and he'd let Sylvie down again. At the top of the stairs he tapped on the arched door and silently opened it, dreading what he might see. He pictured Magus standing there with Jackdaw, both grinning.

Sylvie stood by the window wearing a vivid scarlet cloak. She turned to face him and smiled. She looked stunning. She wore all black underneath – trousers, warm jumper, gloves, suede boots – which accentuated her tall, slim body. The cloak was made of thick velvet with a great hood. Her silver hair spilled out between the scarlet and the black, and her face was alive with excitement.

"Yul!" she whispered. "I was worried you wouldn't come! I'm all ready. Is that alright?"

She gestured to the bed where she'd stuffed an extra blanket and pillow. It was realistic, especially in the half light with the curtains drawn.

"Perfect. Come on, let's go right now."

They slipped out of the wing and into the woods, Sylvie's cloak billowing around her.

"Do you like my new cloak? It's a present from Magus to keep me warm while I moondance for him. Isn't it lovely? And these new clothes and boots. They were all a surprise. He said I must be very good for him tonight and give him all my moon magic. And I mustn't make any fuss afterwards about feeling ill. I can stay in bed for two days if I'm tired but then I have to get back to normal. If I can manage that, he'll buy me some more winter clothes, really beautiful ones. I'm so excited. I'm fed up with Holly laughing at my appearance."

Yul closed his eyes and groaned. He couldn't bear it when she talked like this. The sooner he could get her to Mother Heggy and get the spell lifted, the better. But he had to agree, the cloak was lovely. They reached the tree where he'd tethered the mare and Sylvie jumped with pleasure.

"Are we both going to ride her? We won't be too heavy for her?"

"She's very strong. She belongs to a farmer called Edward, and he probably weighs nearly as much as the two of us put together. Can you ride?"

She shook her head.

"But I want to learn and I'm not scared."

"Well now's your chance, Sylvie. We'll use this fallen trunk here to help us mount. I'll get up first and you sit behind me. You must hold on tight to me."

Soon they were up, Sylvie with her arms round his waist. Feeling her thighs gripping around him and her breasts pushing against his back made Yul quite weak. But he put a firm lid on those feelings and thoughts and concentrated on guiding the mare back along the path towards the glade. Sylvie was chatty and animated, almost too much so, and he remembered how she was at Moon Fullness before the moonrise. This would only get worse until after it had risen.

The woods were misty and damp in the grey afternoon. Most of the leaves had fallen to make a soggy mulch on the woodland floor. Mixed up with the leaves were the empty prickles of sweet chestnut cases, the spiky shells of beech mast, and the split rinds of conker cases. Some yellow sycamore leaves still clung on to their branches, as did the serrated kipper-like leaves of the sweet chestnut, now a deep golden brown. But the sky was visible through the bare branches of other trees, and although he was pleased it was so mild, Yul hoped the rain would hold off.

They reached the little glade, a clearing deep in the woods where emerald green grass grew thickly. They dismounted and Sylvie darted about exclaiming over the dozens of fairy rings in the glade. The little toadstools sprouted in the wet grass in large near-perfect circles. Yul tethered the mare to a tree so she could crop the grass and take shelter if it did start to rain.

"Why have you tied her up?" asked Sylvie. "Are we staying here? Remember I need to be back before it gets dark. You know it's the Moon Fullness tonight, and I told you I must dance at ..."

"Yes, I know," said Yul wearily, thinking that maybe the gag wouldn't be such a bad thing after all. He hated Sylvie under the spell. "Come on, we're going for a little walk up here. There's plenty of time."

She skipped on ahead of him up the path. It wasn't cold and she'd thrown back her hood and given him her gloves to put in his bag. Yul tried to keep her mind off the moonrise by showing her some of the fungi growing on the woodland floor. He remembered that she'd shown an interest in it before.

"See this one, Sylvie? It's the Earth Star. See how it's split into segments like the points of a star."

"It's lovely," she said, bending down and looking carefully at the white star on the dark ground. "Oh, those purple ones – they're Amethyst Deceivers, aren't they?"

"That's right," he said, surveying the great troop of purple-lilac caps. "They're edible. We'll come out mushroom picking one day. And look, there's Velvet Shank. See how smooth and velvety its stalks are? Like the texture of your cloak. Oh, Sylvie, see those through there? Don't ever touch those. That's the Destroying Angel."

124

"Are they poisonous then?"

"Deadly poisonous. Fatal."

"They look quite innocent. Just a white mushroom. I'd never know they were dangerous."

"That's the trouble; some of the most deadly are the most innocent looking."

"I love their names. They sound so beautiful, don't they? Amethyst Deceiver, Velvet Shank, Destroying Angel. You know so much, Yul."

He shrugged, remembering what Mother Heggy had said about his ignorance.

"I know very little compared to you and the other Hallfolk. But I know a lot about Stonewylde and that's what matters to me."

They covered some distance and he managed to keep her distracted for quite a time before she stopped on the path and began to fret.

"I really think we should go back now, Yul. It's getting late. I don't want to make Magus angry. Please let's go back now."

"Just a little further, Sylvie," he coaxed. "We'll get back in good time. I can make the horse gallop if you like."

"Oh yes, I'd like that!" she cried and ran on ahead.

"Look, Sylvie, you must know these!" he said, pointing to a crop of bright red toadstools covered with white sugar crystal spots. They were too brilliant - poisonously scarlet, like something else from a fairytale. The sinister toadstools grew under quiet silver birches; exotic cakes for wicked witches living deep in the woods who made cages in which to fatten up children.

"Yes!" she cried enthusiastically. "I've seen these before. They're Fly Agaric! I always thought they were fatal, but Mother Heggy says she uses them in some of her potions. They have magical properties. And those two old women, Violet and Vetchling, they collect them too."

"Let's see what else we can find," he said, taking her hand in his and leading her deeper into the overgrown woods.

But he could only keep fooling her for so long, and eventually she stopped and refused to go any further. She'd become quite panicky looking at the darkening sky between the branches.

"Please, please, Yul. I have to get back. You don't understand. Magus'll be so angry and I'm scared when he's angry. He frightens me, the way his eyes look at me sometimes. Please can we go back now? You promised you'd get me home in time. He needs my magic tonight."

He wondered how he was actually going to tie her up. It was all very well Mother Heggy saying he was much stronger than her, but he wouldn't use brute force to subjugate her.

"Alright, Sylvie. But on our way back I want to play a game with you. It's a sort of blind man's buff game like we play at some of our celebrations. You must wear this little piece of rope around your wrists. It's great fun."

"Okay, but hurry."

She held out her slim white wrists pressed together in front of her, smiling at him trustingly. He gazed into her exquisitely pretty face, her cheeks pink from the fresh air and her eyes bright, and felt a stab of guilt at the deception. Hands shaking in haste, he bound her wrists tightly together. He used much of the rope, going right up her forearms, and left a length as a halter with which to lead her. Then he took the gag out of his pocket and tied it firmly round her mouth. Her eyes were round with surprise. But it was too late now. She was tied up, he had a lead with which to pull her along, and she couldn't make a noise or question him. He could see the bewilderment on her face. He took her by the shoulders and looked her into her clear grey eyes.

"I'm really sorry to do this, Sylvie. If there was any other way ... But there isn't. I'm going to look after you until the moon has risen and then I'll take you back to the Hall. Magus isn't going to steal your moon magic tonight. I'm sorry to trick you like this."

She started to make muffled noises of protest and pulled away. He tugged the rope bringing her back towards him. She pulled really hard, trying to run in the opposite direction. He yanked the rope and she fell, silver hair spilling everywhere as she hit the ground. He crouched over her trying to avoid the accusation in her eyes.

"I'm sorry, Sylvie. I don't want to hurt you. Are you alright?"

She shook her head violently.

"Where does it hurt?"

She shook her head again. Sighing, he helped her to stand and led her further along the path. It was about half a mile to the tree cage and he wanted to get her there as soon as possible. The light was beginning to fade, although it was very difficult on such a gloomy afternoon to judge the time. Long skeins of mist appeared on the woodland floor wending around the tree trunks. The cobwebs that laced the bare branches and dead bracken were jewelled with falling dew. It was getting darker and colder. She followed for a while fairly docilely, just tugging in defiance on the halter now and again.

But then Sylvie stopped dead without warning. When Yul turned round to see what the matter was now, she swung her arms sideways at his head. The heavy clump of rope around her wrists hit him hard on the temple. He saw stars for a few seconds, the world turning black with shooting red and yellow flashes.

She took her chance. Yanking the rope from his limp hands, she made a dash for it back the way they'd come. He stumbled, trying to grab the rope, slowed by his dizziness from the blow to the head. She was very quick but it wasn't easy for her to run with her hands tied awkwardly in front of her. He soon caught her up and leapt at her, knocking her down and landing on top of her. She felt lithe and wriggly underneath him, squirming around onto her back to fight him. She thrashed about, trying to push him off and hit him in the face again with her bound wrists. She fought and growled like a captured wildcat.

Yul struggled upright and straddled her frantically wriggling body, finally keeping her still by using his weight to control her. He remembered how effective it had been when Buzz had sat astride him like this. Her eyes screamed fury at him. He was sure that if she'd been free and had a weapon, she'd have tried to kill him. The moongaziness combined with the hypnosis had made her lose all reason. His head throbbed painfully where she'd hit him.

He gazed down at her lying stretched out under him. Her bound wrists were pulled above her head, his knees pinning her upper arms hard to the ground. He could feel her rib cage digging into him. It must be so uncomfortable and squashed for her. He wondered what on earth to do next. They were almost there. He knew if he took any of his weight off her for a second she'd squirm and try to escape. But he couldn't spend the next few hours sitting on her like this. She was gasping for breath through the gag and he knew he was crushing her badly.

Eventually, he told her that she'd have to behave or else he'd hit her like she'd hit him. The words stuck in his throat but he had to get her to the tree cage and fast. Darkness was falling. Soon the moon would rise and then she'd really start. It would take more than his weight to control her then.

He pulled himself off her and hauled her to her feet quite roughly, so she could see he meant business. He wound most of the halter of rope around her, pinning her bound arms down across her stomach so she couldn't hit him again. Then holding her from behind, he pushed her along. She resisted all the way, jerking and fighting. In the end his patience wore thin and he became annoyed with her. She was making it so difficult and he was only trying to protect her. He shoved her along, making her stumble, prodding her hard when she wouldn't move. She was so stubborn and he became rougher with her as his irritation increased. At last he could see the tree cage up ahead in the half-light. Relief flooded him. Now he just had to get her in there and the entrance sealed.

Yul felt the moment when she understood his intent. She thrashed about and squealed, digging the heels of her pretty suede boots into the earth. The scarlet cloak was driving him mad for he kept getting tangled in it. With a snarl of anger he wrenched open the fastening at the neck and ripped it off her. It was now much easier to grab her bodily and lift her off the ground, especially with her arms bound to her. Despite her height, she was very light. He shoved her forcefully through the gap between the trunks of the tree cage, bundling her in and trying to avoid her kicking feet. He no longer worried about hurting her.

He knew she banged her head on the trunk and scraped her leg as she was thrust through the gap. But he was beyond caring. He pushed her in hard so she fell down in a heap inside the small cage, giving him time to quickly bind the thicker rope around the two trunks and seal the opening. His hands shook as he wrapped the rope around and around, leaving no gap at all for her to escape.

"Try getting out of that!" he snapped triumphantly, breathless with anger and exertion. His head was really painful and he gingerly felt the lump growing there. She hadn't tried to get up from the crumpled heap where she lay, but he knew she was conscious for her eyes watched him, glaring at him in the twilight. Yul turned his back on her and went to sit some distance away, drinking from the water bottle he'd brought here earlier. He was shaking and made a conscious effort to calm down. He was so angry that he felt like keeping her tied up and gagged in the cage all night, just to teach her a lesson.

Eventually he felt his breathing return to normal. The anger evaporated. All he felt now was a dull throb on the temple where she'd hit him, and a weariness in his heart. Miserably he got up and went over to the tree cage. Sylvie was hunched uncomfortably, her hands still tied to her stomach, a huddled black figure with the gag tight around her mouth. Her hair was all tangled up around the gag, spilling in a silver mass into her eyes and face where she couldn't brush it away. She looked like a small wild animal, caught in a trap and waiting to be killed.

In the gloom, he saw that her eyes were desperate. She was pitiful and his desire to hurt and punish her vanished in an instant. She trembled almost convulsively and he realised her cloak was still lying outside the cage where he'd flung it in anger. Yul tried to push it through the gaps to cover her, but it just fell in beside her. He put his hands through and pulled it over her, but she wriggled so it fell off again. He wondered if the moon was rising yet. Her eyes were unfocussed now, enormous and shining, gazing at nothing. She must have been very uncomfortable but she didn't seem to notice anything. Sighing, he sat down with his back to the cage and hung his head guiltily, not wanting to watch her captive misery.

At the Hall, all hell had broken loose. Magus had called in at the Tudor Wing earlier in the afternoon and Miranda had assured him that Sylvie was fast asleep in her room. He was pleased to hear this and stopped to chat for a few minutes.

"How are you? Everything alright?"

"I'm fine thank you, Magus. I missed you while you were away. I never seem to spend any time with you nowadays."

"I know," he replied, perching on the arm of the sofa where she sat knitting. He stroked her long red hair absent-mindedly. "There's so much on at the moment. I've got a lot of business deals going through, which will mean greater revenue for Stonewylde. I'm also trying to set up the new building projects that I want to start after the Solstice. There aren't enough hours in the day right now. I'm so tired."

"Poor you," she said softly, rubbing his leg where it lay, long and muscular, next to her on the arm of the sofa. She was desperate for his company. "Is there anything I can do to help? I can write letters and reports, things like that."

He laughed at this and shook his head.

"No, it's not the sort of stuff anyone can help with. It's all up here." He tapped his forehead. "How you can help is by looking after that daughter of yours properly and making sure she dances up at Mooncliffe every Moon Fullness. You have no idea how vital that is to me, Miranda. You must make sure she's fit and healthy for it every month. You need to keep her weight up and not let her roam about wasting energy. I want her healthy and strong and I'm counting on you to make sure she is."

"Of course," she smiled. "I know you have her best interests at heart. She's sleeping now, like you wanted. She'll be fine for tonight."

"Good. I'm pleased with you, Miranda. I'll try and spend some time with you in December if I can fit it in."

"Oh yes!" she said breathlessly. "That would be wonderful. I miss you so much."

She laid her head against his thigh and sighed. He chuckled and reached down to caress her, feeling her melt against him.

"Not that long until the baby's due, is it? Three months? Then I shall have to make you pregnant all over again."

She tipped her head back and gazed up at him adoringly, wanting nothing more than to bear his babies.

"Anyway, I'll be back at about four o'clock to collect Sylvie. Make sure she's ready for me and wrapped up warmly in that new cloak I bought her. She'll be compliant this month so there won't be any problems."

He patted her swollen belly and stood up, stretching. He smiled down at her and left.

But when he returned later he found Miranda white and trembling with fear.

"What's happened?" he asked, gripping her shoulders to make her look at him.

"She's not in her room."

"Where is she then? In the bathroom?"

"No. Magus, she's ... she's gone."

"GONE? What do you mean, gone?"

"She's not in her room."

"You've already said that! Where is she?"

"I don't know!"

She burst into tears, screwing her eyes up like a child and crying pitifully. With a rough shake he released her shoulders, making her stumble, and strode past her towards Sylvie's bedroom. At the moment when he let out a roar of rage, Clip came into the sitting room, wanting to check Sylvie was going to be warm enough up at Mooncliffe.

"What's going on here?" he asked, glancing nervously towards the open door. "What's happened?"

Miranda stood sobbing into her hands, her red hair falling over her face. Clip stared at her, his face suddenly white as if he'd seen something from the grave. Magus marched furiously back into the room, his face dark as thunder.

"I'll tell you what's happened! This stupid bloody cow has let Sylvie escape! WHERE IS SHE?"

"I don't know, Magus!" she sobbed. "I'd tell you if I knew. I thought she was asleep but she was playing a trick. I'm so sorry."

"You will be! The one thing I ask you to do - the only thing I want from you - is to look after that girl. And you're too bloody stupid to even manage that!"

He roared at her, his deep voice frighteningly loud. His face was almost purple as the blood pumped to his head. Miranda was terrified.

"Come on, Sol ..." began Clip, but Magus turned on him angrily.

"And you can bloody keep out of it, you drugged-up, useless bastard! Since when did you say anything worth listening to?"

He turned back to Miranda and advanced on her, his head lowered belligerently.

"What time *exactly* did you last see her?"

As Magus stepped menacingly forward she stepped away from him, backing towards the sofa.

"I ... I don't know for sure. I think ... maybe about half past two? But ..."

"What do you mean you don't know for sure?" he screamed. "Think! THINK! I need to know exactly! I need to work out how much time she's had to get away and where she could be now. THINK!"

"I don't know!" she sobbed. "I thought she was in there but ..."

"You stupid bitch! Stop that bloody snivelling and answer me properly! When did you last see Sylvie?"

Miranda had backed away so her legs were now against the sofa and she could go no further. He towered over her aggressively, his breathing heavy, hands clenching with fury.

He looked at her blotchy, distraught face and snapped completely. With a snarl he took another step forward, his hand raised as if he would strike her. She fell back onto the sofa in an ungainly heap, curling up to protect the baby. Magus stood glaring down as if he'd like to throttle her. His chest heaved and his face was utterly remorseless.

"Have you any idea of what you've done this afternoon?" he raged. "Of the consequences of your stupidity and ineptitude? No, I don't suppose so. You're too busy fawning all over me and gushing on about your bloody pregnancy. I told you how vital it was that I take Sylvie to Mooncliffe. I've stressed it again and again. But thanks to your failure to manage the one simple thing I want from you ..."

He turned away from her, his hands shaking with fury, his mouth a thin white line.

"I can't bear the sight of you!" he hissed. "I tell you, Miranda, if you weren't pregnant ..."

"But you love me!" she cried. "You said I was special to you. You said this afternoon you wanted more children with me."

He turned back to her and laughed harshly at this.

"Love you? Special?" His voice dropped to venomous calm. "There's only one reason for making you pregnant and keeping you at Stonewylde. Think about it, Miranda. Work it out. Goddess, how someone as dreary as you ever gave birth to a girl as magical as Sylvie is beyond me."

She shrivelled into herself at his cruelty, shrinking from the vitriol of his vicious tongue.

"Please, Magus!" she sobbed, her voice high and strangled with tears. "Please don't do this to me. I love you!"

His face twisted into a sneer of contempt and he laughed again. His eyes were black diamonds, glittering hard and cold.

"You love me? Of course you do! You and every other woman I take. But you're the only one fool enough to imagine I love them in return. Why on earth would I love you?"

She stared up at him and finally understood. Something inside her quietly died and she bowed her head.

"You've gone too far this time, Sol!" cried Clip. "Get out

of here! Leave her alone!"

"With pleasure!" he spat. "I want nothing more to do with her. You're welcome to her, brother! Not that you'd be of use to any woman, an impotent fool like you."

He lashed them both with a look of disgust and turned on his heel, storming out of the room and almost smashing the door from its hinges. Clip shut the door properly behind him and went to comfort Miranda. She was so distressed that she even allowed Clip to bathe her swollen eyes and hold her gently while she cried as if her world had ended.

Magus raced to the stables and bellowed at Tom to saddle up Nightwing. While he stood impatiently, kicking at the cobbles in the stable yard, he yanked the walkie-talkie from his pocket. Tom and the other stable lads heard him yelling at Jackdaw.

"She's bloody gone missing! She's not with you at Mooncliffe? No, I thought not. It's that little shit Yul! He must've taken her somewhere. If you see him, kill him. I mean it, Jack. Forget what I said yesterday. Kill him! I'm riding up to the stone on the hill where she likes to go. You hurry down and look round the Village, and try his cottage. See if his bloody mother knows where they are. Keep me informed."

He thrust the instrument back in his pocket and yelled at Tom.

"Come on, man! Get a bloody move on!"

He snatched the reins from the ostler and leapt up into the saddle. Nightwing rolled his eyes and reared up. Magus pulled viciously on the reins, shouting abuse at him, and got the stallion under control. He grabbed the whip from Tom's outstretched hand and slashing at his horse's flank, clattered out of the yard.

Tom quickly saddled another horse and called to the stable boys to hurry down to the Village behind him.

"Where are you going, sir?" called one of the boys, scared by the frightening turn of events. None of them had ever seen Magus like this before.

"To Maizie's cottage. I don't want that brute Jackdaw turning up there and terrorizing the poor woman. One of you

134

lads take a horse and go and find Edward. Bring him to the Village too."

He rode out of the stables and the boys ran after him.

The light was almost gone as Magus reached Hare Stone. He saw immediately that Sylvie wasn't there and roared to the sky in pure fury. Nightwing reared again, maddened by his ill treatment. His delicate mouth had been cut by Magus' aggressive handling and his flank slashed again and again by the whip. But Magus was a superb horseman and managed to keep his seat, curbing Nightwing skilfully if brutally. Wheeling him around, he kicked the stallion down towards the Village cursing everything that lived and breathed.

The scene in Yul's cottage was ugly. Jackdaw stood in the parlour with Maizie before him, her chin raised and defiance in her eyes. Tom stood beside her protectively, trying to calm her down. All six children were crowded in the kitchen where she'd pushed them, frightened for their safety. The scene was reminiscent of something from the days of Alwyn's reign of terror.

"I say again, I have no idea where he is and I wouldn't tell you even if I did!" Maizie said, voice trembling and cheeks burning scarlet. "How dare you come into my home and start questioning me?"

"Magus' orders," replied Jackdaw, cracking his knuckles. "Look, woman, I need to know where the boy is. I'm going to find out. You'd do well to tell me now and save yourself a lot of grief."

"Get out and leave her alone!" said Tom angrily. "You were meant to be banished! You can't come back here and start ordering us folk about."

Jackdaw laughed at this, a harsh and mirthless bark. His blue eyes were alight with excitement. This was what he enjoyed most.

"Shut up, you old git. One more word out of you and I'll rupture your kidneys. What are you doing here anyway? You should be up at the stables knee deep in horse shit, not chatting up lonely widows, you dirty old bugger. Now listen darlin', I'll ask you for the last time …"

"I know where they might be!" cried Rosie from the kitchen, pushing herself forward.

"No, Rosie!"

"I think they've gone down to the beach!"

Jackdaw pulled her out of the kitchen and looked down into her pretty face, as flushed as her mother's.

"Ah, a sister! Yeah, you're very like him. So what makes you think they've gone down there? You better not be lying, girl!"

She shrugged, shaking her dark curls from her eyes exactly as Yul did.

"This morning I thought I heard Yul saying to a boy in the Village that he was going to the beach later on with his sweetheart. I don't want to say the wrong thing and I'm not sure. But 'tis where courting couples go at the Moon Fullness sometimes, to the caves down there. To be private like."

Jackdaw stared at her, his ugly face furrowed with concentration. Perspiration beaded his bald head and trickled down his pierced face. The room was rank with the stench of his excited sweat.

"Yeah, I remember them caves. But why are you helping me when your mother won't?"

"Oh, I'm not helping you," said Rosie guilelessly, flicking her curls back and wriggling her shoulders. "I want to help Magus."

Jackdaw barked with laughter at this and chucked her under the chin with a dirty finger, leering into her face.

"And I'm sure he'll be grateful," he said.

At that moment Magus burst into the cottage. He took in the scene quickly and shouted at Jackdaw to get down to the beach and check the caves.

"Right, you girl! Up to Mooncliffe!" he yelled, grabbing Rosie by the arm and pulling her towards the door.

"WHY?" screamed Maizie. "What are you doing? Leave my daughter alone!"

"I'm testing the whole lot of you stupid bloody Villagers.

There must be some silly girl who gets moongazy at the Moon Fullness. I'm going to find out tonight. That rock is going to be charged up by somebody, whatever happens. You, Tom, knock on every door and get all the girls in the Village to go up there immediately. Every one! There's no time to waste. The moon's rising right now! Punishment tomorrow for any family who refuses to obey me. MOVE!!"

Yul was trying to ignore the muffled cries coming from behind him. The Owl Moon must be rising for she was frantic. She squirmed around on the nest of leaves, unable to stand, unable to cry out. It was pitiful to hear and he put his hands over his ears to stop the noise. It was quite dark but he was scared to light the lantern in case Magus or Jackdaw were out looking for them. He wished he could silence her completely, but the gag was as tight as it could be tied and there was nothing more he could do. The noises of distress went on and on and in the end he stood up and walked away, unable to bear it any longer. All around the owls hooted and called amongst the trees, eerie in the deepening darkness.

Up at Mooncliffe Magus stood tall by the great moon rock, his arms folded and face grim. The cliff top was crowded. Girls of all ages were gathered together, with their anxious families looking on. Everyone was scared, not used to being shouted at, herded like cattle and commanded like dogs. Many of the girls were crying as Jackdaw lifted them one by one onto the moon rock and left them standing there, while Magus looked for any sign of the jerking and shuddering that affected Sylvie. It was dark, for clouds obscured the sky and the full moon, but Jackdaw had rigged up a powerful lantern torch using his car battery. The effect was a harsh spotlight on each poor child as she stood alone and scared on the rock.

"Alright, when you've been tested, go back home!" shouted Magus, getting more irate by the minute at the lack of results. "Come on, get a move on. Next!"

There was a background of angry muttering, and one comment rose above the general unrest.

"What about the Hallfolk girls? Why is it just the Villagers?"

"Good point," said Magus loudly. He took out the walkie-talkie and got through to Martin at the Hall, ordering all the girls there to be sent straight away. This silenced the muttering for a while, but made the sounds of children crying even more obvious.

Then a little girl of about five years old was wrenched from her mother's arms by Jackdaw and swung up onto the rock. She cried and cried, shaking with terror and cold. Magus watched intently as she stood sobbing her heart out, her shawl slipping from her shoulders. Her mother stepped forward, trying to reach her, but Jackdaw yanked at her arm to stop her.

"Let me get her, please," begged the woman, her heart breaking at the sound of her little girl crying so pitifully.

"Get back," growled Jackdaw. "Magus ain't finished with her yet."

"I can't decide if she's just shaking from crying or really shaking properly," muttered Magus. He glared around at the crowd in exasperation. "Sacred Mother, I wish they'd all stop this bloody bawling!"

"Shall I shut her up?" asked Jackdaw.

"NO! Don't you touch her!" screamed the mother, trying to push past him. Casually, without even thinking what he was doing, Jackdaw grabbed the woman by the throat and held her at arm's length. She started to choke and there was a roar from the crowd as everyone recalled Lily's fate.

Out of nowhere came the black crow, flying into the bright spotlight in a flurry of feathers and flapping. The crow launched itself at Jackdaw's face. He released the woman, who scrambled up onto the rock and scooped her little girl to safety. Jackdaw hit out frantically at the crow just as he'd done at Samhain in the Stone Labyrinth, trying to thump it away from his face. The crow attacked again and again, pecking and clawing, stabbing with its vicious beak. Its raucous cries of attack mingled with the man's oaths and yells. Then Jackdaw screamed, long and piercing. He doubled over clutching at his eye. Dark blood trickled between his fingers. The crowd shrank back in horror as the man stumbled about in the harsh spotlight, screaming in agony.

Still the crow attacked, pecking and tearing at Jackdaw's hands. He fell to his knees and the crow landed on his head, its claws digging in to the shiny skin that covered his skull. The sharp beak stabbed down repeatedly, slashing at Jackdaw's wounded eye. Magus stepped forward, as horrified at the terrible sight as the Villagers. He picked up one of the stone eggs and tried to bludgeon the crow with it. The crow cawed loudly and Jackdaw twisted round at the sound. The egg came down with a heavy thud, not on the crow but on the back of his bald skull.

Jackdaw cried out, a low howl of anguish. Completely disorientated, he clambered to his feet again. With the bird latched onto his head he staggered about, maddened and clumsy with pain. Thick blood oozed from the messy eye socket. He screamed and stumbled, and then all seemed to happen in slow motion. He tripped and started to fall. The crow spread its great wings and took off. Jackdaw slowly toppled over backwards, his arms flailing wildly. His bald head cracked down full force on the edge of the great white moon rock and split open as easily as eggshell.

Yul approached the tree cage with trepidation. Sylvie was silent, or so he'd thought, but as he got nearer he heard little mewing sounds of misery. He could see nothing in the darkness.

"Sylvie!" he said softly. "Sylvie, it's me. I'm going to light the lantern now. It'll seem bright at first so close your eyes."

In the soft light he saw she was still curled at an awkward angle. She must have been extremely uncomfortable with her hands bound tightly to her body and the gag tied hard around her mouth. She was uncovered by the cloak and trembling violently. Her eyes looked up at him in desperation, begging him to release her. Her distress was terrible to witness.

Fumbling with guilty haste Yul untied the thick rope that fastened the cage. He reached in to pull her out but she couldn't move. She'd been lying awkwardly for so long that her legs were numb. He half climbed into the cage himself, squeezing through the gap, and untied the tight knot of the gag. Her mouth was white and unmoving. She could only stare up at him in mute misery. Yul was almost crying by now, wondering why he'd gone off and left her at her most desperate time. He had great trouble unbinding the rope, for he had first to unwind it from around her body where he'd wrapped it. He managed this, then with her wrists still bound, he pulled her half upright and dragged her out through the narrow gap between the trunks of the cage. He lifted her as she slipped through the gap and stood her upright. She crumpled at his feet, her legs unable to take her weight.

Yul felt worse now than ever before. Last month at the moongazing he'd watched Magus put her through hours of suffering. This month he himself had done exactly the same to her. He'd never forgive himself for this. He pulled the beautiful scarlet cloak out of the cage and tried to wrap it around her as she lay motionless on the earth. He knelt over her, fumbling at the bindings around her wrists, wondering why he'd tied the rope so very tightly. Eventually it unravelled to reveal wrists swollen and bruised, damaged right up to the elbows. Her hands were very cold and white. He scooped her up and sat down with his back against the tree cage, gathering her into his lap. He wrapped the cloak around her as she curled into him and held her in his arms, rocking her gently, chafing her hands and kissing her head. His tears fell silently into her silver hair.

The Villagers had scattered, parents trying to cover their children's eyes to protect them from the hideous scene at the moon stone. The air was full of the children's terrible crying and the shocked, hushed voices of the adults. Nobody could believe what they'd just witnessed. Magus stood in silent disbelief, gazing down in the harsh spotlight at the blood-splattered rock and the body that lay sprawled on the grass. The crowd started to head down to the Village, meeting the group of Hallfolk girls on their way up the cliff path.

"Don't go up there," people warned, shaking their heads, and the Hallfolk turned back when they heard what had happened.

By common consensus the Villagers trooped into the Great Barn, feeling the need to be together at such a time of crisis. Hot drinks were made and children wrapped in warm blankets. People were very angry as the shock of Jackdaw's death lessened and the full impact of what Magus had done tonight began to sink in.

"He's got no right to put our children through that."

"Who does he think he is, dragging us up there in the middle o' winter?"

"Aye, and why was that Jackdaw back anyway? He's banished!"

"How dare he touch our girls, force 'em up on the rock!"

"'Tis what he's been doing to that lovely girl Sylvie every month."

"That crow was Mother Heggy's, you know."

"Where's Yul? He should be here now."

"He must be off hiding the poor maid away so Magus can't get at her again."

Eventually Tom climbed onto the dais where the musicians played at the celebrations. Everyone quietened down, wanting to hear what he had to say.

"Folk, I'm not one for speeches. But we need to think on what's to be done after this terrible night. Something's happened to Magus. He's been good to us in the past, right enough, but he's changed. The man's turned bad, evil, just like his father afore him."

He paused to let the growls of agreement die down.

"At the stables tonight I heard him on that there walkie-talkie thing speaking to Jackdaw. He told Jackdaw to kill Yul!"

There was a roar of disapproval at this. Tom raised his hands to quieten them.

"I know, I know. 'Tisn't the first time it's happened neither. Twice now that boy's been locked up in the stone byre by the stables for days on end. He's been beaten, starved and tortured. First time Magus had Alwyn to help him, second time it were Jackdaw. That poor boy has suffered, I can tell you. You all seen the state of him when he came back to us. We know what Magus tried to do to him at Samhain. Magus must be scared o' Yul to treat him like that. Must see the lad as a threat. Yul's no ordinary Village boy but neither is he Hallfolk. We all know now that he's Magus' son, not Alwyn's. Pardon my impertinence, Maizie, for being personal here. We know 'twas Mother Heggy's crow that killed Jackdaw tonight. And we all remember what happened at the last Summer Solstice, when the crow sat on Yul's shoulder and Magus dropped the sacred fire. Some of us know there was a prophecy, many years ago, about Yul."

The Villagers buzzed excitedly about this and again Tom quietened them. Edward then joined him up on the dais and took over. He knew the people would do as he said, for he was used to managing and leading.

"Listen well now, Village folk. We must bide our time. We must wait patiently, go about our business as normal. We must keep Yul safe until the time is right. And most of all, we must not make Magus angry. He's not right any more and who knows what he might do next. 'Tis nearly the Winter Solstice, when Yul will turn sixteen. I reckon things will fall into place then. But until then, we must keep our heads down. When the time is right, Goddess willing, we will have a new worthy magus to be the guardian of Stonewylde, to lead us in our festivals and our celebrations. To once again bring up the magic from Mother Earth and share it amongst the community. I seen for myself the boy being blessed with the Earth Magic, and 'tis a sight to behold. We will stand together and wait until Yul can become our new magus, for the good of Stonewylde! For the folk of Stonewylde!"

There was cheering and clapping at this as the people felt themselves bound together with a new sense of solidarity and purpose. Gradually the Villagers began to leave the Great Barn, heading for their cottages to put their exhausted and traumatised children to bed.

Yul felt Sylvie responding to his body heat and the gentle

chafing of her hands and wrists. He knew he must get her back home soon, for it was becoming colder and she should be tucked up safely in bed. She was no longer trembling but lay docilely in his lap, her head against his chest, curled up like a kitten. She rarely spoke much after the moongaziness, and he realised that she wasn't going to come round any more than this. Carefully he got up and found that with a bit of help she could now stand. He picked up the lantern, leaving everything else to collect another time. With his arm around Sylvie's waist to support her, he led her back through the woods to the glade where Edward's grey mare waited patiently.

They rode back slowly, Sylvie sitting in front this time so Yul could hold on to her. He let the mare find her way in the darkness until the lights of the Hall were visible ahead. Yul extinguished the lantern and he lifted Sylvie down, light as a quilt of goose down, and carried her towards the back door of the Tudor Wing. He saw lights in her room and was scared of what he may find, but knew he had to take her up there. She was as vague as ever and couldn't possibly manage it herself. He opened the door and climbed the narrow stairs, almost tripping over her cloak hanging down. He pushed the arched door, which swung open to reveal Miranda sitting silently by the window.

She was perfectly still in the soft lamplight, her long red hair hanging down over her shoulders. Her eyes were so puffy they'd almost disappeared. What had gone on here tonight? She rose as he entered the room.

"Yul!" she said softly, her voice raw. She gestured for him to put Sylvie on her bed. He did so and stood back, unsure of what to do next.

"Sylvie, darling," Miranda whispered. "You're back now."

Sylvie's eyes were shut and she seemed to be sleeping. Her mother tugged off the black suede boots and unfastened the cloak, pulling it out from underneath her. She tucked Sylvie under the bed covers and turned to Yul, her head slightly bowed to conceal her swollen eyes.

"Thank you," she said.

He shifted uncomfortably.

143

"I'm afraid I hurt Sylvie tonight. I was trying to protect her but I ended up harming her. I'm very sorry, ma'am."

She shook her head and looked down at the floor, hiding behind the curtain of hair.

"Thank you, Yul. I'm sorry I misjudged you. I'm grateful to you."

He nodded, feeling that if he spoke he might embarrass himself by crying. It had been a terrible night and all he wanted was to get home. With a final glance at Sylvie lying peacefully in her bed, he left down the back stairs and rode the grey mare back through the foggy November night to the Village.

On the cobbles outside the Great Barn, the Villagers milled around as they continued to discuss the rousing talk they'd just heard. The men headed for the Jack in the Green to speak further over a pot of cider, whilst the women gathered their children together to take them home. The Village buzzed with eagerness and speculation. Only Maizie seemed unaffected by the excitement stirred up by Tom and Edward's speeches.

As she led her children back to the cottage, Leveret fast asleep in her arms, Maizie felt her heart heavy in her chest. She alone recognised the enormity of what the men had said tonight in the Barn. As she'd done so many times since Yul's birth, Maizie cursed Mother Heggy and her prophecy. She knew just how iron-willed and utterly ruthless Magus could be. It was too much to ask a young lad to take him on. Maizie alone seemed to understand that the fight ahead was unfairly matched and the outcome far from assured. She ignored the excited chatter of all those around her, and once again shuddered in fear for the life of her eldest son.

CHAPTER EIGHT

Just before dawn the next morning an ill-assorted group gathered on the cliff-top a little way from the disc of white stone. A chill wind whipped their hair and cloaks as seagulls screamed and drifted around them. Magus stood granite-faced before the mound of wood, hastily assembled during the night by Martin and a couple of young servants. Jackdaw's body lay within the pile, hidden beneath a piece of hemp cloth. No embroidered pentangle for him, nor the community's comfort for the bereaved. Vetchling huddled into her sister Violet, her dirty face grimed with tears for her son. Her daughter, Jackdaw's sister Starling, supported her on the other side, squat and bellicose. Martin stood beside them with his young wife, and three small boys looked fearfully on.

The wood smelt strongly of the resin that Martin had splashed over the funeral pyre to ensure a thorough blaze. Magus glanced at the group who mourned the passing on of the most hated man at Stonewylde. Not the normal send-off, and it must be done quickly, for the sooner it was over the sooner the Villagers could put the incident behind them.

He produced a lighter from beneath his cloak and bent over the pyre. The wind extinguished the tiny flame instantly, and Magus cursed as he tried again and again to set fire to the body and its cradle of branches. Martin stepped forward to shield him, and at last there was a sharp crackle as the wood ignited. The flames flared wildly to one side as the salty wind gusted, but the pyre burnt well, the heat and smoke causing the group to step back and the little boys to stare in fascination.

Standing tall on the desolate cliff-top, the black cloak flaring out behind him, Magus looked up into the leaden grey sky. His face was as bleak as the cruel sea far below.

"Dark Angel, take the soul of Jackdaw now, before the sun rises, to the Otherworld. He was killed before his time and we ask that you accompany his soul as he passes through the veil. He will be missed by his family. He served me well."

Vetchling let out a wail as the fire consumed the body of her son. Starling patted her mother's arm and clasped Jay, Jackdaw's young son, to her great thigh. She ignored her own small boy who stood next to Martin's child, sucking a filthy thumb and gazing with vacant eyes at the blaze.

"'Twas Heggy's crow that killed my boy!" Vetchling cried. "She sent it to do her bidding. May the Dark Angel take her and all!"

"Aye, sister, but on whose account was the crow sent? 'Tis that dark-haired brat who's to blame for this. Maizie's bastard – he's the one!"

"You speak right, Violet. The Angel take his soul too."

Magus' dark eyes rested on her wrinkled face and he nodded.

"Four weeks," he said softly, his words stolen by the wind. "Four weeks until the Solstice and then at last I shall be free of him."

The white gulls screamed around their heads as the fire burnt away to nothing, leaving no trace of Jackdaw's presence at Stonewylde.

"Mum, aren't you coming down to breakfast?"

Sylvie stood uncertainly outside her mother's bedroom.

"No," came the muffled reply. "Go on down without me. I'm not hungry."

Sylvie frowned. She felt disorientated this morning. She'd been horrified to wake up and find herself badly bruised and aching all over. Her wrists and lower arms were agony. The skin was swollen and chafed red and her upper arms hurt too. Her leg and all down one side of her body was scraped and sore, and there was a large blue lump on her forehead. Her ribs hurt if she breathed too deeply. She had vague memories of Yul pulling and pushing her, of being bound and gagged and shoved into a cage. She remembered his anger and her desperation to escape; to go to Mooncliffe and dance for Magus. She knew Yul had treated her badly but was at a loss to explain it. She'd hoped that her mother would shed some light on what had happened. Magus must be so angry with her. She'd promised to give him all her moon magic and she'd broken that promise.

"Can I come in, Mum? I want to talk about last night."

"No! Go away, Sylvie. *Please*. Just leave me alone."

"Are you alright?"

"Go to breakfast and your lessons, Sylvie, and leave me in peace."

All day Sylvie waited in trepidation for Magus' summons. He'd be furious, she knew, but it wasn't her fault. She hid her injuries as best she could, pulling her jumper sleeves down as far as they'd go to conceal her wrists and shielding her forehead behind her hair. But Magus was nowhere to be seen. The summons never came, and eventually when lessons were over she returned to the Tudor wing to start the pile of homework that awaited her. In her bedroom she discovered a large and shiny bolt attached to the arched staircase door, a brass padlock securing it shut. Miranda was still in her room and Sylvie began to feel worried.

Eventually she ignored her mother's wishes to be left alone and went into the darkened bedroom anyway. Miranda lay curled up on her bed, and Sylvie was shocked to see her looking so dishevelled. Miranda's face was puffy and her eyes dead. She didn't want to talk. All she would say was that it was over between her and Magus. She refused to speak of what had happened the night before, other than the fact that Yul had brought Sylvie back quite late and had apologised for hurting her. Miranda didn't even ask where she was hurt. She simply closed her eyes and instructed Sylvie to shut the door behind her.

The atmosphere in the Village was strange. People went about their business as usual but it was as if everyone held their breath. The events of the previous night were discussed in shocked voices. In the cold light of day, nobody could quite believe what had happened up on the cliff-top. Everyone was worried that Magus would turn up, clattering over the cobbles on Nightwing, harrying them and maybe even punishing them for daring to speak out against him. The planned Story Web was cancelled and there was a feeling of anti-climax after the excitement of the night before. As Yul walked through the Village he sensed a change in attitude towards him. Many people nodded almost in deference, whilst others glanced at him fearfully as if he spelt danger. He made his way up the path to Mother Heggy's hovel, anxious to unload his guilt.

"Couldn't be helped," she said firmly, a blackened clay pipe clamped between her gums. "'Twas that or the rock. At least she's not weak and drained today, and he has none o' her quicksilver flowing in his veins."

Yul nodded. He knew she was right. But he remembered Sylvie's wrists when he'd finally unbound the ropes, and the way she'd banged and scraped herself against the trunks as he'd thrust her so roughly into the cage. He also remembered his anger with her. He couldn't justify that, nor banish the terrible thought that he was becoming like his father. Heggy surveyed him and chuckled.

"Aye, boy, you are your father's son, right enough. And you must watch yourself in the future. You like things your own way just a mite too much, and you brook no argument with them that don't agree with you. But you're not cruel, Yul, and you love the bright one with your soul and your heart. Put it behind you and think now on what's to be done. Four weeks till the Solstice. Four weeks to prepare. Build up your strength, my boy, and make your plans. Take yourself up into the land and open your heart to the song of Stonewylde. The Goddess herself will help you prepare."

The next day Hazel collared Sylvie at breakfast. Her normally attractive face was grim and frowning.

"Why didn't you come for your weigh-in yesterday?" she demanded. "I'll see you this morning before lessons start."

As Sylvie faced the doctor in her office in the hospital wing, she thought sadly of how Hazel had once been her friend. She remembered the kindness of the young intern in that awful London hospital; the only friendly face amongst the wolf-pack. Hazel had been so warm and caring then. What had Magus said to make her so cold? Sylvie stepped down off the scales and Hazel tapped the figures into her computer.

"You're not gaining. Eat properly. Don't start messing around again. Else I'll be forced to keep you in the hospital under constant supervision."

Sylvie nodded glumly, keeping her head down to hide the nasty bruise on her forehead.

"I saw Magus before breakfast," Hazel continued, "and all I can say, Sylvie, is I hope you feel guilty."

Her head shot up. Was Mother Heggy's spell working? She tried not to think of the tiny crescent of silver hair.

"That poor man. After all he's done for you, I don't know how you can repay him like this. I don't understand how it works, but you know that your moongaziness helps him to keep his strength up. Without it he seems to become weak. He's in a terrible state since the full moon. I'm really quite concerned. He had a message for you. He said that nothing had changed, even though you let him down so badly after promising to help him. You must continue to catch up with your school work and on no account are you to leave the Hall. He was adamant about that. Also you are to eat properly, and I shall be monitoring that. Do you understand?"

"Yes. Doesn't he want to see me?"

She still couldn't believe she'd get off without a lecture.

"No he does not," Hazel shook her head. Her eyes were cold as she stood up from her desk, and she glared at Sylvie. "He doesn't want to see anyone. He's shut himself up in his rooms and he just wants to be left alone. I've never known him like this before. And it's all thanks to you."

The next few days dragged on, the pressure on Sylvie so relentless that she wanted at times to scream. The teachers continued to hound her in every lesson. Magus had done a good job on them too, she decided. She was constantly humiliated in front of her peers. They seized the chance to join the adults in making Sylvie the scapegoat of the class and butt of every joke.

Holly had a field day. She also used Sylvie's lack of smart winter clothes as a weapon against her. The new clothes that Magus had promised her after the Owl Moon never materialised, for she hadn't moondanced for him. She was forced to continue wearing her thin summer skirts and dresses with old jumpers to keep warm. None of last year's winter clothes fitted since she'd grown so much taller, and now that she was restricted to the Hall she couldn't even try the Village dressmakers. Hazel watched her at meal times, although it was nowhere near as bad as the force-feeding Magus had subjected her to. Sylvie stopped being sick after every meal, although she still found the constant monitoring hard to bear.

She dreaded the evenings up in the Tudor wing with Miranda moping in her bedroom. Her mother wouldn't go downstairs and face people. She wasn't teaching any of her classes and now had trays of food sent up at meal-times, which she picked at half-heartedly. She'd grown wan and dull-eyed, crying constantly and carping at Sylvie when she wasn't lying listlessly on her bed. Clip had called in briefly and reversed the hypnosis he'd subjected them both to, apologising for his weakness at giving in to his half-brother's demands. He promised to call in again after he'd spent a few days out in the open. He said he had much thinking to do.

Sylvie's real distress, however, was caused by Yul. She hadn't seen him since the Owl Moon and still didn't understand why she was so injured, or what had actually happened that night. She didn't know that Yul had tried to visit but had found the downstairs door bolted from the inside, rendering his new key useless. On Magus' orders, Martin had instructed the servants to inform him if Yul was seen anywhere near the grounds, and also to keep watch on Sylvie and ensure she didn't leave the Hall.

As the days passed and the swollen skin on her wrists and forearms turned to deep black bruising, she became increasingly upset. She couldn't hide the bruises easily, for all her sleeves were far too short. Her upper arms were marked too and her ribs were painful when she breathed deeply. The scraped skin down her side and on her thigh scabbed over and the lump on her head turned purple. She felt a wreck, her body damaged and her clothes thin and too small. She dreaded her lessons and dreaded spending time anywhere near Miranda. Life seemed unbearable.

Several days later she returned to the Tudor wing after an awful day of Holly's vindictive teasing to find Clip and her mother discussing the future. Since Clip's kindness towards her at the last full moon, when her dream had been blown apart by Magus' cruelty, Miranda had warmed slightly to the wispy man. They both looked up as Sylvie entered the room despondently, clutching the heavy pile of books and folders.

"Come and sit down," said Miranda. "We're talking about options for the future."

Clip smiled at Sylvie, sensing the girl's utter dejection. His eyes were sad and she thought he looked old and tired.

"Cheer up," he said. "It's not as bad as that, Sylvie."

"It is," she replied. "In fact it's worse. I'm working really hard at school now but I still haven't caught up with everything I've missed. It's not my fault but nobody seems to care about that. I'm sick of feeling stupid."

"Well it may not be for much longer," said Miranda. She sat hunched on the sofa, her beautiful red hair lank and dull, her eyes lifeless. "I think it's time we considered going back to the Outside World."

Sylvie's heart almost burst in her chest at this.

"NO! Mum, no! We can't! I don't ever want to leave Stonewylde!"

"Well I do. There's nothing for me here. Magus ... Magus has made it very plain how he feels about me, and how he felt about me all along. I feel a complete and utter fool. I don't know if I can continue to live under his roof. It's too humiliating."

"Mum we can't leave! We've no money anyway, you've

said that yourself before. Where would we go? It's impossible!"

"I've told your mother that if you really wanted to leave," said Clip softly, "then I'd help you. Remember, Sylvie, that Stonewylde does legally belong to me. And although I don't use money as such, I do have access to a large account. I don't want you to leave, but if you insisted then of course I'd help you out. I'd find you somewhere to live and support you until your mother's able to work again. Miranda's had no salary since she came here, and anyway, I feel morally responsible for your plight. My brother has treated you both appallingly and I'm very ashamed of the part I played in it."

"I don't want to leave!" cried Sylvie desperately. "Please, Clip, don't do this."

"I think the decision is mine to make," said Miranda. "I need to consider it carefully. But I really can't see a future here, not now I know the truth about Magus. It's too painful for me."

"But what about me?" wailed Sylvie. "Don't I have any say in the matter? It's my life too. I won't go, Mum. You leave if you must, but I won't."

"No, Sylvie, that's not one of the options. If we do go, then we leave together. As I said, I need to think about it. But if things are as bad as you make out, surely you'd be better off in the Outside World. We could put Stonewylde behind us and make a fresh start – you, me and the baby."

As Sylvie lay in bed that night listening to the wind pick up outside, she thought of what her mother had said. Maybe she was right. Maybe it was time to start again. Miranda wasn't the only one whose idyll had been shattered. Stonewylde wasn't the paradise Sylvie had thought. She had no friends but many enemies and she couldn't keep up with the relentless school work. She'd missed so much both since coming here and before that in London. She doubted now that she'd ever fill in all the gaps in time for the exams. She'd fail everything miserably and everyone would be furious with her. Magus was determined to leech her energy every month on the moon rock, and worst of all, Yul appeared to have turned against her. If he'd only come and explained why he'd hurt her so badly that night and what exactly had happened, she might have been able to forgive him. But as it was, she felt let down and bewildered.

And there was worse to come. The Solstice was fast approaching, and the thought of what would happen between Yul and Magus filled her with horror. She wanted no part of it, knowing that one of them must die. She'd said that it was her battle too and that she wanted to help. But could she live with the guilt that she'd contributed to a man's death by stealing a lock of his childhood hair? Or could she live under Magus' dominion if he should win, knowing the boy she loved had died partly because of his involvement with her? Either option seemed awful. Maybe it would be easier to leave now and let the events at Stonewylde unfold without her.

Yul stood with his back to Hare Stone and surveyed the sweep of land that filled his vision and his soul – the flanks of the Earth Goddess. The breeze ruffled his hair, his curls long and unkempt from the lengthy trek among the hills and valleys of Stonewylde. He was dirty and hungry after roaming the land for a couple of days, but had needed to get away from people and set his mind free. He was living in limbo, aware of time passing. Every rotation of the Earth brought him closer to the fulfilment of his destiny at the Solstice in three weeks' time. He knew that his entire life had been leading to the event ahead, although he understood that the outcome was far from assured. Mother Heggy had stressed to him that what she'd seen at his birth was just one possibility. Nothing was fixed. In his heart he knew he was the true magus. Stonewylde called him to lead the folk and guard the land. But he also acknowledged Magus' power and intelligence. He didn't make the mistake of underestimating the man whom he now accepted as being his father.

With a final gaze around the panorama of green hills and grey skies, Yul touched the great stone reverently and made to leave the magical spot where the moon spirals were so strong.

He paused, suddenly remembering the time he'd lain with Sylvie on the grass here in the warm summer sun, gazing at the tiny pulse beating in her throat. Unbidden, another image flooded his mind. Sylvie lying curled in the belly of the Goddess, pale and still, the tiny hare of yew wood clasped in a lifeless hand. He shook his head to clear such macabre thoughts, and sent his love across the boulders and through the woodland to the Hall. He hoped she would feel it and understand.

Yul made his way to the dolmen further along the Dragon's Back ridgeway where he'd slept for the past couple of nights. It was dry and sheltered, if cold, in the Neolithic stone building. He'd trapped and skinned a rabbit earlier, and would now roast it over a fire. One more night out in the open, he decided, and then he'd go back to the Village for a while. He wanted to be around during the Dark Moon in a week's time. Hopefully Sylvie would be permitted to join the other women in the Great Barn. He'd been told that she was forbidden from leaving the Hall, but surely Magus wouldn't break with tradition and stop her from doing that. He might get the chance to see her outside on the Village Green and explain what had happened on the night of the Owl Moon. He hoped that she'd forgiven him for his rough treatment of her. He had no idea how ugly her injuries were and would have been mortified if he'd known.

The smoke trickling from the open mouth of the dolmen alarmed him. Although he'd collected wood earlier, he'd lit no fire. As he approached, Yul saw Clip's tall angular frame standing in the entrance and he almost turned around and disappeared back into the hills. But knowing that from now on he must face up to whatever waited for him, he pressed on up the incline and joined his half-uncle by the great stones.

"Blessings, Yul," said Clip. "I hope you don't mind, but I've lit your firewood. I've brewed some tea. Come and join me."

Clip was a regular visitor to the dolmen and kept a few basic necessities in the back of the cave-like structure. They sat one each side of the fire in the entrance, gazing out at the view below them and sipping from chipped pottery mugs.

"The magic is strong for me here," said Clip softly. "I always feel that the Stone Circle is the mind of Stonewylde, but this place is the heart."

"And the Village Green is the soul," said Yul, ill at ease with this enigmatic man. There were times when he felt drawn to Clip and his shamanic gift, but he also knew too well of the man's weaknesses.

"Yes, I can see that. The Green Man – he's your spirit guide, you know. You would feel his presence powerfully on the Green."

"Under the yew."

Clip nodded, and watched Yul through the smoke that curled between them. He saw echoes of his brother in the strong face that gazed out across the land. Yul's cheekbones, nose and jaw were as chiselled as Magus' and spoke of the same strength of character and determination.

"You would make a worthy magus," said Clip. "The Earth Magic is in you. The Goddess has chosen you. I can feel it. The time is ripe, I know. I have been shown. My brother has had his day. He's become excessive in his cruelty. I thought he had that side of his nature under control, but lately … You're a brave young man, and should you defeat him at the Solstice, I will support you."

Yul glanced at him in surprise. Clip was struck by the beauty of the boy's deep grey eyes. Yul nodded, and then added more wood to the fire. He began to prepare the rabbit on the spit, and Clip watched him carefully, admiring his practicality and economy of actions.

If only his brother had accepted this boy as his son, how different things could have been. Yul might have tempered his father's hard heart and brought out the kindness and fullness of spirit that Clip was sure were locked away inside Magus' steely personality. Magus had never loved anybody but he could have loved this boy, and through that love become a better person. But it was too late for that and instead, there was room for only one of them at Stonewylde.

Magus lay in his black marble bath, the fragrant water bubbling gently around him. His eyes were closed and he dreamed of steak, bloody and tender. His mouth watered. Not long now and he'd be able to eat a decent meal. It was almost a week since the funeral on the cliff-top following the fiasco at Mooncliffe. His iron will had stood him in good stead as he'd starved himself since then, eating just enough to remain functioning whilst he spent every waking hour working in his rooms. He'd worked diligently, closing many deals and setting up new ones. Throughout the self-enforced exile from everyday life, he'd let it be known that he was languishing on his sick bed unable to throw off a mystery illness.

He smiled to himself at the thought of the three weeks ahead. Sylvie was buckling under the strain, he'd been informed, and struggling with the mountain of school work piled on her over the past weeks. He knew she'd had no contact with Yul. Martin had ensured that she was watched every minute of the day and the bolted door had prevented any visits from the bastard upstart. He could imagine the atmosphere in her rooms at present, with Miranda moping around like a kicked dog. Today he'd launch the plan that would bring his moongazy girl to heel once and for all. He stood up and stepped out of the circular bath, wrapping himself in a thick robe. Shaving at the black basin, he surveyed his hollowed face with satisfaction. He looked dreadful.

The students sat around in the music room sipping at coffee or fruit juice during break time. Sylvie was half hidden in the window seat, gazing out over the lawns with unfocussed eyes. She felt fragile this morning. She'd had a big argument the evening before about leaving Stonewylde. Miranda hadn't yet decided for sure. Sylvie thought privately that her mother was still clinging to a shred of hope that Magus would take pity on her and tell her it had all been a misunderstanding. Although Miranda hadn't gone into details, Sylvie had worked out what had happened on the night of the full moon. Magus must have lost his temper and finally shattered her ridiculous illusions.

Sylvie found it hard to believe that Miranda had laboured under her misconceptions for so long. Hadn't she noticed the way he was with the women who surrounded him? Had she really deluded herself into thinking he cared more for her than any of the other women who fell at his feet?

Last night Sylvie had argued yet again the case for staying put. Having now thought carefully about it, she'd decided that she couldn't leave here. The alternative was too terrible to contemplate. Back in the Outside World, with schools, shops, traffic, pollution, grey-skinned people scurrying about their business. How would she ever fit back into that sort of society? She was unhappy at the moment due to the pressure of school work and her peer group's unkindness, but after the Solstice things would change. And of course there was Yul. As if she'd picked up on Sylvie's thoughts, Holly approached and sat beside her on the window seat.

"Wakey wakey, Sylvie. No time for napping now. It's your favourite lesson next with William. I hope you've done that stats homework or he'll go mad."

Sylvie looked away and shrugged.

"Oh dear, are we a little down in the dumps today? I wonder why? Is it because Magus has abandoned you? Just when you were thinking you were well in there. That's what he does, Sylvie. Takes up with someone for a while and then drops them. You're not so special after all, are you? And no contact with Yul either. Are you fretting under your house arrest? It would drive me mad, not being able to go out."

"Go away, Holly."

"Still upset about Yul kissing me? It's not long till our Rite of Adulthood. I'm so excited about that."

"You really haven't got a clue, have you Holly? You have no idea what's going to happen at the Winter Solstice."

"Why? What is going to happen?"

"Never mind," said Sylvie wearily, gathering her books and files and standing up. She looked down at Holly, pretty and immaculately turned out. The girl smiled nastily up at her, spitefulness animating her features.

"The only thing that's going to happen is I shall celebrate

my coming of age with Yul. I'll think of you, Miss Frumpy, as we drink the special mead and eat the ceremony cakes. I'll toast you as we lie together on the rabbit-fur rugs next to the Solstice bonfire to keep ourselves warm while we make love."

She rose too, barely reaching Sylvie's chin. Her brown eyes raked Sylvie from head to toe.

"How can you bear to walk about looking like that, Sylvie? I'd lock myself in my room if I looked such a tatty mess. No wonder Magus has lost interest. He's a man of expensive tastes and you look even worse than the Village girls. At least their clothes fit them."

"Alright, we'll move on now to revising standard index notation," said William, scribbling a jumble of numbers on the board. "Sylvie, come up and convert this number to standard index form please. This is an easy example to start us off, so I'm sure even you'll have no trouble."

She stood before the white board, her back to the group of students who sat around the couple of large tables. She could feel their anticipation and knew that William was going to have fun with her today. He'd never be allowed to get away with this victimisation at any school in the Outside World. She gazed blankly at the squiggles on the board's shiny surface. They meant nothing to her at all. She'd obviously missed this teaching too.

"Convert the number to standard index form," repeated William. "For crying out loud, girl, just have a try! We learn through our mistakes. So take a risk! If you're wrong I can show you where to put it right."

But it wasn't as simple as that. If she was wrong he'd spend the rest of the lesson referring back to her mistake until she wanted to shrivel with humiliation. He must have made some kind of gesture behind her back, for the others burst out laughing simultaneously.

"I don't know," said Sylvie woodenly. "I don't have the faintest idea. I think I missed this work when you covered it."

"Of course! How silly of me to have forgotten that. Every single time we turn to a new topic for revision – and I stress the word revision – you trot out the same lame excuse. Is there actually anything in the maths syllabus you do know?"

"Probably not," said Sylvie, turning to go back to her seat.

"Not so fast! Let's have a little try, shall we? Let's see if there's any aspect of mathematics where you feel you might have just the slightest inkling of understanding."

Sylvie stood with her head bowed, feeling the sharp stabs as many pairs of bright eyes watched avidly. Her heart thumped in her chest with anger at this treatment. She was tempted to hurl the whiteboard marker pen at William's sneering face.

"Telling the time?" called out Holly, flicking back her hair. "Adding up? Counting?"

There was another burst of laughter.

"Now, now, Holly. Let's not be unkind," said William. "How about some simple ..."

The door opened and Hazel looked in.

"Excuse me," she said. "Magus wants to see Sylvie straight away."

Sylvie had never imagined the summons would bring such relief. She hastily gathered her things and stumbled from the room, to the whispered barbs of Holly and her friends. William simply glared, instructing the class to start the revision exercise.

"Why does he want to see me now?" asked Sylvie as they crossed the entrance hall and headed for the great staircase. Hazel shrugged.

"I have no idea. He hasn't seen anyone for over a week now, not even me. I'm seriously concerned for his health. He called me in just now and asked for some anti-depressants. Then he said he wanted to see you."

They climbed the stairs and Hazel paused, looking hard at Sylvie.

"I'm counting on you to do something to help him. Make sure you don't upset him. I've never seen him like this before and I'm worried. Try to get him to eat if you can."

They stood before the stone arch and Hazel knocked quietly on the oak door, then left Sylvie to face the man alone.

Magus' exotic scent filled the huge room, enveloping Sylvie as she stepped across the thick carpet. A fire crackled in the arched stone hearth and pale sunlight filtered through the diamond-paned windows. He lay on the leather sofa before the fire, a silk cushion beneath his head and cashmere rug draped over him. He looked vulnerable and exhausted. Gone were the arrogance and power. His face was gaunt, the cheekbones sharp, making him look more like Yul than ever. There were dark shadows under his eyes and the lines around his mouth were etched deeper. Magus looked like a man who'd been suffering, a man in torment. He smiled slightly, his deep brown eyes soft as she approached. He raised his arms weakly to pull her down for a light kiss on the cheek. Then he indicated an armchair nearby where the late November sunlight fell onto her face.

He gazed at her until she became uncomfortable.

"I'm sorry to hear you've been ill," she said finally to break the silence. He grimaced.

"Now I know how you feel after the moondancing," he said. "I'm so weak and I haven't been able to eat."

"But why? What's wrong with you?"

He shrugged and his dark eyes locked into hers.

"I need your moon magic, Sylvie. You promised to come with me but you let me down. And now I'm like this."

"I'm sorry," she whispered. "I didn't mean to."

She wondered if he saw through her. All she could think about was the lock of hair and the Dark Moon spell. She hadn't believed in it before, but looking now at the fragile man lying so pathetically on the sofa in his pyjamas, she knew that this was all her doing. She knew it was nothing to do with the moondancing. He was just using that as an excuse to make her feel guilty. He had no idea of the truth behind his frailty.

"You look beautiful this morning, Sylvie."

She shook her head, wanting none of his compliments.

"I was told earlier I looked a tatty mess."

He raised an eyebrow at this.

"Your hair shines in the sunlight like spun silver. I've

never seen anyone more exquisite. I can feel my spirits lifting. Why didn't I send for you before?"

He rose shakily from the sofa and bent to throw a couple of logs on the fire. In his dark silk pyjamas he looked lean and starved. The open neckline revealed collarbones and hollows not normally visible. He crouched by the hearth and looked up into her eyes. The arrogance may have gone but the charisma remained, deepened by pathos.

"I need you, Sylvie. Will you stay for a little while and talk with me? Cheer me up?"

"Of course. Especially given the alternative."

He lay back down on the sofa again, shutting his eyes momentarily as if in pain.

"Which is?"

"Maths. With William. I'm not doing too well at the moment."

He nodded sympathetically.

"Forget maths then and stay here."

He closed his eyes again weakly and Sylvie glanced around the enormous room in fascination. It was so luxurious, and last time she'd been here there hadn't been the opportunity to see it properly. Magus had surrounded himself with beautiful things and the Tudor setting was superb. She was over-awed by the grandeur and opulence. It was such a contrast to Clip's mediaeval tower with its shabby furnishings and strange collection of ethnic objects.

"How did you get that nasty bruise on your forehead?"

He was watching her as she gazed around.

"Oh … I bumped it. An accident."

"I see. And how's your poor mother?"

"Very depressed."

He put a hand to his temple and groaned.

"I don't think she'll ever forgive me for losing my temper like that. I really did shout at her. I was so angry with her for letting you go wandering off into the night when you were moongazy. You know how dangerous that is. I was furious at her negligence. She thinks only of the baby nowadays and nothing of your welfare. But I've been too ill since to go back and try to make amends with her."

"She looks as awful as you do."

"Poor Miranda. She always did have unrealistic expectations about our relationship, even though I never pretended anything otherwise."

Sylvie nodded at this, for it was perfectly true.

"I was angry with her but I never wanted to hurt her. I'd like to make it up, but I doubt she'd listen to me now, if her heart's set against me. My temper's always been my downfall."

He shook his head ruefully and despite herself, Sylvie felt sympathy for him. He'd lost so much weight and he looked hollow and rather tragic.

"Can I get you anything?" she asked. "Would you like a drink?"

"Yes, that would be nice. There's a fridge over there, behind the panelling. A glass of mineral water please. Have something yourself if you like."

She busied herself at the fridge and brought him over a glass of iced water. He took it from her outstretched hand, but then grasped her fingers.

"Hold on … Sylvie! What on earth is this?"

He stared at her wrist, where her jumper failed to reach, then took hold of the other one and examined that too. He peeled the sleeves back and gently traced the deep black bruising around her slim wrists, all the way from the base of her palms up her arms to the elbows. Her skin was very fair which made it look even worse.

"This is terrible! What happened?"

She blushed, not knowing what to say.

"Who's done this to you? Who was it?"

"I … I don't know."

"Oh come on, you don't get injuries like this without knowing about it. It must have been terribly painful. When did it happen?"

"On the night of the Moon Fullness."

"Just as I said! You go wandering off and you get hurt. But this was no accident, was it? I can see now. These are rope marks. Somebody's tied you up, tethered you. Haven't they?"

She nodded, not wanting to get Yul into trouble but knowing there was no other rational explanation for the pattern of bruising.

"And I know who it was. Yul! Wasn't it?"

She nodded again. Magus shook his head, his face turning even paler. She looked into his eyes fearfully. They glittered with fury.

"How dare he treat you like this? What an awful thing to do to someone!"

"Oh no," she said quickly, "it wasn't like that. I think he was trying to protect me."

"Protect you? From what?"

"From … from you. From going up to Mooncliffe with you."

"But why? You wanted to come up there with me, didn't you? I remember you saying so. You said you'd give me your magic willingly. Didn't you?"

"Yes, but you made Clip hypnotise me!" she said. "You promised you wouldn't."

"Not really hypnotise, Sylvie. Just suggestions to help ease the discomfort for you. And that's not the point. How dare that boy tie you up to prevent you coming to me! I can't bear to think of it. And I suppose the bruise on your head was caused by him too? Sacred Mother, but he's brutal! Any other injuries I should know about?"

He saw her glance involuntarily at her leg.

"Go on, show me."

Feeling embarrassed, she pulled up the cotton skirt slightly and rolled down her long woolly sock to show him the sore scraping all the way down from thigh to ankle. Magus gave a low whistle and looked at her in distress.

"I won't have Village boys – or anyone, for that matter – doing this and getting away with it. I shall punish him as soon as I'm up and about."

"No, Magus, please don't! He didn't mean to, I know!"

"But how did he give you that horrible injury to your

leg?"

"He put me in … a sort of cage, I think."

"WHAT? He imprisoned you as well as tying you up? Is there anything more the boy did to you that night that I ought to be aware of?"

"No, and it's not how you're making it out to be. He wouldn't hurt me deliberately."

As she said this, Sylvie had a flash of Yul shoving her hard along the path and bundling her roughly into the tree cage. Her words rang false in her ears. He may have been acting to protect her, but Yul had hurt her in anger. Magus shook his head and frowned, picking up on her confusion.

"I know you feel weak after moondancing for me, Sylvie, but I'd never hurt you like this. You know that. Now can you see why I warned you away from him? I always said he was too rough for you. There's something I must show you. Something that will help you understand why I've forbidden you to have anything to do with him. Maybe you'll believe me then. That boy is brutal and dangerous. But I feel too ill to deal with it now. We'll talk about it later. It's distressing to see someone as special and delicate as you knocked about by a Village lout like him. I'm exhausted. Could you leave me now to rest?"

"Of course. I'm sorry if I've tired you."

"Would you come back this evening to have supper with me? I can't face eating with all those people downstairs in the Dining Hall. I've been off my food for days now. But if you were here, Sylvie, I may discover my appetite again. Would you mind?"

Sylvie nodded. How could she possibly refuse such a request?

CHAPTER NINE

And that was how Magus manoeuvred Sylvie, over the coming days, into spending her time constantly by his side. When she eventually realised what was happening, Miranda hated it, but she couldn't bear the thought of facing him and having a confrontation. Sylvie didn't tell her how Magus had said he wanted to make amends. Surely it was better for her mother finally to be free of her illusions. Magus would never love her, Sylvie was positive, and in the long run it was kinder to leave her as she was. She'd get over the hurt and at least see him with realistic eyes. Sylvie could never imagine Magus being tied to one woman, and Miranda would never be happy sharing him. Sylvie smothered her twinges of conscience. It was much kinder to let her mother continue to believe that Magus wanted nothing more to do with her.

When she returned that evening to have supper with him, Sylvie found him dressed casually in one of the loose white linen Village shirts, looking as strained and pale as he'd done earlier. Supper arrived via the dumb waiter, concealed in the wooden panelling of the interior wall.

"I'm sorry, Sylvie, I feel too weak to serve you and I really can't do with the bother of summoning a servant. Would you do the honours?"

She carried the dishes over to the intimate dining table in its own alcove, set earlier with linen, silver and candles. The light meal was delicious but Magus only toyed with his food. Sylvie found it ironic that their roles had been reversed in this way; she was now the one urging him to eat more. She told him then of how she'd suffered from his force-feeding, and he apologised.

"I'll never do that again," he promised. "I had no idea

165

how awful it is to eat when you're feeling so delicate. I only wanted to build you up so the moondancing wasn't as debilitating for you. I'm sorry, Sylvie. I'm sorry for anything I've ever done to make you suffer. You should be treated like a princess."

Afterwards Sylvie cleared the dishes back into the dumb waiter and pressed the switch for the tray to descend to the floor below. Magus produced a disc and fed it into a machine connected to the huge screen of his television.

"Come and sit next to me," he said, patting the soft leather sofa. "I mentioned earlier that I wanted to show you something. This is distressing, and I'm sorry to break the pleasant mood. But I think you should see it. Your injuries from that boy have upset me a great deal. I've been thinking about it all afternoon. You need to understand why I've been so adamant about you having no contact with him. I know you think I was being high-handed, Sylvie, in forbidding you to fraternise with him. But you really don't know the full picture."

Sylvie glanced at him. Magus' face was serious and she noticed his hands shook slightly. She felt a sudden rush of pity for him. This man was different from the golden god-like figure who demanded obedience so forcefully. Now he was quiet and almost humble, clearly suffering in his weakened state.

"These are photos taken of Buzz after his fight with Yul in the summer, not long after Lammas. You may recall the incident. Buzz was admitted to the hospital wing and Hazel photographed his injuries extensively, recording these images over a period of time as he began to heal. I wanted a record of Yul's brutality. At that point, you see, I wasn't intending to punish Buzz further. Yul had already done that, as you will see. Buzz had only kissed the Village girl and fumbled about with her blouse. Nothing more than that had taken place, by the girl's own admission. Yet the Villagers were up in arms about it. I'd hoped that by showing them these photos of Buzz's appalling injuries, they'd see that he'd had punishment enough for his misdemeanour. It wasn't until he attacked you too that I realised he probably had intended to take it further with the girl after all."

Magus paused, the control in his hand, and ignoring Sylvie's look of scepticism, continued.

"Anyway, luckily I have this record to show you. I want you to look carefully, Sylvie, however upsetting it may be. I want you to see what sort of a beast lies beneath Yul's boyish charm. Remember how much larger Buzz is than him, and try to imagine therefore the sheer viciousness and violence of the assault. Yul is not normal, that's for sure. He has the brutality of someone with a severe personality disorder, someone mentally unhinged. And remember when you see these images that Yul was totally unharmed in the fight, other than his hands. You'll see only too clearly why they were damaged."

Sylvie was then shown the most terrible series of injuries she'd ever witnessed. Hazel had catalogued Buzz's suffering meticulously and Sylvie watched in horrified fascination. She saw the way that time had created an animation of vivid discolouration and grotesque swelling, before finally beginning to heal the damage. She'd had no idea of Buzz's disfigurement, only seeing him a month later when most of the visible injuries had all but healed.

She was sickened at the sight of his face: the eyes puffed-up like dark plums, his nose bent and swollen, his mouth like a piece of raw meat. His body was mottled with a camouflage pattern of deep bruising that passed through every shade before eventually fading to a dull yellow. Finally she could stand no more, and Magus turned off the slide show of photos. He turned to look into her eyes.

"Do you understand a little better now? And appreciate why the sight of your injuries has upset me so much? They're nothing compared to Buzz's of course. But nevertheless, they indicate that Yul would have no qualms about hurting you too if he thought it was warranted. Has he done anything else to you, Sylvie?"

She swallowed, wanting to defend Yul but feeling unable to do so, given the appalling sights she'd just witnessed. She couldn't believe he'd inflicted such dreadful damage on another person.

"My upper arms and ribcage are quite painful. He pinned me to the ground and crushed me, I think. I don't remember it too well because the moon was close to rising and I was frantic. I'm scraped all down the side of my body, not just my leg. And he gagged me. My mouth was sore for a while, although there weren't any marks. That's all, I think."

Magus nodded slowly.

"And what about ... how can I put this ... in passion? Has he done anything to violate you? Of a sexual nature, I mean."

Sylvie blushed scarlet. She thought of their kisses, of the increasing desire she felt for him. She recalled the tentative caresses they'd shared. And she remembered particularly the night when he'd come to her bedroom and had pulled her down on top of him on her bed. She shook her head, avoiding Magus' eye. Yul had never done anything she hadn't wanted. He'd been the one to hold back when her emotions overwhelmed her natural reticence.

"I can see that something has gone on between you," said Magus quietly, shaking his head sadly. "Hopefully it hasn't gone too far. I imagine you're thinking it was mutual. That Yul wasn't forcing himself on you. But just remember, Sylvie, the power of the Earth Magic. I know only too well the effect it has, not only on the recipient, but on all who come into contact with it. It's extremely powerful stuff. It's the very essence of Stonewylde, of nature's wild, procreative forces. Yul will use the Earth Magic to overcome any shyness or reluctance you may feel. I speak from experience here, Sylvie. I've never been turned down by any woman. In fact I've turned over-eager women away. I'm not fool enough to imagine it's just my charm and good looks that excite them. Remember that with Yul. Since he's stolen my Earth Magic, he has access to all that sexual energy and you'd find it impossible to resist any advances he may make."

Sylvie swallowed hard at this. She knew it to be true. She'd felt the compelling force in Yul after the ceremonies and his rituals at sunrise and sunset. But surely there was more to it than that? He loved her and wanted her so much, and that was nothing to do with any green magic of Stonewylde. And she'd felt the same about him. She shook her head and turned away from Magus, staring into the blazing fire. He got up slowly and turned off the television screen. Pouring them both a small glass of mead, he sat quietly next to her on the sofa whilst they sipped at it.

"I'm sorry, Sylvie. What I've said has upset you. But you need to be in possession of the facts. Go away and think about it tonight. Will you visit me again tomorrow if I send for you? I feel so much better for seeing you today, and at last I've managed to eat something. I'm feeling stronger already and I'm very grateful to you."

Back in her room, Sylvie found it impossible to concentrate on the pile of homework. The mead and heat of the fire had made her body relax. Her mind was reeling with the horrific images she'd seen on the screen and Magus' words of warning about Yul's passion. Eventually she pushed the books away and tried to sleep. She moved about restlessly for ages as sleep eluded her. She was worried that Magus was manipulating her, but worried too that he spoke the truth. If only she could see Yul to speak to him.

Magus was as gentle and charming the next day, sending for her in the middle of the morning during a History lesson. Once again Holly hissed with spite as Sylvie bundled up her things and left the school room. She followed Martin up the stairs, not dreading the encounter as she'd done the previous day, but still wary of Magus and any further revelations he might make today. She needn't have worried. He seemed a little brighter and they ate lunch together at the dining table looking out over the grounds. He spoke of the early days of his leadership of Stonewylde and some of the difficulties he'd faced trying to put right the years of neglect. She felt a grudging respect for him as she understood more fully just what he'd achieved.

"Stonewylde is my life," he said softly, sipping at his glass of water as the food lay largely untouched on his plate. "I'd never voluntarily give up my guardianship of the place."

"Can't you manage a little more of your food?" Sylvie asked, not wanting to discuss the forthcoming conflict. Magus was still pale and drawn and his eyes were weary. His hands trembled as he pushed the plate away and she felt a pang of pity for him. The sun glinted suddenly on his blond hair and she almost choked on her mouthful as an image of the tiny lock of child's hair rose unbidden into her mind. She wondered if there was any way to reverse Mother Heggy's awful spell. It was one thing going along with all the talk of destroying Magus, but quite another to see the weakness and suffering of the man himself as he sat quietly in the sunlight, talking of his hopes and dreams for Stonewylde.

"No, I can't," he said. "I just can't face it."

He lay on the sofa after lunch and closed his eyes. Sylvie sat fidgeting, worried about her lessons. It was maths again this afternoon and she didn't want to arrive half way through. Not after leaving early yesterday before William had finished his daily bout of mortification. He'd be angry enough without lateness today, and she hadn't managed to finish the homework last night. He was going to really lay into her. She wondered about creeping out whilst Magus slept, but didn't want to upset him.

"Do you want to go, Sylvie?" he asked, opening his eyes.

"Sorry, did I disturb you? I'm just worried about my classes this afternoon. If I don't go now I'm going to be late."

"What have you got next?"

"Maths."

"Would you rather go to maths or stay here with me?"

She laughed at this.

"I'd rather walk across hot coals than go to maths."

"That bad? Stay with me, then. I feel much better when you're here. I'm so weak since that terrible last Moon Fullness when Yul prevented you from coming to me. Perhaps I'm picking up some of your energy now?"

"I don't think it works like that," she said doubtfully. "It's not like the Earth Magic."

"Then maybe it's just your presence. Whatever the cause, I don't feel so terribly depressed when you're around. Would you mind staying?"

She needed little persuasion to miss another session on standard index form or any other horror that William might humiliate her over. She spent a peaceful afternoon sitting on the long sofa reading a book from the pile on the table, whilst Magus rested beside her. He lay with his head against her leg, saying that being close to her helped his recovery. He was so weak and listless that he no longer seemed a threat, and she found some comfort in knowing she was helping him. Anything to lessen her guilt over the spell. As the afternoon grew dark, she fed the fire and lit the lamps, pulling the huge oak shutters across the long expanse of windows. It was cosy in the great room and Magus watched her moving quietly about.

"I like you being here, Sylvie," he said. "I'm feeling much better. Are you alright about missing school for a few days?"

She came over and sat down on the floor, hugging her knees and gazing into the fire.

"I'm alright about it. I hate it. It was you who were so cross about me missing school and my lack of progress."

He chuckled.

"Yes, I was. I thought you were malingering. Now I know better. I'd be a hypocrite to chastise you now for taking to your bed for a week and eating nothing. It's exactly what I've done. Have you caught up with the schoolwork yet? I heard you'd been putting in a lot of effort recently."

She shook her head, feeling a welling up of the despair that any thought of school now inspired.

"I've tried so hard. I've worked and worked, but there are so many gaps. It's not just since I started moondancing for you. I missed almost two years of school in London because of my illness and allergies and the bullying." Her voice started to crack and she swallowed hard. "I hadn't realised how little I knew until all this revision started. I feel stupid and thick, and I'd always thought I was alright."

"Don't be silly. You're not stupid at all."

"Well that's how the teachers here have been making me feel. Completely useless. And the others – Holly and her gang. They tease me about it and laugh every time I can't answer a question or get a poor mark in a test. I can't ..."

To her surprise, she burst into tears, bowing her head over her knees and sobbing. Magus leant over to stroke her hair.

"Don't cry, Sylvie," he said gently. "It's not the end of the world. It's only schoolwork."

"But I'm useless!" she sobbed. "I can't do anything. They all laugh at me and William picks on me and I can't bear it any longer!"

All the frustration and misery of the last few weeks since the work had piled up came flooding out and she couldn't stop crying. Magus slid down onto the floor next to her, sitting with his back against the sofa. He put an arm around her shaking shoulders and pulled her in close to him, enfolding her in soft linen and heavy scent. Gradually she relaxed into his embrace and felt the unique comfort of being held by someone big and strong. He stroked her hair gently, a small smile on his lips.

"Sylvie, stop a minute and listen to me. I can make it all better. Listen."

She managed to stop crying and sat quietly.

"If you like, I can make a call on the intercom to your tutor. I imagine he'll be in his room changing for dinner. I can tell him that we've decided to defer your exams for a year. You could take some time off now, catch up with everything you missed last year, and then start this year again next September. It wouldn't matter at all. Would you like me to do that?"

She stared at him incredulously, hope flaring inside her.

"Are you allowed to do that?" she gasped.

"Sylvie, I can do anything I want. I'm in charge here, remember? Shall I make that call now?"

She nodded, unable to believe that at a single stroke he could remove the relentless and crushing stress that had blighted her life since Samhain.

"There's one condition."

"Yes?"

"You'll keep me company until I'm better again. You'll

look after me and come here every day to cheer me up. Is that a deal?"

She smiled, sniffing and gulping back the tears, her heart light with relief. She nodded happily and he bent to kiss her forehead.

"Silly thing," he said fondly. "If you'd only told me how much you were suffering I could've done this long ago. I want you to be happy, Sylvie. I'll do whatever I can to make you happy. You've been so good to me the past couple of days. I won't forget it."

Martin stoked up the fire and turned to his master, who sat at the desk tapping into a keyboard.

"Are you ready for that steak now, sir?"

"Is she back in her room?"

"Yes, sir. All tucked up for the night, I would imagine."

"Fine. Send the food up then. Goddess, but it's been a long haul. A decent bottle of wine too. And Martin ..."

"Yes sir?"

"When I've finished, bring me a woman."

"Anyone in particular, sir? The young doctor perhaps?"

"No," he frowned. "She'll talk and fuss too much. She thinks I'm seriously ill. No Hallfolk. It could get back to Sylvie. Get me a Village girl, someone fresh. And a moon egg. Make a detour to the cliff on your way to the Village. You've got one of the padlock keys, haven't you? Use a bag or you'll drain some of it."

"Very good, sir. Anything else? Do you want me to wait up and take the girl back later?"

"No ... no, I'll keep her till the morning. Be ready to escort her down the back stairs and away first thing, though. Sylvie will be joining me for breakfast tomorrow."

Martin smiled and plumped up the cushions along the sofa.

"Enjoy your evening, sir."

"I'm sure I will, Martin. I deserve it. This past week of abstinence has been hell."

"You can't just miss a year of school!" said Miranda angrily.

"Not miss it, Mum. Defer it, he said. I'll go back and do this year again next September."

"But I don't want you to do that! Magus should've asked me first."

"I don't think he wants to speak to you," said Sylvie, feeling a prickle of guilt at the lie. Miranda's face fell and she looked down at her knitting. "Please, Mum, don't get funny about it. I can't keep up, and this way I'll get better results when I do take my exams."

"What about if we leave?"

"Come on, Mum. You know we can't leave. Anyway, my schooling would be even worse then. How could I start at a new school now, half way through my final year? Please, don't make a fuss. I feel so relieved. It's like a great weight has been lifted suddenly and I can straighten my back again."

"It just annoys me that he thinks he can make these decisions without even consulting me. I'm your mother after all! What were you doing in his room anyway? Did he send for you?"

Sylvie looked away guiltily.

"I've been spending a bit of time there over the past couple of days. Magus has been ill and he asked me to keep him company."

Miranda swallowed, keeping her head down. She'd never imagined she'd feel such violent resentment towards her own daughter. She looked up to see Sylvie's eyes shining with happiness as she sorted out her school books and folders and put them tidily into the book shelf in their sitting room.

"I don't know what he's playing at," Miranda said slowly, "but be very careful, Sylvie. Whatever you do, don't get fooled by him like I did."

"Mum, I've always known what he's like. It was you who were blind to it, not me. Remember the arguments we used to have about him? When I told you there was another side to him and you wouldn't believe me? I don't trust him at all, but he's been very sweet the last few days and it won't do any harm spending time with him. I can find out what his plans are for the Solstice maybe. There's stuff that's been going on ... things with Yul, about the future. I've got to stop it before it's too late. I don't want anything more to do with it."

Sylvie was relieved when there was a knock on the door to their rooms the next morning and she found a maid standing outside with a pile of their clean laundry. It was Rowan, the girl who'd been the May Queen at Beltane all those months ago. She was now quite heavily pregnant, and glowed with vitality and ripeness. Sylvie smiled tentatively, but the laundry maid refused to meet her eye.

"Thank you," said Sylvie. "I'd been hoping these would come back soon. I've got nothing else to wear. "

The new black trousers and jumper were the only things that fitted her properly and she'd wanted to wear them for days. Magus noticed too, when she joined him for breakfast. His eyes followed her about the room. The slim black outfit set her figure off perfectly and her hair shone in a silver cloud almost down to her waist. She sensed a change in him today. His eyes sparkled and glowed with the old lazy charm. As she brought the plate of croissants to the table, he caught hold of her hand and examined her wrists again.

"Still there, I see."

"Bruises take ages to fade on me," she said, looking down into his dark eyes. "But they don't hurt as much now and my ribs are fine when I breathe deeply."

"Good," he said. "I don't like his marks on you. Come and sit down so we can eat. I feel ravenous today."

She watched in bemusement as he consumed a couple of croissants in quick succession.

"Your appetite's come back!" she said. "You look almost normal today."

"It's because you're here with me," he said, smiling across the table at her. "I feel infinitely better. What power you have, Sylvie, to cure someone just by your presence."

She frowned at this, not convinced.

"You seem different today," she said. "There's something

else ... Did you get a good night's sleep?"

His face split into a grin, and he looked so like Yul.

"I had a wonderful night, Sylvie. Absolutely wonderful."

After breakfast he took her over to the screen at his desk and sat down with her.

"We're going to order you a new winter wardrobe," he said. She stared at him in wonder. He laughed and hugged her. "Don't look so shocked! I said I'd buy you new clothes after the Owl Moon."

"Yes but ... I didn't moondance for you."

"That wasn't your fault, Sylvie. I can see the pain and suffering you went through trying to escape that damn boy's clutches. You'd have danced for me if you could have. So I'll keep my side of the deal. There are several websites for department stores that do a courier service, so we can get some clothes quickly for you. And I'd like to get some decent designer things. Some really special outfits to do justice to your beauty. They may take a little longer to arrive. You'll need shoes and boots too, and maybe some jewellery? Perfume and cosmetics? Let's go on a virtual shopping trip and see what lovely things we can find for you."

Two hours later Sylvie sat in the window seat gazing out at the wintry sky. She couldn't believe what had just happened. They'd visited several sites and Magus had urged her to choose whatever caught her fancy. At first she'd been shy, not sure if he'd approve of her taste, not certain how much she was allowed to spend. He sensed her awkwardness and had hugged her again.

"I love your lack of greed," he'd said. "You're not avaricious in the slightest. I've seen some of the girls here with rich parents indulging in spending frenzies that shocked even me, who's not renowned for restraint when it comes to money. But you, Sylvie ... you're delightful. You make me want to buy you the earth."

"But is it alright to order so much? This will cost a fortune."

"Sylvie, I'm worth a fortune. I have considerable personal

176

wealth. Remember my company in London? It's extremely successful and there's money pouring in from all sorts of ventures. I'm a very rich man and I can't think of a better way of spending it than buying things for you. You're so appreciative."

She smiled shyly at him. She'd never in her life had money, and certainly never been able to splash out on fashionable clothes. She'd always had to make do with second hand things. Anything new she'd been bought had been cheap and shoddy. This was a different world.

Magus had taken over as they shopped, realising her lack of experience when it came to serious spending. He'd ordered item after item, urging her to choose which colour she preferred and accessories to match. She had no idea how much money he'd spent on her, for after a while the figures meant nothing and she lost count. Magus didn't even seem to look at the price of anything anyway. She felt a thrill deep in her stomach at the exhilaration of such extravagance. When they'd finally finished, they stood up and he'd taken her hands in his, gazing down into her moonstone eyes.

"You've given me a lot of pleasure this morning," he said softly.

"No ... no, you've been the kind one. Thank you!" she smiled. "Thank you, thank you!"

He chuckled and held her close in a brief hug, kissing the top of her head.

"This is just the beginning," he said. "Your life is going to change so much, my moongazy girl. I want to spoil you, pamper you. I want to indulge your every whim."

She giggled at this.

"No, Sylvie, I mean it. You know how desperately I need your moon magic. You know you're the only one who can give me what I crave. And in return, you shall never want for anything. Every month you'll dance for me on the rock, and you'll see what a generous and grateful man I can be. You shall be my princess, and everyone will know just how special you are. Just what you mean to me."

Now she sat on the window seat as they waited for lunch, and her heart began to sink. She'd got caught up in the excitement of buying beautiful new clothes, things that would make Holly and her gang go green with envy. But the meaning of Magus' words now trickled through her self-delusion. He'd spoken as if she'd be with him for ever more, as if they'd be living at the Hall with the whole future spread before them. A future patterned by the thirteen full moons when she'd go up to Mooncliffe willingly and stand on that rock, pain shooting through her body as the stone beneath drank her magic.

Maybe Magus was imagining she'd get used to it. And maybe over time he'd let her stay there just long enough to feed him what he needed, with no extra stones to fill. But he wouldn't be alive after the Solstice! The thought sliced through the fantasy he'd created. He had no idea what Yul had planned for him in less than three weeks' time.

She still didn't trust Magus, but realized she was warming to him. He'd treated her very kindly over the past few days, just as he'd treated her when she first came to Stonewylde. He could be a gentle and congenial person when he wanted to be. She remembered how he'd healed her in the woods. How could she now play a part in his destruction? Just by keeping quiet she was helping to bring about his death.

She thought then of Yul, and realised it was the first time she'd done so today. If she warned Magus of what was to come, what would happen to Yul? Would Magus really kill him, as Yul believed? It was impossible to imagine this generous man setting out to murder his own son. Yul must be mistaken. True, Magus hated him. And he wouldn't tolerate Yul's challenge to his supremacy. Maybe she could negotiate between them, help them to come to some arrangement? She'd give Magus her moon magic every month and he'd leave Yul alone and allow them to see each other. She needed to speak to Yul and try to sort this out.

After lunch Magus decided they needed some fresh air and told her to fetch her cloak. He fastened the clasp around her neck, releasing her great swathe of hair from where it had become caught. He let it slip through his fingers in silky strands. His eyes were bright as he gazed down at her.

"You are lovely," he murmured, his eyes roaming her face. She felt a pang as she wore the scarlet cloak for only the second time, remembering the previous occasion with Yul. She wondered what he was doing now. Magus took her arm in his and they went downstairs together side by side. Several people in the entrance hall looked up at the striking pair descending the great stairs. Sylvie was gratified to see that one of them was Rainbow. This would get back to Holly. Hazel was there too, and she greeted them at the foot of the stairs.

"You're better!" she exclaimed, looking up at Magus with a twisted half smile. Sylvie felt sympathy for the doctor. Her eyes held the same expression that her mother's had done. Sylvie knew it could only lead to heartache.

"I am indeed," he smiled, putting an arm round Sylvie's shoulders. "All thanks to this little moon goddess."

Hazel's eyes followed them as they swept past her, and Sylvie felt the young doctor's pain.

They went into the formal garden with the gravel paths, clipped yews and stone statues. The December sky was like lead and a chilly wind flicked at them, stinging their cheeks and eyes.

"I wish I'd brought my gloves!" said Sylvie, and Magus took one of her hands in his. He began to tell her the history of this garden and formal gardens in general. He talked of the Renaissance ideology, of the concept of imposing order and symmetry on the chaos of nature. He was eloquent and knowledgeable. She listened to his lively conversation and found herself wondering if it would pall after a while, living with someone so clever, or whether it would always be entertaining and stimulating.

"Of course, you'd have to visit Italy and France to see the best examples of those Renaissance gardens. When the weather is a bit warmer, maybe March or April, we could go and visit if you like. We could spend a month or so in Europe, travelling and touring. What do you think?"

"Oh yes!" she exclaimed, forgetting that if Yul was successful, Magus would no longer be alive in the spring. "I've never been abroad before."

"What? Oh Sylvie, in that case, we must start soon! We can go wherever you want. We'll look on the globe in my office when we get back. I shall take you to such wonderful places …"

And then, at that precise moment, in the order and symmetry of the formal Italianate garden with its raked gravel and perfect hedges, Sylvie started to think seriously about what life with Magus would actually be like. Life with a very wealthy man. Life with a man who'd been everywhere and done everything and wanted to share it all with her. Life with a man who could have any woman he wanted, but who believed her to be unique.

Sylvie knew she had something he wanted more than anything in the world. It was something he couldn't take away from her, but would have to accept in small portions every month. She knew too that when she channelled the moon magic for him it was painful and debilitating. But would it be worth enduring that pain in order to keep a man like him in thrall? Would it be worth the sacrifice in order to live like a princess?

CHAPTER TEN

Sylvie awoke the next morning and stretched in her bed, luxuriating in the knowledge that there were no more lessons to face for a while. All the pressure was off. After weeks of being ostracised and ridiculed by her peers, nagged and censured by the adults, it was lovely to be spending time with someone who appreciated her company and found her delightful. She hopped out of bed eager to start the new day. She wore the black outfit again, unable to bear the thought of her scruffy old clothes. Holly had been right. What must Magus have thought of her floral skirts, bobbly old jumpers and woolly socks? Hopefully today the courier service would bring some of the new things they'd ordered. Her heart jumped with excitement at the prospect. She decided to go straight to his rooms now for breakfast. After all, she must keep her side of the deal.

But as she left the bathroom and made for the door that led into the corridor outside, Miranda emerged from her bedroom in her dressing gown. The pregnancy, now in the last months, had suddenly become hugely apparent. The bump was enormous and she was starting to put on weight everywhere, her arms and legs puffy with extra flesh. Even her face seemed bloated, and her beautiful chestnut-red hair had become quite lank. Gone was the sparkle and vivacity, to be replaced by a heavy dullness. Sylvie felt sorry for her. It must be awful carrying that great bulge around and knowing that you looked so ungainly.

"Are you going to breakfast?" asked Miranda, shuffling across the sitting room in her slippers to draw the curtains. Sylvie nodded.

"Hold on and I'll come down with you. I'm feeling a little

more like facing the world now."

"That's good, Mum," said Sylvie, her heart sinking. "I'm so pleased for you. But I can't ... I'm sorry, I'm not going down to the Dining Hall. I'm having breakfast in Magus' rooms."

Miranda frowned at her.

"Has he sent for you then? I didn't hear a knock."

"No, but ... he said he wanted me to keep him company until he's better. He's ordered me some winter clothes and that was the deal."

"I see. So he's arranged for you to miss a whole year of school just so you can prance about in new clothes and keep him amused, has he?"

"No Mum, it's not like that. He says I've helped to make him better. I must go. I promised."

"But what about me, Sylvie? I'd really like you beside me as I go downstairs and face all those people again. I'm dreading the looks and comments. They must all have guessed what's happened. I feel so humiliated. I need some support and I thought you'd be happy to help me."

Sylvie looked away guiltily. She wanted to sip fresh orange juice from crystal glass and talk with Magus; bask in his warmth and appreciation. She certainly didn't want to walk into the Dining Hall next to her heavily pregnant mother. Everyone would stare. Gossip must be rife, and she really didn't need any more aggravation. Not now that everything was so rosy.

"I'm really sorry, Mum. I've promised Magus I'll spend the next few days with him. I can't go back on that."

"I think you've spent quite enough time with him lately. He doesn't own you. We'll send a message to say you're busy today."

"No!"

"But you don't enjoy going there, surely? Not after what he's done to all of us. You, and me, and Yul."

"Well, no, but he isn't that bad. I mean, I know he hurt you and Yul, but he hasn't actually done anything to me."

"What about Mooncliffe? Have you forgotten what he put

182

you through? Clip's told me all about it. It's dreadful that Magus used you like that. And what about your awful weakness afterwards?"

"That wasn't his fault really. It's what the moongaziness does to me. He tried to make it less painful for me, but ..."

"Just listen to yourself, Sylvie! He's got you exactly where he wants you, eating from the palm of his hand. You are so shallow! What about poor Yul? I thought you were "in love" with him. Where's your sense of loyalty?"

Sylvie felt herself flushing angrily.

"Alright then, Mum. I'll go now and tell Magus that I can't come because you said I must have breakfast with you instead."

"No, Sylvie, only if you want to! I'm not forcing you. I thought you'd want to help me. That you'd be pleased I was feeling ready to face the world again. I thought you hated Magus as much as we all do. It seems I was wrong."

"No. Well ... yes. I mean, I've got to know him better over the last few days and he's not as horrible as I thought. He really likes me. And he's actually very good company."

"Of course he is! That's why I fell in love with him. I'm not a complete fool, Sylvie. You know how strong and independent I used to be. I would never have fallen for him if he'd treated me badly from the start. Magus is charming and flattering and funny while he's still hunting you down. But you wait till he's got his claws into you. Then the charm and flattery just evaporate and you see just how cold and cruel he is inside. You saw it happen to me, Sylvie."

"I know, Mum, but ..."

"But in your own arrogance, you think it'll be different with you! You think you're special. You think you're the one he'll change his ways for."

"No, Mum, you've got it all wrong. I don't think of him in that way. Not like you and all the others do. It's different, my relationship with him."

"Oh don't make me laugh, Sylvie! Of course it isn't different! You've got a crush on him and you're naïve enough to think he feels something for you. You're playing with fire.

You're much, much too young for him. He'll chew you up and spit you out like all the rest."

"No he won't! It's not like that with him and me. Honestly, Mum, he's different with me. He can't do enough for me. He watches me all the time, can't take his eyes off me. Not that I want anything like that, of course, but he really thinks I'm unique. He said so."

"For God's sake, girl, you're only fifteen! What on earth would you have to offer a man like that? And don't say your pretty face, please! Nubile girls are ten a penny to him. He can have any girl or woman he wants, here or anywhere else. You're not that special!"

"Oh but I am," said Sylvie softly, stung to anger by her mother's brutal honesty. "I'm the only one who can give him what he really needs. I'm the only one who's moongazy. He'll do anything for my gift of moon magic. To Magus, I'm one of a kind."

Miranda stared at her daughter, wanting very much to slap the smugness off her lovely face but knowing that would not be a good move. Sylvie gave her a little smile, and slipped on her black suede boots. She flounced out of the sitting room, shutting the door just a fraction too hard.

But when Sylvie tapped on the great oak door there was no reply, and she didn't like to go in without permission. Where was he? She stood uncertainly by the stone arch, unsure of what to do now. She couldn't go back to her room, not after the row with her mother, nor could she go down to the Dining Hall for breakfast. She looked down over the balustrade of the stair case to see if he was in the entrance hall below. She saw the gleam of blond hair and thought for a moment it was him, but it was Martin who looked up. He climbed the staircase slowly, watching Sylvie.

"Were you looking for the master, miss?" he asked deferentially, his grey eyes cold.

"Yes ... I thought ... I was going to join him for breakfast."

"Really? Did he invite you?"

"No, not exactly, but I thought ... oh well, I must have

misunderstood."

"Yes, miss, you must have. Magus had breakfast long ago and then went riding."

"Oh. I see."

"I expect he'll send for you when he wants you. He's a busy man. He'll let you know when he has time for you."

Sylvie flushed and looked down at her feet. She felt a fool. Martin gave a small smile.

"Will that be all, miss?"

His meaning was clear and she nodded, moving away from the oak door. She decided to go and do some work in the library, having nowhere else to go now. She sat in the window seat of the silent room surrounded by thousands of books. She waited all morning for Magus to return and come looking for her. At lunch time she thought about going to the Dining Hall but again didn't want to face everyone.

So Sylvie stayed where she was, becoming more impatient and frustrated as time wore on. Why hadn't he sent for her? After all the time they'd spent together recently and the great fuss he'd made of her, she felt now as if he'd stood her up. Eventually she'd had enough of hanging around waiting for him. She'd go upstairs and see if one of the luxurious bathrooms was free. She closed the books she'd been reading and stood up, just as the door opened. Holly walked in.

"Well, well, it's Queen Sylvie herself," she sneered, shutting the door behind her.

"Leave me alone, Holly," said Sylvie. The girl came over and faced her across the antique writing table, head cocked to one side. Her eyes danced with malice.

"How do you do it, Sylvie?" she asked. "We're all dying to know. While Magus is away, you've got Yul running round after you with secret assignations under the trees in the Village Green. Then Magus comes back and you're shut up alone in his rooms all day with him, and he doesn't even come out for meals. And now we hear you're excused from school. What's your secret? We'd love to know."

"I'm sure you would. But even if you did, it wouldn't help you, Holly. You've either got it or you haven't."

Holly's face twisted dangerously, her cat's eyes narrowing.

"You're a smug little bitch and I hate you! We all hate you!"

"It's mutual."

"Now that you're tied up with Magus, I think I'll pay Yul a visit. Take up where we left off under the chestnut tree."

Sylvie shrugged, tossing her long silver hair behind her shoulders. She felt good in her svelte black outfit. She could see the jealousy fizzing in Holly's eyes and smiled.

"You'll be wasting your time, Holly. Yul doesn't want to know. He only kissed you because you tried to blackmail him. But it won't work again. He really can't stand you. I'm afraid he only wants me, Holly, so bad luck."

"You wait, you cow!" hissed Holly. "I'm going to wipe that smug arrogance off your face! Once Magus gets bored of you, I'll make your life a misery. I promise you that."

Sylvie laughed, heading for the door.

"Well don't hold your breath, Holly. Magus is far from bored with me. Quite the opposite! It's a pity he likes to keep me all to himself up in his rooms, else you'd be able to see just how special I am to him!"

When Sylvie returned to her room, Miranda was nowhere to be seen and she breathed a sigh of relief. Then she noticed a note from Magus on the table asking her to join him for dinner in his rooms at eight o'clock. She was pleased, but cross that she'd wasted the whole day moping about waiting for him. She trooped off down the wing to see if the white bathroom was free.

Sylvie lay in the marble bath, her head emerging from a sea of fragrant foam. Her thoughts drifted as she relaxed in the hot, silky water. She remembered how she'd brought Yul here on the eve of the Summer Solstice after she'd rescued him from the quarry. He'd been overwhelmed by the grandeur of the place. Poor Yul. He had no idea at all of the luxury of the Hall and the lifestyle here. He was out of place anywhere other than the Village and his woods. It wasn't his fault, of course, just the way things were. She remembered how she'd once longed to live a simple life in the Village. She smiled at the notion and felt the hot steam bring beads of perspiration to her pink face as she luxuriated in the white marble tub.

When Sylvie walked into the room in her bath robe, glowing and smelling lovely, Miranda wordlessly handed her another note from Magus, just delivered by Harold. Sylvie's heart sank thinking he was cancelling the dinner. She didn't relish the prospect of an evening with her crabby mother. But instead he asked if she would wear the evening dress that had arrived that day. Sylvie saw then the boxes lying on the table and hurried to rip them open, crying out with delight as she removed the tissue paper.

Miranda sat down and picked up her knitting, pointedly ignoring Sylvie's rapture as she examined the beautiful new things. The dress was sleeveless, a deep shimmering green of watered silk, cut on the bias. There was a black pashmina of the finest texture imaginable, elegant high-heeled shoes and lovely underwear. Sylvie felt like Cinderella as she took the things into her room to get changed.

Magus greeted her with a glass of amber mead. He wore a dark suit over a black shirt and looked strikingly attractive, his illness now passed but his face still hollowed and interesting. His blond hair gleamed in the candlelight, for the room was lit by many tiny flames. He smiled, kissing her cheek lightly, his black eyes glittering. Sylvie felt nervous standing in the figure-hugging dress, her neck, shoulders and arms exposed. He'd removed the pashmina as she entered the room and she felt embarrassed, unused to such a sophisticated style of dress. She was also very conscious of the disfiguring purple bruises on her wrists and arms. Her hair fell like a curtain of silk to her waist and she felt Magus' eyes on her, taking in every detail of her appearance. He toasted her and drank down the mead in one go, whilst she sipped at hers. She loved the taste of it but knew it made her dreamy and drowsy.

A log fire blazed in the great fireplace and they went to stand by it, for Sylvie was shivering slightly.

"Have you had a good day?" he asked, pouring them another glass of mead from a crystal decanter.

"Yes, very good thanks. I worked in the library. Research for my history coursework. For next year of course."

"Good. I missed you today, Sylvie. I've been out riding for most of the day. I needed the air and the exercise after being cooped up in here for so long. And Nightwing needed a good hard ride too. That horse forgets his manners if I neglect him for too long. But I've blown my cobwebs away now and reminded Nightwing of who's the master."

"I rode a horse with Yul recently."

It was a silly thing to say, but she had a ridiculous urge to make him jealous. She was still annoyed that he'd abandoned her all day without letting her know.

"Really?" He seemed unperturbed. "I didn't think the boy had a horse."

"He borrowed it. An enormous white one."

"A grey. That would probably be Edward's. That's interesting to know he's been helping Yul. Drink up, Sylvie. The mead will warm you. Let me pour you another one. So you shared the same horse, did you?"

She nodded, sipping the third glass of mead and knowing she must slow down. She'd eaten nothing all day and could feel her body becoming warm and tingly. Everything seemed a little unreal. He smiled at her, eyes bright and fathomless.

"How intimate. Was this at the Moon Fullness?"

"Yes. We went through the woods and I felt as if we were part of a fairytale. It was all misty, and there were amazing red toadstools everywhere."

"And tell me, did you ride to the cage he kept you in? I'm intrigued by this cage. I can't imagine how he came by such a thing."

"We rode quite a way and then he tied the horse up in a clearing in the wood. The cage was just a bit further on."

"A metal cage?"

"No, it was made out of tree."

"A wooden cage?"

"No, a tree cage."

"Ah yes, of course! I know the tree cages. I used to go there as a boy. Had great fun up there!" He laughed. "What a brilliant idea. But he had to tie you up first to get you in there, I would imagine. That's how you were injured."

"Yes, I guess so."

Sylvie put the empty glass down on a small table and stood looking into the flames of the fire. She suddenly felt very weary and wondered why she was here at all. Magus must have sensed the change in her mood for he pulled a bell rope by the fire. Almost immediately there was a discreet buzz from the dumb waiter.

"Go and sit at the dining table over there," he said, nodding towards the beautifully laid table. A great silver candelabra glowed on the snowy linen, making the cutlery and glass twinkle. He opened the panel and began to bring dishes of food over. Sylvie watched in a detached way as he looked after her every need, serving her tiny portions, fussing over the napkin on her lap, pouring her some iced water.

"I don't want you getting drunk," he said, smiling. "You can have some more mead later, but I think you've had enough for now, don't you? And see, Sylvie, I'm not over-feeding you any more. This isn't too much, is it? Now we've ordered all those new clothes you mustn't put on any weight or nothing will fit."

She enjoyed the meal and felt her spirits revive as she ate. After a while she began to sparkle. She laughed, joked, teased him, and by the end of the meal had cast aside all her earlier misgivings. She still felt slightly removed from the scene as if somebody else was in her body, but the sensation was quite pleasant. Then Magus got up and took a jewellery box from the mantelpiece.

"I almost forgot. These arrived today. I thought they'd complement that dress."

He opened the box to reveal a necklace and bracelet of opals and diamonds. They were exquisite, gleaming and glittering in the candlelight. Sylvie gasped, unable to speak. She'd never even dreamed of owning such jewels. They must be extremely valuable. She smiled at him incredulously.

189

"Lift your hair from your neck and I'll fasten the necklace," he said gently, smiling at the disbelief on her face. He stood behind her as she raised the mass of hair with both hands. Very carefully he circled her neck with the jewels and closed the clasp, bending to brush the soft skin of her nape with his lips. She shuddered involuntarily and his eyes gleamed.

"Now give me your wrist, Sylvie," he whispered, and started to fasten the beautiful bracelet on her.

"These bruises are so ugly," she said, looking at the livid marks on her slim white arms. "They spoil the effect of the dress and the jewels."

"Oh I wouldn't agree at all," he murmured, kissing the inside of her wrist. He looked into her eyes, his nostrils flaring slightly as he breathed in her scent. "There's something quite intriguing about such juxtaposition."

"What do you mean? You're not saying that you like the bruises, surely?"

"I merely meant they remind me why you should be here with me and not hiding in the woods with some Village boy. Wouldn't you agree?"

"Oh Magus, don't make me say ..."

"Would you really rather be out in the cold now? Can you hear the wind? It's horrible out there. And so warm and cosy in here, so intimate. Come on, if you've had enough to eat. We'll go and sit on the sofa near the fire and keep you warm."

"I've got the pashmina."

"No, don't put that on," he said softly. "I like to see your skin."

They sat together on the leather sofa sipping at another glass of mead as music played softly in the background. Sylvie felt relaxed and happy, mellowed by the mead and fine meal. Magus knew her interests and how to impress her, and chatted easily, engaging her in the conversation and making her laugh. She felt warm and safe in the comfort of his luxurious rooms, with the great log fire burning and the soft leather of the sofa cradling her body. Gradually she curled into him as the effect of the mead overcame any vestiges of shyness. He slid an arm around her and held her gently, careful to keep his touch very light. He looked down at the silver head on his chest and smiled to himself in satisfaction. This was proving easier than he'd imagined.

"I enjoy your company so much, Sylvie. You have such an enquiring mind and you're very well informed for someone so young."

She smiled, her head nestled into him. He stroked her hair softly, enjoying the pure silkiness of it, the way it slipped and entwined itself around his fingers. Then he picked up one of her hands and ran his long fingers from the palm slowly up to the inside of her elbow and back down again, tracing the bruised skin with a touch like swansdown.

"There's one thing that puzzles me, Sylvie."

"What's that?" she murmured, feeling quite sleepy.

"You're such an intelligent girl. You clearly enjoy intellectual conversation, and you've said you find me interesting."

"Mmn?"

She was very relaxed; the touch on her arm was so subtle.

"What do you find to talk about with Yul, I wonder? What has he done, or seen, or read? What does he know? He's never left this estate and barely left the Village. Never read a book, never seen a film. He must be very dull and uninformed. I'd have thought, intellectually at least, you were a million miles beyond him."

Sylvie swallowed. The caressing on her arm stopped. She realised she'd hardly thought about Yul all day. She felt guilty and pulled herself from the comfortable cradle of Magus' arms. Her mass of hair tumbled everywhere as she sat upright, face flushed.

"We always find things to talk about. And often we don't need to talk at all. It's just good being together."

He held up her wrist and examined the bruises. His dark eyes met hers in a mocking gaze.

"I see. And yet despite such spiritual compatibility this strong, silent one manages to inflict these terrible injuries on you. He imprisons you in a cage, cracks you over the head, takes the skin off one side of your body, and almost breaks your ribs as you lie crushed beneath his weight. Do you enjoy him treating you roughly?"

"No, of course not! And it's never happened before. It was only because of the moongaziness. He never meant to hurt me I'm sure."

"I understand. Well, I just hope that he has the intellect and intelligence to satisfy you in the future. There's nothing worse than being saddled with some ignorant dullard who bores you witless. You'll find the Neanderthal brutishness will begin to pall after a while."

She stood up, stung by his sarcasm, and felt the room sway.

"I think I'll go now," she said tightly.

"Alright, Sylvie," he said smoothly. "You do that, if you've had enough of my company. But you should pop into my bathroom first and do something about your hair and your face. Your mother might get the wrong idea if she sees you looking like that."

Angrily she went through to the black marble bathroom and gasped when she saw herself reflected many times over in the gilt mirrors all around her. Her cheeks were very flushed, her eyes unnaturally bright and her hair was messed up all around her head. She did indeed look as if she'd been doing something she shouldn't.

When she returned several minutes later, smoothed and cooled down with cold water, he'd poured them both another drink.

"Just have this before you go," he said, smiling. "I'm sorry, Sylvie. I didn't mean to upset you. I was only teasing. You mustn't rise to the bait. But I really don't think he's worthy of you. A simple Village lout and a princess like you – it's all wrong. You deserve the very best."

"Please don't be nasty about him," she said, accepting the glass from him and sitting down again. "I enjoy coming here while you're getting better, but you know I like him and I don't want to hear you say horrible things about him."

He shrugged.

"I don't like the horrible things he's done to you. Drink your mead."

She swallowed obediently.

"Anyway, how can you call him a simple Village lout? I thought he was your son."

"He is. But he's still a lout. Relax, Sylvie. Stop being cross with me. Come here and snuggle up again. It makes me feel better having you close."

She put her empty glass on the side table, her head spinning. She knew she'd had far too much to drink. The mead was powerful and she wasn't used to drinking alcohol. She rested her head against Magus and he held her lightly. She felt warm and drowsy in the heat from the fire.

"Yul's very like you, you know," she murmured, her eyelids heavy.

"Maybe he is," said Magus softly. "But why make do with a copy when you can have the original?"

Sylvie awoke late the next morning on Magus' sofa, the pashmina draped over her. Her head throbbed and her eyes wouldn't focus at first. She sat up feeling confused, and as the reality of the situation hit her, horribly embarrassed. The clock said it was almost mid-day and there was no sign of Magus. The fire had burnt out but had not yet been re-laid. Her hair hung in her face, and when she looked in the mirror over the mantelpiece, she saw her eyes were smudged dark with mascara. What a mess. She crept back to the Tudor wing, hoping she wouldn't meet anyone on the way. She still wore the evening dress and jewels, and it was obvious she'd spent the night out of her own room. She was lucky. The only person she saw was Martin. He composed his face into a respectful smile as he passed her in the corridor.

"Good afternoon, miss. I hope you slept well."

"Er … yes, thank you, Martin."

"Are the master's rooms now available to be cleaned?"

"Yes, of course. I'm sorry if I held anyone up with their work."

Miranda was waiting in their rooms in fine fettle,

accusations ready to hurl.

"I promise it's not what you're thinking, Mum! We'd eaten dinner, had some mead, and we were sitting on the sofa by the fire. The next thing I knew it was morning. I feel very embarrassed. I must have dropped off to sleep and I've only just woken up. I don't know where Magus is. So don't give me a hard time, please."

Miranda could see Sylvie was telling the truth, but glared at her daughter as she unwrapped the soft pashmina.

"What on earth are those? Are they real?"

She touched the milky opals and brilliant diamonds around Sylvie's throat, her face twisted as if she'd swallowed something sour.

"They were a present. I'm sure they're real. Can you imagine Magus buying fakes?"

Miranda turned away, her throat tight.

"Go and get changed and wash that make-up off your face," she spat. "You look like a slut, Sylvie, coming back in such a mess and dripping with jewels. What on earth would people think if they saw you like this? I hope nobody did see you?"

"Only Martin."

"That's a relief. Hurry up and we'll go down to lunch."

"Oh no, Mum, I couldn't face lunch. My head hurts."

So Miranda went alone to lunch, and then down to the Village for the afternoon to join the women in the Nursery. Sylvie was delighted that she'd started going out again. It was just what her mother needed and would stop her carping on about Magus all the time. Sylvie thought she might go for a walk herself but she still felt sleepy. She had a rest on her bed and before she knew it, Harold was knocking on the door. He carried a couple of boxes and seemed a little awkward with her, clearly not wanting to engage in conversation. There was also another note from Magus, inviting her to join him as soon as possible and stay for dinner. It was getting dark, almost four o'clock, and Sylvie realised she'd slept for most of the day. She felt satiated with sleep, lazy and languorous.

Dressed in another set of new clothes, Sylvie went along to Magus' rooms. He was on the phone but smiled and waved her to the sofa. She kicked off her boots and lay down, picking up a book to read. She could hear Magus' voice in the background, rattling away in a foreign language she didn't recognise.

"Sorry," he said eventually, coming over to her and kissing her briefly on the lips. She recoiled slightly. He usually kissed her cheek. She looked up at him wide-eyed and he smiled down at her.

"You look very well rested. Good night's sleep on my sofa?"

She flushed at this.

"I'm sorry. I don't even remember falling asleep."

"I don't mind. I thought it best to let you sleep on rather than wake you up and send you back to your cold bed. You looked so cosy curled up here by the fire. And it was lovely to watch you while I ate breakfast. I hope Miranda didn't mind."

"Well, yes, she did. But we sorted it out."

"Good. How is she? Will she speak to me yet?"

Sylvie realised that she didn't really want Miranda speaking to him at the moment. She was enjoying coming here every day and Miranda would just complicate things.

"No, she never wants to speak to you again."

He laughed.

"Well that's going to be difficult, seeing as how we live under the same roof. She'll come round, I'm sure. I just don't want her giving you a hard time about anything. You've had a bad experience recently with all the teachers hounding you. If you have any problems with your mother, let me deal with her. I expect she's a little jealous of you at the moment."

"Yes, I suppose she is. She says I'm shallow."

He sat down next to her and put his arm round her, squeezing her affectionately.

"I've never met a girl less shallow than you, Sylvie. Don't listen to her. Oh, by the way, we had a big delivery today. Look over there. All those parcels are for you."

"Wow!!"

She was quite overwhelmed with the amount of things he'd bought her. It hadn't seemed so much when they were sitting at the computer, but there were boxes and boxes, with the clothes inside all beautifully wrapped in tissue paper.

"I don't think it will all fit into my wardrobe," she said, as they stood looking at the piles of unpacked clothes and shoes.

"I thought you might say that," he smiled, passing her a glass of mead. "So I've organised a room for you just down the corridor beyond my bedroom. You can keep all your new things in there. And it'll be a bolt hole for you too if Miranda's on your back. You really don't need a jealous mother going on at you all the time, nagging and telling you off. Pregnant women can be quite irrational at times. You're practically grown up now and you need to be more independent of her."

"Thank you, Magus," she said. "You're so kind to me."

"Not at all. You've given me so much pleasure, Sylvie in the past few days. Buying for you is a delight. I want to buy you the world. Being rich for the sake of it is no fun, but being able to treat you to whatever you want gives me such a buzz."

He poured some more mead and sat working again at his desk for a while. Sylvie lay on the sofa by the fire, sipping her drink and reading. They ate a leisurely dinner and watched a film, and she felt herself becoming drowsy after a while. She knew she should get up and go back to her room, but it was so comfortable here. She curled up against Magus and he stroked her hair and played with the long silky strands. She felt her eyes closing, and he shifted so that she lay more heavily against him. His scent was heavenly and his hands very gentle as they soothed her to sleep. She drifted away.

When she awoke the following afternoon, Magus had just come back from a ride. His cheeks and eyes glowed and he looked bright with well-being. Sylvie had been dreaming about Mother Heggy and the crow. Now, looking at Magus bursting with health and vitality, she realised what a load of rubbish the idea of a banishing spell was. She couldn't believe she'd been ridiculous enough to take it all so seriously. She smiled lazily up at him and stretched, her body arching like a cat's on the sofa. He gazed down, his eyes slowly travelling the length of her.

"Have you been asleep all this time?" he laughed. "You look so content there. No need to get up if you don't want to. Do you want any lunch?"

"No thanks, I'm not really hungry. Just a bit woozy."

"Oh dear, then you won't want this."

He'd brought her over a glass of mead, glowing gold in the weak sunlight that streamed through the windows. Smiling, she took it from him and laid her head back languidly on the pile of silk cushions, sipping its fiery sweetness. She was getting quite a taste for it.

"Let me run you a bath, Sylvie," he said, refilling her glass a little later. "You lie there and I'll call you when it's ready."

She sipped and sighed, wriggling her toes with pleasure, picturing the black marble bathroom. She wondered idly what Miranda was doing today. Probably down in the Village again talking babies. An image of Yul flitted through her brain and she felt a twinge of guilt. She'd hardly thought of him at all in the last couple of days. Her head was so heavy from all the sleep and spoiling. She didn't want to think of him now; it was too much effort. Much easier to finish off her drink and sink into a little snooze whilst Magus ran the bath for her. She closed her eyes and basked in the warmth of the December afternoon sun and the heat of the log fire.

Sylvie must have drifted off for she was awoken by a knock on the door. Magus was still in the bathroom, so she called for the visitor to come in. Hazel entered, her eyes sweeping the room and missing nothing. Sylvie tried to sit up but felt a little dizzy from the mead, so remained spread out on the sofa in disarray. She smiled up at Hazel, hoping she'd be a little friendlier now. The doctor stared down at her stonily.

"Where's Magus?" she asked. She stared at Sylvie lying dreamily in her expensive new clothes, cheeks flushed and silver hair spilling everywhere, an empty glass on the floor beside her.

"In the bathroom I think," said Sylvie, waving vaguely in the direction of the other rooms.

"Are you drunk?"

"No! Of course I'm not."

"Sylvie! Your bath ... oh, Hazel."

Magus strode into the room and frowned at the young woman.

"To what do we owe the pleasure of this visit? I thought I'd always made it very clear that anyone who wishes to see me phones through first on the intercom or checks with Martin that it's convenient. Never just turn up here unannounced."

Hazel gazed up at him, her eyes begging for kindness.

"I'm sorry. I just wanted to make sure that Sylvie was alright."

"Well of course she's alright. Why wouldn't she be?"

"It's just that ... you were concerned about her health before and you wanted me to check her daily. She hasn't turned up for her weigh-in for several days now."

"Oh that!" Magus shook his head. "No, I don't need you monitoring her any more. She's under my personal care now."

"She looks a little thinner," said Hazel, glancing down at where Sylvie lay stretched out.

"She's fine. I've stopped forcing her to eat. It was making her sick. I'm not worried about her weight any more. If she wants to be slim, that's fine by me. Isn't that right, Sylvie?"

She smiled up at him and nodded.

"And are you fully recovered, Magus? You called me in a week ago and asked for anti-depressants. But you're looking well now."

He brushed Sylvie's hair with his fingertips, and Hazel saw the way the girl gazed up at him, her soft grey eyes slightly unfocussed. She was definitely thinner and Hazel understood only too well what was going on here.

"As you say, I'm well now. Fully recovered thanks to Sylvie's attentions. So if that's all, Hazel?"

The doctor turned on her heel, smarting with humiliation. She felt like an intruder on an intimate scene, although it was clear that Sylvie wasn't being coerced into anything. Not yet anyway. Magus was so clever. And the worst thing of all, thought Hazel bitterly, was that she'd have given anything to be in Sylvie's place.

"Sylvie, you're going to have to leave tomorrow."

"No! Why? I don't want to."

It was two days since Hazel's visit and Sylvie still hadn't left Magus' rooms. The hours had passed in a pleasant haze. Sylvie gazed at him now with drowsy eyes, reluctant to make any effort to move at all.

"It's the Dark Moon tomorrow. You need to go to the Great Barn with the other women."

"Oh no, I'd forgotten about that," she groaned. "What a pain. Do I have to go? I really can't be bothered. I want to stay here."

"You'd better go. Tongues will start wagging if you don't. You can come straight back to me in the evenings though, so it won't be too bad. You'll miss me and I'll be waiting here for you. Ready to pamper you."

She twisted on the sofa and looked up into his dark eyes, deep and heavy as he gazed down at her.

He ran his hand down the side of her body as she lay curled against him. He stroked the bones in her hip, down her flanks, then up again into the hollow of her waist and along her arm. He lifted her languid hand and examined her wrist.

"His marks are beginning to fade. I don't ever want anyone else's marks on you again. I don't need to tie you with rope to keep you by my side. We both know you belong to me."

He raised her hand to his lips and she wriggled with pleasure. Sylvie closed her eyes dreamily, sighing. She wanted to sleep now for she felt so lethargic. But he tugged at her hair and pinched her until she opened her eyes again. She could see the muscle in his cheek twitching. She remembered him looking like this before, sitting on her bed in the Tudor wing stroking her hair as he came to say goodnight to her. She'd felt terrified then, and wondered how she could ever have been scared of him. He was so kind and gentle when he was pleased with her. It was easy to control him and keep him happy. She knew exactly what she was doing.

"Let me sleep," she mumbled. "I'm tired."

"You can't be tired. You haven't done anything all week other than lie around in here. Wake up, Sylvie! I need to talk to you."

"What?"

"I don't want you mixing with the Villagers tomorrow in the Great Barn. You will sit with the Hallfolk where you belong. If you're going to be my princess, you must behave accordingly."

"But the Hallfolk girls don't like me."

"Don't be silly. Of course they like you. They may be a little jealous, but just ignore it."

"No really, it's much worse than that. They've been ganging up on me all summer and autumn. They say the most awful things to me. Holly's the worst. She really hates me."

"Does she? Would you like me to send her away?"

She looked up at him startled, her head leaning against his thigh as she lay on the sofa, her hair cascading over his lap. He gazed down at her impassively, one hand lightly fingering her throat and the sharp line of her jawbone.

"What - banish her?"

"Not exactly banish. But I could send her away from Stonewylde to live with her parents in the Outside World. Holly's father is my cousin."

"Would you really send her away just to please me?"

"Sylvie, my angel, when are you going to realise? I would do anything to please you. Anything at all. You only have to say what you want and it's yours."

She smiled, feeling a thrill of power, but shook her head.

"No, don't send her away. She's been awful to me but I can deal with her."

"I'll speak to her, then. I'll speak to all of them. But you're not to sit with the Villagers tomorrow, do you understand?"

His fingers played on her throat, kneading the tender skin gently.

"But Magus, I usually ..."

"No! It stops now. I will give you the earth, Sylvie, but you must obey me. That's the deal. You do as I tell you." He looked down into her eyes. His face was lit by the flickering firelight, hollowing his cheeks and making his dark eyes glow.

"You might see Yul tomorrow."

She looked away, feeling guilty. She'd barely thought about Yul lately. He'd just faded into the background of her consciousness, now that her days and nights were filled with indolence and luxury.

"You understand, don't you Sylvie, that to enjoy all this you will have to give him up completely?"

She didn't respond and kept her eyelids lowered. His thumb traced the outline of her lips.

"Sylvie, you can't expect this level of privilege and still enjoy your bit of rough on the side."

"He's not my bit of rough!"

"Oh I think he is. And Sylvie, there's another thing, while we're on the subject of Yul. I believe he has some silly notion about taking over from me as magus. I've never heard anything more ridiculous! Tomorrow, when you tell him it's finished between you both, you can also tell him this. If there's any nonsense at the Solstice, he'll be banished from Stonewylde."

"You couldn't do that to him!"

"But I could," he said quietly. "I am the magus and I can banish whosoever I wish. I've put up with a lot of aggravation from that boy, but no more. He's overstepped the mark with this." He tapped her wrists. "How dare he prevent you from being with me? Next Moon Fullness, in two weeks' time, we'll be up there at Mooncliffe together, just you and me. I'll do everything in my power to make it less uncomfortable for you. You know I don't want you to suffer. You're to tell him all this tomorrow when you say goodbye to him. Any attempts at a coup and he's out for good. You will do this for me, Sylvie. To please me and to show me that you'll obey me."

She started to sit up. His hand on her throat restrained her, and then resumed its caressing as she sank back down again.

"Don't go, Sylvie. You don't want to go back to that small, cold bedroom and suffer a long lecture from your mother, do you? She hasn't seen you for days and she'll be raring to go.

You know how you like to fall asleep on the sofa with me looking after you. Stay here with me."

"But Magus, I can't obey you," she said in a small voice. "I can't give Yul up. I'm sorry but I just can't."

His mouth hardened and something in his eyes changed, glittering as brilliantly as diamond as he looked down at her.

"Oh come now! Did you really think you could live so intimately with me in my private rooms, with every single thing your heart desires, every need anticipated and served by me personally, and still carry on with that Village boy as well? You surely can't have thought that, Sylvie. You must've realised that if you belong to me, I don't share. You're mine and mine alone. So you won't defy me. You will say goodbye to him tomorrow, and end your ridiculous liaison once and for all. Now let's have a glass of mead and then get some sleep."

He poured Sylvie a large glassful and let her sit up to drink it. Then he laid her back down on the sofa and turned off the lights. He stroked her face and hair in the half darkness of the dying fire, waiting for her to fall asleep so he could go to his bed. His face was tense and angry but this wasn't revealed in his touch.

Eventually he felt her body relax into sleep, and he sighed. They were almost there now. He'd played her so carefully and skilfully. He thought of how easy it was usually, getting what he wanted, and grimaced. Sylvie was different, but what he needed from her was different too. He remembered Jackdaw's words: the toughest nuts to crack are always the sweetest. And he remembered something else he'd heard his own father once say, a long time ago.

A moongazy girl is hard to find, but worth more than all the riches in the world for the unique gift that she brings.

CHAPTER ELEVEN

Magus awoke Sylvie the next morning and made her get off the sofa. She was grumpy, not used to waking up before mid-day now. She refused breakfast and sat in the window seat, wearing yesterday's clothes, with a cup of coffee. Her head ached and she scowled at the floor. Magus had clearly been up and about for a while and was curt and business-like.

"I've spoken to Holly and the other girls. You won't have any more trouble from them. They've gone down to the Barn already. You'd better get down there soon. It's almost ten o'clock."

Sylvie ignored him and stared out of the window. He frowned and moved across to stand over her, his hand heavy on her shoulder.

"Remember what I said last night. Sit with the girls and don't mix with the Villagers other than to be polite. If Yul's hanging around outside waiting for you, you may speak to him for a few minutes. Tell him that it's all over between the two of you. Then come back with the other Hallfolk girls. As soon as you get back, come straight up here to my rooms. I'll be waiting. I've a special present for you tonight. Have you got all that, Sylvie?"

She nodded sullenly, sipping her coffee noisily.

"Stop making that disgusting noise and answer me properly!"

She glared at him.

"Yes!"

He stared out of the window at the grey December morning, then looked back at her.

"Are you sulking because of Yul?"

"No."

"Then what's the matter?"

"My head hurts. And my stomach aches. It is the Dark Moon, you know."

"Of course. I'll get you something for that."

He returned from his dressing room with a pill.

"Poor darling, this'll help you. Now give me a hug and show me you're not sulking."

Reluctantly she stood before him, angry with him and angry with herself. She didn't know what to do about Yul. She was ashamed to admit that she'd hardly thought of him during the past week or so since Magus had been keeping her in his rooms. The days and nights had passed in a blur. She hadn't been able to face up to the fact that this man, with whom she was becoming so intimate, may actually be dead in two weeks' time. The whole thing was barbaric. It just couldn't happen; she had to persuade Yul against it.

And what about Yul himself? Now that she had such a special relationship with Magus, was there any room for Yul in her life? Sylvie dreaded seeing him today and had never imagined she'd feel like that. What was he going to think of her? She'd betrayed him by allowing Magus to lure her into this alternative world of pampering and indulgence. She felt so drowsy. She didn't want to leave the comfort of these rooms to trek down in the cold, wintry morning to the Village. She didn't want to face up to reality. It'd be so much easier and more pleasant just to stay here and go back to sleep in front of the fire.

"Come here, Sylvie."

Magus held out his arms and pulled her in close, kissing the top of her head and holding her against his broad chest. His cashmere jumper under her cheek was soft and he smelt gorgeous. Sylvie put her arms around him and hugged him back. It was like embracing a great pillar of protection. She snuggled her face into his jumper contentedly, feeling her irritability and tension begin to lessen.

"That's better," he murmured. "Don't be grumpy, my sweet girl. It won't be as bad as you think."

He stroked her hair gently, and she found his touch

soothing and reassuring.

"I don't want to go down there!" she said petulantly. "It's cold and grey and I'll have to sit and talk with those girls all day and do stupid sewing or something equally tedious. It's boring and I don't want to go. I want to stay here with you."

"But you have to go, Sylvie. It's the Dark Moon. All menstruating women go to the Barn. You know it's one of our customs. I take it you are menstruating?"

"I usually start around mid-day," she said. "Please let me stay here with you, Magus. You said I could have whatever I wanted and that's what I want. Please?"

He laughed at this, still holding her close.

"You can have whatever you want, of course, but you also have to obey me. I want you to go just to show everyone you're fine. They'll be wondering what's happened to you. And if you don't go they might even think you're pregnant."

Sylvie gulped. That hadn't occurred to her. He smiled at her embarrassment.

"Would you like me to take you down in a car, so you won't get cold?"

She nodded, closing her eyes and clinging on to him. If only she could just curl up on the sofa by the fire and forget everything.

"Go into your room and get yourself ready. Make sure you wear your new clothes and look elegant. I'll drive you down to the Village in fifteen minutes."

The room Magus had given her was a little further down the corridor, and could also be reached through the interconnecting doors of his rooms. It was fairly grand and comfortable, and now full of the gifts he'd bought her. Some of the new clothes hung in the wardrobes but many were still spilling out of their boxes and tissue paper, strewn over the bed. The dressing table was littered with bottles of perfume, cosmetics, make-up sets and the jewellery he'd given her. Shoes and boots lay all over the floor.

The four poster bed remained unslept in. Sylvie spent every night on his sofa by the fire, soothed to sleep by the mead and his touch. She looked around at the mess and knew she should make the effort to at least put away all the expensive things he'd bought her. She sighed. Maybe one of the servants would do it.

Sylvie returned to his sitting room smartly dressed, with her hair brushed and wearing a little make-up to hide the pallor. Magus nodded approvingly, and handed her a glass of mead.

"I know it's a little early in the day, but it'll help you relax until the pill starts to work. And I know how you enjoy mead. This one's brewed with blackberries. Tonight you can have lilac blossom."

Sylvie drank it down, the warm sweet liquid like nectar in her mouth. She loved the way it made her feel so languid and calm. She could live on the stuff.

"You look absolutely lovely, Sylvie. Designer clothes really suit you. Hazel was right, you have lost a little weight this week. I think I prefer you like this, all willowy and thin. The clothes hang perfectly on you, like those beautiful girls one sees on the catwalk. I was wrong to force-feed you and I shan't do it again."

Giving her a final hug, he put the scarlet cloak round her shoulders and led her down the wide staircase to the hall below. Several servants looked up curiously as they came down, but quickly glanced away when Magus' dark eyes rested on them. Sylvie felt odd being out again, having spent so much time closeted in his rooms.

He ushered her through the grand entrance hall and porch, and onto the gravel drive. The silver Rolls Royce was waiting, its engine running quietly. Magus opened the front passenger door for her. Sylvie sank into the fine leather seat, enveloped in the softness of it, savouring the expensive smell. The last time she'd been in this car, she realised suddenly, was the day they'd arrived here. She remembered sitting in the back seat and catching Magus' eye in the driver's mirror as they passed through the gates and entered the world of Stonewylde. As he went round to the driver's seat, she closed her eyes, feeling a little strange and disorientated.

"I love this car," she said as they purred away down the

drive. "It's just perfect."

He chuckled and patted her knee. She felt like a rich man's plaything basking in such luxury, wearing her expensive clothes and perfume.

"After the Yule celebrations I'll take you up to London for a few days. Not the London you know, of course. I'll show you my world. We can shop in Knightsbridge, go to concerts, the ballet and the theatre. Stay in my house in Mayfair. We'll drive up in the Rolls if you like."

She nodded, excited at the thought of such a treat and forgetting the reality of the situation. The drive down to the Village took only minutes in the car. They pulled up on the cobbles outside the Great Barn. Magus switched off the engine and turned to face her. The Village Green looked cold and muddy, the trees encircling it starkly bare except for the dark yew tree. The cottages seemed huddled in on themselves. Smoke rose from every chimney and a cold wind swept the grey skies.

Sylvie's eyes filled suddenly with tears which spilled down her pale cheeks.

"Please don't make me go in there, Magus," she whispered. "I really don't want to do this."

He took her chin in his hand and gazed at her. She was vulnerable and scared, he could see that. He'd groomed her well over the past couple of weeks. He knew how she'd slowly relinquished her loyalty to the boy, lapping up the luxury and flattery he'd heaped upon her and betraying the devotion she'd felt towards his son. Today would be the final cutting of ties. It was painful for her he knew, but he'd handled her expertly and she was ready to do it. It had to come from her. Once she'd broken the bond with the boy, she'd be alone and in need of his nurture and attention. She'd fall into his hand like a ripe peach. There'd be no question of duress. She herself would have made the choice, and would be all the more desperate for affection because of it. And all the more willing to give him what he needed.

"You have to do this, Sylvie," he said softly. "Face the women in the Barn. Show them what you've become – my princess. My favoured one. And if Yul is waiting for you, you must face that too. Just tell him it's all over and then leave. Promise me you won't linger or get drawn into arguments. And swear to me, Sylvie, that you won't go anywhere near him. Don't let him touch you. I absolutely forbid that."

He held her gaze and she saw something new in his eyes; a nakedness that frightened her with its intensity. And Sylvie realized then that maybe she didn't know what she was doing after all. This man's passion was volcanic and she'd made the mistake of thinking she was strolling through foothills.

"Swear to me!"

"I won't let him touch me," she whispered. "I'll say what I have to and come straight home."

She bowed her head and he smiled, exhaling sharply. He patted her leg and leant across her to open the door. A cold blast of air entered the warm cocoon of the Rolls.

"Are you feeling any better now?" he asked solicitously. "Headache and stomach ache gone?"

Sylvie nodded, for they'd vanished and she was floating on a cloud. Her head was light and uncluttered and her body felt hollow and empty but good. She gave him a small smile. Magus leant over and brushed his lips against hers, his breath warm on her mouth.

"Don't let me down today, my moongazy girl. You know this is what you really want. What you were born for."

She slid from the car. With a little wave, and feeling as if her feet didn't belong to her, she pushed open one of the double doors to the Great Barn and went inside. The warmth and noise of many women hit her and she stopped dead, feeling confused. A sea of faces stared up at her, arriving late and looking startlingly beautiful in her scarlet cloak. She stood there, unsure of what to do, overwhelmed by a sense of unreality. But then a group of Hallfolk girls came rushing up to her smiling brightly and all talking at once. They took off her cloak, admiring it, and hung it on the pegs with the other coats. They led her over to where they sat on the cushions, stitching the quilt they'd started last month. They hadn't got very far.

"Are you feeling alright, Sylvie?" asked Dawn, noticing Sylvie's pale face and unfocussed eyes.

"Yes thanks, I'm fine," said Sylvie.

She felt very awkward with them. She caught Holly's eye and the girl gave her a strained smile.

"It's so good to see you again, Sylvie," she said in a high, unnatural voice. "We've been wondering where you were recently."

Sylvie noticed her eyes were red and swollen.

"I don't know why," she replied. "You saw me only last week. In the library, if you remember. You called me an arrogant bitch and said you'd make my life a misery when Magus became bored of me."

Several of the girls gasped at this and Holly stared at the floor, unable to look Sylvie in the face.

"I'm sure she didn't mean it!" said July quickly. "You know how silly Holly can be."

"She meant it alright," said Sylvie. "She's never made any secret of the fact that she hates me."

"That's all in the past now," said Dawn. "Isn't it, Holly?"

Holly nodded, still unable to look up. Sylvie realised she was crying. She shrugged. The scene was becoming increasingly dreamlike as the effects of the pill kicked in.

There was a little silence and then the Hallfolk girls started to make conversation, talking about the planned ski trip due to take place after the Yule celebrations.

"Are you coming, Sylvie? Most of the Hallfolk go every year."

She shook her head, trying to stitch one of the patchwork pieces but finding her fingers weren't working properly.

"I don't think so. Magus has just said we'll be spending a few days in London, but he hasn't mentioned skiing."

The girls exchanged glances at this but were careful to be discreet.

"I love those boots, Sylvie," said Rainbow. "They are gorgeous."

"And your trousers and that top. You look great."

"Thanks."

"Are they all new? Did you go away for some serious shopping?"

"No, Magus bought them for me on the Internet."

"We saw all the boxes being carried up to his rooms and we wondered. Has he bought you lots of stuff?"

"Yes, loads. There's so much it's just lying about everywhere all over my new room."

More glances were exchanged.

"You are lucky, Sylvie."

She looked up at the group of blond girls watching her so carefully, their eyes bright with envy.

"We're really sorry we were horrible to you before," said Wren.

"We were just upset about Buzz being banished," said July.

"We thought it was your fault, but we realise now it wasn't. Magus has told us the truth, and he's explained a lot of things. We're all sorry and we hope you'll forgive us."

"Well, of course. But it really doesn't matter. I don't care."

"It does matter!" said Holly. "I want to be friends, Sylvie. Can I get you a drink?"

She insisted, despite Sylvie's protestations. When she'd gone, Sylvie shook her head.

"Is something up with Holly? She looks like she's been crying all morning."

"She has," said Rainbow. "Magus told us all off, but he really laid into Holly. It was so scary! He grabbed her shoulders and shouted right in her face. He was really loud and nasty. I thought he was going to hit her and so did she. And he said if she was ever mean to you again he'd banish her instantly, just like he did with Buzz. She's very frightened."

"Please don't tell him we told you that," said Dawn, frowning at Rainbow. Sylvie merely smiled and accepted the drink that Holly brought her.

Later on, when she went to the lavatories attached to the Great Barn, Rosie followed her in.

"Blessings, Sylvie! I was hoping you'd sit with us again.

'Twas fun last month."

"I know, I wanted to but I'm under orders today to sit with the Hallfolk girls. I'm sorry, Rosie. I'd much rather be with you."

"Oh well, can't be helped. Not much longer, eh? I've a message from Yul. He's been so worried about you. We've heard all sorts from the servants. 'Tis said you sleep in Magus' rooms every night and never come out."

"I sleep on his sofa."

"Of course, that's what they said."

"How do they know?"

"They go in every morning to clean and lay the fire, and they find you fast asleep on the sofa. They call you Sleeping Beauty."

Sylvie felt annoyed at this.

"It's not really their business where I sleep, is it?" she said stiffly.

"Well, no. Anyway, Yul will be outside at the usual place, he said, just after sunset. He'll come straight down from the Circle. Is that alright?"

"Yes, but Rosie … "

"What's wrong?"

Sylvie shook her head. How could she tell this sweet girl that she was going to finish with her brother this evening? She remembered Rosie's words, spoken back in the summer in this very place, about not hurting Yul. How could she explain this? She cringed with guilt at what she had to do. Her only comfort was in knowing that this way there may possibly be no confrontation at the Solstice.

"Nothing, Rosie. It doesn't matter."

Many Village women started to leave just before the sun set, wanting to get home before dark to start cooking. Sylvie had long given up trying to sew, and was curled on a large floor cushion by one of the fires. She knew that Hazel was looking at her from across the Barn. The doctor had been watching all day, but hadn't approached her. Sylvie's stomach ached with the cramps. The effects of the pill and mead had long worn off.

She felt a little sick and had barely eaten anything. Her headache had returned too. The last thing she wanted now was to have to meet Yul under the yew tree in the cold, dark evening. What was she going to say to him?

"Are you coming back to the Hall now, Sylvie?" asked Dawn, packing up the sewing for tomorrow. Sylvie lifted her head and shook it wretchedly.

"We'll wait for you till you're ready to go."

"Well you'll have to wait a while. I need to see Yul outside a bit later."

"That's alright. We'll wait here like Magus said."

Sylvie shrugged. She didn't really care if she inconvenienced them. Magus had said she must talk to Yul and she knew she had to get it over and done with. How could she face him? What was she going to say? Shivering under her cloak, she left the Barn and crossed the Village Green to the yew tree. It was windy and very cold after the warmth of the Barn.

Yul was leaning against the massive trunk, taller than ever. Sylvie couldn't see his face in the darkness, but as she approached he stood upright and wordlessly pulled her into his arms. He wrapped her in a tight embrace, cradling her as if she were the most precious thing in the world. She stood like a stone carving in his arms, her heart shrieking with despair. She must tell him she no longer wanted him. She must deny everything she'd felt for him; the love between them that had been growing since the spring when she'd first watched him digging her back garden.

Sylvie suddenly recalled the time she'd found him down by the river, wrapped in his cloak of loneliness and misery. She remembered how her heart had cried out to him then, wanting to light the darkness that filled his spirit. The bond between them – that flash of telepathic understanding that had connected her soul to his – now snapped into place. With his powerful arms around her and his heart drumming in her ear, Sylvie could feel his brightness and life-force, the essence of him that called to her and joined them as one. The trappings of Magus started to unravel under the blaze of love that raged inside Yul. Sylvie hugged him back fiercely. How could she even have imagined it was over between them? He felt perfect in her arms.

Yul kissed her gently, murmuring her name, covering her face with small urgent kisses. She melted into him, loving the smell of him, the feel of his skin and hair against hers. His kisses became hungrier. All the old emotions came flooding back as she kissed him deeply, losing herself in the darkness. How could she have forgotten this magic? How could she have ever doubted the strength of their attachment? She clung to him tightly, feeling his leanness and energy. Eventually they pulled apart. He took her face in his hands and peered at her in the darkness. She was trembling violently.

"I've missed you, Sylvie, my moon angel," he said softly. "I love you so much. I've missed you every day, every hour, every single minute. You've been in my mind all the time."

He bent and started to kiss her again, saving her from having to lie to him. For Sylvie hadn't thought of him constantly, nor had she missed him. She'd denied him, betrayed him. She'd agreed to give him up forever. Her mother had been right all along. She was shallow. Shallow and naive, easily swayed by Magus and his excessive wealth and generosity. A few new outfits and she'd dropped Yul as if their love was nothing. She hated herself. Then she remembered the girls waiting in the Barn, and Magus waiting up at the Hall, and reluctantly pulled away.

"Yul, I don't have long. The Hallfolk girls are in the Barn and I've got to walk up with them. He's waiting for me."

"I bet he is," muttered Yul. "I've heard about how you're virtually a prisoner in his rooms. He hasn't hurt you, has he?"

"No, no, not at all. He's been very kind to me."

"Bastard! Remember what he's done to all of us. Don't get taken in by him, Sylvie."

Too late for that, she thought. She took one of his hands in hers and held it to her cheek. She'd forgotten the raw energy of Yul; the feeling that together they could set the world alight. She'd forgotten the sheer excitement and magnetism of him.

"Yul, I'm sorry. I've got to tell you something. I can't go

through with our plan. Things have changed. You mustn't kill Magus. You can't. I know he's treated you badly but you really can't kill him. I don't want to be a part of it."

"What?" he said incredulously. "Treated me badly? Sylvie, he tried to kill me! If you could have seen him at Samhain in that labyrinth. He was going to burn me alive. And before that, up at Mooncliffe. He stuffed so many cakes down my throat I nearly died of poisoning. And that's not to mention what he did to me in the byre back in the summer. If I don't kill Magus this Solstice, he'll kill me. It's that simple. Is that what you want?"

"No, of course not. But I don't think he feels like that any more. It's different now. As long as you don't try to take him on, he won't do anything to you. I'll speak to him; make him promise he won't hurt you. He'll do what I ask. He wants to please me."

He pulled away from her angrily, his eyes flashing in the gloom.

"Are you completely daft? He doesn't want to please anyone but himself. Whatever he says to you will be a lie. You're back under the spell, aren't you? I thought Clip wasn't going to do that again."

"No, you're wrong. I haven't even seen Clip."

"Then Magus has put his own spell on you. He's been working on you. Has he talked to you about the next Moon Fullness, by any chance?"

"Well yes, but ..."

"There you are then! That's all he's interested in – feeding on your moon magic. He knows he has to get it this month or he's finished."

"Stop being silly, Yul. Yes, he does want me to go up there with him, but it's not as drastic as you make out. I was thinking, if I just went up with him this month to keep him happy, then I ...."

"Sacred Mother!" he shouted, spinning around and stamping his boot into the ground. "What has he done to you? Have you forgotten already what it feels like when you're standing on that rock? Don't you remember how much it hurts you? He's tricked you, Sylvie. I don't know what he's been saying to you but you're under his influence. You MUSTN'T go up there with him! If he gets your moon magic then I'm dead. He'll be too powerful for me. Please, Sylvie, listen to me!"

He grabbed hold of her shoulders and shook her. She shrugged him off angrily.

"Don't touch me like that! I've only just about healed from the last time you had a go at me. Don't start manhandling me again!"

He stepped back and stared at her, unable to read her expression in the near darkness. All was silent save for his uneven breathing as he struggled to control himself.

"I'm sorry I hurt you last month, Sylvie. You know why it happened."

"I know you didn't want Magus to take me to Mooncliffe. But you didn't have to be so brutal! I know what you're like now, Yul. I've seen photos of what you did to Buzz. They were absolutely horrific. You obviously have a violent streak, and I think maybe you're more of a danger to me than Magus is."

Yul hung his head.

"I never meant to hurt you. You hurt me too that night, you know. You attacked me and almost knocked me out. I had to get you in the cage else you'd have run off into the woods. And as for Buzz – I know I gave him a bad beating, but he'd have done the same to me if he'd got in first. He was much heavier than me, remember. I had to go in hard and bring him down before he got the upper hand. And he had it coming, Sylvie. If you could've seen the way he'd beaten me over the years, when we were younger. He's always been so much bigger and stronger than me. He was a great big blond Hallfolk boy and I was always quite small and skinny. He used to bring his gang along and get them to hold me down while he hit me. He deserved everything I did to him that day, believe me."

"Maybe he did. But there's another side to you I didn't know about. I won't go along with this violence. I won't be part of killing Magus. It's barbaric, all this talk of killing. Magus is a civilised, educated man and you're not. He's shown me a different world and I'm not sure of anything any longer."

Yul stood before her silently. He reached out to her but she brushed his hand away impatiently.

"Don't you love me any more, Sylvie?" he asked, his voice strangled with pain. "What's happened?"

"I don't know. I thought … I'm just not sure now. I'm sick of this conflict. I'm being torn in half."

"But you said … I thought we loved each other? I thought we belonged together? Sylvie, please! Without that there's nothing. You're the reason I must do this."

"*No I'm not*! I'm not some prize to be fought over! And don't use me as an excuse to justify your violence. I don't want to know any more. I was going to finish with you tonight, Yul. I'm sorry but that's the truth. Magus persuaded me. Then when I saw you and we kissed … I realised I still loved you. But that's not a good enough reason for this battle of yours with Magus. He's not a bad man, not deep inside. There's another side to him I've seen now. He's kind and he's fun. And he's your father, for goodness' sake! Why can't we sort this out? I could …"

But he'd turned away, choking on his tears. He'd never expected this. He stumbled a few steps away from her and sank to his knees on the earth, hunched over and crying into his hands. Sylvie looked at him helplessly. She still felt sick and hollow, as if she wasn't really there at all. Her head throbbed mercilessly.

"I've got to get back, Yul. There'll be trouble if I'm out any longer. I'm so sorry to upset you. Maybe we can talk tomorrow if I can slip away."

She went over to him and put her hand on his shoulder. He shook with silent sobs as if his heart was breaking.

"I never once doubted you," he choked. "I never thought you'd do this to me. You were the one person in my life I counted on …"

"Please, Yul, stop! I do love you. It's just … I can't agree with this killing. Magus has been good to me. He cares for me."

He cried out at this and leapt to his feet, angrily wiping his face with the butt of his palms.

"You've been deceived, Sylvie! He's evil and he's going to make you suffer. How can you be so *blind*? If you ..."

"I've got to go. He'll be cross if I don't get back."
She started to walk away, her stomach aching and head pounding.

"Sylvie! Come back tomorrow! We can't leave it like this. Tomorrow mid-day. I'll be waiting. Promise me you'll come."

"I'll try," she said over her shoulder. "But I can't promise."

"She's turned against me!" Yul cried, sinking onto the hard chair. "She doesn't love me like she did. What can I do?"

He felt a wrenching pain in his chest that stifled his breath. Mother Heggy nodded in sympathy. She rocked in her chair, a thick hairy shawl clutched around her and the familiar shapeless hat pulled low on her head. On her feet she wore ancient hobnailed boots and her dress was little more than a thick grey sack reaching her ankles. Somebody kind had recently knitted her some fingerless mittens. They covered her gnarled hands, leaving only the filthy nails poking out like horny talons. The skin on her face was furrowed like a field and just as dirty. Her features had caved in on themselves, so her nose curved into her puckered mouth and her whiskered chin rose up to meet her nose. She was very old indeed. The crow perched precariously on the back of her chair. Its beady black eyes blinked rapidly and its sharp beak nodded in time with her rocking.

"She still loves you as always, my dark one," Mother Heggy wheezed. "She's deceived, but not for ever. He cannot mask the evil for ever. She will shine clear. Have faith in her, my boy."

"But she's fallen under his spell! I can't stand it knowing she's with him night and day. He's so powerful and clever and she's only a young girl. She's too open and trusting. She has no idea just how evil he is. I can't bear it!"

"Two weeks, Yul. Only two more weeks. But she still has much to endure, the poor child. Trapped in his golden cage. 'Tis as well she is strong and clever herself."

"Tonight she brushed me off. She said she might go to Mooncliffe with Magus to keep him happy."

"NO!" screeched Mother Heggy. "Oh no, she must not do that! She is in danger. Five, I see - always five."

"Five what? What do you mean?"

"In the leaves, in the bones, in the ashes and in the runes and cards. Everywhere that I seek the truth, I see five. Five deaths at Stonewylde this Solstice. Not one, but five!"

Yul stared at her in horror. Her face was creased into an expression of fear and bewilderment as she rocked in her chair.

"Five deaths? Are you sure, Mother Heggy? Who will die?"

"I don't know. Maybe 'tis not yet decided. But Sylvie must not go to Mooncliffe! 'Twould give him the power and strength to fight you and maybe defeat you. And 'twill be the Moon Fullness in the Winter Solstice. The brightness in the darkness. The moon magic will be more powerful than ever, and maybe strange too as 'tis during an eclipse. You recall what happened to my poor Raven up there at the eclipse. The same may happen to Sylvie, if he gets her on that rock. Remember my words, Yul. Five deaths!"

CHAPTER TWELVE

When Sylvie returned to Magus' rooms, weary and depressed, he had everything ready as promised. She was ushered straight into his black marble bathroom where the circular bath brimmed with hot, fragrant foam. She slipped into the water with a groan of relief, and lay there sipping mead. All she wanted was to block the horrible events of the day from her mind and forget everything. Much later she emerged, glowing and relaxed, wearing a pair of black silk pyjamas he'd laid out for her. They were newly arrived that day; a brief camisole top with shoe-string straps and wide, loose trouser bottoms. She wrapped her hair in a white towel and carried the empty glass back into the sitting room. Magus was on the sofa reading some papers but rose as she padded in on bare feet.

"Sylvie, you are exquisitely beautiful," he murmured, pouring her another drink. He sat on the sofa and pulled her down onto a cushion at his feet. He unwrapped the turban, and with a large comb started to detangle her hair as the warmth of the blazing log fire dried it to pure silver silk. Sylvie became drowsy from the heat, the hot bath and two large drinks on an empty stomach.

"Are you hungry yet?" he asked, still playing with her hair, teasing it out so the strands slipped around his fingers.

"No, not at all," she mumbled, eyes closed. "Just sleepy."

"Lie down here while I eat then," he said. "I'm starving. Come and join me if you change your mind. When I've finished I'll give you that special present."

She nodded and crawled onto the sofa, falling instantly asleep on the soft leather.

Later, when Magus had finished dinner, he took his glass

over and looked down at her curled up fast asleep. The black camisole top showed off her pale arms and shoulders to perfection. Her hair tumbled around her delicate face, flushed slightly from the heat. He closed his eyes briefly and took a deep breath. Then he sat beside her and smoothed the hair off her face, calling her name. Eventually she opened her eyes, drowsy and confused.

"Wake up, my darling girl. Are you sure you don't want to eat?"

She shook her head, still half asleep.

"I've got you some more mead here."

She was so sleepy, taking the glass with numb fingers and nearly spilling it.

"Steady," he said, holding the mead to her lips. "Just drink it down so I can get rid of the glass. There, good girl."

She could barely sit up and leant against his shoulder, her hair spilling over his chest and into his lap. Magus held her close, stroking her slim bare arm. Her skin was as silky as her hair. He felt a jolt of pleasure at the beautiful perfection of her; at the possession of such a prize.

"Now tell me, Sylvie," he murmured, "everything that happened while you were away from me. I missed you today. I've grown used to keeping you by my side."

He had to shake her to keep her awake, and in a muddle she began to tell him about her day in the Barn.

"So the girls were friendly, were they?" he asked. "Did they treat you well?"

"Yes," she mumbled. "They were nice to me."

"And Holly? Was she suitably contrite? She bloody well better've been, after what I said to her."

"Yes, she was alright."

"Only alright? In that case, I'd better have another word with her in the morning."

"She tried hard to be friendly."

"And so she should."

Then came the part she'd been dreading. Sylvie couldn't think straight but knew that she must. The room was spinning and she felt very confused, her mind a jumble of what had really happened and what she should say had happened. All she could think of was Yul on his knees sobbing silently into his hands.

"And Yul? You were back late, so you must've spoken with him. What happened?"

"Nothing," she said quickly. Too quickly. "Nothing at all. He just said he'd missed me."

"Missed you? Did you tell him it was over between the two of you?"

"Yes, yes I did."

"And was he upset?"

"Yes, very upset."

"Did he get close to you? Did he touch you?"

"No," she whispered, keeping her head down. She sat very still, hardly daring to breath.

"So he didn't even try to get close? I can't believe that. I don't think you're telling me the truth, Sylvie," said Magus softly. "Did he try to kiss you?"

Even in her confused state she sensed the edge to his voice and how his body had tensed like a steel coil.

"No."

"DON'T LIE TO ME!" he shouted, turning on her and grabbing her arms hard. He shook her and she flopped like a rag doll, her hair flying out about her. He released her suddenly and she shrank back into the corner of the sofa, huddling as small as she could, her eyes now wide open. He leaned over her until his face was only centimetres away from hers. His black eyes glittered dangerously, boring into her terrified gaze. She bowed her head.

"I'll ask you again, and you'd better tell me the truth this time. Did he kiss you?"

"Yes," she whispered, unable to meet his eye.

Magus took a deep breath.

"Look at me, Sylvie. Look at me! That's better. Now tell me this. When he kissed you, did you enjoy it?"

She stared at him like a rabbit caught in headlights, trembling and white-faced.

"Yes," she whispered once more.

He grabbed her upper arms again very hard, deliberately squeezing and pinching the soft flesh in a grip like a vice. She cried out in pain but didn't dare try to pull away. He kept her gaze locked into his as he dug his fingers viciously into her skin.

"You will never kiss him again," he said, very softly. "You've let me down, Sylvie. You've disappointed me. I won't forget this. I hope you told him you'd be spending the Moon Fullness with me."

"Yes," she gasped. Her upper arms were agony and she whimpered in distress. With a final sharp dig, he let go.

"Good. And now, my moongazy girl, let me give you your present. Not that you deserve it. I should be punishing you for disobeying me, not giving you gifts. But this is the Dark Moon and I want you to have this tonight."

Magus reached down and picked up a large square jewellery box, with an exclusive Bond Street jeweller's name and logo embossed in gold leaf onto the velvet. Sylvie sat hunched in fear, her arms on fire with pain, trying not to cry. Smiling at her as if he'd never hurt her at all, Magus carefully opened the box to reveal a necklet such as she'd never seen before. In the firelight it sparkled with a fire of its own that dazzled the eye. It was a choker, very high and studded with hundreds of diamonds, each one glittering with prismatic light. It was open and she saw four long clasps that slid into holes on the other side to fasten it. There was a tiny gold key too, nestling in the velvet, with its own chain. With delicate fingers Magus picked the collar up and opened it fully.

"Sit up, girl," he commanded. "Lift your hair off your neck."

He reached across and fitted it round her throat. He snapped it shut, and she heard the clasps sliding in and clicking into the holes. He took the key and locked it shut. The thick collar was a snug fit around her slim neck and twinkled beautifully as it caught the light.

"Now let your hair go. Oh yes, that is exquisite. Do you like it, Sylvie?"

"Yes, thank you very much," she croaked.

"That's good. Because now I've locked it, you won't be able to get it off again. It's on permanently unless I choose to unlock it. Which I don't intend to do, seeing as it cost me thousands and thousands." He put the chain round his neck and slid the key under his shirt. "I'm having two wrist bands made for you as well, to match your collar. You'll sparkle like a princess. And you'll never forget that you belong to me. What do you think of that, Sylvie?"

She shook her head in confusion, still unable to believe what he'd just done to her.

"I don't ... I mean, thank you, Magus. Thank you."

"Poor child, you sound so dry. I'll let you have just one more drink and then you can lie down and go to sleep."

He poured her another glass and watched as she drank it down. Her head was really spinning now, the room going in and out of focus. Her stomach was hollow with hunger and the tops of her arms throbbed. He gazed at her with heavy eyes that gleamed darkly.

"Are you feeling alright, Sylvie? There, just lie down here and let me stroke your hair, how you like it. You go to sleep now, there's a good girl."

He ran his fingertips down the purple bruising that had appeared in blotches and lumps on the delicate white skin of her upper arms.

"You do bruise easily, don't you, my sweet? I didn't mean to mark you, but you have to understand what happens if you disobey me. I'd warned you that you couldn't carry on with that boy, yet you deliberately defied me. I get angry, Sylvie, very angry, if people disobey me. You'll have to learn your lesson, my darling. Now go to sleep."

She was awoken by a kiss on each eyelid and smiled, dreaming still of Yul who'd haunted her all night. She slowly opened her eyes and found herself staring into black eyes that seemed to suck her soul into a maelstrom of darkness. She blinked in shock and recoiled.

"Good morning, my dearest girl. Feeling better today, I hope?"

Sylvie struggled to sit up, the black pashmina with which he covered her every night falling off and her blonde hair tumbling about her in a tangled mass. She felt terrible, her head pounding and stomach hurting. Her throat was as dry as bark.

"Good morning," she mumbled, blinking at him in the bright morning sunlight. It was far too early for her.

"Go and have a quick shower and get dressed," he said. "I'll start breakfast without you, if you don't mind. I've been up for ages and I'm hungry."

She sat up, holding her head in her hands. The heavy diamond collar felt strange round her neck, rubbing the tender skin sore.

"Hurry up, Sylvie. The girls have gone down to the Barn already. I'll give you a lift again if you get a move on. Oh, and make sure you cover those arms up. I don't want everyone seeing how angry you made me."

When she returned to the table, feeling a little fresher and much more awake, there was hardly anything left to eat. Sylvie felt very hungry, having eaten virtually nothing the day before.

"Can I ring for some more please?" she asked, gulping down coffee and the one remaining croissant. Magus looked up from the newspaper he was reading, the harsh sunlight etching shadows and hollows on his handsome face.

"Oh no, Sylvie, there isn't time now. You should be down at the Barn already. But look, there's plenty of coffee left. Actually, I've just thought – I've got some cakes here. If you're hungry still, have one of these."

He passed her over a cake tin and she looked at the speckled cakes inside.

"But aren't these the special ceremony cakes?" she asked, remembering what had happened that night to Yul up at Mooncliffe.

"No, they're just some saffron cakes that Marigold makes for me. They're delicious. But if you don't want one …"

"Yes, I do, please. I'm starving."

He put one onto her plate and watched as she ate it,

washed down with coffee. He smiled, folding the newspaper, and got up from the table.

"Good girl. Right then, let's get you down to the Barn. Your collar looks beautiful, by the way. It's catching the sunlight and sparkling everywhere."

She touched the heavy band round her neck and found she couldn't look him in the eye. He was acting as if nothing had happened last night; as if he hadn't hurt her at all. If he'd only say sorry for losing his temper or show some remorse for his cruelty. But the most frightening thing was that he hadn't actually lost his temper. The viciousness had been controlled. Sylvie wanted to confront him about it. She wanted to protest at the outrageous way that he'd treated her, but she simply didn't dare.

"It was very generous of you, Magus. Thank you."

"You know I like to spend money on you. Just make sure you deserve it. No more disobedience today or this time you will certainly be punished. If the boy's out there at the end of the day, ignore him and come straight home to me. Don't even speak to him. Do you understand?"

"Yes."

Sylvie stood up, desperate to get out of the room that was transforming all around her into a cage. Magus came round the table and took hold of her shoulders, looking deep into her pale grey eyes. She was unable to look away. There was something different about him today. A dark fire that she hadn't noticed before.

"You haven't apologised yet for making me so angry with you last night."

His hands slid deliberately down from her shoulders to her slim upper arms. He held them lightly, exerting a subtle pressure on the swollen, bruised skin. Sylvie flinched and her eyes widened. She saw his black eyes, fixed on hers, register her pain. Something flared inside him. She saw it clearly. And in that split second he lost her forever. She could never forgive that flicker of pleasure. With a small squeeze, making her gasp sharply, he smiled.

"Well?"

She wanted to cry.

"I'm very sorry. Sorry I made you angry."

"That's better. Make sure you behave appropriately today and remember what I said to you last night. I won't be so lenient if you ever disobey me again. Come on then, we must get going."

Sylvie got through the morning in a blur, everything seeming strangely unreal. Some of the women appeared weird and distorted, but when she looked twice, returned to normal. The Hallfolk girls were all over her again and Holly was even more upset than yesterday. She had a red mark across her face, with four points bright against her cheek. Every time Sylvie looked up at her, the mark seemed to pulsate like a blood-red jelly fish. Sylvie knew that she wasn't right. It must be the cake Magus had given her, for why else would she be floating like a ghost above the ground?

"What happened to your face, Holly?" she asked in a voice that didn't sound like hers. Holly stared at the floor.

"It was Magus," piped Rainbow. "He told her off again this morning, and when she tried to say something back he slapped her hard round the face. He was really horrible. We don't envy you, Sylvie, being alone with him up in his rooms day and night. We used to think you were so lucky, but not any more. Magus is a bit of a monster, isn't he?"

"Ssh!" hissed Dawn, looking worried. "Don't say things like that, Rainbow. Holly's fine."

"Yes, I am," said Holly quickly. "I'm fine. Nothing's wrong at all."

As mid-day approached, Sylvie wondered how she was going to get outside to see Yul without anyone noticing. The effects of the cake were beginning to wear off but everything still appeared slightly surreal. Hazel came over to where Sylvie lay on the cushions, gazing up at the rafters in a daze while the girls chattered around her. The doctor loomed overhead, and Sylvie stared up at her face. Time slipped and she imagined she was back in her London hospital bed with the intern doing her rounds.

"Good morning, doctor. How are you today?"

Hazel crouched down and scanned Sylvie's face, her expression concerned. She took one of Sylvie's wrists and felt the pulse.

"What's happened to you, Sylvie? What's been going on?"

"I've been very silly," she muttered. "I got it all wrong. I made a big, big mistake."

"Are you eating? What's he given you? Your pupils are dilated. Sylvie, can you understand me?"

She nodded weakly.

"I'm alright. I'm sorry Magus doesn't want you any more, Hazel. I saw your eyes the other day. You're hurting badly."

Hazel looked away.

"We've all made a big mistake, I think," she said quietly, "and learnt our lesson. But I'm worried about you, Sylvie. Tell me what he's been doing to you."

"It's alright. The Solstice will be here soon."

"What? You're hallucinating, aren't you?"

The doctor stood up, uncertain what to do for the best. She knew the girl had been drugged, and she'd seen her drunk the other day. But what could she do? Magus was not to be challenged by anyone, even the doctor.

"It's okay, Hazel. Really. Don't worry about me."

Shaking her head, Hazel glanced down at the prone girl in consternation.

"I'll go and see your mother tonight when I get back. We'll sort something out. You can't carry on like this. You shouldn't be alone with him in his rooms."

The time came for lunch to be served, and Sylvie saw an opportunity to get out while everyone queued up for food. She was upset to be missing lunch because she was very hungry, but it couldn't be helped. She must see Yul. While the girls went over to the food tables she went to the lavatories, and then slipped out of a side door.

It was a cold December day and she hadn't put on her cloak, knowing she was less obvious without it. She walked quickly round the Green on unsteady legs, keeping close to the trees so as to be unobtrusive, and reached the yew. The branches hung down so low and thickly it was impossible to see underneath to the trunk. But as she ducked under a bough she saw Yul's boots and her heart jumped with relief.

It was wonderful to see his face again, for last night she hadn't seen him clearly at all. His hair was longer, hanging down in curls almost to his shoulders, and he looked somehow older. His eyes were clear and bright as they fixed on her. She read the anguish in his look, the fear of being hurt all over again. She stumbled towards him and he took her tentatively in his arms. As she clung to him she felt his heart beating wildly against her.

"Yul, I really only have a few minutes," she mumbled against his chest. "I've got to be back soon. I can't risk him finding out I've seen you today. Yul, please!"

The desperation in her voice made him pull away and look carefully at her.

"Are you alright, Sylvie? Your eyes look funny. What's happened?"

"He gave me a cake for breakfast. I think it was the same as the ones he forced you to eat. I feel strange."

Yul's face darkened with anger. He took her by the arms and she winced, yelping with pain.

"What? Did I hurt you?"

He rolled up one of the sleeves of her jumper, blanching as he saw the faded bruising on her forearms.

"Is that what I did to you?" he whispered.

She nodded. He pulled the sleeve up higher and saw the fresh, livid marks on her upper arm, swollen into welts and turning black now as the bruises started to develop fully. She felt him shaking.

"He's done this to you? That's it! I'm going to get him right now! I ..."

"No, wait! Wait till the Solstice, when the time's right. I'll be okay. He did this because I kissed you yesterday. As long as I obey him he won't hurt me, Yul. It's better to hold on as we planned. But I must go now. If he finds out from the girls

228

that I've seen you he really will do something awful to me, I know it. I'm so sorry about yesterday. I was wrong and I've been stupid. He deceived me, made me think he was kind and caring. He's almost impossible to resist when he's being nice and I was taken in by him. But I saw something in his eyes today. Something that I won't forget."

"I can't let you go back to him, Sylvie," said Yul desperately, holding her close. "You're not safe."

"I am, really, and it's only for what … twelve days now? I can manage that." She gently extricated herself from his arms.

"Goddess, I want to kill him!" muttered Yul. "I can't bear to think of you trapped in there with him."

"It's alright. I'll be fine and at least he's off your back. But be careful and Yul, whatever happens … make sure he doesn't get me at the Moon Fullness, please. You were right. He's counting on taking my moon magic to power himself up. And I don't want to give it to him ever again."

Nobody seemed to realise she'd been missing, but her rumbling stomach was a nuisance all afternoon. Holly spent a great deal of time trying to be friendly, falling over herself to be nice to Sylvie.

"Holly, you're trying too hard. Leave me alone."

"Sorry. But please don't push me away, Sylvie. I want to be friends. I'm so very sorry for all the things I said to you. Please don't hate me."

"I don't hate you," said Sylvie wearily.

Holly looked at her with frightened eyes. Sylvie didn't have the heart to enjoy her victory over the erstwhile bully. Holly was too pathetic to gloat over. When it was time to leave, Sylvie got ready with the other Hallfolk girls and they left together. Nobody noticed the tall, blond man waiting silently in the shadows by the side of the Great Barn. He smiled as Sylvie headed straight up the track towards the Hall, and urged the black stallion onto the Green for a circuit of the trees. It was as well for Sylvie that she hadn't thought to slip away and disobey him. He'd have caught her red-handed.

The next few days passed by slowly for Sylvie, still being kept prisoner in Magus' rooms. He decided she needn't go to the Great Barn for the full four days, as not everyone did. Now that Sylvie had seen through Magus' false charm, she became more aware of how she was being manipulated. She was underfed and hungry, drunk and drugged, and constantly sleepy from the roaring fire and hot baths. She knew it was all part of the control he was exercising over her to keep her weak. He didn't want her to think lucidly or stand up to him. He needed her compliant and docile as the full moon and the Solstice approached. But she thought that if she went along with it, he wouldn't hurt her again. He'd believe his plan was working and wouldn't bother Yul either. It was just for the next few days. Soon they'd all be free of him forever. Any qualms she'd had about finishing him off had vanished.

One afternoon Clip came knocking on the door. Sylvie hadn't been awake long and was curled up trying to read a book. She'd already had two glasses of mead. There'd be no food until dinner that evening, unless she asked for a cake. Her stomach hurt badly and her hands shook. She couldn't focus on the page. Magus sat working at his desk in the corner of the room, well away from the blazing fire. He'd barely spoken to her today. Some days he was all over her, unable to resist stroking her and playing with her hair. Other days he was curt and cold and seemed almost to hate her. She didn't know which frightened her the most.

When the knock came, Magus looked up sharply, annoyed at being disturbed. He was even angrier to see Clip, who breezed into the room and sat down on the sofa without waiting to be invited.

"I'm busy, Clip," he said tersely. "I'll have to see you some other time."

"Don't worry, it's just a social call. I'll talk to Sylvie."

He smiled at her, but his eyes registered shock at the sight of her. She blinked at him, confused and not sure if he was really there. She was sure her food last night had been spiced and she was still seeing strange things.

"Are you alright, Sylvie? Your mother's been worried about you. She hasn't seen you for ages."

"I'm fine thank you," mumbled Sylvie.

"You've lost a lot of weight since I last saw you. Are you eating enough?"

Magus strode over from his desk and perched on the arm of her chair. He rested his hand proprietarily on her shoulder and glared at his half-brother.

"Of course she's eating enough! She's fine, and you can tell Miranda that. Was there anything else?"

"Yes, I'd like to take Sylvie for a little walk to stretch her legs. It's very hot and stuffy in here. Do you fancy that, Sylvie?"

"No she doesn't!" said Magus sharply. "She's perfectly happy here."

"I would like some fresh air," she whispered, and Clip noticed how Magus's hand on her thin shoulder tightened into a white-knuckled grip. She closed her eyes and winced.

"Then we'll go for a walk later," Magus said smoothly. "I'm expecting a very important call any minute from Japan, which is going to take some time. I really can't leave the room right now."

"I wasn't asking you to come, Sol," laughed Clip, and held his hand out to Sylvie. "Come on, young lady. Put your shoes on and get your cloak. It's quite mild out today."

Magus started to protest angrily but then the phone rang and there was nothing he could do. Clip quickly hustled Sylvie out, supporting her discreetly as she stumbled and swayed against him.

"For Goddess' sake, what's he done to you?" he muttered furiously as they hurried towards the stairs. "We'll go to your mother's rooms. Cherry!"

He'd seen Cherry below in the hall, and half carried Sylvie down the stairs.

"Cherry, I'm taking her over to Miranda in the Tudor wing. We don't have a lot of time. Get her something to eat quickly – anything - and bring it there, would you?"

"Yes, sir, yes," said Cherry. "Poor little mite."

Miranda hugged Sylvie as if she would snap her in half. Then she held her daughter at arm's length and surveyed her carefully.

"I've been so worried about you, darling. Oh, look at the state of you! It's even worse than Hazel told us. Is she drunk, Clip?"

He nodded, guiding the swaying girl to an armchair in the tiny sitting room. She sank gratefully into its depths, a pathetic huddle with her pale face and vague eyes.

"He's obviously dosing her up with mead to keep her quiet and obedient. Hazel was right. And Yul's told us about the cakes. I know only too well just what they can do to you. Is that right, Sylvie? Has he been feeding you too much mead and those special cakes? "

She closed her eyes wearily as the sitting room revolved around her like a carousel.

"And I'm so hungry," she whispered. "I've barely had anything to eat in the past few days. He's starving me."

"He always goes too far!" Clip barked angrily. "I understand he wants you where he can keep an eye on you, but there's no need for this cruelty. Can't he see how he's damaging your health?"

Miranda took one of Sylvie's limp hands in hers.

"I can't bear to see you like this. Has he hurt you?"

"No, not really. He says I'm his princess. He's given me so many presents. Don't worry, Mum."

"But I do! I hate you being in there at his mercy. It's not right. I think ..."

There was a knock and Cherry bustled in with a tray.

"'Tisn't much. I hope this will do," she said, and stood back to watch as Sylvie devoured the sandwiches and glass of milk. Her plump face was filled with concern and she shook her head in disapproval.

"Miss Sylvie, I could leave food in that room he's given you," she said. "I was thinking - I can get in there through the door from the corridor. I've got a key on my master key-ring. I could leave the food hidden somewhere."

Sylvie looked up at Cherry with unfocussed eyes and

nodded slowly.

"Would that work, Sylvie?" asked Clip gently. "Can you go to your room for a little while to eat, without Magus noticing?"

"I don't know... I sleep on his sofa and I use his black bathroom. I spend all day and evening in the big sitting room with him. I'm only allowed to go into my room to get dressed when I wake up. But Magus goes in there too every day. He always lays out the clothes that he's chosen for me to wear each day."

"I'll be careful," Cherry promised. "I'll leave a tray under the bed. He'd never look there. 'Twon't be much, but more than you're getting now."

"Thank you, Cherry," said Clip. "That'll really help."

Miranda leant over to kiss her pale daughter, tears in her eyes.

"Sylvie, I'm so very sorry about everything. I've failed you. I've let you down and now ..."

"Don't, Mum. I'm sorry too. I was horrible to you. I must have hurt you so much."

"We've both been manipulated and used. But he won't come between us again." She turned to Clip. "We've got to get her out now. I can't stand by and let him do this."

"But Miranda, you know what we've all agreed. Whilst Sylvie's staying in his rooms, he's staying in there too. You know we said that ..."

"I don't care! I can't bear this. She's not safe with him."

"I honestly believe she is," he said, concern creasing his craggy face. "It's not in his interest to harm her, not with the Moon Fullness so close. He's keeping her quiet and weak, but he won't harm her. We need him complacent and convinced that all is well. If we take Sylvie out now, he's going to be furious and then he'll start snooping about. We can't have him doing that and discovering what's going on. Not now the Solstice is so close. There's too much at stake here to alter our plans now."

"But what if ..."

"Mum, I'm alright, really," interrupted Sylvie, a bit

brighter now she'd eaten some food. "Please, I want to do my bit to help. What's been going on? Have you got everything organised for the Solstice? What's going to happen?"

"Oh Miss Sylvie, 'tis so exciting!" said Cherry, clasping her chubby hands together. "There's all sorts o' ..."

"Ssh, Cherry," said Clip. "It's best Sylvie doesn't know what's planned. We don't want her blurting something out by mistake, do we? And Sylvie, we must go out to the garden now. As soon as Sol's off the phone he'll come looking for you."

Sylvie and her mother kissed goodbye, Miranda clinging tearfully to her thin daughter, and Clip led her down the back stairs. They made their way quickly to the formal garden, Sylvie now much steadier on her feet. The cool winter air revived her too, and she realised just how intoxicated she'd been. They strolled around the gravel paths between the clipped bushes. Sylvie breathed deeply of the fresh air, making the most of this unexpected freedom from her prison.

She smiled gratefully at Clip.

"Thank you for rescuing me," she said. "I was so pleased to see you today."

"It's about time I did something to help," he replied. "You have no idea how guilty I feel, Sylvie. I should never have hypnotised you or taken any of your moon magic. I feel dreadful about it."

Sylvie squeezed his hand, feeling the old warmth towards him that she'd felt right from the start.

"Don't worry, Clip," she said. "I understand how hard it is to go against his wishes. I know you've never meant to harm me."

"But I shouldn't have been so weak," he said ruefully. "I've always been scared of my half-brother. All my life I've never been able to stand up to him. I know exactly what Sol is like. I really admire you, Sylvie my dear, for what you're enduring, being with him day and night. He's absolutely obsessive and it must be dreadful for you."

"It was alright until he found out I'd kissed Yul at the Dark Moon. Then he turned really nasty with me. He likes to play cat and mouse. Sometimes kind and sometimes cruel. I never know how he's going to treat me from one day to the next. He seems to enjoy watching me suffer."

Clip nodded.

"He does. He's always been like that, ever since he was a boy. You're a brave girl, Sylvie. But I really don't think he'll harm you. I wouldn't dream of leaving you with him if I thought you were in any danger. Just try to keep him happy, and whatever you do, don't stand up to him or cross him in any way. Don't give him any reason to hurt you. Go along with him and obey him. It's only for five more days. The Solstice is almost here! And after that ..."

"SYLVIE!"

Magus' voice was furious. He strode up to them and took hold of Sylvie, putting his arm round her. She leant against him and looked up at him guilelessly.

"I'm so pleased you came, Magus," she mumbled. "Please take me back. I feel so weak."

"Of course, my darling."

He scooped her up into his arms as if she weighed nothing, and started to walk back to the Hall with Clip trailing along beside him.

"You're a fool, Clip! I told you she shouldn't go out. It's much too cold for her. She's very delicate."

"You've changed your tune! When I think back to that last Moon Fullness when you took her to Mooncliffe ... And you won't be saying she's too delicate next week on the eve of the Solstice, will you?"

"That's different. And she'll be better wrapped up then. Now go away, and don't come barging in to my rooms like that again. I'll see you tomorrow morning, about eleven o'clock, in my office. We need to discuss the Solstice ceremony, and also make arrangements for the Story Web at Yule."

"Fine. I've got some good ideas for that. See you tomorrow. Goodbye, Sylvie. I'm sorry if the walk was too much for you."

Back in the grand sitting room, with the fire roaring,

Magus laid Sylvie gently on the sofa and removed her cloak. She closed her eyes, trying to hide the excitement she felt bubbling inside her. He poured her a goblet of mead and sat by her, holding the crystal glass to her lips.

"There, you'll feel better with this inside you. Drink it all up now. You should never have gone outside with him. Don't ever do that again. You mustn't go anywhere without my permission."

"I'm sorry," she said. "I just wanted some fresh air. I was silly to go without you."

He smiled and smoothed her hair, then fingered her neck and the choker.

"Just remember what this collar symbolises, Sylvie. You belong to me. You must stay by my side at all times and you must never stray."

CHAPTER THIRTEEN

The next morning Sylvie was awoken once more by kisses. She pretended to be asleep, desperately hoping he'd go away. When the kisses touched her lips she opened her eyes wide in horror, and saw not hard black eyes, but deep smoky-grey ones.

"Yul!"

Sylvie struggled to sit up but he pushed her back down and kissed her again, holding her face in his strong hands. It felt so good and she wrapped her arms around him, pulling him in closer, kissing him back. She wondered if she was dreaming this, because he shouldn't be here. They were in Magus' rooms! Where was Magus? She pushed him off in panic and sat up.

"Why are you here, Yul? What's happening? Is this it? Is it the Moon Fullness?"

He smiled, smoothing her mass of silky hair back from her face.

"Not yet. Magus is downstairs in his office with Clip, discussing the Solstice. We've got half an hour at most. The door to the corridor's locked, you know. He's actually locked you in, Sylvie. You really are a prisoner here. But I came in through your room with Cherry's key, right down the corridor, and then up through all these connecting rooms. I'll leave the same way and down the back stairs. Here, I've got you some breakfast."

Sylvie wolfed down the bacon sandwiches and gulped at the milk whilst he watched her, horrified at the sight of her but trying not to show it. She wore another pair of the black silk pyjamas which Magus liked to dress her in. Although the bottoms covered her, the skimpy top showed just how thin she'd become. Her collar bones jutted out, her shoulders were pointed and her arms were much too skinny. Her jaw bone and cheekbones were unnaturally prominent. The huge diamond collar, so thick around her neck, sparkled in the sunlight pouring in through the windows. Her silver hair cascaded around her shoulders and down to her waist in a tangle. He couldn't bear the thought of Magus seeing her like this every night and morning, so exposed and defenceless. Yet more desirable than ever in her vulnerability.

She looked up at him, chewing frantically on the sandwich.

"Stop staring at me," she said with her mouth full.

"I can't help it. You're too beautiful."

She smiled, swigging down the milk.

"You can bring me breakfast in bed any time you like," she said, finishing the last crumb of the sandwich and licking her fingers. "Oh that was lovely!"

"I'll have to go, Sylvie. It's all so close now; I don't want to risk anything going wrong at this stage."

Yul held her gently, not wanting to squeeze her too hard. He tried not to look at the livid bruising all around her upper arms. It was too upsetting and he'd go mad with anger, spoiling their brief time together.

"I love you, Sylvie. Remember that over the next few days. On the afternoon of the Moon Fullness, be prepared to leave when you're told to. We've got everything organised. There are so many people who … well, never mind that now. Go along with whatever Magus wants you to do so he thinks everything's fine. But remember that whatever happens you won't be going to Mooncliffe. I've sworn an oath on that. I'd die before I let you down. I'd never betray you."

Sylvie nodded, clinging onto him, burying her face in his curls. She loved him. How could she have almost given him up for that man? She felt so ashamed of herself. Yul might never betray her, but she'd betrayed him. She started to cry.

"Don't! Please don't, Sylvie," he begged. "I won't be able to leave if you're crying. It breaks my heart to see you trapped here in his lair, at his mercy. I hate you being used like this.

It's been decided that this is the best way, but I don't like it. It's as if you're the sacrifice to keep him contented and unworried. But we can't see any other way to make him stay up here at the Hall and away from Village. He mustn't find out what's going on behind his back. How everyone's turned against him. Dry your eyes, Sylvie, please. I feel so bad about this."

"I just wish it was all over," she whispered. "I want to be with you, Yul, and feel safe."

"We'll be together very soon. Just imagine - we'll be able to see each other openly and whenever we like. No more secret meetings. Nobody will try to keep us apart and we'll be just like any other sweethearts. I can't wait!"

He kissed her tears, tasting their saltiness.

"Lie down as if you're asleep. And try to look hungry."

"I am hungry! It'll take more than a bacon sandwich to fill me up."

He gazed down as she lay back on the sofa, her hair spread out in a fan of silver. She smiled up at him and his legs tingled with weakness and longing. There was something magical about her that drove him wild with a fierce hunger. How could Magus resist her? That was what worried him. Surely he wasn't alone in feeling this craving for her?

That night Sylvie had a nightmare. Maybe because she'd eaten proper food that day, the mead hadn't sent her to sleep as soundly as it usually did. She dreamed terrible dreams. She was being chased through the maze in the formal garden by Magus, who wielded a double-headed axe made of white stone. He was mad, his eyes manic, his mouth open in a rictus of rage. He'd turned into the Minotaur. All around the maze snakes writhed, silver and black, hissing up at her with forked tongues and needle-like fangs. Sylvie sat up screaming, kicking the pashmina to the floor, flailing her arms wildly.

Magus came rushing in, which showed how loudly she'd screamed. There was a dressing room and bathroom between this room and his bedroom, yet he'd heard her clearly. He raced over to the sofa and scooped her into his arms, holding her tight.

"It's alright, Sylvie," he said soothingly. "It's alright, my darling, I'm here."

"Who are you?" she whimpered, still thrashing about trying to escape. In the near darkness lit only by the glowing embers of the fire, she saw the gleam of his blond hair. *"No! Not you! I hate you! I want Yul! Where's Yul?"*

She fought him, trying to get out of his grip, punching at him and wriggling wildly. Magus grasped her by the arms exactly where he knew it would hurt most, and shook her till her head snapped back and forth.

"Be quiet, you stupid bloody girl! Be quiet!"

She screamed with the pain as he squeezed her damaged arms. He released her to slap her hard round the face. That quietened her. She fell back gasping for air, trying to catch her breath after the screaming and sobbing.

Magus got up and turned on the lamps, flooding the room with soft light. He found her goblet and filled it with mead.

"Drink this," he commanded. "All of it. Then we're going to have a talk, you and I, and put things straight once and for all."

Sylvie forced the drink down her throat, feeling the familiar warm sensation as it hit her stomach. She shivered with fear and cold, unable to remember what she'd said while she was dreaming. She closed her eyes. She was living in one terrible nightmare.

Magus had gone to his dressing room and returned wearing a heavily emroidered black silk robe. He sat next to Sylvie on the sofa with a glass of brandy in his hand and stared into the amber pool.

"I'm sick of this attachment you have to Yul," he said finally, in a cold, clipped voice. "It's been going on a long time, despite me telling you repeatedly to stop. You've persistently disobeyed and defied me over him. I thought, the other night when you made me so angry, that we'd cleared up the matter once and for all. I explained to you that to deserve this level of pampering and privilege, to earn the right to have your every desire and whim taken care of by me personally, the one thing I require from you is obedience. And I made it abundantly clear that any feelings you once had for that boy were to be erased for ever. Did I make that clear or not?"

"Yes, Magus, you did," she whispered, her voice quavering.

He turned his gaze to her and stared, his eyes narrowed and merciless. Sylvie trembled. She was terrified. She had no idea what he might do to her next. It could be anything. She recalled the flare of pleasure in his eyes as he'd witnessed her pain, and knew he was capable of any kind of cruelty. She thought of Yul, at his mercy twice in the stone byre for days on end, with Alwyn and then Jackdaw to assist in the long slow torture. She understood fully now just how Yul must have felt, and why he would never be dissuaded from destroying this man. To have someone enjoying your pain was the worst experience ever.

Magus poured her another goblet of mead. She didn't want it but maybe she'd need to be dead to the world. She began to drink, forcing it down. She started to feel slightly sick and her mouth was slow. Her face stung where he'd slapped her so hard.

"Right then, Sylvie. I'm now going to enlighten you as to exactly why I'm so adamant that this relationship with Yul finishes. I know he's kissed you. Presumably it's happened on several occasions?"

"Yes," she whispered, remembering Yul's presence only that morning.

"Has it gone any further than that?"

"No!"

"But judging from the way you're so obsessed with the damned boy, doubtless it would, sooner or later. He'll be sixteen soon, and so will you next summer. And you and he must never, ever have a sexual relationship."

He turned on the sofa so he was facing her, staring straight at her. She tried to look away but he reached across and took her chin in his hand. He examined the bright red slap mark on her cheek and shook his head sadly.

"Why do you make me do it?" he asked. "I really don't

want to hurt you. You're so stupid to make me angry, knowing the consequences. When will you learn?"

"I'm sorry," she said. "I'll try harder."

"Very wise. Now, listen to me, Sylvie. And look at me. I want to see your eyes. It's a sad and sorry tale and one that I'd hoped to spare you. But because of the way you've been behaving, I'm afraid I can't. I have no choice. You shall have to be told the full truth."

His hand gripped her chin as he spoke, telling her of what had happened in some woods, one autumn, many years ago. He told her how he'd attended a masked ball, invited by a business associate. He was bored, wishing he was back at Stonewylde to watch the Harvest Moon rise at Mooncliffe where he always liked to go. A young and pretty red-haired girl in a fairy costume caught his eye, and before he knew it they were heading for the woods together. She was a little tipsy and all over him, eager and giggly. One thing led to another and they made love in the woods on a carpet of fallen leaves under the red September moon. It was a pleasant experience for them both, and afterwards they went back into the party and joined in the dancing, little guessing the consequences of their union.

Magus watched Sylvie's eyes closely. He knew she was slow because of the two glasses of mead she'd drunk in quick succession on top of the others she'd had throughout the evening. He also knew she was cold and scared, and not really thinking straight. But he was delighted to witness the exact moment when Sylvie fully understood the implications of what he was saying.

He was her father; that was shock enough. He saw that fact registering and being accepted with horror. But the next realisation – that was the one he enjoyed the most. It hit her, more powerful and devastating than any physical punishment he could inflict on her. He watched the intense pain and sorrow blossom into a bloom of utter despair.

If Magus was her father, then Yul must be her half-brother.

The following day Sylvie woke very late, having been awake for much of the night. The afternoon passed in a haze of misery and mead. Magus plied her constantly with the drink and she gladly accepted it, wanting only to obliterate consciousness. She was numb inside, unable now to cry, although she'd shed enough tears during the night. At dinner that evening she found it hard to swallow even the meagre portion he'd served her. Magus was so solicitous, constantly enquiring if she was alright, patting her gently, smiling sadly. She felt a powerful desire to stab him with her dinner knife, for she knew he was revelling in every moment of her suffering. The mead and her unhappiness made her bolder than she'd been of late. She really didn't care if he chose to hurt her. Nothing could hurt more than this. Nothing mattered any longer.

"If you knew you were my father, why didn't you say so in the beginning?"

"I didn't know then. It wasn't until quite recently that Miranda told me the circumstances of your conception. Then I realised."

"Does she know it was you?"

"No, not yet. But she'll have to be told."

"What about Yul? He must be told too."

Sylvie knew what this news would do to him. Yul loved her as fiercely and deeply as she loved him, maybe even more so. He couldn't be her brother. It was too cruel to believe. And yet it all made sense; why she had the silver hair, why she looked so much like Raven, Magus' mother, and why she was moongazy. Everyone had said her father must be Hallfolk. Who'd have thought it was the magus himself?

She found that she hated him, the discovery of her father's identity after all these years bringing no rush of love or happiness. The revelation strengthened her determination that the plan would go ahead regardless. She and Yul had no future together, but they must rid Stonewylde of this evil man and send him off to the Outside World. Or the Otherworld. Yul would still be the new magus. The only difference now was that he'd stand alone without her as his partner.

"I want to be the one to tell Yul, not you," she said, imagining how Magus would relish Yul's pain.

'That's a good idea," he said gently, and she frowned at him. The capitulation was too easy. "I'll arrange it for tomorrow. He can come here to see you. And now, my dear daughter, I have yet another present for you, arrived today."

She shut her eyes and groaned. She'd come to loathe his presents. A whole mountain of boxes had been delivered earlier containing the latest clothes he'd ordered in a smaller size. Magus had insisted she try some of them on and was pleased that they fitted her. She was stick thin and he said again how it suited her. He'd admired her as he forced her to parade around the room for him, saying she was his catwalk girl. He'd obviously settle for her as a trophy daughter if she couldn't be his trophy partner.

He brought out another Bond Street jeweller's box and opened it to reveal two heavy bracelets to match the choker. They were very wide and studded with diamonds. He clipped them round her slender wrists. They snapped shut like the collar, and once again he locked them using his gold key. They felt like handcuffs, which she supposed was the idea. A collar and handcuffs. His property and his prisoner.

"Do you like them, Sylvie?" he said, stroking her arm.

"No I hate them!" she cried, jerking her arm away from him. "And don't touch me! You make my skin crawl. If you're my father you shouldn't be touching me like that!"

He laughed and the sound made her shudder.

"Touching you like what exactly? I've never behaved inappropriately towards you, Sylvie, not once. Think about it. If you've misinterpreted my actions, maybe the fault lies with you. Maybe it was you who thought of me in that way. If so, you must quell those feelings now, however difficult that may be. You must never think of me like that."

He laughed at her look of disgust and slid his arm around her, pulling her close to him and ignoring her tight-lipped resistance.

"I'm so proud to have such a beautiful daughter," he murmured. "My sparkling princess."

Sylvie drank mead all evening until she could no longer even sit up, but sleep eluded her. The room was spinning and she felt nauseous. Magus was a blur, a noise in the corner of her consciousness, and nothing was real any more. She knew suddenly that she was going to be sick and lurched to his bathroom, stumbling into furniture on the way. She just made it and retched violently into the toilet bowl. Magus was there, holding her hair back, his arm around her waist as she heaved. Because the contents of her stomach were almost totally liquid, the experience was fairly brief, but all the more painful. Eventually she swayed upright, clammy and deathly white.

"Please let me go back to my mother," she begged.

"Absolutely not. You stay with me."

"Then can I sleep in my room down the corridor?" she asked. "I just want to lie down on a proper bed."

"No, my darling," he said. "I like you on the sofa where I can sit with you. Come on, back we go."

He picked her up and carried her back to the sofa where the fire still blazed. He laid her down and sat next to her, his hand on her hair. Sylvie looked up at him, her face ashen and her eyes dull with grief.

"Why do you treat me like this?" she said softly. "Why are you so cruel to me?"

He chuckled, his fingers still playing with her hair. His eyes were hard as he gazed at her, burning with the darkness she'd grown to dread.

"Cruel? You're the one who's cruel. When you had that nightmare and I came running in immediately to comfort you, you rejected me. I could've loved you, Sylvie. I've never loved a woman before, as a partner or as a daughter. I've never loved anyone in fact. But I thought I loved you. And you've thrown it back in my face, all of it. You shall pay for that, believe me. You'll pay dearly, for you're ungrateful and heartless. I could've given you the earth, you know."

"No, Magus," she whispered. "You couldn't have. The earth isn't yours to give."

He woke her up at midmorning the following day. Sylvie felt even worse than usual, with a throat like sandpaper and head like a drill. Her stomach hurt badly and she'd pulled the muscles with that awful retching the night before. She sat up and rubbed her eyes, the collar and bracelets glinting brightly in the sunlight. Magus sat at the other end of the large sofa watching her struggle to regain consciousness.

"Yul has been sent for," he informed her. "He'll be arriving at the Hall in a while, so I want you up, showered and dressed straight away. You must look your most beautiful when you tell him that you are in fact his sister. I've put out the clothes you're to wear. You'll love the dress. It's one from that mediaeval collection we admired from Milan. Very appropriate, given the setting."

Sylvie did as she was told and after showering, went along to her room. The servants had cleared all the mess a while ago. The room was now immaculate, the wardrobes and chests full of the expensive outfits, her perfume and cosmetics arranged neatly on the large dressing table. The dress she must wear lay spread on the four poster bed, and despite her resentment, she was over-awed at its beauty.

It was of heavy brocade silk, a deep rich purple with a sweetheart neckline and long pointed sleeves. Tiny seed pearls and beads of amethyst were embroidered into the full, flowing skirts. The boned bodice was smooth and silky, with a long line of hooks that must be laced up with thick satin ribbons from the back. Sylvie slipped on the gossamer-fine shift first, then stepped into the heavy dress, pulling it up around her. She froze as Magus appeared in the doorway, his expression inscrutable.

"Go away! I'm getting dressed and I want some privacy."

"Mediaeval clothes weren't designed to be put on unaided," he replied with a smile. "And neither are the modern replicas. It'll be my pleasure to assist you, my lady."

Sylvie slid her arms into the long tight sleeves, her heavy bracelets catching in the material. The points came down over the tops of her hands, but the slashes in the sides of the sleeves revealed the diamonds as she moved her arms. The dress was the ideal foil for the diamond choker around her throat. The neckline sat low on her milky white chest, revealing her delicate collar bones and the heavy, priceless collar.

"Turn around and I'll lace you up," said Magus softly. He began to tug hard on the laces, firmly and methodically pulling the material tighter and tighter as she breathed in. Gradually the dress was fastened to skin-tight, unyielding perfection. Sylvie could barely breathe and certainly couldn't bend, but when she saw her reflection in the full-length mirror, she knew the effect was stunning.

Magus picked up her hairbrush and brushed until her hair shone around her in a silver cloud. He slid her feet into the embroidered slippers that matched the outfit, for she couldn't bend to do this herself, and then surveyed her critically.

"Make-up," he said. "You need to cover up the marks on your cheek. And put on some eye shadow and mascara too. All that crying hasn't done you any favours."

"Why are you making such a fuss about my appearance?" she asked sullenly. "What's it to you? Surely you don't care how I look when I'm seeing Yul alone?"

"Whoever said you're seeing Yul alone?" he asked.

"Well I'm not telling him in front of you!" she said, smoothing foundation into her skin to cover the faint but tell-tale imprint of his hand on her cheek.

When she was made-up to his satisfaction, they left her room and returned to the sitting room. Sylvie stood by the windows, ignoring him, looking out across the lawns and trees to the wintry hills beyond. She yearned to be free from the prison of this room. It was so long since she'd been outside, at liberty to roam where she wanted and enjoy the fresh air. She remembered walking with Yul around Stonewylde; in the woods, the ridgeway, the Stone Circle, the hill at Hare Stone.

As the memories flooded in she felt as if her heart had turned to stone. They'd never be together like that again. She thought of Yul's curly dark hair, always falling in his face, full of bits of wood and leaves. His grey eyes, slanted and long-lashed, smouldering with tightly controlled passion as he watched her. His body, long-limbed and slim but strong too, and so very tough and resilient, bearing witness to the beatings and cruelty he'd been subjected to all his life. She remembered his beautiful golden brown back criss-crossed with ugly scars, and his hands, long-fingered and square nailed, often dirty but always so gentle.

A sob escaped her throat and then Sylvie dissolved into tears, finally understanding fully that these thoughts, these memories, were now forbidden and denied. She could still love him – nothing would ever stop that – but it must be a sister's love. She could never again feel that melting sensation as he kissed her or touched her. She must never hunger for him, long for him, as she'd done for so many months, always with the certain knowledge that one day her longing would be fulfilled. She sobbed silently as if her heart would break, the bones of the corset tightening as she cried.

Magus came and stood close behind her, gently holding her arms. The bruises were hidden under the silk but he knew exactly where they were. He exerted the tiniest pressure and she caught her breath sharply.

"I really think you should pull yourself together, Sylvie," he said softly, as her body convulsed with suppressed sobs. "You'll still be able to see him, after all. In fact, you'll be seeing him in a few minutes and I want you calm and composed. So be a good girl and stop this silly blubbering. You'll smudge your make-up if you carry on like this."

He gripped her arms a little harder, pinching on the damaged flesh under the tight silk sleeves until she could no longer keep silent but cried out in pain.

"Leave me alone!" she sobbed. "I hate you! I wish you were dead!"

He laughed at this, letting her go and turning her round to face him. He put a finger under her chin and tipped her face up so their eyes met, hers soft and grey and full of tears, his black and gleaming. He took a handkerchief from his pocket and carefully wiped around her eyes.

"I do enjoy a girl with spirit. So much more fun. You'll learn to love me, Sylvie. When I decide to be kind to you again, you'll lap it up and come running back like a little kitten, desperate for my attention. Think how keen you were only a week or so ago. How much you enjoyed all the pampering and fuss. But of course you didn't know then that you were my daughter. Anyway, it's almost time to go downstairs."

"Why? What for?"

"For you to tell Yul that you're his sister, just like you wanted."

At that moment there was a discreet knock and Martin came in. He ignored Sylvie, his face expressionless.

"All is ready, sir," he said.

"Thank you, Martin. Come on then, my moongazy girl. Time to make your announcement."

"I want to see Yul alone!" she cried, shaking his hand from her elbow.

"Oh no, Sylvie. Such an important announcement must be made to everyone. Or everyone that matters, anyway. Come on!"

She began to struggle and Martin stepped forward, his grey eyes cold.

"Would you like some assistance, sir?" he asked quietly.

Magus shook his head and spun Sylvie to face him, thrusting his face into hers.

"Do you want us to carry you downstairs kicking and screaming, you stupid girl?" he demanded curtly. "Stop this behaviour at once or you'll suffer for it later. You know I mean it, Sylvie."

He grasped her bruised arm and she had no choice but to move, for the pain was excruciating. She followed Martin down the stairs, with Magus behind prodding her in the back.

"But I want to tell Yul alone! Please, Magus!"

"You'll do as you're told, girl. Move yourself!"

Then she understood his intentions. They entered the mediaeval Galleried Hall, the place where Magus regularly held his court of justice. The great room, with its stone-flagged floor, vaulted ceiling and oak-panelled walls, was filling up with Hallfolk. They milled around, arriving through various arched doors that led into the vast area. As Magus and Sylvie made their entrance, everyone fell silent. She faltered and stopped, horrified at the sight of such a large crowd to witness such an intimate moment. But the vicious grip, so agonizing on her upper arm, forced her forward towards the dais at the far end of the hall. The great carved chair, like a throne, stood empty and waiting for Magus. An ornate stool had been placed at its foot. Magus guided her up onto the dais and indicated she should sit on the stool.

Sylvie felt as if she were on a film set. Everything seemed staged and unreal. Her purple silk dress, fitting like a tight glove around the bodice and flowing in the heavy skirts, swirled in a mass of pearls and amethyst around her. She sat down carefully, straight backed, as the rigid steel bones in the bodice bit into her ribs and waist. She couldn't breathe properly and had to take small, shallow breaths which made her feel dizzy. Her hair fell about her face and shoulders almost down to her waist in a shining silver veil. The thick diamond collar and wristlets glittered brightly, startling against her very white skin. The bones in her face were fine and sharp like delicately carved alabaster.

Sylvie sat perfectly still, her grey moonstone gaze fixed on the half-hidden carvings of Green Men and dancing hares up in the high vaulted roof. It was as if she were a fairy-tale princess and not made of flesh and blood at all. Every single eye in the great room was on her. She had the rare gift of true beauty and everyone feasted greedily on it.

Magus relaxed on the throne chair, enjoying the attention Sylvie was attracting. She was an exceptional trophy. He revelled in her charismatic beauty, her air of tragedy and torment. Reluctantly he dragged his eyes away and looked around at the crowds of Hallfolk, all of them related to him in some way. Nearly everyone was blond and there was a definite genetic link, clearly visible when they gathered together like this.

And then Yul arrived, dark and different, but also one of them. It was apparent in his cheekbones, the way he held his head, his long limbs, his nose and jaw. Magus had never before seen it as clearly as now, with the boy surrounded by his kin. But Yul shone brighter than any of them. Something fine and honed glowed from deep within. Something magical crackled in an aura about him.

All eyes had turned to watch Yul's arrival through one of the arched doors. He wore his festival clothes, the flowing white shirt and black trousers and boots giving him too a mediaeval air. He strode in and stopped, unsure of what was expected of him but not nervous or awkward in the slightest. He stood straight, chin raised proudly, shaking the curls from his eyes in the familiar mannerism.

Then he saw Sylvie on the dais. Magus noticed with satisfaction the effect she had on him. Yul's body stretched, seeming to yearn towards her. His eyes brightened and his lips parted. None of this was wasted on Magus, so perceptive and astute. It was plain that the boy was absolutely in love with her, which made the forthcoming revelation even more delightful.

The buzz of noise that had greeted Yul's arrival died down. All eyes now turned to Magus, who'd summoned them there. He stood up, tall and commanding, and expectancy throbbed in the air.

"Blessings to you, my Hallfolk," he began, his deep voice filling the great room. "Thank you for gathering here today at such short notice, and welcome to all the visitors who've come early for the festival. I wanted to speak to you before the Winter Solstice ceremony and the Yule celebrations and holiday. I know most of you are leaving for Switzerland after the twelve days of Yule for our annual skiing trip. Sylvie and I may join you some time later in January."

There was a burst of excited chatter at this news, for everyone had been hoping Magus would come. He raised a hand for silence.

"There are two important pieces of news to tell you all. The first I believe most of you will already have heard, but I wanted to make it official. The young man you see standing there, whom you've known as Yul, a Village boy training to be a woodsman, is in fact my son and therefore a member of the

Hallfolk."

There was a great eruption of noise as people turned to each other. Behind one of the many arched doorways leading into the Galleried Hall, two women who didn't belong at the gathering met each other's eye.

"Has to tell the truth now, don't he? Got no choice any more, and after all those years of hiding it!"

Cherry pursed her lips and nodded, jowls quivering.

"Aye, sister. But our Yul ain't no Hallfolk! Look at him now, so handsome and full o' the magic. Better than all o' that lot put together!"

"So what's all this about then?" said Marigold. "What's Magus playing at now? I don't like this, not one bit. He knows there's something going on. He's heard something, and I bet 'tis from Martin, miserable old sod."

They both looked across the crowded hall at Martin, standing tall and sombre in another doorway and watching the proceedings intently. His eyes were on Yul, and his expression was one of bitterness.

"He hates Yul, don't he? Look at his face! We must be careful, sister. If Martin gets any wind o' the plans afoot, he could spoil everything."

"Aye, Marigold. He'd snitch straight off. Go running to Magus telling tales. And Goddess help us all if Magus finds out what the folk got planned. We must guard our tongues, right enough."

"'Tis not long now. Not long till our Yul takes his rightful place."

"We won't be hiding away like this then, will we? Skulking in corners and not being allowed to show our faces. Us Villagers'll take our rightful places too."

"Aye, if all goes well. But I don't know … something's not right here. Magus is too clever. Oh, I feel for that poor maid. Look at her now. What's he done to her?"

Yul too stared across at Sylvie, who sat bolt upright as pale as death. Her eyes found his and he poured his love to her across the room, ignoring the noise and the people, sending a silent message of comfort and adoration. But he saw there were tears in her eyes. They sparkled in the sunlight shining down on her in a shaft of bright blue through one of the stained glass windows. She was bathed in medieval azure light as if someone from the past had shone a blue-filtered spotlight on her. She shook her head sorrowfully, her message back to him unclear.

"It's unusual for one of the Hallfolk to have been raised in the Village all his life, for normally a Hallchild is brought up here at the age of eight," Magus continued. "Unless of course he's completely daft. But there's no doubt that Yul is my son and I want now to formally acknowledge this. After the celebration he'll be coming to live with us at the Hall. He and Sylvie have a strong attachment, and I know that they like to spend as much time together as possible. With Yul living here under the same roof, they can see each other as often as they wish."

There was more chatter, for nobody could understand Magus' thinking. Everyone had assumed that Magus wanted Sylvie for himself. He'd kept her up in his rooms for two weeks now, barely allowing her out. They'd all seen the boxes and boxes of presents that had arrived for her. The diamond jewels she now wore were clearly priceless. Why was he handing her on a plate to his son?

Yul too was utterly confused. He frowned at Magus and looked across at Sylvie for enlightenment. But she was staring down at her hands in her lap, and he realised from the slight shaking of her shoulders that she was crying. Something terrible had happened, he was sure. Magus was playing with them, pretending to free them as he prepared to pounce. Yul could bear it no longer. He'd come along today in answer to the summons only because Clip had advised him to. They'd thought it best to keep Magus happy. But he wasn't taking any orders from Magus, nor playing the victim in his cat and mouse games. He'd gone beyond that. Yul stepped forward and called out in a voice very like Magus', deep and clear.

"I am your son and there's no doubt of that, as you say. But as for being one of the Hallfolk – I tell you all now, I will never, *ever* be Hallfolk! I'm proud to be a Villager, the lifeblood of Stonewylde. I will *not* be coming to live at the Hall. I don't belong here and I don't want to belong here. And Sylvie and I will see each other where and when we wish, not under your roof and by your say so."

His deep grey eyes flashed and Magus, lounging on the throne up on the dais, smiled lazily. Yul thought again of the silver cat of his nightmares, and shivered. Something bad was going to happen. Magus was too purring and complacent.

"Of course, this is all a shock to Yul," he replied smoothly. "He didn't know why I summoned him here this morning. He didn't know I was going to acknowledge him in public as my son, nor invite him to live here. Such grandeur must seem daunting to someone raised in the Village, and we'll make allowances for him. But Yul, there is something else you must learn today. Sylvie already knows, and she especially insisted on being the one to tell you personally."

He smiled again at Yul, his dark eyes hooded and heavy with veiled menace like a cobra about to strike. Yul straightened himself, preparing to take whatever Magus gave. He knew that look of excited cruelty only too well.

"Sylvie, stand up," commanded Magus.

She obeyed, swaying slightly like a slim reed in the breeze. The amethysts and pearls in her skirts caught the light, the diamonds sparkled and her hair shimmered around her. She glittered like a star. People caught their breath at her perfection. Sylvie slowly raised her eyes to meet Yul's, and he read in them all her sorrow and pity. What had she done? His heart began to hammer in his chest as the dread grew inside him. What on earth had happened? He had the most terrible, awful premonition of what was to come. She'd submitted to Magus, maybe as a deal to stop the imminent conflict or maybe by force. He'd taken her as the latest in his long line of women. She was too young, of course, but only by six months. And Magus made his own rules.

Yul's fingers flexed and he steeled himself, ready to kill. There was a path from where he stood in the middle of the hall to where Sylvie stood on the dais. People had instinctively parted to make a way through. He hesitatingly began to step towards her, terrified of what she was about to say, worried too that she may faint away altogether. She was as white as death and looked alarmingly fragile.

"Tell him, Sylvie," said Magus, a small smile on his lips. "Tell him the news."

Yul stopped a few steps away from her, the dais balancing their heights so their eyes were level. She brushed the tears from her cheeks with the back of her jewelled hand and glanced towards Magus in supplication. He nodded at her encouragingly.

"Go on, Sylvie. You wanted to tell him yourself. Everyone's waiting to hear."

She swallowed, and cleared her throat in the absolute silence.

"Last night," she said, in a small voice, "Magus told me something terrible. But ... I can't ..."

"Tell him, girl!"

She tried again, her voice faltering.

"He told me ... the truth is ... it was him, Magus, who ... who forced himself on my mother in the woods when she was only a girl. It was him who made her pregnant. Which means that he is ... my father too."

She saw the shock flash in Yul's eyes, and then the light die as the truth hit him, just as it had hit her the night before.

Magus had risen angrily and seized one of her arms. She cried out as he gripped her hard.

"That's not what I said!" he shouted. "I don't force girls! You've twisted it!"

"Let go of her!" roared Yul and leapt forward to pull Sylvie from his grasp.

"My mother *was* forced!" cried Sylvie, flinching before Magus' fury. "It wasn't all nice like you told me. She was only a young girl and she didn't want that! She wasn't willing. *You're* the one who's tried to twist it!"

"NO!"

"Yes," came a clear voice from above, cutting through the stunned silence. "What Sylvie says is true. It was rape."

There was a collective gasp and every head in the hall

looked up. Miranda stood above in the gallery which ran around one wall. Her red hair gleamed as she held onto the balustrade and gazed down at them all.

"Thank you for inviting me too, Magus," she said quietly, but in a voice that carried right across the hall packed with shocked faces. "And just as well you did, for as Sylvie says, you're twisting the facts a little."

"We'll discuss this later, Miranda," hissed Magus, his face like thunder. His moment of sticking the knife into Yul was now completely ruined.

"I'm sorry but as you wished to make Sylvie's parentage such a public affair, I don't think you should pull away from the truth at this point," replied Miranda coolly, her chin tipped with defiance.

Sylvie had sunk down onto her stool, and stared up at her mother with admiration. This was the old Miranda, the woman who stood up for herself and fought back at the rough deal life had given her. Yul had stepped forward and taken one of Sylvie's hands in his. She felt him trembling and knew that she was doing exactly the same.

"Everyone may leave now!" called Magus. "I …"

"Not so fast!" cried Miranda. "We were talking about how I was raped in the woods at the age of fifteen, and how I conceived Sylvie that night."

"I do *not* rape girls!" bellowed Magus, his pride at stake. "Everyone here will testify to that! I have never, *ever* had to force anyone."

"That's true," came another voice, similar to Magus'. Clip stepped out from behind Miranda in the gallery. He surveyed the pool of upturned faces and his brother's murderous expression. "You've never forced anyone in your life, Sol. As you say, you've never had to. But I have. It was *me* who took poor Miranda's virginity that night, not you. Sylvie is *my* daughter!"

There was another explosion of noise, and Yul stared at Sylvie, his eyes flaring with hope. Was it true? Cousins? And only half cousins at that! She looked up at him, the same frantic hope in her eyes.

Magus was beside himself. He paced the dais like a caged panther, desperate to go up into the gallery to silence them, but not wanting to leave the hall to do so.

"Don't be ridiculous, Clip! You're a shaman. You're celibate!" he raged. "And you couldn't make love to anyone even if you wanted to. You know you've never been able to."

"Never been able to here at Stonewylde, with you mocking me and taunting me," said Clip calmly. He leant over the balustrade and met his brother's eye unflinchingly. "You had to be the best at everything, didn't you, Sol? You even made that into a competition and I couldn't compete with you. You're right - I couldn't do it. But once, just once, at that dreadful fancy dress party in the Outside World, I saw a lovely young girl dressed like a fairy princess. She knew nothing about me or you or Stonewylde. She knew nothing about my previous attempts and my failures. She knew nothing of the way you'd teased and taunted me for my lack of success. She was innocent and untouched, unable to judge me and find me inadequate. And I managed to make love to her, under the red Harvest Moon in the woods. At least, to me it was making love, a dream come true. But to her it was rape. And I never imagined a child would come of it."

"Is this true, Mum?" cried Sylvie, staring up at them. "Is Clip my father, and not Magus?"

"Yes, Sylvie, it's true," said Miranda, looking down at her beautiful daughter on the dais, all bathed in blue light from the stained glass. "Clip realised who I was on the night of the last full moon, after Magus shouted at me and humiliated me, and showed his true colours. The memory clicked into place and Clip suddenly put it all together."

"It was when Miranda cried and her long red hair fell over her hands," said Clip ruefully. "I've never, ever forgotten that. It's an image that's haunted me all these years. That poor girl standing up afterwards, all covered in leaves and earth. She cried into her hands with her lovely hair hanging over her face. I've always felt guilty about it. I'm so sorry, Sylvie. This is a terrible way to find out that I'm your father. I'm so very sorry that it had to be like this."

The Galleried Hall erupted as the Hallfolk began to discuss these extraordinary revelations. Sylvie had risen again and flung her arms around Yul, who held her tightly as if he'd never let her go.

"I love you," she whispered, in the mayhem and noise around them. "I love you more than anything in the world, Yul. I thought I'd lost you for ever, but now ..."

"Do you want me to get you out?" he whispered back. "I hate you being here in this vipers' nest. I can take you away now, Sylvie."

"No, it's only three more days. I'll hold on. It's almost over. Best to wait for the right time, like the prophecy said."

She looked up and her eye fell on the Green Man in the stained glass window above. She smiled, hugging Yul tighter, and kissed his cheek. Miranda and Clip had left the gallery and were on their way down. Excited noise from the startled Hallfolk rose like a cloud of bees ready to swarm. Magus stepped forward and roughly pulled Sylvie away from Yul.

"Don't touch her, boy! Upstairs now, Sylvie!"

Yul looked Magus in the eye, his steely grey gaze steady.

"Three more days," he said softly. "Under red and blue, the fruit of your passion will rise up against you, with the folk behind, at the time of brightness in darkness, in the place of bones and death. You have three more days, Magus of Stonewylde. Three more days until I kill you."

CHAPTER FOURTEEN

Magus leant against a standing stone watching the boy on the rock. It was still half-light, the sky a palette of lavender and mauve with a hint of pink. A cold breeze rippled across Magus' cheeks, numbing his lips, but the boy seemed oblivious to it. He sat cross-legged and straight-backed on the Altar Stone facing the lightest part of the sky, his eyes closed. Dressed in browns and muddy greens, his hair long and curly, he looked like some sort of woodland spirit. Like the Green Man.

As Magus watched, a curious spectrum of emotions flickered inside him. Strongest of all was hatred. If he'd been able to kill the boy right then, he'd have done so without hesitation. He remembered the moment when Yul had been born by that very same stone almost exactly sixteen years ago. It was just after the sun had set and the full moon had risen. The blue moon at the Solstice. This was a highly unusual conjunction, with rare magic afoot. At this point the ceremony was at its most mystical and powerful.

Magus remembered the scene so clearly; the dark Circle packed with silent people, all lit by the flickering light of the great Solstice Fire. The young dark-haired girl crouching on the earth had moaned in a long drawn-out wail of agony, unable to stifle the sounds of her labour any longer. Then the unmistakeable, primeval howl of a new born baby echoed around the sacred circle. Mother Heggy had cried out her wild prophecy as she cut the cord with her white-handled knife. Triumphantly she delivered the baby, still bloody, onto the Altar Stone.

Magus recalled the cold whisper of destiny in his heart as he'd picked up the tiny child, hot and velvet skinned from the

259

womb, and thought to smash its skull on the Altar Stone. But Mother Heggy had risen up like a ragged spectre and screamed her summoning spell. She called on the Dark Angel to bind the child with his shadowy protection, to keep him safe from the evil intent of his father. Suddenly a thick mist had swirled into the Stone Circle, bringing spirits from the Otherworld and a deathly cold unlike any winter chill.

Magus shuddered now at the fearful memory; the awful paralysis that had stilled his hands as he clutched the screaming child. The crone had snatched the baby from him and completed the magical words that would ensure Magus' death if he ever tried to kill his child. Magus had felt the cold presence of the Dark Angel at his shoulder, and had known then the incredible power of the Wise Woman. But she'd paid for the powerful magic invoked that night. Her abilities had waned, as if everything had been drained from her, used up by that terrible deed of summoning the Angel of Death.

Now, as Magus looked at the young man sitting on the Altar Stone, he felt the hatred flowing in his heart as strong and blood-red as ever. The binding spell that Mother Heggy had cast that night at the Winter Solstice blue moon was to enable Yul to grow up in safety. The spell would be over and finished at sunset on the eve of the Winter Solstice, as the boy at last attained adulthood. Finally Yul would be alone and unprotected. Magus smiled at the thought. Then he'd kill him.

The sky was palest apricot to the south east horizon where the sun would soon rise. Shredded ribbons of cloud lay above the skyline, glittering pink and bright, mirroring the sun that had yet to clear the rim of the earth. Yul's body yearned towards the horizon. His hollow-cheeked face was serene, his eyes shut. Suddenly great rays of golden light beamed up around the skyline and the boy's eyes flashed open as the light washed over him.

Magus frowned in disbelief, blinking in the blinding light. It seemed that Yul himself glowed, giving out light and brightness. He stood in a fluid movement, facing the glorious sun, his slim frame arched to accept the caress of light. Magus felt something moving, a rumbling beneath his feet. The glowing boy quivered as the force thrust up in an explosion of energy from below the Circle, through the silicate molecules of rock and into his body. Sparks shot from his outstretched fingertips and his hair stirred with a crackling charge. Yul shuddered violently as he received the energy bestowed upon him by the earth and sun's aligned magnetic fields. He stood several minutes longer as the sun glittered brighter and brighter, rising in the pink sky. Then with a respectful bow he jumped lightly from the rock, as if gravity had been altered just for him.

Magus was overwhelmed at what he'd witnessed. Such power! And it wasn't even a festival. Even in his early days he'd never been so powerfully blessed. He stepped forward into the arena of the Stone Circle. Yul turned to him, his eyes burning like stars. Magus felt the confidence and magic surging within the boy.

"I want to speak to you, Yul."

"You are."

"Come and sit on the stone."

"It's a sacred altar, not a seat. I'll stand."

"Very well. I want to speak to you about the future of Stonewylde. I want to see if together we can work something out which will benefit the whole community. For I see now just how very strongly the Earth Goddess loves you."

"And no longer loves you. Which is why you want to share my power. You're a stealer of energy. Sylvie's moon magic and my Earth Magic. If the Goddess wanted you to share her magic, she'd still be blessing you. But it's stopped and you're finished. Don't try to pull me down in your death throes."

"Very poetic," said Magus with raised eyebrows. "Where did a Village lout like you learn to speak with such eloquence?"

"I speak from the heart and the soul. I don't echo others' wisdom."

Magus watched the boy with something like amusement. Yul had blossomed; metamorphosed from a simple Village boy into a powerful young magician. He'd be no push-over.

"Yul, you have no concept of what it is to be Magus of Stonewylde. It's more than just standing on a rock as the sun rises and feeling your fingers tingle. It's about leadership of the people, stewardship of the land, guardianship of the magic. Yes, I'll grant you, the Goddess loves you and you've been abundantly blessed with the magic. But that's not enough on its own."

Yul shrugged and Magus gesticulated impatiently.

"Listen to me, Yul! You need wisdom and experience. You can't even read and write. You haven't the remotest idea how much organisation and paperwork is involved in running this place. You've heard tales of how bad it was in the days of my father, my uncle and their father too, when the cottages were falling down in disrepair and the people always cold and hungry. That was due to poor management and lack of organisation. I've spent all my adult life putting that right. I'm very good at it. I have a wealth of experience and knowledge. I'm also a very rich man, thanks to my business interests in London, and I use much of my personal wealth to subsidise the community. How could you possibly do all this? You wouldn't know where to start."

Yul looked at his father and knew that what he said was true. But he also knew that a compromise with this man wasn't possible. He shook his head.

"I don't know how to run a community. But there are many people here to help me, and I'll learn. Besides, being magus doesn't have to mean managing the community alone just because you've done it that way. The magus is the magician, the wise one. The one who is blessed with the Earth Magic. And that's me, as you must have just seen. I didn't choose it or ask for it, but it's come to me and I accept the responsibility that goes with the power. So save your breath, because whatever you say cannot change any of what is going to happen."

"Are you angry because I tried to lie to you about Sylvie?"

"I'm angry about everything you've ever done to Sylvie."

"Can you understand why I pretended she was your sister? I'm sure you can, and remember, by doing that I was also denying myself."

Yul shrugged again.

"You don't really want Sylvie. All you want is to feed on her moon magic. You don't get the Earth Magic any longer so you steal her gift."

"That's true, but only because it benefits the community. When I've tasted her magic, I'm full of energy and power. I can work for hours and hours on end. The moon eggs she makes for me are better than food or drink or sex. They give me everything I need. Have you felt their power? I have some left up at Mooncliffe. We'll go up there and you can feel just how strong they are. It's different from the Earth Magic, more exciting and wild somehow."

"The moon magic isn't yours to experience. It's for Stonewylde. Sylvie's been brought here to channel it into the earth at the place where the spirals are strong. She must forge the union between the earth and the moon. But you block it. You make it flow into the moon rocks to satisfy your craving. You can't do that! You've become evil and greedy. You're interested only in your own needs, not those of Stonewylde. And that's why you're finished."

Magus sighed. He turned so that he stood face to face with Yul, who was only very slightly shorter than him now. It seemed only a few months ago that he'd been looking down at a boy. A tousle-haired, surly boy who defied him with his smouldering eyes and curled lip. And now he faced a young man who pulsed with power and confidence.

"Yul, together we could run this place like it's never been run before! I have the wisdom and experience, the money and the knowledge. You have the Earth Magic and the energy, the youth and the power. Think of it – father and son, ruling together in harmony. And you could have Sylvie. The day after tomorrow, you'll be an adult. You can have any woman you choose, Yul. And I'd let you have Sylvie, even though she's a little young. A moongazy girl is special and something to be prized above any other woman. She's unique and magical, but I'd be prepared to give her to you. I'd let you have her to prove to you just how much I'm willing to sacrifice for the good of Stonewylde."

The sun had risen quite high now and shone into the Circle, its glittering mid-winter light gilding everything it touched. As Magus watched, the sunlight turned the boy's skin to gold, his dark curls to glossy sable. Yul laughed, his eyes flashing sparks as he looked at the shadowed face of the great man before him.

"How can you possibly think I'd ever want to work with you? How can you think I'd let you be any part of my life? All you've ever wanted is my death. And as for offering me Sylvie – she's not yours to give away. You can't offer her as a bribe to get what you want. *She* has chosen *me*. She's unique and magical, you're right there. I'm the luckiest person on this earth to have her love. *You* don't come into it at all!"

His grey eyes flicked over his father with contempt.

"Two more days, Magus of Stonewylde."

Yul turned and left the Stone Circle, heading for the Village.

Magus walked up to Mooncliffe and gazed out to sea, still struggling to rein in his anger. It was cold and breezy, the wind whipping the sea into sparkling waves that danced in the sunlight. He was furious at the cavalier way in which Yul had rejected his offer of partnership. But as he calmed down, he decided that maybe it was just as well. It had been a silly, spur of the moment decision to spare the boy's life and suggest a joint rule. It could never have worked. And he didn't think he could bear to have let Yul have his moongazy girl. To be forced to watch them together. Sylvie might think it was Yul she loved, but he'd enjoy showing her the error of her ways.

He climbed onto the great moon rock and felt only a slight flicker of the moon magic. It was almost two months since Sylvie had danced here for him. He thrilled with excitement at the thought of the Moon Fullness the night after this, on the eve of the Winter Solstice. It would be particularly strong, a mixture of moon energy and solstice power. He'd drain every drop of moon magic from the girl. It would serve her right for her ingratitude. He'd bring her to heel and break her spirit, whatever it took. Once he'd killed Yul, it would be so much easier. And he'd savour every moment of her misery.

Magus jumped off the moon rock and went over to the two wooden chests. The used eggs were heaped all around them in a great pile of sparkling white stone. He knew there were six moon eggs left because after last month's fiasco he'd been rationing them carefully. He hadn't touched one for ages now. He knew how crucial it was that he had power for the Winter Solstice when he must kill Yul. If by any terrible misfortune he didn't manage to get Sylvie up here first to energise the moon rock and the eggs, at least with these six eggs left he'd still be powerful enough to defeat the boy. Yul had such an unfair advantage, he thought angrily, with all that stolen Earth Magic inside him.

Magus pulled the padlock key from his pocket. One chest was empty, and he opened the other one. Yes, six of the moon eggs remained, nestling together in a glorious heap of pure moon magic. And now, he decided, he'd treat himself as he was feeling so low. He needed a boost of energy. He felt angry and tired, drained from the humiliating experience yesterday morning in front of all the Hallfolk. And livid with that damned boy and his arrogance just now in the Stone Circle.

Sylvie was waiting for him up in his rooms, probably awake by now and crying pathetically in a corner. He'd been a little harsh with her since the incident in the Galleried Hall. She was a captive target and he'd vented his fury on her, even though it was Clip and Yul he'd have liked to get his hands on. A moon egg would make him feel so much better. He must get himself under control. He mustn't break her completely before the full moon tomorrow or she'd never be able to satisfy his need for moon magic. He'd bring Martin to help tomorrow night with all the eggs. There'd be no trouble getting Sylvie up here as she was far too weak to fight him and she weighed next to nothing. And should that jumped-up brat of his try to intervene this month and rescue her, he'd be in for a nasty shock. Magus smiled grimly. He had that covered.

He reached into the chest for an egg. He braced himself

for the jolt of energy that would flow into his arm when he touched it, for the quicksilver flood that would course throughout his body as the magic spread. This would continue for hours on end if he held on to the egg. There was no other sensation like it on earth. His long fingers curled around the white, sparkly rock. Nothing happened. He frowned in disbelief and snatched up the egg. No magic at all! He tossed it down onto the pile outside the chest. He must have put a used one back in the chest by mistake. Now he only had five.

Magus picked up another one and yelled in dismay when he realised that this too was dead. Dreading what he was going to discover, he touched the remaining four eggs one by one. With a scream of pure rage he stumbled back, unable to believe it. They were all dead! Somebody had switched the eggs! Now he had no power at all until tomorrow night, when Sylvie would stand on the rock for him again. What if something went wrong? There was no back-up now. His vision dimmed as wave after wave of fury pounded in his head and down into his abdomen. Somebody had dared to steal from him, to trick him! It had to be Yul.

It was afternoon and Sylvie had been awake for a while. It had been a living hell in this room since yesterday morning, when they'd returned from Miranda and Clip's revelation in the hall. Magus had been terrifying, ranting like a madman and throwing things around the room. He'd shouted at her, pushed, slapped and shaken her throughout the day and night. The very sight of her seemed to fuel his anger. When Clip had tried to come in he'd yelled at him and locked the door. Sylvie had been cooped up with Magus, entirely at his mercy, and was grateful for the mead which at least dulled her fear and enabled her to slip from reality.

She hoped today would be slightly better. Perhaps he'd have calmed down. She got up from the sofa and went through the chain of rooms to her bedroom to get dressed. She looked under the bed and found a tray waiting for her. Laughing with delight, for she'd eaten virtually nothing the day before thanks to Magus's vicious anger, she tucked into the food. She wondered how she'd have managed over the past few days without Cherry's help.

Returning to the sitting room, Sylvie flung open the windows to get some air in the place. It made her shiver but was better than the usual stifling stuffiness. Although it was cold, she welcomed the lack of roaring heat that made her so drowsy and weak. She felt she was living a nightmare. Her only consolation was that there were less than two more days to be endured – the rest of today and tomorrow. Tomorrow night was the Moon Fullness when she'd be rescued. She could get through anything, knowing that the end was now in sight.

Sylvie looked out of the window at the blue sky, cold and crisp in the December sunshine. Wood pigeons called softly and repetitively in the delicate pattern of the trees' bare branches. She thought suddenly of Professor Siskin up in Oxford. She had an image of a large, comfortable room, as ancient as this one. The old man sat at a desk in an oriel window, gazing out at the cloistered green below. She felt, in one of her occasional flashes of intuitive empathy, his infinite sadness and longing. She understood then, in that moment, just how passionately the professor loved Stonewylde and how very much he missed being here. In the autumn she'd decided to bring him back to Stonewylde as soon as Magus was gone. So why not invite him home for the Solstice? He could then see Yul become the new magus and be a part of the transition himself. She remembered how taken he'd been with Yul, and his preoccupation with both the ancient Green Man of Stonewylde and the wood henge of the Village Green.

Magus must have been gone for some time, but if she was quick there may be time to e-mail the professor. She hurried through the rooms to her bedroom at the end, looking around frantically for her computer. She knew she'd brought it here ages ago, when she'd thought she may be able to do some school work.

She found it and hurried all the way back to the sitting room where she could access the Internet. She wasn't sure if it would work further down the long wing. Sylvie wrote an e-mail to the professor briefly explaining the new turn of events. She suggested that he travel to Stonewylde tomorrow, ready for the celebrations the following day at the Solstice, and that he move to Stonewylde permanently when Yul became the new magus. Her fingers trembled as they flew across the keyboard, making stupid spelling mistakes in her nervousness. At last she was able to send the message and took a deep breath of relief.

Sylvie stuffed the computer back in its bag, not daring to wait for a reply, and then remembered what was in the side pocket. She unzipped it and carefully drew out her precious photo of Yul. Just what she needed to give her heart now. She sat down on the window seat and gazed longingly at the beloved face smiling dreamily out at her from a halo of leaves. Yul's deep grey eyes stared into hers and she felt a great surge of love for him, so powerful and overwhelming that tears came to her eyes. If anything were to happen to him tomorrow night at the Moon Fullness … If anything were to go wrong …

Sylvie heard the key turning in the lock of the great oak door and hastily slid the photo between the pages of a book lying on the cushions. She held the book in trembling hands and pretended to read, the weak midwinter sun washing her face. The heavy door was flung open and Magus crashed in. She'd never seen him so angry and her heart leapt frantically in her chest. His face was mottled with anger, his lips a thin white line. He strode over to where she shrank in the seat and grabbing her wrist, yanked her to her feet. The book fell to the floor and he kicked it right across the room.

"WHERE ARE MY MOON EGGS?" he roared into her face.

Cherry returned to the kitchens pale and shaken. She banged the tray onto the enormous scrubbed table and looked around the crowded room for her sister. The vast area was filled with Villagers. They scurried about preparing the next meal for the Hallfolk, whose numbers were hugely swollen by the extra visitors who'd arrived for the Winter Solstice and Yule celebrations. The white-aproned servants worked diligently at their tasks, with a flushed and sweating Marigold bellowing orders and chivvying everyone in sight.

"Oh dear Goddess, I don't like the turn o' things," said Cherry, shaking her head.

"What? What's ado, sister? Clover, do NOT put the egg whites in that bowl! What are you thinking of? And hurry along with them parsnips, April. They should be in the stove by now!"

"'Tis the master. I never seen him like this before. He's gone barking mad!"

"Why? What's happened? No, Clover! Not that one! Cherry, I don't have time now. You see how rushed 'tis in here. Tell me later, my dear."

"I know, but I'm that worried for the little maiden. He wouldn't let her eat any o' these sandwiches he ordered, but she's still knocking back the mead on his say so. She looks so poorly. Worse than when she came here a nine-month ago. And he's got that glint in his eye – you know what I mean, Marigold. The man's gone dog-demented, almost foaming at the mouth. I fear for that poor girl trapped all alone in there with him. 'Tain't right."

"Well, 'tis not for much longer now."

"Aye, and just as well. Don't reckon she'd last much longer, way she looks now. He's a wicked man. He deserves everything that's coming."

"True enough. And at least we won't have to cook all that fancy stuff them bloody Hallfolk clamour for at Yule. Plain, wholesome Stonewylde fayre and nought else, after Solstice Eve. About time too!"

Old Greenbough yelled grumpily across the Circle at the men finishing off the great Solstice Bonfire. Like the one in the summer, it was built towards the edge of the Circle at the opposite side from the Altar Stone. There was a platform with a beacon to be lit, and a ladder in the centre with a tiny entrance. The woodsmen were filling in the gaps between the large branches that formed the outer framework, and Greenbough stomped around issuing orders and muttering complaints.

"I miss Yul, I really do," he said to nobody in particular. "Like a squirrel he was, the way he would race up and down the bonfire. Nobody else comes close."

"Aye, well, he won't be building no more o' these, will he, sir? Not when he's our new magus," mumbled a huge man, chopping up extra wood for padding out the fire.

"Ssh!" hissed Greenbough, glancing at the Hallfolk who were with Merewen and a group of Villagers putting the finishing touches to the paintings on the stones. Fennel looked up sharply. He glanced at his sister, Rainbow, and they raised their eyebrows at each other. They felt the strange atmosphere in the Circle – suppressed excitement, anticipation, and also fear.

But they continued their painting: mistletoe, holly and ivy, and the rising sun picked out in gleaming gold. The Altar Stone was decorated with evergreens round its base, and there were torches and braziers all around the great Stone Circle. The entire Winter Solstice festival was a celebration of the return of light, the coming of the sun.

"Do you reckon what they've been saying at the Hall is true?" whispered Rainbow. "That Yul is going to become the new magus tomorrow night?"

"I don't know," muttered Fennel, "but I bloody well hope not. Village bastard! I wish Buzz was still here so we could give him a good thrashing like we used to."

"But what will happen to Magus? I don't understand. How can Yul just take over? Magus would never let that happen. You know how fierce and powerful he is."

"I don't know, Rainbow. It's just a load of stupid Village talk I expect. We'll be celebrating the Solstice as usual tomorrow and Yule for the next week. Then off to Switzerland. Don't worry about it. Yul's just a Village peasant and nothing will come of all this bloody daft gossip."

They fell silent as Merewen approached, filthy in her paint-stained overalls, curly hair springing in profusion from her no-nonsense face.

"Good, nice work. Rainbow, come and help me over at

the big stone behind the altar. I need your fine hand."

Rainbow glanced in surprise at her teacher as they surveyed the largest of the stones. Merewen had outlined an image totally out of place at the Winter Solstice.

"I don't understand! Why on earth are we painting a Green Man?"

But Merewen merely smiled and handed her a paintbrush.

Down in the Village there was a great deal of activity. The Great Barn was being decorated ready for the feasting and dancing that would begin the following night. At Yule the partying and celebrating continued for twelve days. There were dances, dramas, singing, musical events and games, as well as much feasting and drinking. The Barn was decorated with evergreens and many candles. By the enormous fireplace lay the decorated Yule Log, ready to be lit.

Every cottage in the Village had an evergreen wreath on its front door, representing the wheel of the year. Yule candles stood in parlour windows to welcome the return of the sun. The trees around the Village Green had been hung with small lanterns to be lit each night. There was an air of anticipation trembling amongst the bare branches and trunks of the trees that formed the circle. The children ran wildly around the Green in their warm homespun jackets. They spoke excitedly of the Yule elves, dressed in green leaves, who'd visit their homes tomorrow night. They'd leave little gifts in the knitted socks hanging over every hearth; honeyed cobnuts and creamy fudge, and trinkets such as a carved animal or bead necklace.

In the cottages and at the Village bakers and butchers, people were busy cooking and preparing food for the feasts. This was the time when people over-ate and indulged in treats. Every household was filled with the fragrance of herbs and spices, the mouth watering aroma of baking. Tomorrow was the Frost Moon and every Villager was aware of its significance. Of what must take place before the sun rose the following morning.

In the cottage down the lane, Maizie tried to concentrate on her baking. When Sweyn and Gefrin, the two youngest boys, came tearing into the kitchen for the umpteenth time and knocked Leveret flying, she finally snapped.

"Get out, you little brats!" she shrieked, cuffing at them. "Get out of here and don't come back till I've finished the baking!"

Rosie was busy polishing everyone's festival boots in the parlour. She came hurrying in, alarmed at the note of hysteria in her mother's voice. She found Maizie crying into the bowl of flour whilst Leveret howled on the floor.

"Oh Mother, don't cry! Geoffrey! Gregory! Take the boys down to the Green to play. And keep them there."

She scooped up Leveret and put an arm round her mother's shaking shoulders.

"He'll be alright, Mother. Don't cry. Yul will be alright."

"We don't know that, Rosie! Magus is strong and clever, and Yul's only a boy, for all his new power. I can't bear it!"

"But think of the prophecy, Mother. You know what Edward and Tom and everyone's been saying, about this being the right way. How 'twas destined to be since Yul's birth."

"Aye, Rosie, I know that damn prophecy! It's been ringing in my ears for sixteen years. Don't mean it'll come to pass though. Old Heggy was a Wise Woman, but where are her powers now? She can't help our Yul. He's on his own."

"No, Mother. He has the folk behind him, just like the prophecy foretold. He's got lots o' help."

"You're wrong there, my girl. Oh aye, I know the folk are behind him, and want Magus dead as much as we do. I know we've all been meeting and planning and hatching. All that talk about what will be when Magus is dead and gone. All the dreams for Stonewylde run by the Villagers. But in the end 'tis Yul who must face Magus alone. 'Tis my boy who must bring this all about. That's what's going round in my head like a ferret in a trap. My poor son, only a lad, up against that strong and desperate man. I don't think Yul stands a chance."

Preparations for Yule were also taking place at the Hall. As in the Barn, evergreens hung everywhere and the Galleried Hall was particularly beautiful. The ancient vaulted roof and the balustrade of the gallery were woven with ivy and holly, and great bunches of mistletoe hung in white-berried magical splendour over every arched doorway. There were myriads of candles on massive wrought iron candle-trees standing in the corners. A huge evergreen tree had been decorated with tiny carved animals and birds and woven straw fairies and elves, all hanging from the tree with scarlet ribbons. The only concession to the twenty-first century was the silver, twinkling lights that sparkled amongst the branches. Another great Yule Log lay in the long hearth, decorated like the one in the Village with skeins of ivy and straw birds.

The Hallfolk went to the Great Barn for many of the celebrations, dances and feasting, but they also held their own private celebrations here. Galloping around the Barn with the Villagers and quaffing cider and hearty food was all very well, but there was a lot to be said for the more refined pleasures of the Hall. Fine champagne and imported delicacies were enjoyed throughout the Twelve Days of Yule by Hallfolk, whose sophisticated palates craved more subtle pleasures.

The atmosphere in the Hall was expectant, but also uneasy. Somehow the servants' gossip had become common knowledge and there was much speculation. Most Hallfolk were loyal to Magus but many had become disillusioned with him. He'd been harsh and uncaring recently. He seemed irrational and even a little unhinged at times. The sinister events of Samhain were known to all, even though Magus had glossed over what had really happened. The sight of Sylvie the other day in the Galleried Hall, clearly underfed and ill, had worried people. Many privately thought that it was time for a new magus. But there was also fear that they'd lose their privileges and lives of ease if a young Villager were to take over the reins of leadership. Yul may be Hallfolk by blood but he certainly wasn't one of them. Below stairs there was a fever of excitement amongst the servants, and a fervent hope that the Hallfolk would definitely lose their lives of ease.

"May I come in for a quick word please, sir?"
Magus glanced up as Martin slid silently into his office.

The man was so deferential. Magus acknowledged ruefully that he certainly needed something to help calm him down, and Martin was probably the best antidote for his rage. He'd spent it on Sylvie of course, but every time he thought about the missing eggs, he felt the fury rise up again.

"Of course, Martin. What can I do for you?"

"Please forgive me being personal, sir, but I've been wondering … Yesterday Master Clip told us he was the father of Miss Sylvie. I wondered if that was really true?"

Magus frowned, not wishing to be reminded of the fiasco in the Galleried Hall, and his awful humiliation at being unmasked as a liar.

"I imagine so. It seems probable, and he and Miranda are agreed on it. Why do you ask, Martin?"

"Well, sir. I always thought that although Master Clip owns Stonewylde, passed on by his father Basil, that as he had no children himself, 'twould pass on to you one day. But if he has a daughter, then I expect she would be the heir."

"What a strange thing to ask. Whatever made you think of that, Martin?"

"My mother, sir. I visited her last night and she and my Aunt Vetchling were talking about it."

"I see. And how is Old Violet?"

Martin's nose wrinkled with distaste at the memory of the filthy cottage shared by his mother Violet and her sister. Vetchling's daughter Starling also lived there, with her own small son and her brother Jackdaw's son. The cottage was a little way out of the Village and the family were generally ostracised by the Villagers. The three women were not popular.

"She's well enough, sir. Busy baking ceremony cakes for the Solstice of course."

"Good. And tell me, Martin … what's the general feeling about this coming Solstice? I mean this business about Yul and that ridiculous prophecy that's unfortunately been raked up again. Are people talking much about it?"

Martin eyed Magus carefully. He knew he was treading on eggshells here, for the master was touchy at the moment.

"I don't get to hear much of the tittle-tattle, sir. Not in my position. The servants always whisper in corners, o' course. And stop when they see me coming."

"What about Violet and Vetchling, and Starling for that matter? Have they heard anything?"

Martin shook his head firmly.

"My mother's family are treated shockingly, sir, and that's a fact. Villagers cross the road to avoid them. 'Tis on account of Jackdaw, of course, but 'tis not right. Not for a woman of my mother's position. She should be respected, not insulted."

"I promise you, Martin, that once this Solstice is over, things will change at Stonewylde. Loyalty will be rewarded. And betrayal will be severely dealt with."

"Have you seen what is to come? What will unfold?" asked Mother Heggy, peering almost sightlessly at the blond man in the chair opposite her. He shook his head, eyeing the crow on the table warily. He knew what the crow had done at the last full moon up at Mooncliffe.

"I've seen very little lately," he replied. "My gift, such as it is, seems to have deserted me in recent months."

The crone nodded, and creakily bent forward to take his hands in hers. He flinched, frightened of her. All his life he'd been scared of this woman. He knew she hated him, and had done so since his moment of conception. She gazed at him with milky eyes and crooned softly as she rocked.

"Your father was a bad man," she mumbled eventually. "He took what he shouldn't have. He violated what was forbidden. And you, born under the eclipse – you should have been truly gifted. But you too took what you shouldn't have. You've suffered for that, right enough."

Clip nodded. He sat silently, reflecting on his plight. Mother Heggy sighed.

"But now you have another chance. You must protect your daughter. You must do what is right."

"I will! I want to do what's right. I've never wanted to hurt anyone."

"Aye, you speak the truth. You have the gentleness of my

275

Raven in you, I see it clear. What you did under that Harvest Moon – 'twas destiny. The silver girl had to be conceived. The moongazy maiden had to return to Stonewylde to dance the spirals. But she is in great danger, the bright one, caged as she is. I feel it strong, yet 'tis not clear. My power has all but gone. The binding spell is almost over, its magic spent. Tomorrow my dark one will stand alone and I fear for him too."

It was silent save for the crackling of the meagre fire in the hearth and the creaking of the rocking chair. Clip felt himself drawn to the old Wise Woman and wished then that he'd talked with her before this. He'd always been too scared to approach her, knowing how she cursed him and his brother. When Yul had said that Mother Heggy wanted to see him, he'd been terrified of the encounter. But now he felt the old magic in her, the knowledge and wisdom of a true witch. He could have learnt so much from her over the years if he'd only had the courage to seek her out. He resolved to forge a bond with her and visit regularly from now on.

"Beware of your brother," she whispered suddenly, her grip tightening. "He has evil in his heart. He is the serpent that creeps."

"I've always been wary of my brother," he replied. "I know he's evil. I long for his reign to be over."

"No," she said. "I speak not of him. The other brother. *He* is a danger to you."

Clip frowned at her, but then she began to moan softly, a strange noise that made his skin horripilate. The old woman peered under the table, and he bent to see what she was staring at. The scraggy black cat was under there, growling low, its mangy tail lashing. Laid out carefully in a neat row were five dead rats, their throats torn. The cat glared malignantly, daring anyone to touch his trophies.

"Five! Always five!" croaked Mother Heggy. She clutched at her dirty shawl in fear, her gnarled fingers scrabbling on the worn fabric. "Five deaths at the Solstice! Five souls for the Dark Angel, and I know not whose!"

CHAPTER FIFTEEN

The day of December 20th finally dawned. Yul received his energy not on the Altar Stone as usual, but in the dolmen up in the hills by the woods. He sat in the ancient temple feeling the power spiral up from beneath him as the sun rose above the horizon. This was the energy of the earth dragon of old, the serpent lines of green magic that lay deep in the ground, waiting to be drawn upon by those wise ones with special ability. He'd spent the night in the dolmen, not trusting Magus to leave him alone. There could have been a midnight raid on his cottage or a surprise visit to the Stone Circle at sunrise.

Yul sat for a while, deep in thought. Tonight was the brightness in the darkness. Full moon at the Winter Solstice. The prophecy would be realised by this time tomorrow, if it was to happen. And if not – he would be dead from trying. He had to rise up against his father. He had no choice, for those words had greeted his birth and blighted his childhood. Sunset this afternoon was the time for fulfilment.

Yul's clear grey eyes roamed across the body of the woman before him, clothed in her winter robe. Trees sprang from her head, and the hills formed her shoulder and hip as she lay on her side. The curve of her waist was the valley, and the ancient tumuli her breasts. The Goddess in the landscape lay silent and still, spread before him as he looked out from his vantage point on the hill. This was the woman who held the gift of life in her womb, latent now in the depths of winter, but ready to be born once the returning sun resumed its warm caresses in the spring. This was Stonewylde, whom he must guard and cherish. For he was the chosen one. The magus.

Yul thought then of Sylvie, the other woman who needed

277

his protection. She too was part of the synergy of Stonewylde. As ever, just thinking about her made his bones melt. He loved her more than life itself. Tonight he was prepared to die for her. Should everything go wrong and she be put in danger, he'd give his life to save her from Magus.

"Bring hand guns and rifles. Yes, with night sights. You shouldn't need them, but ... yes, exactly. Knives? Yes, good idea. Whatever you usually prefer to work with, although remember the element of surprise will be crucial here as it'll all take place out in the open. Definitely camouflage gear, yes. Cuffs too, and rope. Now, when you get here you'll be stopped at the Gate House. They'll be expecting you. Wait there. They'll ring through to me and I'll come up and get you, and brief you fully ... Yes ... About two p.m. ... Alright, I see, but absolutely no later than three p.m. That's very important. You have to be in position before sunset at four. See you later, then. ... Yes, I understand ... Yes, and the other half on completion. Fine. See you at three."

Sylvie shut her eyes and pretended to be asleep as Magus came over to the sofa. Her heart clutched with terror at what she'd overheard. He was bringing in a hired man to help him tonight. Guns and knives! Yul wouldn't stand a chance. She had to get warning to him somehow. Inside she quaked with fear but tried to keep still as Magus looked down at her. He ran his fingers delicately over her cheekbone and she stirred slightly.

"Wake up, sleepy head," he said gently. "Breakfast will be coming soon and I'm sure you're hungry."

He knelt and stroked the hair away from her face, then leant forward and softly kissed her cheek. She was enveloped in the exotic smell of him, and remembered with shame how there'd been a brief time when that smell had thrilled her. She opened her eyes quickly to prevent any further intimacy and gazed at him in trepidation. He'd been so very cruel to her yesterday. Was he still playing cat and mouse?

But Magus was kindness itself this morning; a different person from the man of the previous night who'd made her drink until she was sick, who'd shouted at her and threatened her with torture on the rock at Mooncliffe. He went off to run a bath for her as they waited for breakfast to arrive.

With shaking hands Sylvie ran to his desk and grabbed a pen and a scrap of paper. She must get a message to Yul. Someone was arriving this afternoon with guns, camouflage gear and knives! She couldn't bear to think of it. Magus had said the element of surprise was crucial. She must warn him. Fingers trembling, she scribbled a note to Clip and crumpled it small in her hand. The black silk pyjamas she wore had no pockets in which to hide a note. She thought frantically – would the servants bring the food up themselves, or would they use the dumb waiter? She usually missed breakfast and had no idea. She decided they'd probably use the dumb waiter as the food would be hot and it was quicker way that way.

Her hands shook uncontrollably as she yanked open the concealed panel. She saw with relief that the small lift was up here and not downstairs. She put the note inside, knowing that the servants would find it. She hoped desperately that they'd pass it on to Clip, who'd make sure Yul was warned.

"What are you doing?"

"I … I thought I heard the food coming, but it wasn't."

"Are you very hungry?"

"Yes, I am."

"Come here."

She padded reluctantly across in bare feet to where he now stood by the window. The sun had risen and was sparkling the melting frost into dew on the lawn to the south-east. He pulled her to him, wrapping his arms around her, feeling her thin shoulders and arms as he cradled her head against his chest.

"I'm sorry, Sylvie. I've treated you cruelly and I'm truly sorry. Something inside me - it takes over sometimes and I can't stop. It's not your fault, any of this, but you've born the brunt of my anger and frustration over the past month. Look at the state of you. I've starved you deliberately and now you're so thin. And your poor arms, these horrific black bruises. You're beautiful and delicate but I've tried to make you ugly. I hope you'll be able to forgive me eventually."

She stood perfectly still, her skin crawling where he touched her. His fingers gently but insistently probed her back, feeling through the flesh for her bones. He traced her shoulder blades and the vertebrae in her spine. He sighed and squeezed her tightly for a moment. Then he held her a little away from him and tipped her face up to his. His gaze was soft and he groaned.

"Oh Sylvie, what have I done to you? I'm sorry for mistreating you, my lovely girl. I've been brutal to you. Clip always says I go too far and he's right. But I'm not a bad person. Not deep down inside. You must help me bring out my better nature and bury my darkness."

To her horror he bent to kiss her lips. She jerked back, every muscle in her body screaming resistance, but he held her firmly. He put one hand behind her head, bringing her face inexorably towards his. His eyes gleamed as he closed in. She felt his mouth move on hers, his lips firm and insistent, his tongue adamant. She started to struggle, trying to pull away from his hungry kiss. Relief flooded through her as the buzz of the dumb waiter signalled the arrival of breakfast. With another groan he pulled back, his eyes heavy-lidded and glazed. He smiled ruefully at her.

"We'll continue that delightful activity later on. I've held back for far too long and Goddess knows why. You're clearly a beautiful woman now and no longer a girl. But you're hungry, my darling, and I must feed you. Go and sit down and I'll bring breakfast over."

He served her at the table, waiting on her hand and foot, piling food onto her plate from the silver serving dishes. Sylvie enjoyed the first proper meal she'd had for a long time, all thoughts of the kiss pushed to the back of her mind. She sat in her black silk pyjamas, blond hair everywhere and diamonds sparkling, and tucked in to her food ravenously. Then she soaked in the bath he'd run and felt a great deal better than she'd done for ages.

As she lay in the bubbling black marble tub she suddenly understood. Of course! It was the Moon Fullness tonight.

Magus wanted her able to cope with the ordeal that awaited her this evening on the moon rock. All this was just to make her a little stronger. She realised again just how calculating and cruel he was. He could turn the kindness on and off at will. But she knew it wasn't for much longer, and that thought gave her courage. Just a few more hours to endure.

Professor Siskin watched the countryside roll by outside the window of his first class carriage. A modest suitcase and precious computer bag were his only luggage. The latter now sat on his knees as he gazed out of the window, unable to concentrate on his work. Since receiving the e-mail from Sylvie yesterday, he'd been desperately excited. He hadn't spent the Winter Solstice at Stonewylde since Sol became magus many years ago.

He muttered to himself and received odd looks from other passengers, but the old professor was oblivious to this. He was going home! Sylvie was a lovely girl, he thought, and a worthy heir to Stonewylde. She was kind and caring, and passionate in her love of the place. As for Yul … Siskin pulled out his copy of the photo he'd taken of the boy and felt that thrill of recognition all over again. He knew for sure he was looking at the Green Man. The very one whose return to Stonewylde would ensure that all would be well and all would prosper. The Magus and the Maiden, the Green Man and the May Queen, the Earth Magic and the moon magic. Stonewylde hadn't had anything like this for a long time. Centuries in fact. The good times were about to begin. Siskin smiled joyfully. He'd be there to herald the dawn of the new magus and the return of the sun.

When Sylvie returned to the sitting room from her bath, she found the fire had been re-laid and was now blazing in the great hearth. The room had been cleaned too. She could smell the beeswax polish and the carpet looked freshly vacuumed. Magus was at his desk working as usual, and looked up as she entered.

"Refreshing bath? Sit down and I'll dry your hair for

you."

Her heart sank. This involved him fiddling about with her hair and her neck, and after the attempted kiss this morning, she was scared of what might happen next. She could tell that he was unstable at the moment, living on a knife-edge of normality but capable of going completely over the edge with minimal provocation. She was absolutely terrified of him today. There was something in his eyes – a desperation that she hadn't seen there before. He knew his time may be coming to an end. Tonight the prophecy might be fulfilled and he'd be finished. He might feel he had nothing to lose.

Sylvie found her large comb and sat on a cushion in front of the sofa, the fire roaring its heat at her. She crossed her legs, tucking her bare feet under her, and straightened her back. Magus came and sat on the sofa behind her and teased out the long strands of hair, like wet string falling to her shoulders in a jumble. His fingers were gentle.

He seemed calm enough and Sylvie started to relax. The fire made her cheeks flush but was also drying her hair quickly, so he'd have to release her soon. She was just beginning to feel that everything would be alright after all when she noticed the book she'd been reading yesterday. She remembered with a jolt the train of events. She'd thrust the photo of Yul inside its pages quickly. Magus had entered the room with a crash, grabbed the book from her and thrown it to the floor, before violently kicking it right across the room. The servant who'd cleaned the room this morning must have picked it up. It now lay on a small table in direct view of the sofa. Where was the photo? She knew that in Magus' present state of volatility, the sight of Yul might tip him over.

She realised he was talking to her and dragged her mind back to the present.

"I'd like to buy you a horse in the spring," he was saying. "I'll teach you to ride myself, and then we can ride all over Stonewylde together. You said you liked horses, didn't you?"

"Yes," she said quickly, thinking of her strange ride with Yul on the milk-white horse through the misty woods full of red toadstools. "I've always wanted to learn to ride."

"I'll buy you a beautiful horse," he said. "A really gentle but intelligent mare. I suspect you'll be a natural."

His fingers raked through her hair onto her scalp, massaging with a confident touch.

"And we'll go abroad too, as I promised you before. Wherever you want to go. You can swim in the clearest, warmest waters. I shall enjoy showing you all the wonders and beauties of the world."

She didn't know how to respond to this, so kept quiet. He scooped up all her hair into one handful and raised it from her neck. He touched the heavy diamond choker, feeling where it chafed her skin.

"Is this sore? Does it rub you?"

"Yes, all the time. It's really uncomfortable when I'm trying to sleep. It cuts into me."

"Oh well, I'm sure you'll get used to it. It's like a new saddle or bridle on a horse. Always rubs a bit at first while it's being broken in."

His long fingers slid round the choker, caressing her neck and throat. She held her breath, desperately hoping he'd be distracted by something and stop. His thumbs on the back of her neck began to massage, moving to her shoulders. He flicked the thin silk straps down, so he had a clear run on her skin. Sylvie knew she must move and get out of this situation fast. She pulled away slightly and pretended to cough. He stopped the massage and waited until she'd finished. Then he reached forward and cupped a hand under her chin. He tipped her head right back against the sofa so that she was looking backwards, her throat arched and fully extended, right into his upside down face. He looked almost demonic, round the wrong way. His dark eyes gleamed with that black light and his smile was strange.

He traced her feathery eyebrows and stroked her jaw line. She could see the muscle in his cheek twitching.

"You are mine," he said thickly. "My own moongazy girl. So special and magical. Nobody else will ever have you, Sylvie. You belong to me."

His fingers slid down to the choker on her arched throat,

now biting into her windpipe. He caressed the delicate skin, feeling tenderly where it was chafed.

"Sylvie," he groaned, "What have you done to me? I've never felt like this before. It's more than just wanting you. It's deeper than that, much deeper. You're the only woman in the world who can give me what I need. I long for you like I've never longed for anyone else. You've no idea of the torment I'm going through. And today ... today it's more powerful than ever before. Maybe because of the full moon tonight. Maybe your magic is stronger. I'm on fire today with this awful burning need for you."

With a swift movement Magus rose from the sofa and stood before her on the hearth. He bent and took her hands in his, pulling her upright. The diamond cuffs glittered on her wrists, and her hair, now dry and silky, cascaded over her shoulders in a silver mass.

He stood opposite her, holding her hands loosely in his, gazing at her. Her cheeks were flushed from the fire. Sylvie watched him with bright, fearful eyes, scared of what was coming next. His breathing was heavy and she recognised the expression in his eyes. She'd seen it in Yul's eyes too. He started to close in and she pulled backwards, trying to get away. He tugged and she pulled, shaking her head, her eyes wide with fear.

"Sylvie, please ..."

"No!"

"I love you, Sylvie. I never thought I'd say those words, but I do."

"You don't love me! If you loved me you wouldn't treat me like this. You've been so cruel to me!"

"The only reason I've been cruel is *because* I love you. It's so strong it hurts, and it makes me want to hurt you too. You torture me with your coldness and indifference. If you would just show me some warmth, some gratitude for all I've given you. Look at you! You're dripping with my diamonds; they're worth thousands of pounds. Any other girl would die for those diamonds."

"I hate them! They cut into me and hurt me, like you do. I

don't want your love, Magus. Your love is selfish and cruel, and ..."

"Come here, Sylvie. Let me kiss you properly. You're so innocent. You don't know anything. And I know all there is to know. You wait until I've shown you what making love is all about. When you've flown and touched the stars, then tell me you don't want my love. Come here, Sylvie."

He tugged sharply so she stumbled into him and wrapped his arms fiercely around her, crushing her attempts to struggle from his grasp. She closed her eyes, praying desperately for some miracle to save her. She knew his steely determination to have his own way at all times. She also knew of his legendary passion, his need for women. He'd hardly left the room for days. He must be ready to explode. Nothing she said or did would make any difference. He was relentless. She could feel how he craved her. He was trembling as he held her close. He bent his head to kiss her, his eyes boring into hers.

The intercom buzzed sharply and insistently. Sylvie felt him tense like a steel spring.

"Bloody hell!"

Magus strode over to the phone on his desk, practically ripping it from the connection.

"This had better be bloody important!" he yelled, face scarlet with anger. "What? Oh, yes, we'll be down, Martin. I'd forgotten, yes. Ten minutes. Give them all some more mead and wait for us."

He slammed the receiver down and glared at Sylvie as if it were her fault.

"We're eating lunch downstairs today. I hadn't realised it was so late. Go and get dressed. I've already laid out the clothes you're to wear on your bed. And put some make up on too. I want you to look especially beautiful. Be quick, girl!"

Gratefully, Sylvie slipped past him and through the rooms to get to her bedroom. She saw the dress of midnight blue crepe de chine and elegant high heeled shoes, and knew she was to be paraded again in front of the Hallfolk, just as he'd tried to do in the Galleried Hall. He'd even put out the ivory silk underwear she was to wear. She felt a boiling up of resentment inside. How did he think she could bear to live like this, with every detail of her life controlled by him? But there was no time now for rebellion for he was clearly in a hurry. She tugged off the silk pyjamas and slipped into the underwear, then stepped into the dress. She could hear him coming through the connecting rooms and struggled to zip it up before he came in. She quickly moved away from the untouched bed and sat on the stool before the dressing table, picking up her mascara.

"Hurry up, Sylvie!" he said. "They're all waiting for us in the Dining Hall."

He stood behind her as she put on some makeup, watching her movements, his eyes meeting hers in the mirror. She rose and his gaze swept down her, noting the skin tight fit of the dress and the way it accentuated her figure. He smiled, his eyes still burning with desire, and ran his hand down the side of her ribs and into the hollow of her tiny waist.

"Perfect. Now come on. We're very late."

He took her hand and led her down the wide staircase to the great Dining Hall where all the Hallfolk had gathered for lunch. It was packed with the extra visitors. The noisy room fell silent as they entered. Sylvie held his arm as she'd been ordered as they swept in. Magus smiled graciously around him, greeting people and nodding, but Sylvie remained silent and impassive. She wasn't going to pretend she was enjoying this.

Magus led her to the head of the high table where an extra place had been laid next to his. He seated her attentively, fussing over her, his message to the Hallfolk very clear. She refused wine or mead and he couldn't force her in front of everyone. When lunch was served she ate hungrily. She didn't care that people were staring as she wolfed down the food. She felt all eyes upon her; the people she knew, and many visitors who hadn't seen her before, or barely recognised her as the young newcomer of earlier in the year. Of her mother and Clip, there was no sign at all.

Sylvie's peer group watched her the whole time with undisguised envy. They were too far down the table, and some on other tables, to make conversation with her. But they followed her every move, staring at the expensive dress and the heavy diamond choker and wristbands that glittered as she moved. They commented to each other on her thinness and beauty, and her air of complete detachment from everyone, including Magus himself. Each of them would have loved to have been in her place, sitting alongside a man so clearly obsessed. He too watched her closely, frowning as she accepted a large second helping.

"Don't overdo it, Sylvie," he said quietly. "I've just told you that you're perfect."

"I'm hungry!" she retorted. "You've been starving me. I need food."

"Yes, but you'll make yourself sick."

"It'll make a change from you making me sick with all that mead. Leave me alone, Magus. I'll eat what I want."

"Don't speak to me like that, Sylvie," he said very softly. "You might get away with it here, in front of all these people, but you know I'll make you pay for it later."

She glared at him and continued eating, knowing it was annoying him and feeling glad. When this was all over, she vowed that she'd never miss a meal again.

Yul raced up the track to Mother Heggy's cottage. He was very busy today but knew he must see her. It was turning colder, he noted, although the sun shone brightly. There'd be a frost tonight, he was sure, which was appropriate as the full moon of December was known as the Frost Moon. He must make sure Sylvie was warm enough. He knocked at the tumbledown door and went in.

Mother Heggy was crouched in a corner poking at something on the floor. She peered up at him and rose creakily to her feet, her back still bent almost double. She shuffled towards him, and surprisingly, embraced him. She felt like a tiny bird. Beneath the layers of grimy, ancient clothing, there was barely anything left of her.

"The time is here," she wheezed. "The brightness in the darkness. 'Tis all up to you now, Yul. Are you ready for it?"

287

He nodded. "I am. Everything's in place. Will you come to the sunrise ceremony tomorrow morning, Mother Heggy? I'd love you to be there."

She shook her grizzled head.

"'Tis too cold for me, Yul. I can't be out in the cold and dark. Maybe the Summer Solstice, when Sylvie becomes sixteen. 'Twill be warmer then."

"Alright. But we'll both come and see you later on tomorrow. You'll be looking at the new magus then!"

She felt the excitement and certainty flowing in him, but shook her head again.

"I need your help, Yul. Will you drag the table over to the wall?"

"Yes … but why?"

He pulled the heavy oak table, scraping it along the uneven flagstone floor. She picked up an ancient besom and began to sweep to one side the debris that littered the floor.

"That's why," she said breathlessly, pointing to the floor. "You do it for me, Yul. I feel so weary today."

She sank into the rocking chair whilst he swept the floor, with the crow crouched on the table watching. Yul saw marks scratched into the flagstones. Gradually a large pentangle within a circle was revealed. He automatically made the sign in the air, touching his heart to signify that his spirit and the elements were as one, bound by the same laws and the same love of the Goddess.

"There, Mother Heggy. Anything else?"

She pointed to the things she needed, and he set up the magic circle ready for her. He placed a small candle in a green glass jar at each point of the pentangle, and a bowl of salt in the centre. He knew she'd sprinkle it around the circle in a careful trail from within, before she started her ceremony. This would keep the dark forces at bay and protect her inside her circle. He placed the symbolic objects at each point of the star, next to the candles. There was one each for the four elements – earth, air, fire and water. And of course one for the spirit, the fifth element. He placed matches and a taper next to the salt for her to light the candles. Finally he put in a cushion for her to sit upon within the inner pentagon formed by the lines of the pentangle.

He surveyed the magical space marked on the floor and respectfully stepped out of it. He himself didn't cast the circle or call upon the elements. He didn't need to. He felt the power of nature everywhere. The Earth Goddess spoke to him directly through the green magic at the special places all over Stonewylde. Clip needed the spirals within the dolmen and the ridgeway. Sylvie needed the full moon and the magic on the hill marked by the Hare Stone. Many people simply needed a wood, a beach, a hill top, or just blue sky on a sunny day. And others, like Mother Heggy, cast their circles with salt and flame and called upon the powers to visit them and bless them. Yul respected each way of communing with the force of nature, the magic of creation, the life energy that throbbed and snaked and sparkled everywhere all over the earth. Each to their own. There were many paths to the divine destination.

"Blessings, Yul. You are a good lad. I'm proud of you. I shall be within the circle here tonight as the sun sets and the moon rises. I shall do all I can to help you. No! Don't say you need none o' my help! We all want that man dead. If I can call upon any of the forces, then I will. Don't imagine tonight will be easy, Yul. Don't think that because I made that prophecy sixteen years ago, 'twill all come to pass."

Mother Heggy sighed heavily and the crow hopped onto her lap. She stroked its glossy plumage with a twisted finger.

"Your father is still very powerful. That man has elements on his side that only he can use. There are ancient echoes of energy and ancient story patterns still in play. Nought is set in stone. You could fail tonight, my dark one. Sylvie could be taken tonight. Anything could happen, Yul. Don't make the mistake of thinking all will go to plan, just because Stonewylde loves you. Stonewylde has had her dark times afore. Terrible times when all seemed lost and gone. 'Tis possible we will enter those dark times again."

Yul stared at her, worry creasing his face. He knelt before her as she crouched in the rocking chair and took her withered hands in his young, strong ones. He looked into her milky eyes, his fierce spirit blazing from within.

"Thank you for your wisdom, Mother Heggy. I heed what you say. I won't make the mistake of over-confidence, nor of under-estimating him. I'll do my best and fight my hardest. If I should fail tonight, please help Sylvie. She'll need you."

The old crone nodded.

"Go now, Yul. I must sleep for a while. I feel so tired and 'twill be a difficult night. I will look out for the bright one, just as I've looked out for you, the dark one. Bright blessings, young magus."

She made the sign of the pentangle over his head, and prayed silently to the Goddess to keep him safe. After he'd gone she rose slowly, muttering to herself, and began to prepare what she needed for the night ahead. She was very frightened. Earlier that morning she'd found five black feathers lying on her doorstep. The scrying glass would not reveal to her what would happen that evening at sunset, when her binding spell was finally unravelled. Despite a lifetime of magic and practising the craft, she was now as much in the dark as the next person. Except for the message of five. That was as clear as spring water.

"This is all my fault," said Hazel sadly as she removed the cuff from Miranda's upper arm. "Your blood pressure's a bit high. Hardly surprising."

Miranda rolled down her sleeve and patted Hazel's hand.

"It's *not* your fault. Don't even think it."

"But I brought you here! It was my idea."

"And what was the alternative? Leave Sylvie to die in London? Come on, Hazel. You did what you thought best, and despite everything, I'm pleased you did."

She looked down at the enormous mound of her pregnancy and sighed. The baby was kicking again and had been agitated all day. She and Hazel had shared lunch in the hospital wing whilst she had her check-up, unable to face the clamour of the Dining Hall and the oblivious Hallfolk.

"Try to get some rest, Miranda. You look exhausted."

"Tomorrow, when this whole nightmare is over, I'll rest.

Clip's coming to fetch me in a minute. You know where we're going."

She stood up and held her arms out to Hazel, who bent in an awkward hug around Miranda's belly. She felt the young doctor sobbing silently, the strain of the past weeks coming out at this unexpected show of affection.

"I'm so sorry," Hazel mumbled. "So very sorry it all turned out like this. I was completely fooled by him. I was horrible to poor Sylvie, blaming her for everything. And all the time he'd been making her suffer terribly every Moon Fullness and none of us believed her."

"We're all guilty of that. It's even worse for me. I'm her mother and I should've been protecting her. Do you think she's alright? I'm still so worried about her up there alone with him. Clip is sure Magus won't harm her, but …"

Hazel pulled away and found a tissue.

"I'm sure she is. And only a couple more hours now. She'll be safe soon."

"But what if it goes wrong this evening? Why won't Yul do what we all wanted? He should have agreed to what everyone suggested. How can he possibly do this alone?"

Hazel shook her head.

"That boy – or rather, young man – is as determined and iron-willed as his father. He insists he must be the one to take Magus on. He says it's part of the prophecy and it won't work if he has any help. It has to be one to one. What can we do?"

"He'll make a good magus, I'm sure," said Miranda. "There's something very special and powerful about Yul."

"Green magic. Yul has the green magic now and that's why he's so adamant about what must happen tonight. With the Goddess on his side, how could he fail?"

As soon as the long lunch was over Magus dragged Sylvie upstairs again. Once they were in his rooms with the door shut he turned on her, his face furious.

"You need to learn how to behave, young lady! When I allow you downstairs to mix with the Hallfolk, you will be sociable and gracious, both to them and to me. You are never to speak to me in that disrespectful way again in front of them. And you're never to be greedy again either, stuffing food down your throat as fast as you can. If you behave like that when I let you out, then you won't go out at all. You'll stay locked in these rooms until your manners improve. Do you understand?"

She nodded, her earlier defiance gone now that they were alone again. She looked out of the window. It was still bright and sunny, although the wind looked as if it might be chilly.

"I want to go out for a walk," she said. "You haven't let me outside for ages. I need some fresh air."

"Well you can't. You'll get plenty of fresh air tonight."

"Can I get changed then? This dress is too tight. It's cutting into me."

"That's because you ate too much. No, you can keep it on. If it's uncomfortable it serves you right. Maybe it'll teach you not to be so greedy. I want you to rest for the afternoon. Here, sit down and read your book."

He picked up the book where it lay on the table and handed it to her. She took it carefully, not sure if the photo was still inside. She went over to the window seat and he followed her over, unable to leave her alone.

There was a discreet knock at the door and Martin appeared. He stood respectfully before Magus, paying no attention to Sylvie.

"You said you wanted to speak to me after lunch, sir."

"Yes, it's about tonight at Mooncliffe."

Martin's glance flicked to Sylvie.

"I'd be glad to assist you, sir."

"Of course. I want you to go up there now and stack all the eggs around the rock."

"Yes, sir. Will that be all?"

"No – take a couple of blankets too, and the little pavilion. And the brazier and wood for a fire. I'll need to keep my moongazy girl warm. She's going to be there most of the night." Magus patted her knee. "I did warn you, Sylvie. It's going to be a heavy night."

She turned her head away, looking out of the window and

ignoring him. Magus smiled and looked up at Martin, standing so impassive and cold-eyed.

"Oh, and one more thing, Martin."

"Yes, sir?"

"Take the other things up there too."

"The usual, sir?"

"Yes, the usual. The silk cushions, the candles ... you know what's required."

The stony-faced man nodded and gave a small smile.

"I know what's required. And if I might say so sir – about time too."

When he'd gone, Magus turned to Sylvie. The blood had drained from her face.

"Did you understand that?"

"Yes."

"I can't wait any longer, Sylvie. I'm burning up for you. It's like a fire inside me and it hurts. I've heard that my father was like this with my mother. It's all to do with being moongazy. You just don't know the effect you have on me."

She sat very still, her heart thumping with fear. What if everything went wrong tonight? She had faith in Yul, but things had gone wrong before. And she remembered the earlier phone call. Magus had help coming soon. What if they over-powered Yul? She started to cry softly, the tears rolling down her cheeks and smudging her make-up.

"Don't cry, my darling. I'll be so gentle, I promise. I love you, Sylvie. And after tonight, you'll love me. I can guarantee that."

"How can you do this if you love me?" she choked, wiping the tears away impatiently. "I don't want you and I'm too young. I'm not ready for this. There are so many others here. You know you can have anyone you want at Stonewylde."

"But I don't want anyone else. It's *you* I crave. You're the only one who can feed the stones and give me the moon magic I need. And you're the only one I want to make love to. Nobody else will do. I just can't wait another six months, Sylvie. I thought I could but I can't. I'm sorry."

He pulled out his handkerchief and gently wiped away the tears and mascara. He smiled at her ruefully.

"I don't think I've ever had this reaction before when I tell a girl she's been chosen for the Moon Fullness. Please don't cry, Sylvie. You'll learn to love me. Let me get you some mead."

She groaned as he went over to the cabinet and found her crystal goblet. She couldn't stand it. Still clutching the book, she gazed out through the diamond paned glass across the garden, like a bird imprisoned in a cage. She knew that out there the whole community was busy preparing for the Solstice. She knew that Yul would be getting ready for whatever he'd planned for her rescue. She also knew that what happened tonight would determine the rest of her life.

If Yul failed, she'd never escape Magus' clutches. He'd keep her cooped up as a virtual prisoner, starved into submission whenever he felt like it and controlled in every way. He'd shower her with gifts, dress her in expensive clothes and jewels, parade her as a prized possession, but he'd never allow her any freedom. He'd control and dominate her every minute, binding her with his love and his hatred. For despite these protestations of love, she knew he hated her as well for her coldness towards him. She'd slowly wither under his obsessive captivity, like a wild bird trapped in a gilded cage.

Magus came back with the mead, moving across the floor like a great panther. She looked up into his face, so attractive with his strong features and dark eyes, his silvery blond hair emphasising the perfection of his chiselled cheekbones and jaw. He was tall and muscular, every woman's dream of a desirable man. Yet he filled her with loathing and dread. He smiled at her as he held out the crystal goblet, his eyes bright with admiration.

"Here you are, my moongazy girl. You look beautiful sitting there like that against the light. I feel ..."

At that moment the photo, still between the pages of the book in Sylvie's hands, slipped out and fell to the floor. She gasped and tried to cover it with her foot in a futile gesture.

Magus frowned and put the glass down on a side table. He bent and picked up the white rectangle from under her foot.

He turned it over and stared into the face of the Green Man. He saw the foliage in an aura around the head, the thick dark curls full of vegetation. The skin was smeared green and brown from lichen and earth. And the eyes! Those clear, grey eyes, slanted and long-lashed, gazed out with such clarity, such knowledge.

Magus knew then, in that moment, that Sylvie would never love him. This boy was the one she wanted, the only one she would ever love. He, Magus of Stonewylde, was nothing to her and never could be. With a roar of pure animal rage, he ripped the photo in two.

"Why?" he bellowed. *"Why him? Why not me?"*

He ripped the photo in two again, and then again, throwing the pieces on the floor and grinding them under his boot in a paroxysm of fury. He grabbed the crystal goblet and flung it across the room. It hit the great television screen and smashed with an explosion of glass and amber liquid. His chest heaved with anger and passion as he glared down at Sylvie, his hands clenching and unclenching, his breathing heavy. She curled up as small as she could into the corner of the window seat, her face white and eyes enormous with terror. He fell to his knees before her, taking her shoulders in his hands and gripping her tightly. His eyes were wild and his face hollow. His voice was low and trembled with deep emotion.

"You cut me to the bone, Sylvie. I've told you how I feel about you. I laid myself open to you, offered you something I've never offered anyone before. All I ask for is your love. Why is that so difficult? Every single woman I've ever met has been mine for the taking. Nobody has ever turned their back on me, not wanted me. Why are you so different? How can you love that boy and not me?"

His voice cracked in anguish and she thought for a terrible moment he was going to cry. She stared at him, mute with fear. He felt her trembling beneath his hands. Suddenly a white hot rage welled up inside him and with it an overpowering urge to hurt her really badly. To hit her and hit her until she was nothing but a piece of battered debris, her beauty ruined and her spirit smashed. His hands flexed on her shoulders as the desire to destroy her flooded through him. He could do it. It would be so easy. Then he saw a pulse beating frantically in her white throat above the diamond choker, like a small bird trapped.

With a groan he let her go, pushing her violently away from him. She fell back hard against the window. His face was dark with unspent rage and pain. He looked down at the fragments of photo beneath his feet for a long moment and took a deep breath. Then he looked up at Sylvie, his face now under control, his voice like steel.

"Because you love this boy, I'm going to kill him slowly. Have no doubt of that, Sylvie. He'll die tonight at my hand and at my pleasure. And then, on the rock, I will make you pay. No gentleness and no love. You'll pay every day for the rest of your life for hurting me like this. You'll wish then that you'd loved me while you had the chance. Before you forced my love for you to turn to hate. You'll wish it with all your heart, my girl."

Siskin climbed into a taxi at the station and tipped the porter who'd helped with his suitcase. The porter looked askance at the dapper little man, something from a bygone era with his patent leather shoes, brushed overcoat and hat.

"Stonewylde please," said Siskin, closing the car door.

"Where's that to then, sir?" asked the taxi driver, clearly a Dorset man.

Siskin sighed, but in his heart was glad that somewhere the size of Stonewylde had managed to remain unknown even to locals, blanketed in mystery and invisibility from the Outside World.

"Take the main road out of town and I'll direct you," replied Siskin. "It's about an hour away."

He sat back in the taxi and smiled to himself. Not long now, and he'd be home where he belonged.

CHAPTER SIXTEEN

The intercom on Magus' desk buzzed. He covered the room in a few long strides and jabbed the switch, picking up the receiver.

"Yes? ... Good. No, no stay there. I'll be with you in about twenty minutes."

Sylvie looked away quickly as he came over to her. The hired man must have arrived at the Gate House. She hoped desperately that her message had got through to Yul. The alternative was too awful to contemplate.

"I have to go out for a while," he said, standing over her as she huddled in the window seat. "I'll be gone for an hour or so. I want you to lie down and rest."

He reached across and smoothed down her hair, and despite his earlier cruel words, there was gentleness once again in his touch. He took her chin in one hand and looked into her eyes. She was so very beautiful, and so very vulnerable. He felt the desire to protect her and to violate her in equal measures. He gave her a tight smile and patted her cheek.

"After this solstice, Sylvie, things will be very different. That boy Yul will be gone and you will in time forget him. You'll live with me, by my side constantly day and night, and you'll learn to love me. After tonight I know the Earth Magic will return to me. Together you and I will be so powerful. A partnership such as Stonewylde has never known before."

He sighed and taking her hand, pulled her up from the seat and guided her over to the sofa. He pushed her down gently onto the soft leather and made her stretch out.

"Try to get a little sleep, Sylvie. You've a long night ahead of you. I'll be back to collect you before sunset."

He perched on the edge of the sofa and took one of her

hands in his, examining her bitten nails.

"You're like an unpolished jewel, Sylvie. Under my guidance and expertise, you'll learn to glitter and sparkle. I shall enjoy working on you, polishing and refining you until you reach perfection. I shall devote myself to you. A moongazy girl is hard to find and I shall never, ever let you go. Remember that, Sylvie. I'll be with you always. Forever."

He bent and kissed her on the lips. His scent filled her nostrils as he lingered, seeming loathe to leave. Then he rose and his gaze swept her one last time.

"I'll be back for you, Sylvie."

"Goodbye, Magus," she whispered.

She heard the key turn in the lock, and knew that she was captive.

As soon as he'd gone, she jumped up and raced over to the dumb waiter, wrenching open the panelling. The note had gone! Yul must know the danger he was in. As long as the message had got through to him. She hurried down through the rooms to her own room to get changed into warm clothes. She wished she knew what the plan was. There wasn't that much time till sunset and Magus wouldn't take long to drive up to the Gate House and back. The sky was still bright but she was starting to get twitchy. She could feel the familiar sensation beginning to prickle under her skin. She heard the intercom buzzing back down in the sitting room. She hesitated, for she wasn't allowed to answer the phone or intercom. But then she thought it might be for her; something to do with her rescue. So she raced back through all the rooms, hair flying, and reached the phone before it stopped buzzing.

"Magus, sir?"

"No, it's Sylvie."

"What? Oh, well I need to speak to Magus."

"He's not here. He's gone out."

"He can't have! No, no he can't have!"

The line went dead. She assumed the Villager on the other end didn't use the phone much. It buzzed again.

"I'm sorry, miss. 'Tis Tom here. Tom from the stables. I need to speak to Magus to tell him that Yul's been here."

"Tom, is this part of the plan? Yul's plan?"

"Aye, miss, you could say that. But if Magus ain't there, I don't know what to do. Where is he then?"

"He's gone up to the Gate House. In a car, I suppose, if you haven't seen him. There's someone coming, a man with guns and knives, and I think he's coming to kill Yul. I sent a note to Clip this morning. I thought you'd all know about it by now."

"No, miss, we ain't heard nothing. With guns and knives? That's bad. Well, I don't know what to do now. We thought the master'd be with you. I don't know what to say. You just be ready, miss, to leave very soon."

Sylvie felt sick with fear and her agitation increased as the hour of sunset drew nearer. She went to collect her cloak from the wardrobe, and as she passed again through the rooms, she glanced outside. The sun was low in the sky and the shadows very long. Her heart beat fast and her hands trembled. Where was Yul? Magus would be back soon with this man. She was terribly scared.

When she returned to the sitting room, she didn't at first notice the figure standing in the shadows. Her heart jumped as the blond head turned at the sound of her approach. It was Martin! He stared at her and she felt uncomfortable under his expressionless scrutiny.

"Hello, Martin. I ... what are you doing here?"

"I've completed the preparations at Mooncliffe. All is in place for the night ahead."

"But why are you here? I don't need babysitting. Go back downstairs, please."

He shook his head, pulling a scrap of paper from his pocket. With a plunge of despair, Sylvie recognised her note.

"You think to escape! You're the moongazy maiden and should be honoured to serve. Yet you've been plotting and scheming with those who stand against our Magus. But I shall make sure that you're ready and waiting for the master."

He smiled and Sylvie shivered. How was Yul to rescue her now? She went over to the window and looked out. The sky was turning pink. It wouldn't be long.

"Martin, you really don't need to stay here. I'm ready, as you can see. I've changed into my warm clothes."

Martin chuckled at this, and the sinister sound made her flesh creep.

Silently a dark figure appeared in the doorway of the connecting room. Sylvie looked up, her heart jolting again. It was Clip. He wore his dark cloak full of black birds' feathers and held his ash staff, the one that had transformed into the Rainbow Snake all those months ago. He looked out of place here in Magus' domain, a strange man with his long, wispy hair and pale grey eyes. Eyes just like her own. He smiled at her and held out his hand.

"Come, Sylvie, my lovely daughter. I've come to take you moondancing."

"No!" cried Martin, stepping out from the shadows. "She's for Magus! All is prepared."

Clip turned and stared at the tall blond man so very similar to himself.

"No, Martin. She's not for Magus."

"Yes! She must be taken tonight, at the brightness in the darkness! The magic is strong and powerful and Magus must take his fill tonight on the stone of snakes at Mooncliffe. Then she will be bound to him. She will never break free. Her magic will be his for ever more!"

Clip frowned.

"Those are your mother's words, Martin. What evil is she up to now? Come here."

Reluctantly Martin stepped forward until he and Clip were level with each other. Sylvie gasped. She'd never seen them so close together before. Clip stared hard at Martin.

"Look at me! You will sit down, Martin, and ..."

"Oh no! You won't catch me like that!" he cried, looking away and holding a hand up to block Clip's view of him. "Keep away and don't try your tricks on me!"

He rushed over to Sylvie and grabbed her roughly.

"Stay with me, girl," he hissed. "Don't defy the master or it'll be worse for you."

"Let her go!" commanded Clip, striding towards them.

"How *dare* you do this, Martin!"

"I don't take my orders from you!" he said contemptuously. "You're not the master! You're a poor thin shadow, not worthy even to walk behind him. He'll be back any minute now and then we'll see how you cower when he raises his voice to you. Just as you've always done. Keep away from this girl. 'Tis her destiny to be bound by the snakes of the rock. 'Tis her destiny to feed their hunger. And to give the master what he craves."

Clip raised his ash staff and began to spin it around him. The black-feathered cloak flew out in a vast circular wing of darkness and Martin gazed spell-bound, his grip on Sylvie loosening. Clip swung the staff in a great blurred arc and with a mighty crack caught Martin on the side of the head. He fell like a tree, straight down and almost in slow motion. Sylvie cried out in horror.

"No time for that!" barked Clip. "Come on! Magus'll be back any minute!"

Together they hurried through the connecting rooms until they came to her bedroom. They flung open the door out into the long corridor, and rushed along towards the back stairs.

"Where are we going?" cried Sylvie, clasping the cloak around her to stop it tangling in her legs.

"To Woodland Cottage, where you lived when you first came here. Then as the sun sets, we'll make our way up to Hare Stone. That's where Yul wants you to go."

"Will he be there waiting for me?"

"No, he's dealing with Magus. He wants you safe whatever the outcome of their conflict. I'll be taking care of you tonight, Sylvie. It's about time I looked out for your welfare."

She smiled at this, and hurried to keep up with his long strides.

"Where's Jack then? Are we gonna see him tonight" asked the hard faced man in the front seat next to Magus.

"No, he's not here right now," replied Magus evenly. "That's why I've had to call on your services for this job, else

I'd have used him. But he'd left me your number and recommended you. Now remember, keep away from the girl. Don't go anywhere near her. She's not quite right at the moment. All you must do is patrol the area around the cliff top and capture the boy when he makes an appearance. He'll be trying to get to the girl and he won't be expecting you there. You've got handcuffs and rope like we agreed? Capture him, cuff him and gag him, and then keep him out of my way. "

"So you don't want the boy done over at all?" said the man, frowning. "I thought you wanted him taken out. Why bring all this kit then?"

"I want him captured. If he's got weapons and you think he's about to seriously injure me, or manage somehow to take the girl away, then yes, you can kill him. But I'd rather hoped to have that pleasure myself. We'll take the boy up to the Stone Circle later on. That's where I want to take his life. I'll need you two along in case he has any misguided followers with him. Feel free to deal with them by all means."

"Right you are. You got that, Bob?"

He turned around to his colleague in the back seat, and rolled his eyes, his message clear.

"We're approaching the Hall now. We'll collect the girl and get straight up to the cliff top."

"Nice pile," muttered the heavier man in the back seat of the Landrover, eyeing the grand stately home. "Very nice."

Magus pulled up and led them inside, heading upstairs. The two men, both wearing combat gear and carrying long gun cases, looked incongruous in the mediaeval setting of the Hall. The place was deserted as everyone had gone to the Stone Circle for the brief ritual at sunset and moonrise, marking the eve of the Winter Solstice. Magus had arranged for Clip to conduct the ceremony, although unbeknown to Magus, Clip had found a last minute substitute to do the honours. Magus hurried up the stairs, unlocked the door to his rooms and ushered the hired men inside. He was annoyed to find Sylvie gone from the sofa where she should be sleeping. He called her angrily.

Then he discovered Martin lying unconscious in the

shadows behind the table near the window, and cried out in fury. He saw the great lump on the side of his head and ran through the rooms shouting for Sylvie. When he realised she wasn't there and that the door from her bedroom to the outside corridor was open, he went pale and let out a scream of pure rage. As he raced back through to the sitting room where the hired men were waiting, the intercom began to buzz.

"YES?" he yelled.

"Sir, Magus, 'tis the boy Yul!" began Tom, relieved that at last the master had returned so he could put his part of the plan into motion.

"What about him? Is this Tom? Have you seen him?"

"Aye sir, he's been here in the stables and he's took Nightwing. He ..."

"WHAT? Why did you let him do that, you bloody fool?"

"He said you gave permission, sir. But I weren't sure and I tried to phone you to check, sir, but you been away. I kept trying."

Magus slammed his fist on the desk, white with fury. He took a deep breath.

"Alright, Tom. He's taken Nightwing. Did you see Sylvie? The young girl."

"Oh yes, sir," said Tom quickly, adjusting the plan to cope with the new train of events. "She was with him. He took her on the horse too."

"WHAT? I don't believe I'm hearing this! And you didn't think to stop them?"

"As I said, sir, he told me he had your permission. And seeing as how he's your son, and she's Master Clip's daughter, I didn't think 'twas my place to say ..."

"I will deal with you tomorrow, Tom, when this is all over. Saddle me up another horse! I'm on my way down now. I'll find them at Hill Stone, no doubt."

"Well, sir, I was just about to say, I think I know where they've gone."

"Why the hell didn't you say so before? Where?"

"Well, they was arguing, sir. Miss Sylvie said she wanted to go to Hare Stone, wherever that is. Maybe she meant Hill

Stone. But young Yul, he weren't having none of it. He said they were going to Quarrycleave."

"*Quarrycleave?*"

"Aye, sir. He definitely said Quarrycleave. I was standing right with them while they was talking. Felt awkward, I did, listening in. He told her there was a special stone up there that she could dance on for him. They argued a bit and she cried and he shouted at her. Quite harsh he was with her, and she was very upset. Then she said alright, she'd do it for him as 'twas his birthday, just the once. Those were her very words, sir"

"The sly, cunning, little *bastard*! All that crap he gave me yesterday, and he wants her moon magic too! Alright, Tom, I won't need a horse. I'll drive up there in the Landrover, and then I can take my associates here too."

He slammed the phone town, quivering with anger. His eyes flashed dangerously as he spoke to the two men.

"Change of plan! We're driving up to the quarry. The boy's on horseback and he's got the girl. He's taking her to a tall stone at the head of the quarry. Under no circumstances whatsoever are you to approach that stone or touch the girl. Do you understand? I want the boy captured as we discussed before. More than ever now I want to kill him myself, so don't go firing guns or anything like that. Just catch him and tie him up. Now come on, let's get a move on. The moon will be rising soon."

On their way out, the men caught each other's eye. They grimaced to each other and shook their heads. As they followed Magus down the stairs, they held back slightly and managed to whisper hoarsely to each other.

"Don't like the sound of this, Bob. It ain't what he told us on the phone. This is all very dodgy."

"Shall we get out now? Cut our losses? We got half the cash, after all."

"Nah, let's go along and see how it pans out. Might be alright. But if it starts getting too funny, we'll get out. Bloke's completely off his bloody head."

At the Gate House, the two Villagers on duty were surprised when a taxi pulled up and Professor Siskin got out. They recognised him of course, but had no idea he was due to visit.

"All the Hallfolk coming for the Solstice have already arrived, sir," said one of them, carrying his case into the Gate House. "We weren't expecting you. There ain't no car here to take you down to the Hall. And you just missed Magus."

"No matter!" said Siskin brightly, breathing the late afternoon air deeply and beaming with happiness. "Ah, but it's good to be home! I'll come in and have a cup of tea with you two chaps, if you don't mind."

"Course, sir. And I'll phone down to the Hall and get someone to drive up and collect you."

"No hurry. And I'm happy to travel in horse and cart if necessary. I'm actually not going to the Hall first anyway. I wanted to go to the Jack in the Green and have a glass or two of cider."

"Very wise, sir. Wouldn't mind one myself."

Mother Heggy took a jar from a shelf and poured some of the thick liquid into a heavy goblet. She added another thinner liquid and stirred in a sprinkle of desiccated herbs, then carefully hobbled over to place the goblet inside the pentangle next to the salt and matches. She took a small cake wrapped in a piece of linen, and her clay pipe and herbal tobacco, and put these too inside the magic circle. The light was fading fast. She put extra logs onto her fire, knowing that the chill would be bad later on. Once the circle was cast she wouldn't be able to leave it until the rituals were finished.

Finally, she opened a little black box and removed the figure, taking it into the circle with her. She pursed her lips and summoned the crow, who hopped delicately inside with her, sitting at the head of the star. Mother Heggy picked up the bowl of salt, and muttering the incantations, began to sprinkle it carefully in an unbroken circle onto the circumference marked out on the flagstones. She was now protected within the circle. Then with great difficulty she sat down on the cushion in the centre, feeling her ancient joints and ligaments crack in protest. She lit the taper and reached to light the five candles in the points of the pentangle. Now she could summon the elements. Now the ceremony could begin. The crow blinked.

At Woodland Cottage, Miranda sat in an armchair by the fire watching her daughter pace the room. She and Clip had discussed Sylvie's terrible revelation that a hired thug had arrived to help Magus kill Yul. They realised there was nothing they could do now for the plan was already in action. There was no way they could get in touch with Yul. They just had to trust in Yul's strength and ability to take care of himself. Clip looked out of the window.

"Sun's going down," he announced. "We'll go up there soon, Sylvie."

She nodded, the tension becoming unbearable. She tingled and prickled and her feet moved of their own accord. She wanted to get out, to go up high.

Up, up high on the hill with the beautiful moongazy hares dancing with me round and round in a spiral. I am a moon angel and I spread my wings and I fly, fly round the great marker stone. I feel the moon magic enter my soul and I feed the Earth Mother. I am the moongazy girl and I must dance. I was born to dance for the earth and the moon and to bring the moon magic to Stonewylde!

She rushed to the door and tried to wrench it open.

"Steady," said Clip, taking her arm. "You need to wrap up warm first."

She turned her face to him but her eyes were completely blank, the pale grey irises with their dark rings unworldly. She was listening, but not to him, and then she tried to push past him. Miranda got up and put the scarlet cloak around Sylvie, fastening the clasp. She tried to put gloves on her but Sylvie pulled them off angrily.

"Go, go, go! I must go now!"

"Is this how she always gets?" asked Clip. He'd only ever seen her up at Mooncliffe, which was somewhat different, especially when she'd been hypnotised.

"Yes, it is," replied Miranda, remembering all the

incidents in London when Sylvie had become frantic trying to get out onto the balcony of the flat.

"Come on then," said Clip, taking Sylvie's hand in his, and lifting the latch of the door. "We'll be back later on, Miranda. I have no idea what time. Make sure her bed's ready and warm because it's getting cold out there. See you later. You know there are several Villagers outside in the garden keeping an eye on you, and Edward and his group are patrolling all around the area. So don't worry, will you? Everything's going to be fine, I promise."

They walked quickly up the path in the woods, Sylvie tugging at Clip's hand impatiently.

"Quick, quick, quick! The hares are gathering. Hurry!"

As they reached the field at the foot of the hill, Sylvie broke free from his grasp. She ran on ahead through the cold grass and around the boulders, up towards the dark stone outlined against the pale blue sky at the top. The sun was gone; a peachy glow marked its point of departure. A bright star twinkled in the clear sky and the temperature began to drop rapidly as Sylvie raced up the hill, followed by her long legged father. Unseen, Greenbough and the woodsmen with their axes stepped silently out from the wood. They took up their places around the hill, forming a ring of protection for the magical girl in her scarlet cloak.

Up at Quarrycleave there was no ring of protection for Yul. This was his battle and he would face it alone. He desperately hoped his plan to lure Magus away from Sylvie would work. Tom would have done his bit by now, with Edward as back up in case Magus didn't swallow the story. With the woodsmen and Clip guarding Sylvie at Hare Stone she must be safe. That was what mattered more than anything. He'd sworn to her that she'd be safe tonight from Magus, and nothing would prevent that.

He'd ridden up here very fast. Nightwing was glorious! He loved the horse passionately and the horse loved him. Yul had whispered to Nightwing in the stables and without protest the great stallion had allowed the boy to mount. The horse could feel the power and the passion in his young rider and had responded in kind. They'd flown to the quarry like the wind, pounding swiftly along the miles of ridgeway. Silhouetted as the sun sank lower in the sky, the dark boy and the dark horse were as one; sweat and muscles flowing and stretching, hearts pounding in unison. It was the stuff of Yul's dreams.

At the quarry Yul leapt down on light feet, his thighs trembling from the hard ride. He tethered Nightwing loosely to a stunted elder tree. Yul glanced around. They were close to the caravans where Jackdaw had taken such pleasure in humiliating him. He smiled grimly. That all seemed so long ago now. Yul caressed the horse's long head, his hand gentle on the velvet nose. He whispered into Nightwing's flickering ears and the great black horse dipped his head in compliance. He would crop the grass and wait quietly here.

Yul looked up to the hill above him and saw that the sun had just slipped behind the horizon. He took a shuddering breath. Sunset on the eve of the Winter Solstice! The binding spell was finally broken. Mother Heggy's magic no longer cloaked him in protection. Standing at the mouth of the place of bones and death, Yul peered into the shadowy labyrinth ahead and remembered the deadly lure of the place.

The quarry was a place of brooding and menace in the day time; at twilight it took on an even darker atmosphere. The stone was pale and the enormous crater seemed to glow slightly as if the white stone had retained daylight. It was impossible to see from one side of the quarry to the other, for the rock had not been blasted out entirely. There were channels and walls, cliffs and mounds, great boulders lying tumbled everywhere. The place was a massive labyrinth hewn and gouged into the land, a wild jumble of fossil-encrusted rocks and half dressed blocks of stone. Great twisting ropes of ivy snaked up the cliff faces, the glossy leaves covering cracks and crevices and hidden recesses. Yul remembered climbing up those faces in the summer and hacking at the sinuous ivy.

All around lay the debris from the work done under Jackdaw's command. Yul knew through the Village grapevine of the deaths that had occurred just after he'd left Quarrycleave six months ago. Somewhere, under tons of fallen rock, lay the bodies of several men. The men who'd thrown their empty beer cans at him and laughed as Jackdaw forced him to further degradation with each new day. Yul shivered at the thought.

As the light thickened around him and the first stars began to peep, Yul ran lightly along the paths of the tall labyrinth. He twisted his way from the shallow end, where the quarry was no more than a few feet below ground level, to the far end, where there was a high, sheer cliff face leading up to the top of the hill. It was near the summit of this high quarry face that the great snake-stone stood, partner to the disc of rock at Mooncliffe. It was a huge monolith of the same sparkling white stone, with room on top for several people. It had been hewn into a smooth pillar shape that seemed to rise from the rocks around it like a hand thrusting from the grave. Snakes had been carved onto it, massive coiling serpents that writhed around the base and twisted themselves up the rock to the top.

As Yul came closer to the sheer quarry face he turned and followed a path that led up to the side of the crater. He began to climb the tumbled rocks that formed steps and platforms. The path wound up the side and finally Yul reached the base of the snake stone. He used the boulders around it to climb higher and finally leapt up onto the top. He stood, still and silent, surveying the scene in the fast fading light.

Below him, the quarry was a vast stonescape of shadows. The pathways between the rocks were channels of blackness. Anything could be lurking down there in the maze of rock. He felt the menacing atmosphere pressing on his soul. He recalled the awful compulsion he'd succumbed to last summer, saved only by Sylvie's presence and the creatures she'd summoned. There was a feeling of dread here, a feeling of pain, terror and death.

Yul sensed something of the ritual slaughter performed in this hollow place over the ages. But he knew nothing of the remains of many bodies concealed beneath; the bones, skulls and sad fragments of things once held precious by the ancestors of Stonewylde. He knew nothing of the sacrifices of blood and flesh, the torture, killings and murders committed in the name of appeasement and supplication. In the greed and lust for power. All he knew was that the quarry was the place of bones and death. It was the final arena for the prophecy in whose aura he'd lived his whole life. It was the place where tonight he must kill his father, or be killed himself.

The Landrover bumped and jolted up the track leading to the quarry, pot-holed and gullied by years of winter rains and neglect. The two passengers held on tightly as they bounced in their seats. Magus drove like the devil, his face grim. He swore softly under his breath, a continuous stream of invective against Yul, the boy who threatened his power and his very existence as Magus of Stonewylde. He'd had no energy from his moon eggs for many days now. The last eggs, so carefully hoarded and rationed, had been switched. He'd absolutely counted on being up at Mooncliffe with Sylvie tonight, feeding on her moon magic. He desperately needed that energy, now the Earth Goddess no longer gave him any of hers. Without it he was powerless. Without it he was no more than an ordinary man.

But what really filled him with searing rage was the thought of Yul's duplicity and greed. He knew just how much power the boy had, literally at his fingertips. Only yesterday Magus had seen him glow with it, the energy crackling around him, sparking from his fingers and even lifting him from the rock in its force field. He was pumped full of Earth Magic. How could he be so greedy as to want the moon magic as well?

Magus cursed him again, and that ungrateful little bitch. He'd laid his heart open to her, offered her the world, yet she was unwilling to give him the one thing he craved. Instead she was prepared to share her gift with his bastard son who didn't even need it. When he got hold of them tonight, nothing would stop him exacting his revenge. With the two mercenaries to help, he'd kill the boy slowly. And then he'd begin on Sylvie. He wasn't sure which he looked forward to the most.

Clip stood beside the standing stone on the hill top watching his daughter wait for the moonrise. She faced the north-east where the full moon rose at the Winter Solstice; exactly the same place as the Summer Solstice sunrise. The scarlet cloak was flung back as she raised her arms to the heavens. Early stars glittered in the cold night air. The sky was clear and bright, perfect for the Moon Fullness. Sylvie's mass of silver hair flowed around her, spilling onto the scarlet velvet as she stood with her wings held high. She began to sing the strange moondance music. The hares crouching further down the hill raised their long, velvet ears and sat up on their hind legs. The first sliver of bright buttery yellow appeared on the horizon far out to sea. The girl's wild voice soared in glory and the hares gazed with glinting eyes towards the water.

Siskin sat back in the deep oak settle, the noise of the Villagers in the Jack in the Green all around him as he sipped his glass of cider with closed eyes. He was perfectly happy. The men had fallen silent when he'd arrived a little earlier, driven down in a car summoned by the gatekeepers. The last thing the Village men wanted tonight was a member of the Hallfolk in the pub. But Siskin had understood and had produced the photo of Yul from his bag. He'd held it up proudly, inviting all to see.

"This is why I've come!" he said excitedly. "To see this young man take his rightful place as our new magus, as our own Green Man. I'm on your side, chaps! Sylvie invited me here for the Solstice sunrise ceremony tomorrow. But I can't go up to the Hall yet, because Magus doesn't know I'm here. I'd be grateful if you'd let me spend the evening in here with you good folk, keeping out of the way while Yul does battle."

This earned him much back-slapping and the Villagers were delighted to welcome him. They found him some food and settled him in a cosy corner by the fire with a glass of cider. Siskin was happier than he'd been in years. And he was so excited about the ceremony in the morning.

At his feet, Yul could make out the six moon eggs that Edward had brought up earlier. They nestled in the cup-like hollows of the snake stone. The top of the stone was encircled with several such hollows and Yul believed that they'd once all held similar eggs of stone. Maybe Magus had remembered these from his boyhood, which had given him the idea to make the eggs for Sylvie. Yul knew he'd played here as a boy because Mother Heggy had told him.

Or maybe the stone eggs that had once sat in the sockets were from ancient times and long gone. Maybe there'd always been a moongazy girl at Stonewylde, who could be forced to charge the rock here and at Mooncliffe with her powerful moon magic. And maybe there'd always been a magus who received the Earth Magic from the Stone Circle, but stole the girl's magic when his own was gone. Perhaps there was eternal conflict; perhaps patterns and stories came and went, repeated endlessly in the circle of time. Yul didn't know and didn't care. All he hoped was that Sylvie was safely at Hare Stone within her ring of protection, and that Magus would arrive here soon to meet his destiny.

Yul could feel the strange spirals of moon magic in the eggs at his feet. He tried to keep his distance from them. Their magic was cold and liquid, like quicksilver threading around him. It was different to the deep, hot magic of the earth, which felt like molten magma coursing through him. He didn't want any of Sylvie's magic. He needed the earth spirals from below and the sun brushing his face. But the eggs were here to lure Magus, and as he thought this, Yul heard the sound of an engine approaching.

His heart lurched. At last! The plan had worked. Magus had fallen for the ruse. The lights bounced in and out of sight as the Landrover jolted up the track. Then the noise and lights cut out. Yul heard a door slam. No - he heard three doors slam! His heart began to beat very slowly and very hard. Magus had arrived and he hadn't come alone.

CHAPTER SEVENTEEN

"Remember," said Magus softly, "capture and restrain him but don't kill him. And don't touch the girl. Shout if you catch the boy. Sound carries well here. We'll split up now and meet up by the tall stone at the head of the quarry. One of you go round the top to the right, the other to the left. Head uphill towards the summit and watch out for the boulders up there. Don't get too close to the edge either. It's a steep drop. I'll go down through the quarry itself. Keep very quiet until we know where he is. We must surprise him. We'll soon see if he's up with her at the snake-stone yet, or still on his way."

Yul stood on the rock, considering the consequences of three people arriving and how he could fight them all. Suddenly a black shape appeared in the gathering gloom and brushed past him. It uttered a loud caw and circled him. He smiled. Now he too had reinforcements. The crow landed in a flurry on his shoulder, sidestepping and pecking gently at his ear. He murmured to it, grateful to Mother Heggy for sending her emissary. He looked down but could see nothing, for it was dark now. On the horizon, peering over the ridgeway, was the moon, a huge yellow disc slowly emerging from the purple haze. He thought of his beloved Sylvie and imagined her at this moment raising her arms and transforming into a moon angel. The crow croaked in his ear and took off, flying down into the quarry. Yul knew he must follow.

The two men were finding it hard going. Both were tough, and experts in their field, but they were used to operating in city gangland. This terrain was very different and there was no street lighting. The darkness at Stonewylde was absolute for

313

the moon had yet to rise high enough to give out light. They stumbled and faltered, worried about the quarry edge and unsure of where the paths lay. Both wished fervently they'd never agreed to this job.

Magus knew his way around the quarry from years before, but was not as recently familiar with it as Yul. He trod carefully as he moved along the dark corridors of stone, sometimes brushing against the ivy clad walls and occasionally stumbling on small rocks in his path. His anger had turned to an icy resolve. He would hunt the boy down and lash him up, tightly bound and gagged. Then he'd see if Sylvie could charge the great snake-stone, and if so, he'd keep her here and feed off the moon magic to power himself up. Then he'd deal with his son. He wasn't sure yet how he intended to kill Yul, but one thing was definite – it would not be quick and the boy would suffer first. And Sylvie would watch. He smiled to himself in the darkness, sensing the malignance that lurked in the labyrinth of stone. He shivered with a sudden rush of bloodlust. Sixteen years he'd waited for this chance. He couldn't wait to get his hands on the boy and slowly extinguish his life.

Yul climbed lightly down the steps and boulders back into the quarry. His feet remembered the path and he was soon down in the black depths, the moon not yet visible here as it still hung low and golden in the sky. He knew that Magus was somewhere in this maze of stone passages, and he felt certain that the two others with him were up on the top, above the quarry. He'd heard noises from both sides and wondered who Magus had brought with him. They must be Hallfolk, for all the Villagers were now against Magus. He moved silently and stealthily through the high canyons of stone. The crow had disappeared.

The Magus and his two hired warriors hunted the boy, knowing they would find him in this place of death. The warriors were strong men from a clan outside. They wore strange clothing and followed

*different customs. They carried long weapons and had rope to bind
the boy, for they knew they must not kill him. That was the pleasure
of the Magus. They moved slowly as this was not their land and the
paths were strange to them.*

*Down in the stone maze the Magus moved like a grey wolf in the
darkness. He was angry, the blood pumping fiercely in his veins. He
must challenge this young usurper, this threat to his rule, to his
status as head of the clan. Magus wanted to take the moongazy
maiden for himself. She was magical and beautiful. She would bear
him fine sons and bring him even greater power. But the boy had
been enchanted by her magic and wanted her too. Another reason
why he must die tonight. Magus paused and sniffed the air. He
caught the scent of the boy and knew him to be cowering nearby,
somewhere in the darkness. The moon was rising fast. The hour of
death drew near.*

Yul heard a sound and froze. His heart beat loudly in his ears.
He knew that Magus was close by. The ivy was thick at this
point, swarming up the stone walls, and Yul melted back into a
crack in the rock shielded by the leaves. Magus approached
stealthily but not silently. Yul could hear his breathing, deep
and heavy, and his feet made small noises on the loose stones.
Yul could smell him too. The exotic scent he wore mingled
with something more primeval; the fresh sweat of a strong, fit
man hunting his prey. Yul picked up a small stone and threw
it far ahead. Magus paused, then hurried forward, and Yul
grinned to himself.

Mother Heggy moaned and muttered in the centre of her circle,
calling on every power to help the boy tonight. She rocked
back and forth clutching her shawl around her. She'd sent her
crow some time ago, knowing Yul would need all the help she
could give. She'd been told the plan but had no idea what was
happening now in the quarry. She knew only too well of
Magus' strength and intelligence and his utter ruthlessness.
He'd be fighting for his life tonight. He'd stop at nothing to
remove the threat that had haunted him for so long. She

hoped that Sylvie was safe up at Hare Stone. She could see nothing. Her second sight had deserted her completely. She thought again of the five deaths. They were the only thing of which she was sure tonight. She shivered and stared hard at the five green points of light about her. All the candles in the pentangle still burned steadily. Nobody had died yet.

The two men finally met up at the head of the quarry, relieved to find each other in the darkness. The moon had risen fully and now that they could see more clearly, they realised what they were up against. The quarry glowed below them in the moonlight. Somewhere down there amongst the piles of rock and deep channels of shadow was their intended prey. And the man who'd hired them. They both shook their heads, and after a hurried conversation decided to get out while they still could. This wasn't what they'd expected and they both had a bad feeling about it. Together they started to make their way back to the Landrover. Both wondered how their old mate Jack Daw had ever got involved in such a weird set-up as this.

Sylvie danced in the moonlight, her feet brushing the freezing wet grass as she leapt gracefully in spirals around the stone. The hares raced with her, ears back and long hind legs pounding. The barn owl circled overhead and Clip watched in awe. He now appreciated just how she must have suffered being pinned to the rock up at Mooncliffe. To have stood there unable to move must have been torture for her. She needed to be wild; to sing and dance. The brilliant golden moon was higher now, glowing brightly in the cold night air. Sylvie spun around, her cloak and silver hair flying out about her, the diamonds at her throat and wrists sparkling as they caught the light. Below the hill stood the woodsmen, silently gazing up at the magical figure dancing in the moonlight.

The two hired men dodged the boulders that lay strewn everywhere. They were thoroughly spooked, desperate to find the Landrover and escape. They'd hotwire it if that madman had taken the keys. Both felt the menace of the place, the brooding atmosphere of death and fear. They began to panic, looking over their shoulders and glancing down into the hungry shadows below. Something was watching them. Watching and waiting. Hurrying made them clumsy. They kept stumbling and losing their footing. They skirted a clump of stunted trees and boulders, forcing them to go even closer to the edge.

Just as they were passing a twisted elder tree there was a loud caw. A huge black bird flapped out of the branches and flew straight at them. The heavier man lurched to one side but there was nothing to grab onto. Almost in slow motion he started to fall, trying desperately to twist himself back to safety. But too late. With a cry of disbelief he tumbled over the drop into the void. A second later his companion heard the heavy thud as he hit the rock below. The crow continued to call loudly, circling over the quarry. Down below, Yul heard it and knew what had happened. Magus cursed softly.

The remaining man scrambled ahead in a blind panic. He'd been in tough situations before and was no coward, but there was something here that scared him witless. With laboured breath he reached another clump of trees up ahead. Sweat poured into his eyes as he ran, tripping over the stones and pushing himself up again to stumble on. He knew it couldn't be far to the Landrover. At first he thought the black shape in front was the vehicle. Then he realised his mistake.

There was a startled whinny and Nightwing reared up, eyes rolling madly in the bright moonlight. The man cried out in terror, shielding his head with his arms. His rifle clattered to the ground as the great hooves came down hard onto him. He was felled, then trampled on again and again as the agitated stallion tried to rid himself of the mound beneath his feet. Yul heard Nightwing through the darkness. Now it was just the two of them, father and son. Now it could begin.

Inside the pentangle, Mother Heggy sighed as two of the green lights snuffed out almost simultaneously. Two had died. Two deaths on the eve of the Solstice. Three to go.

The moonlight threw everything into monochrome, bleaching all colour and tone away. Black and white. Darkness and brightness. The white of skin and hair and stone: the black of eye and fear and shadow. The Magus and the boy, stalking each other in the place of bones and death. And now something else was here. Something that prowled amongst the boulders and passages. Something raised by the spilling of blood. The two warriors had sacrificed their lives, tempted by the gold which sat uselessly in their pouches. Now their bodies lay broken on the stone, killed by the black creatures of the night. The crow and the dark horse had been summoned by the boy's magic. He felt powerful now, knowing that two were dead. But he was not invincible. As he rejoiced in the death of the warriors, the Magus caught him off guard. With a shout of triumph, the great man caught hold of the boy and held him fast.

Magus slammed Yul into the stone wall, knocking the air from his lungs with a grunt. Yul couldn't get his breath and taking advantage of his incapacity, Magus punched him hard in the stomach. As Yul doubled over in pain, the fist slammed into the side of his face. His head jerked back into the cushion of ivy.

"No escape now, you little bastard!" hissed Magus, pinning Yul by the throat to the stone wall. Although his body screamed silently with pain from the blows, Yul made himself relax, a technique he'd learnt when receiving similar treatment from Alwyn. Magus' grip loosened a little.

"Where's Sylvie?" he demanded, breathing heavily.

"She's hidden," spluttered Yul. "You won't find her."

With a roar of anger, Magus let him drop and spun him around. He grabbed Yul's arm and twisted it up behind his back, then pushed him hard into the wall again, front first. He shoved his full weight into the boy, feeling the crunch and give of skin and bone against solid stone.

"Where is she exactly?"

"She's hiding!" gasped Yul, unable to breathe properly. "I left her so I could find you. She's in one of the caves amongst

318

the stone."

"Why did you bring her here? This is a dangerous place."

"She wanted to give me her moon magic. She said she'd dance for me on the snake stone. As a birthday present."

Magus howled at this as jealousy knifed through him. He couldn't bear to think of Sylvie loving this boy and wanting to please him.

"I shall kill you tonight," whispered Magus, his lips next to Yul's ear. "I shall kill you very slowly in front of Sylvie, you bastard! And then I'll begin *her* punishment."

The moon shone silver white, now high in the sky, and Sylvie at last came to rest. She panted with exertion. She'd been dancing and singing for a long time. She knelt down in the freezing grass and gazed up in silence. The moon was surrounded with a bright halo of silver light, formed by ice crystals up very high in the cold night air. The Frost Moon was beautiful. The hares had stopped racing around and were moongazing too, sitting up on their great hind legs. The barn owl had swooped down on silent feathered wings and now perched on the standing stone, its moon face glowing round and white. Clip saw the dew turning to frost, the diamond drops freezing to silver crystals. His hands and feet were numb. The moon shone down, washing the man, girl, owl and hares with silver magic.

In the pub Professor Siskin stood up a little unsteadily. He'd now had a few glasses of cider, and made his way to the privy out the back. But afterwards, instead of returning straightaway to the warm pub, he decided to take a stroll on the Village Green. A minute or two out in the cold night air would clear his head. The Green was his favourite place in the world. He tottered onto the grass, stiff now with a rime of frost, and looked up. He saw the stars glittering incredibly brightly. Hundreds, thousands, millions and millions of them, so clear at Stonewylde where there was no light pollution. He saw the great face of the full moon shining down, the pale grey hare visible as a shadow on the silver disc.

He wandered right into the middle of the Village Green. He remembered the cricket matches he'd watched here over recent years and all the other Midsummer and Lammas celebrations he'd been permitted to join. And before that, before Sol had become magus, he remembered other festivals; the maypole dancing at Beltane, the labyrinth at Samhain, the archery at Imbolc. The Green held many happy memories for him.

Then he began to go further back and strange images crowded into his head, jostling for attention. People in different clothes dancing, feasting, singing and competing here. He could see and hear them clearly, and as a scholar he recognised the language. It was very old. Then further back still, to a time when there were woods all around for miles and miles. He saw a great wooden structure built to enclose the circle of the sacred grove. Here was the heart of the woodland, the vitality and fertility almost tangible in such a magical place. The trees had been consecrated. He saw the yew, much smaller and younger but the same tree nevertheless. And a great lime tree, such as the one Yul had been resting under when he'd taken the photos.

And here was the Green Man himself! Surely? A young man with dark hair, clad all in green and brown. His skin was mottled with lichen, and leaves formed a halo around his head. The green magic chased and danced about him. He walked from out of the circle of trees, smiling at Siskin. Leaves sprouted from his mouth and nostrils. The old professor felt a strange flutter in his chest, like a bird flexing its wings before it flew away. He sank down to the frosty ground and curled himself up like a child, cradled in the loving bosom of Mother Earth.

The Green Man came close and smiled down at him, his bright eyes flashing warmth and merriment. He held out a hand in invitation. The young Siskin stood up easily, following him into the sacred grove to become one with the ancestors of Stonewylde. The old man's body lay in the frosty grass and slowly froze in the cold, starry night.

In the pentangle a third candle guttered and suddenly extinguished itself. Mother Heggy muttered her incantations and continued to rock backwards and forwards. She had no idea who the Dark Angel had just taken, although she didn't feel it was Magus or either of her special ones. She would surely have known that in her heart. The room was still warm. The wood she'd banked up on the fire had caught hold and was now burning brightly. Firelight flickered around the tiny cottage chasing the darkness from the corners. She raised the goblet and sipped at the drink slowly, then began to nibble at the cake with her bony gums. Two of the green flames still burnt steadily.

The Magus handled the boy very roughly, not caring how he hurt him as he dragged him through the labyrinth towards the Stone of Death – the great stone carved with serpents. But the boy was quick and clever. When they came to an open part of the maze where several paths joined, the boy tricked him. He called beyond to the maiden who was not there at all but dancing to the moon on a hilltop with the sacred hares. The Magus was fooled, looking around frantically for her. In the confusion the boy escaped his grasp. He ran off into the labyrinth and the Magus followed him, screaming with rage at the boy's cunning.

For a long time the man and boy played cat and mouse in the darkness, running from moonlight to shadow and hiding in the pools of blackness. But the boy tired of it. When the moon was risen high, he made his way up to the great Stone of Death. He stood and cried to the Moon Goddess and to his beloved. He cried to the cold night of his love. The Magus heard and hurried to him. He was eager to kill the boy and take the maiden now, while the moon-lust was upon him and the blood pumped hot and hard in his veins.

Magus paused, standing on a boulder below the snake stone. He could see Yul clearly up above him. The figure stood tall on the stone, his head thrown back, face washed in moonlight. His dark hair hung down to his shoulders and the bright moonlight chiselled his face into strong planes and deep hollows. Magus realised with a shock that he was looking no longer at a boy but at a man. A man who seemed to glow in the moonlight. For the first time ever, Magus felt a tingle of fear. Yul pulsed with power and strength. He stood with his legs apart and his face turned to the moon. And he wasn't scared that Magus was on his way up. He wanted this confrontation.

Magus could just make out Sylvie standing behind him. The moonlight shone full onto Yul. In comparison she was faint and shadowy. Magus saw her wild silver hair and her white skin, her thin arms and legs bare in the cold winter's night. He felt a shiver of excitement at the sight of her, his moongazy girl. But he hated her for choosing his son over him. He could never forgive her for loving Yul.

By the time Magus reached the top of the snake stone, only Yul stood there. Magus climbed onto the stone and the two men faced each other. They could see each other clearly in the moonlight. It shone as brightly as the sun, but silver instead of gold. Glittering black eyes locked into smouldering grey ones.

"Where's she gone?"

"She's not here. She's dancing at Hare Stone. Her father's looking after her."

"Don't be bloody stupid! Of course she's here. You said she was."

"I lied. I'd never put Sylvie in danger. I'd never take her moon magic."

"Yes! You *are* a liar! You would take her magic! You *were* taking it. I saw you just now."

"I don't need her magic. I have more than enough of my own. Look – see for yourself."

Yul held out a hand, identical to Magus', and they both saw the tiny sparks coursing from his square finger-tips. Yul reached out to touch him but Magus stepped back, unable to bear the thought of his own son receiving the Earth Magic instead of him. He teetered near the edge of the stone and his eyes rolled in alarm, but then his foot brushed something and he looked down.

"My moon eggs!" he cried, bending and picking up one in

each hand. "I knew it was you who stole them!"

He closed his eyes as the energy began to course through him, like quicksilver in his veins. Nothing came close to this ecstasy, this pulsing explosion of power that went on and on, filling him with silver magic. He smiled and opened his eyes to gaze dreamily at Yul. Sylvie had come back and once again stood in his shadow. She stared at Magus with moon-filled eyes. He raised his hands, clenched around the heavy stone eggs, and showed her.

"See? I got them back after all. You needn't have tried to hold out against me, Sylvie, because I always win in the end. And they are so good. Two at once is out of this world. I'm teeming with moon magic already. I'm taking you back to Mooncliffe to charge up the rest of them. I'm not going another month without this energy."

"What are you talking about?" demanded Yul. "You're mad!"

"Get out of my way! Sylvie's coming with me now. I'll be back for you later when I've finished with her. Father against son, man to man, and the winner takes Stonewylde. I shall enjoy the challenge. But first let me take her to Mooncliffe. She hasn't charged this snake stone at all. Look, she's not jerking and quaking. She's not in any pain. I need to use her for a couple of hours, that's all. Move aside, boy!"

Still holding the eggs, he tried to push past Yul to get to Sylvie. She laughed, shaking her head at him, taunting him. She dared to defy him openly, thinking that Yul would protect her. But she was wrong. He'd force her, for he was so much stronger than her. With a growl of anger at her audacity, he shoved Yul hard out of the way. The boy stumbled but grabbed Magus and righted himself. As he touched Magus, the Earth Magic flashed like a great electric charge. A bolt of pure energy hit Magus and lit him up like a torch. His silver hair stood out on end and his eyeballs sizzled as if they would explode with pain and heat. He cried out in agony and staggered backwards, the heavy eggs in his hands giving his movement further momentum. He teetered as if frozen on the brink of the enormous stone.

He gaped in horror, knowing that he must fall. His terrified eyes met Sylvie's. She threw back her head and laughed, and he saw her small, pointy teeth. Magus knew then that he'd been wrong. It wasn't Sylvie at all who'd taunted him. This moongazy girl was Raven, his own mother. And he realised, in that split second, that the Dark Angel comes in many guises. The Dark Angel can even be bright and silver.

"Yul!" he howled, the name echoing again and again around the stone graveyard in the cold night. There was nothing to grasp onto to stop himself from falling. Yul's hand shot out to save his father, but it was too late. He grabbed only thin air where a second earlier Magus had stood. It was a long way down from the snake stone, at the head of the moonlit quarry. A long way down, still falling, to the jagged rocks that waited like sharp pointed teeth at the bottom.

Blood had been spilled – the blood of three men. Appeasement to the evil that stalked this ancient arena of death and bloodlust. Three lives to satisfy the hunger that prowled the labyrinth in the place of bones and death. The young Magus stood on the Stone of Death and gazed out across the white moonscape of the quarry. The stars glittered in the cold midwinter air. A frost began to dust the land with sparkly silver. The time of the Winter Solstice was approaching. The great Wheel of the Year turned, and the earth turned, and the centuries came around, and time almost stood still, like the sun in the sky at this point in the year. Time stood still, but the ancient patterns played themselves out. The ancient stories clamoured to be retold ...

Stonewylde had a new Magus and the dance could go on.

The crow called and flapped across to circle around him. Yul heard a horse's whinny and remembered Nightwing waiting patiently by the elder tree. With a final glance at the black void that had swallowed his father, Yul jumped down onto the boulders and began to run back to where the horse waited for him. He wanted only to gallop like the wind with Nightwing, away from this place of bones and death, this place of white rock and red blood, and back to the green soul of Stonewylde.

As the fourth green light was suddenly extinguished, Mother Heggy peered at the mangled remains in her clawed hands. It was a tiny wax figure, and bore a lock of soft, silver hair taken long ago from a child's head. She nodded, knowing that the prophecy she had seen, all those years past, had been fulfilled

Under red and blue, the fruit of your passion
Will rise up against you with the folk behind
At the time of brightness in darkness,
In the place of bones and death.

She cackled toothlessly and raised the goblet again, drinking deeply this time, toasting the new magus. She threw the tiny mommet out of her circle and into the blazing fire. It hissed and melted, the lock of blond hair sizzling and giving out a foul stench as it burnt. She gazed at the one green light still burning. Only one left. Who would it be? If Magus was dead, Yul should now be safe. But Sylvie – what of her? Old Mother Heggy felt the cold clutch of fear around her heart. Not her little bright one, not her! She couldn't bear to lose Sylvie. The girl was so precious, just as her Raven had been.

There was a soft knock at the door, making her jump. Probably someone Yul had sent to check that she was alright. Maybe to see if she wanted to come to the sunrise ceremony after all. She shook her head. It was warm in this room, but she knew how cold it was outside. The knock came again.

"Lift the latch and come in!" she croaked, looking up. Her milky eyes widened in surprise at the sight of her unexpected visitor. "Oh, 'tis you! I should've known."

Moonlight silhouetted the robed, hooded figure standing tall and dark on the threshold. She nodded. Now she understood. Mother Heggy gazed into his fathomless eyes and then her head fell to her chest. The fifth green light faltered and snuffed out.

In the darkness before dawn, the Stone Circle was packed tightly with the folk of Stonewylde. The sun was not yet risen on this, the shortest day of the year. But the longest night was now over. Today at the Winter Solstice the sun stood still in the sky at its furthest point in the year. Tomorrow it would start on its return journey towards summer. Soon the ceremony would begin to welcome the sun as it rose in the south-east. The great Solstice Bonfire stood at one edge of the circle. A boy shivered up on the platform by the brazier, waiting to herald the dawn. Harold had been chosen and he held the lighter ready in his hand, nervous at such an honour.

At the Altar Stone, Clip led the chanting and singing and the drummers played the rhythms softly. Clip was resplendent in white robes and a head-dress of mistletoe and ivy. His movements and voice were measured and soothing. The people felt calm and reassured and joined in the singing whole-heartedly. As the sun approached the horizon the tension rose and the drumming picked up speed and insistency.

People's hearts beat faster, the drumbeats reverberating inside their chests. Their heartbeats became as one, a great pulsing rhythm of sunrise and hope. The boy on the fire cried out and lit the flame. The brazier flared brightly and the people chanted, welcoming the return of the sun to their dark lives. The boy climbed down the ladder inside the fire, holding the torch he'd lit in the brazier. But all eyes were on the Long Walk where two figures were approaching.

Yul and Sylvie stepped into the Stone Circle hand in hand. He wore a heavy robe of gold, embroidered with yellow suns for the Winter Solstice, and a great head-dress similar to Clip's of mistletoe, ivy and holly. It sat on his dark curls snugly, the woven foliage seeming to sprout from his head. His beautiful face was solemn but joyful. Next to him walked Sylvie, tall and slender in the dark green robes of Yule. The evergreen material was embroidered with a pattern of leaves and the white berries of mistletoe, red berries of holly, and black berries of ivy. Her glorious silver hair cascaded down, topped by a filigree circlet bearing a silver crescent to signify the Maiden. Her moonstone eyes danced with happiness.

As they came level with the bonfire, Harold emerged from the concealed exit. With a bow he passed the flaming torch to Yul, who held it aloft. He and Sylvie continued on to the Altar

Stone. Sylvie went to stand next to her father whilst Yul climbed the step and stood upon the stone, outstretched arm holding high the Sacred Flame. At that second, the first beams of the sun flashed through the gap in the aligned stones. The golden rays hit Yul and his robe seemed to light up, the golden embroidery glittering and reflecting the brilliant sunlight.

But even more remarkable was what happened to Yul himself. Even he was taken by surprise, for this was unlike anything that he'd experienced before. The sunlight illuminated him and he jolted, as he normally did. He felt the earth energy beneath him start to spiral up through the stone and into his body, but this was stronger, much stronger, than ever before. The very earth seemed to sing, a strange music of rock and soil.

A deep shuddering rumbled beneath the Stone Circle like an earthquake, making the ground tremble and the people shake. It lasted only a brief heart-lurching moment. Then the spiral of Earth Magic shot out of the Altar Stone and swirled around him in a whirlwind, encasing him in pure energy. He radiated light, his robed body and wreathed head haloed with a strange green brightness. The torch in his hand flared brilliant green. His eyes burned like stars as he stood tall, doused in Earth Magic that seemed to set him on fire.

"Folk of Stonewylde," cried Clip, "behold our new Magus! The Green Man has returned to Stonewylde! All will be well! All will prosper! We greet him and offer him our loyalty!"

"MAGUS OF STONEWYLDE!" roared hundreds of voices. "We welcome the Green Man!"

The energy flew around the Circle touching the hearts of every person there. The drums rolled triumphantly and the community burst into song, an ancient song whose words were remembered but no longer understood. The ceremony continued in the crisp morning air, brilliant with sparkling sunlight and a new atmosphere of liberty and joy.

Yul and Sylvie caught each other's eye and smiled, unable to believe that this day had finally dawned. They couldn't wait to be alone together later on, to enjoy each other's company in peace after the terrible recent months.

Sylvie looked around the packed Circle, wondering if Professor Siskin had managed to make it back to Stonewylde after all. She hadn't seen him yet, but as the light glowed brighter by the minute she scanned the faces. She hoped that he'd experienced the amazing moment when the Green Man returned to Stonewylde, just as he'd foretold. She knew the professor's soul belonged here, just as hers did. With his long exile finally over, he'd now find contentment in the place he loved so dearly.

Yul was thinking of Mother Heggy and how he'd promised to visit her today with Sylvie. She'd be so happy to see the pair of them, the grandchildren of her Raven. The man she'd hated since his brutal conception on the snake stone was now dead and gone, and her prophecy had come true. As he thought of Mother Heggy and the part she'd played in this, there was a flapping and a flurry. The great black crow appeared, flying slowly into the sacred Circle. Yul noticed many people make the sign of the pentangle, remembering old Mother Heggy and her natural magic. The crow circled overhead cawing loudly, then alighted in a tumble of feathers onto Sylvie's shoulder. The people nodded. The Wise Woman's crow had spoken. Sylvie belonged by Yul's side.

When it was time for the sharing of cakes and mead the people started to form lines. Moving forward to approach the altar, they were surprised by a change to the routine. They received their cake and mead and found the cakes to be delicious but not spiced with the herbs and extracts that had always made everyone feel so strange and unworldly. The mead was sweet and heady but not laced with anything stronger.

Instead they experienced something infinitely more powerful and enthralling. They went one by one to Yul on the Altar Stone and stood on the step, reaching up to him. Glorious in golden Solstice robes and evergreen winter headdress, he bent and clasped their hands in his. As he touched them, each one received a surge of Earth Magic. He was the channel, the conduit, and he shared the gift with his people so that everyone could experience the wonder of the

Earth Goddess' energy. For this was the true but long forgotten role of the magus, the magician, the wise one.

One by one they came and clasped his hands, all his friends and all the others who'd been unsure of his suitability as the new magus. He gazed into each person's eyes, his grey eyes blazing with energy and light, and gave each one a jolt of the green magic. Maizie and Miranda came up together, both glowing with pride at their children's bravery and triumph. Clip too received the energy from Yul, smiling at him, full of respect for the young man. Clip looked at the handsome dark face before him and knew that Yul would succeed as magus. He was too much his father's son to do otherwise.

Finally, Sylvie came from her place beside the stone. She stood before Yul looking up at him, the black crow on her shoulder. He held his hands out to her and pulled her up from the step to stand next to him on the Altar Stone. Holding hands they faced each other, and the energy flowed in both directions. Green magic and quicksilver. Their eyes locked together as they gazed into each other's souls. The fear, pain and suffering of the past months melted away to nothing, like frost in the sun. Their passion and adoration glimmered around them in an aura, there for all to see. The crow took off and flew to the stone behind, where the image of the Green Man smiled amongst the symbols of the Winter Solstice.

The sun blessed them both, gilding them like bright angels. They looked deep into each other's eyes and time seemed to stand still for a moment. Then moving as one, they fell into a fierce embrace. The folk cheered as they held each other tightly.

Sylvie and Yul felt the cogs of time falling into place. They felt the wheels of fate revolving, and they knew that this was how it was meant to be. The ancient story was told again, the pattern repeated as it always had been throughout the ages in this enchanted place. The Green Man and the moongazy girl, the darkness and the brightness, together again as one.

The true guardians of the magic of Stonewylde.

Read the next book in the Stonewylde Series:

SHADOWS AT STONEWYLDE

For more information about the Stonewylde Series visit the website:
www.stonewylde.com

A note from Kit Berry ...

This was going to be the end. When I started to write of Stonewylde, the book became so vast and complex that I split it into three books and made it into a trilogy. And when I'd come to the point where you are now, it was finished. The story of Yul and Sylvie had been told.

But I felt bereft. I moped about feeling sad and miserable. When my eldest son finished reading the manuscript, he insisted that I continue with the story of Stonewylde. He begged me to carry on and tell of what happened next, after the triumphant events of the Winter Solstice.

So there will be two more books, making the trilogy into a pentalogy. Or as dear old Mother Heggy would have said,

"Five – always five!"

Stonewylde is a place that lives in our dreams and imaginations. For me, and for many readers too (I know this because they've written and told me so!) Stonewylde is a real entity. It's somewhere to escape to in your day dreams. It's the perfect place, a beautiful, enclosed sanctuary where nature has been unharmed and thrives undamaged by modern exploitation. But of course the tension arises because although the place may be idyllic and perfect, people never are.

Magus may have been ousted. Alwyn, Buzz and Jackdaw may have fallen one by one. But human nature being what it is, could there ever be complete harmony and happiness at Stonewylde? The story continues ...

Thank you for coming with me on this journey so far. We'll leave Yul and Sylvie and all the folk of Stonewylde to establish a new way of living. And we'll pick up with them again at some point in the future. You may be surprised at what Stonewylde has become when you read the next book *"Shadows at Stonewylde."* Or maybe not.

Bright blessings to you all!

Enjoyed the Stonewylde Series?

Come and join Kit Berry and many other Stonewylde readers and fans on the Stonewylde Forum! This is the place where you can discuss Stonewylde with like-minded people, and share your views about all sorts of related topics.

Visit the forum at www.stonewyldeforum.com

For more information about the Stonewylde Series visit the website:
www.stonewylde.com